GRIEVING ROYAL

CLUB ROYAL, BOOK THREE

ELOUISE EAST

CONTENTS

To Maria,
For keeping me on point in more ways than one

SUTCLIFFE ROYAL FAMILY

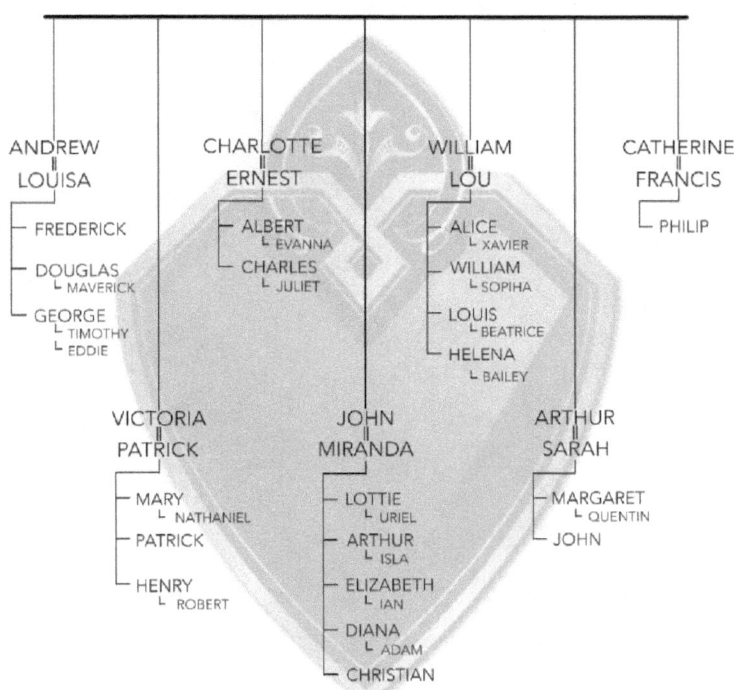

LIST OF CHARACTERS

(ALPHABETICAL ORDER)

Albert, cousin, Charlotte and Ernest's child

Andrew, King of England, George's father

Bella, Eddie's friend

Briony, Timothy's sister

Charles, cousin, Charlotte and Ernest's child

Charlotte, George's aunt

Christian, cousin, John and Miranda's child

Clarice, Club Royal's receptionist

Damon, Frederick's best friend

Denise, Timothy's mother

Derek, Timothy's therapist

Douglas, George's brother, Mav's boyfriend

Eddie, barista

Elton, owner of The Den, friends with George

Frederick, George's brother, heir to the throne

George, third in line to the throne

Henry, cousin, Robert's boyfriend, Victoria and
    Patrick's child

Imogen, Timothy's sister

Jason, George's best friend
Louisa, Queen Consort, George's mother
Maverick, Douglas's boyfriend
Mel, Eddie's friend
Oliver, Club Royal bartender
Parker, Eddie's father
Patrick, Henry's brother
Portia, Queen Louisa's assistant
Randall, King Andrew's assistant
Robert, Henry's boyfriend
Rose, Eddie's mother
Talia, Timothy's sister
Terry, Eddie's friend
Timothy, teacher/therapist
Vincent, sleazy bad guy

GRIEVING ROYAL

1

GEORGE

·

George Sutcliffe stared around him, the energy of Club Royal beating against his body as if it was a physical caress. He fed off it, clenching and stretching his hands to ward off the need to lower his head, close his eyes and soak it all up. Although he was submissive, few people knew about it, and he wanted to keep it that way for the time being. There were too many people who would use it against him.

He fell forward as someone bumped into him from behind, and he turned, ready to curse at them before doing so anyway when he found his brothers grinning at him.

"What the fuck?" His words were sharp but lost some of their heat in the loud music.

He couldn't stay angry at them for long, and Freddie and Douglas's infectious grins had a smile creeping across his face.

"Hey, it's Valentine's Day. Cut out the cursing," Freddie said, slapping his best friend, Damon, on the back.

George raised his eyebrows. "First, what difference does Valentine's Day make? Second, are you drunk?" He glanced between the heir to the throne and Damon, wondering if he'd been dropped into an alternate universe. He couldn't remember the last time he saw his brother drunk.

Damon grimaced. "I may have slipped him an extra shot or two of alcohol tonight. I didn't think it would make much of a difference, but I was wrong."

George grinned. "Wow, my big brother is drunk off his ass! Kudos to you, Damon, but he's going to bitch about it in the morning."

"I know." Damon glanced at Freddie, who had taken to staring around them while weaving back and forth. Damon gripped the back of Freddie's neck to keep him steady. "I'll keep an eye on him, though."

"I thought he was working tonight?" George said.

Douglas grinned. "I called in reinforcements before we plied him with drinks. He's too stressed, but I didn't expect him to drink so many. We better not stay here too long. It might be easier to get him home drunk than when he's sobering up."

"Agreed." George nodded. "I'm done here."

Douglas squeezed his shoulder. "You haven't been here long. Are you sure?"

"Yeah. I'd much prefer to spend the evening with you lot." He laughed. "How sad is that?"

"It is a little sad, but it's also true for me as well." Douglas glanced over his shoulder. "Let me grab Mav, and we'll head out."

Douglas disappeared into the crowd, and Damon and George headed towards the exit with Freddie stumbling along between them. George would have to take a photo before Freddie sobered enough to argue with him. He hadn't seen his brother like this ever because Freddie took his role as heir to the throne seriously. He would never take the chance of being seen like this. Luckily, there was an underground car park for the club, and they should be able to get away without being seen.

"Why were you plying him with drinks?" he asked Damon when they sat Freddie in a chair in the changing rooms. The club's monitors were all part of the royal family and had a separate changing room to keep the security risk to a minimum. Nothing had ever happened as far as George was aware, but it was better to be safe than sorry, his father had always said.

Damon sighed and wiped a hand over his face. "He's stressed about this damn visit he has to go on. He refuses to take me with him because he says he doesn't want to subject me to it; however, I think he needs the support. I wanted him to relax, but maybe I went a bit far."

George spared a glance for his brother, who was resting his head back in the chair and waving his hands in front of his face whilst wearing a big smile. George snorted. "I think he's just fine, although tomorrow…maybe not so much."

Damon groaned and sank into a chair. "He's going to fucking kill me."

"That he might."

George went to his locker and retrieved his clothes, stripping off his leather shirt and throwing it into the hamper. He did the same with his trousers, hopping on one foot until he could get them off. His skin pebbled in the air conditioning after being in the warm leather outfit for the past couple of hours, and he was grateful for the trousers and shirt he replaced them with. He would've preferred a shower, but he didn't want to miss a single minute of "drunk Freddie."

Douglas and Maverick entered the changing room, wrapped around each other and laughing about something.

"How is he?" Douglas asked, coming to stand in front of Freddie.

"Away with the fairies," Damon replied.

George snorted. He slid his phone into his pocket without checking it, his wallet into his other pocket, then slid his jacket over his shoulders and closed his locker. He turned to his family as he unwrapped a love heart packet of sweets—his favourites, that he couldn't be without.

"Right. You lot get yourselves sorted. I'll get brother dear here to swallow some water, and we can get going. I think we're going to have to take a chance and leave Freddie in these clothes because there's no way we're getting him changed when he's like this," George said, popping a sweet into his mouth.

Damon, Douglas and Maverick got changed, and George persuaded Freddie to drink the water by putting it in a shot glass and pretending it was alcohol. He didn't withhold his smile at all because drunk Freddie was adorable. If he could've videoed it and kept it to show at embarrassing moments, he would've, but it was things like that which got leaked to the press.

Despite the rumours circling about the royal family and their connection to Club Royal, nobody had ever officially linked the two. A previous king had created the club decades ago when he decided to take matters into his own hands and have somewhere a little less private for his proclivities. Even

George didn't know the truth of the matter, but from what he could gather, this king had needed to rein in his son and had taken it upon himself to induct him into the BDSM lifestyle. From there, the club grew. In more recent years, the necessity of non-disclosure agreements made things easier to navigate.

"Right. Let's see if we can get his trousers over the top of the leathers. The shirt I'm not so bothered about because we can hide that with a coat, but they will easily see his leather trousers," Douglas said.

"Do you have access to his locker?" George asked. "Because I don't."

"I do," Damon said, pressing his finger to Freddie's locker.

George raised his eyebrows, then shrugged. They were best friends and had been since pre-school. He would've been surprised if they didn't have access to each other's lockers.

With a struggle, they got the trousers over the top, and though it couldn't be comfortable, Freddie didn't seem to care. Damon slid his arm around Freddie's waist and held his arm over his shoulder to carry most of his weight. It wasn't the best ruse, but the two men were close enough friends that being seen like that shouldn't ring too many bells with potential passersby.

They all signed out at the reception desk, Clarice showing no reaction to their ragtag group except for a slight twitch of her mouth. The woman was the best thing to happen to this place, and George wished she would become immortal to ensure she never left. In fact, if she ever wanted to become part of the royal family, he'd happily marry her to ensure she stayed.

By the time they reached the car park, Freddie had begun singing, even though they had tried to shut him up.

"Just get him in the car," Douglas said, opening Freddie's passenger door and helping Damon get the man inside. "Are you okay to drive?" he asked Damon.

"Yes, I had one beer ages ago. Are we heading to Windsor?"

Douglas put his hands on his hips and stared at the floor. "Let's go to Freddie's. Hopefully, we won't have any followers. If you see too many people following you, go to Windsor instead."

Damon nodded and climbed into the driver's seat. Douglas clapped George on the shoulder and climbed into his car with Mav beside him. George sat in his Lexus RC F Coupe and pulled out his phone. He sent messages to Henry, Patrick and Christian, who were their cousins, and let them know what was happening. He couldn't remember if any were working tonight, but if they could make it to Freddie's, they would.

He slid the phone into the holder and turned on the music before reversing out of the space and following in his brothers' wake. It wasn't particularly late, not even midnight, and George didn't feel even a little tired, so having company would be good. The Scandalous Six, as he'd coined their group, could have a get-together tonight. He frowned. He had to think of a new name because there were more of them now. Douglas had Mav, and Henry now had Robert. Damon went wherever Freddie was, so that made nine of them. The Nice Nine. The Nasty Nine. The Naked Nine. *The Naughty Nine.*

George grinned. Perfect. Tonight, the Scandalous Six would be retired, and The Naughty Nine would commence.

The roads were quieter when he got outside the hustle and bustle of London, and when he finally pulled up outside Freddie's cottage—still on Windsor Castle's land but a decent distance away—he found everyone except Christian and Patrick present.

"We need a drink to celebrate," he announced as he entered the house.

Groans abounded, and he grinned while he rummaged through Freddie's bar.

"Dare I ask why we are celebrating?" Henry said from his perch beside Robert, who had his arm around Henry's neck, and they had linked their fingers together over Henry's chest. A slight pang went through George at the sight of it, but he ignored it.

"Because we have graduated from the Scandalous Six Academy," he said, affecting an even posher tone than he usually used. "I never believed it possible, but it is with great joy I announce the retirement of the Scandalous Six." The room applauded, and George held out his hands, calming them down. "With even greater appreciation is the knowledge that the members of the group are banding together to create The Naughty Nine."

George hooted when everyone groaned, paper and cushions flying towards him.

"For god's sake, George," Douglas said at the same time Mav said, "How come you've gone from six to nine? You've only added Robert and me."

George placed a hand on his chest and turned to Damon. "It is with deep regret that I did not include a VIP in my first incarnation. I will forever be humbled by your presence, Sir Damon."

Damon laughed. "I don't think I'll ever be a sir, but thank you for including me."

George glanced at Freddie. "How is he?" His brother lay on the sofa with his legs behind Damon's back, staring up at the ceiling in silence.

Damon shrugged. "He's gone quiet. He's either sobering and wishing he was dead, or he's going to fall asleep."

"Did you get some paracetamol into him?"

Damon nodded. "Luckily, he had no plans tomorrow. I might need to hide from his wrath."

George rubbed his nose, hiding his smile. There was no way Damon could upset Freddie. He had no idea how Freddie would handle a hangover because he'd never had one as far as George had known. His phone chimed, and he put the bottle of wine down, unopened, and checked it.

CHRISTIAN: I can't get away. Say hi to everyone for me. I will get back there as soon as I can. Chin up.

GEORGE: Can you video call?

CHRISTIAN: Better not. I pissed off my father because I returned two days later than I was supposed to. Doesn't matter that the Army wouldn't let me leave.

GEORGE: Well, if you can call or come at any point, you know you're always welcome. If the doors aren't open, the windows will be, lol.

CHRISTIAN: I may take you up on that.

He wished he could help Christian out. His father was an

arsehole, and his mother wasn't much better. It was the reason Christian had gone into the Army in the first place—to get away from his immediate family. The rest of them missed him something fierce, but they all knew why he'd needed to do it.

"Christian can't make it, and I've not heard from Patrick," he said, glancing at Henry, who shrugged.

"I've not seen him today, although Mother mentioned he had an appointment with someone this afternoon."

The moment he said it, George heard the crunch of car tyres on the stone driveway. He stepped to the windows, seeing Patrick's car pulling up alongside the others, and exhaled. He hated not knowing how everyone was doing. It was in his genes to make everyone happy and look after them, but he couldn't always do it, and he hated it.

The door opened, and Patrick greeted everyone as if they'd never been apart.

"Not so loud," Freddie grumbled from where he lay with a hand over his eyes.

George chuckled. "I guess the alcohol is wearing off."

"I didn't drink that much," his brother mumbled.

"Enough that you stumbled around and asked if the stars were twinkling just for you," Douglas said with a grin.

"Fuck off." Freddie held up his middle finger.

"I'm sorry, Freddie. I was trying to help." Damon laid a hand on his arm, and George saw Freddie's mouth twitch.

"Remind me never to ask you for help." Damon flinched at Freddie's words and pulled his hand back, staring at the floor. Freddie cursed and grabbed his hand back. "I didn't mean that the way it sounded. Just not alcohol help. My brain can't stand it."

Damon didn't seem mollified, but he smiled in Freddie's

direction, then returned his focus to the floor. George flicked his gaze between them. They would make a good couple, but he knew they were both straight. He loved reading stories about people who found their soulmates in their best friend. If they had been gay or bisexual, they would've been perfect for each other.

He would've loved to have a friend like that. Although technically, he did, they weren't perfect for each other. Jason Freeman was his best friend and fellow troublemaker. They'd met at primary school and had been firm friends from day one. When they'd become curious as teenagers, they'd fooled around, although never slept together until they were older. They'd found out at that moment that they were incompatible but had remained friends to this day. Jason was the one he could let loose with and be who he wanted to be. The person who wasn't of a royal bloodline. The person who didn't have to abide by certain rules.

Some of those rules, mind, he broke every month when he visited his second club, The Den. No one there knew his identity, and it would stay that way forever. Sometimes, Club Royal was too much for him, and he needed the anonymity of being in a crowd who knew nothing about him. It was he—or rather his alter-ego—who had arranged for Henry to visit the place and had unintentionally pointed him in Robert's direction.

He focused back on the conversations going on around him. If he had to choose anywhere in the world where he had to stay forever, he would choose here. Not necessarily this place, but these people. They were his family, his world, and he would do anything for them.

"So, who wants that drink to celebrate our new venture?" he said, wanting to hear the complaints.

"New venture?" Patrick asked.

"Don't ask!" Henry shouted.

"Zip it!" Douglas said.

"Stop shouting. Fuck!" Freddie stumbled from the room with Damon close on his heels.

The ruckus calmed down to steady chuckles, then George raised his full glass. "To The Naughty Nine!"

2

TIMOTHY

imothy Dixon closed the door behind him and rested back against it. His eyes took in the bright space in front of him, and his shoulders relaxed a fraction more. He was far enough away from his Bristol roots to give him a little peace. Whether it would stay that way was another thing.

His phone rang, and the temptation to ignore it was strong, but he knew his family would wonder if he'd arrived. Pressing the button and closing his eyes, he answered.

"Have you arrived yet? Is it as nice as the pictures show? Do you have a pleasant view? Have you met your neighbours yet?"

"Briony, stop. One question at a time. I can't answer them when you throw them all out at once."

"You could easily remember all of my questions. Answer them and prove me right."

He sighed. "Yes, yes, yes and no."

"Told you." He snorted. "I can't believe you left us on your birthday."

He bit his lip to stop his words from leaving his mouth and moved away from the door. Stepping close to the window, he shoved his free hand into his pocket and studied the view.

"It was the only day I could do it. You know that. Anyway, I'm forty. It's just another year."

He didn't see the point of celebrating another year of his life. Some people didn't get to see the number of years he already had. It wasn't fair. The memories took hold, and Timothy inhaled, focusing on what Briony was saying. He couldn't understand her words, but her voice tethered him to the here and now. By the time his brain had come back online, and he could understand what she was saying, sweat dotted his forehead, and he weaved his way around the boxes and dropped onto the sofa.

"Are you listening?"

"No," he answered.

Briony was quiet, then asked, "Are you back with me?"

"I am now."

"Good." A loud exhale travelled across the line. "I wish you weren't so far away."

He didn't have an answer for her that he hadn't already given her several times. He couldn't work in Bristol any more. There were too many memories. Too many people who knew who he was and what had happened. Too many media hounds wanting a different spin on an old story. At least moving to Windsor had given him some anonymity.

He held the phone tighter to his ear and scrubbed a hand over his scruff, the scratchy sound loud in the silence of his new house. "You're welcome to visit whenever you want to, Bri."

"I'll be taking you up on that sooner than you think. I bet

you have decorating to do. I'll get the girls over there, and we'll be done in no time."

Timothy huffed a laugh and studied the cream-coloured room. "Deal. It's not my taste."

"I saw that from the photos. We'll get a splash of colour in there, and you'll feel more at home."

It meant a lot that Briony said that. He knew his family was unhappy about his decision to up and leave his childhood city, but after what happened, he couldn't stay. They knew that, but it didn't stop them from telling him at every opportunity that he had made a mistake.

"Anyway, I'll let you go now that I know you're there safe. I'll ring you tomorrow, Moth."

He smiled at the nickname he didn't let anyone but his sisters use and said goodbye. He dropped the phone to the seat beside him and surveyed his surroundings. If he ignored the numerous boxes the moving company had left in every room, he could see the potential of the place. The house was enormous and far bigger than he needed for himself, but he'd chosen it, not only because it was on a private road on the outskirts of Windsor, but because it had plenty of space for when his family wanted to visit.

When the settlement had come through, he hadn't wanted to use it at all until his mother persuaded him to buy a house with it instead of giving it away. It made him feel sick that he'd benefitted from someone's death, and the thought lingered all the while as he signed the papers for the place. He hoped the dark cloud hovering over him would eventually leave, but did he deserve to be left in peace?

Timothy stood and paced to the window again, watching the sun sinking towards the horizon. It was quiet here, and that was a bonus. He'd had enough of the media circus following him around all the time.

A knock at the door made him jump, and he frowned. He wasn't expecting anyone, especially at five in the afternoon. His heart raced as he worked his way through the house to the front door. He inhaled and exhaled before opening the door, expecting to have a camera flash in his face.

"Surprise! Happy birthday! I thought I'd bring a celebratory drink and some food."

Timothy relaxed at Portia's voice. She was another reason he'd chosen Windsor to move to. Instead of having to start completely over again, he had her, one of his best friends. They'd met while Portia had spent a term at Bristol University many years ago, and when she'd headed back home, they'd kept in touch. They'd never had a romantic relationship, although Portia had come onto him once, and he'd had to explain he was gay. They laughed about that night often, and if he'd been straight, she would've been a catch.

"Hi. Thanks. I wasn't expecting to see you today. I thought you were working."

Portia stepped inside and kissed his cheek. "I left a few minutes earlier than normal because there was nothing left to do. Win, win." She shook the bottle of what looked to be champagne. "We have a welcome gift from my employer."

Timothy raised his eyebrows. "Oh, wow. Make sure you say thank you."

"So," she said, wandering down the hall and peering into doorways, "where is the kitchen?"

"When you find it, let me know," Timothy joked, following her.

Portia Lavigne was a down-to-earth, girl-next-door, brown-haired bombshell with a cute little fringe that made her look far more serious than Timothy expected it to. She'd only recently had it cut into that style, and it had taken a while for him to get used to seeing her with it. She lived in Windsor with her parents —in their annexe—and spoke French as easily as English. It was probably to do with her parents being French and having moved from France to England when Portia was one.

"Do you have a corkscrew, or are we scouring the drawers in the hopes someone has left one behind?"

She placed the bottle and bag on the breakfast bar and began opening drawers without waiting for Timothy to answer.

He let her look for a moment, then asked, "Why do we need a corkscrew for champagne? Don't we just pop the cork out?"

Portia paused and glanced at him. "How the hell do I know? I've never had champagne."

"I'm sure you've served it before."

"Yes, but I've never opened the bottle myself." She fiddled with the bottle and pulled a face. "You're right."

"You can do the honours."

"Why me? It's your new house."

"You have more practice than me, I'm sure. Besides, I need to find the glasses."

"Shit, I never thought of that." Portia chuckled. "So much for a relaxing evening."

"It will be once we have those. The food we can eat out of the containers. I'm not searching for plates." He checked the boxes and unpacked two glasses. "Although I suppose I'll need something to have breakfast in tomorrow."

"What are your plans for the weekend?" she asked, pouring the fizzy liquid like a pro.

"Getting enough of this unpacked to start work on Monday. I'm a week behind because I couldn't get here last week."

Timothy sipped his drink, wrinkling his nose as the bubbles hit him, then ignored his earlier words and sought the box with the plates in. Bringing back two, he quickly washed and dried them and placed them next to where Portia was pulling out the food.

"I chose Chinese. I hope that's okay."

"It's food, Portia. It's great." He hip-checked her, and they divided the food between them and ventured through the house to find one of the living rooms.

"This place is enormous," Portia said when she'd sat on the sofa and kicked off her shoes, tucking her legs underneath her.

Timothy sighed and glanced around. "It is. I'm probably only going to use three or four rooms in the whole place. I don't know why I let Mum persuade me to buy it."

Portia clucked her tongue. "You know why. Mainly for privacy. You deserve that if nothing else." She inhaled a mouthful before asking, "Have you checked out the bedrooms yet? Are you taking the master one? Papa said it was huge."

He laughed. "It *is* huge. What in this place isn't? And no, I've not checked anything else out. I'd barely closed the door when Briony rang me, and then you turned up."

Portia's dad, Remy, was his contact for helping him check out the place before he signed the contract. Remy had gone to the viewing for him and given him a video tour of the house. It had worked out well, considering he'd been two hours away. The man had been a godsend, though, which reminded him to make a note to send him a gift as a thank you.

Portia made a very un-lady-like noise and held a hand over her mouth, eyes widening. The expression, in addition to the noise, had them cracking up like teenagers. Both had to put their food down until they had calmed.

"Sorry. I've never made that noise before. What I was trying to say was that I'm sorry for turning up unannounced."

Timothy waved her away. "You know I don't mind. You're welcome anytime."

Portia rested her hand on his arm. "I don't want you secluding yourself away. Orlan was wrong, but you're better off without him."

The pain of his breakup came to the forefront, and he rubbed at his chest as if it would ease the ache. He and Orlan had been together for five years before Orlan had left, stating Timothy was never home. The man didn't mean physically. He meant mentally. In some ways, he'd been right, but Timothy could no more ignore his patients than he could his need to eat. To ensure he gave his patients his all, he often brought work home to research and plan, but it was Yanni who Orlan had a problem with.

Yanni had been his patient for around six months before he found out where Timothy lived and began "visiting" more than was suitable for a patient and therapist relationship. Timothy never invited him inside, but he often sat on the steps of the house talking with Yanni, hoping to give him some peace from everything he'd had to deal with in his life.

Unfortunately, Timothy hadn't seen the signs, but Orlan had. Several months after Orlan had left him, Yanni made a decision that changed all their lives irrevocably.

Needing to lock away the images that bombarded him with a frequency he knew was worrying, Timothy dropped his chin to his chest and breathed deeply as his grief shattered him. *He* was worried, and he was a therapist, so he knew he would begin his sessions with someone new here in Windsor. Luckily, he had a lot of contacts.

A hand running through his hair helped ground him and bring him to the present once more. Two flashbacks in one day were not uncommon, but it was more than he wanted.

"Thanks," he said, patting Portia's knees.

"You're welcome." She sat back and clapped her hands to her legs. "How about we find the box for the TV, and I help you set it up so we can watch a movie? And by that, I mean, how about I help you find the box, then watch as you set it up, and I drink more champagne?" She grinned, strained as it was.

"Sounds like a plan I can get behind."

Timothy climbed the stairs of Windsor College and weaved his way through the students until he found his room. He had a little under an hour before his first class, and he wanted to make sure he had everything ready. The teacher he'd replaced was on long-term medical leave. It had been fortuitous for him but not so lucky for the teacher. Timothy had wanted to start last week, straight after half term, but he hadn't been able to. What he had done, though, was teach from afar. He'd sent in work for the class to do to prepare for his arrival today. Time would tell if they had done it or not.

He shut out the hustle and bustle of the corridors and rested his bags on his desk. The classroom was a standard layout with desks set in rows. That wouldn't work for him because he needed the students to see each other in addition to him, so he set about moving the desks into a U shape. It might not work brilliantly, but until he could get a feel for the students, it would do.

Teaching had been second on his list of professions he'd wanted to try when he'd been at college. If he hadn't made it as a therapist, this would have been where he'd settled. Becoming a therapist had taken the top spot because of a kind gentleman who had helped him through his father's death. When he was thirteen, his dad had been killed in a robbery at the supermarket. He'd been there as a customer, picking up some last-minute items for a birthday party that weekend. His father had saved the life of the supermarket assistant at the cost of his own, but Timothy knew his dad would've been happy about that. He wouldn't have let anyone suffer if he didn't have to.

Timothy's therapist had worked with him for almost two years, and Timothy credited the man's patience and words for who he had become. It was because of him that he went into psychology in the first place.

Now that being a therapist was no longer possible, teaching was his future.

As his class filed into the room, he could see the confusion in their eyes at the new layout, but he smiled and let them settle down before saying anything.

"Welcome, class. It's nice to finally put a face to a name. Let me quickly do the register, so I can figure out who you all are." He ran down the list of names, looking up after each one to acknowledge which person it was. "Great. So, as you know, I'm Mr Dixon, and I will finish up your A-Level

Psychology course this year. Before we begin, does anyone have any questions for me?"

A girl put her hand up, and he nodded for her to speak. "Why have you moved the desks?"

He smiled. "My way of teaching isn't just about what you read or hear from me. I open the class to discussions, to debates, and to understand everything about what I'll be teaching you, you need to study body language. Who better than your fellow students to practise on?" He grinned at their widening eyes. "Don't worry. We're not going to determine your deepest, darkest secrets." He paused. "Yet."

A chuckle rounded the room. A boy put his hand up. "Why do we need to learn more about body language? It was in the first term of this course."

"Good question and I'm going to throw the question back at you as a class. Why do *you* think we need to learn more about body language?"

"Because we might have forgotten a lot?"

"That's a good reason. Why else?" When no one else said anything, he prompted, "What do we do every day?"

"Go to college."

"Okay, if we take that answer, what do you do at college?" He crossed his arms over his chest and leaned back against his desk, crossing his ankles.

"Learn."

"Read."

"Study."

He prodded again. "And how do you do these things?"

"The teachers give us information."

"How do they give you the information?" They were getting closer.

"They tell us or give us sheets of paper or get us to read the textbooks."

He smiled. "And what is that doing? What is the teacher doing?" He waited, hoping it would click.

"They're communicating."

He pointed at the student and stood. "Yes! Going back to my original question, why do you think we need to learn more about body language?"

"Because it's a way of communicating."

He clapped his hands together. "Exactly. Communication is something we do every second of every minute of every day. Even when we are silent, our bodies are speaking for us. It is next to impossible—except for those highly trained—for someone to stay completely still with no bodily tells to let us know how they're feeling." He glanced around them. "Let's try it. I want you to keep still and quiet until I say otherwise. I will go round the class and pick on a few of you," he winked, "to show what you probably don't realise you're doing. Is anyone uncomfortable with that idea?" They all shook their heads. "Okay, start now."

He waited for a few seconds before he started.

"Emily, you're eager to know more. Daniel, you're tired. Lee, you're competitive. Anya, you have a headache." He glanced around for one more victim. "Isobel, you want to have your nails redone."

Laughter followed. "How do we know if you're right?"

Timothy smiled. "Let's go round. Emily, I said you're eager to know more. Do you know how I know that?" Emily looked down at herself as if she could see what he did but shook her head. "You were tapping your finger on the table. It shows eagerness or impatience, but I chose to think you want to be here, so erred on the side of eagerness." She nodded.

"What about me?" Lee asked.

Timothy chuckled and wagged his finger. "Wait your turn. Daniel, you're tired. Your blinking speed slowed down. No falling asleep just yet." Daniel nodded his head with a smile. "Lee, you're competitive. Your body was rigid, as if you didn't want to lose the game. Sometimes, by withholding body language, you give away just as much."

"How did you know Anya had a headache? That's more internal, isn't it?" Emily asked.

Timothy nodded. "It is, but there are still tells. A twitch in the temple, narrowing of her eyes as pain goes through her head, breathing out slowly to stop the nausea. I could be wrong. Am I?" he asked Anya.

"No. I have a blinding headache." She chuckled.

"Have you taken something for it?"

"Yes. Just before class."

"Good. Make sure you drink plenty." She nodded. He looked at his last victim. "Isobel and your nails. You keep trying to hide your hands. I can see you have your nails done, but I noticed one of them is chipped. That would annoy *me* if I was in your place." Chuckles rounded the room again. "Does that answer your questions about why body language is so important?"

"Because even when someone says nothing, they could be saying everything."

"Spot on, Emily. Spot on."

3

____

EDDIE

ddie Ward filled the mug with the coffee mixture he'd made and, with a smile, set it on the tray on the counter for the customer to take. He read down the receipt on the next tray and set about making the three drinks needed to complete that order. The noise surrounding him was a warm blanket, settling his nerves and reminding him of where he was. It was only the occasional cup or plate crashing to the floor that made him startle now, which was a great thing as far as he and his therapist were concerned.

The routine of his work helped, too. Working full-time as a barista in a coffee shop might not be what most people consider a career, but he had never felt more at home than he did when he was there. Even his home with his parents had been more strained than work, but that was to be expected when they'd found out what had happened between him and Talon almost a year ago. He'd decided to tell them some details after his therapist explained it would be easier for them to deal with the nightmares he'd been having if they knew a little about the abuse he'd suffered and his triggers.

Those triggers were almost non-existent now, but he'd moved out of the house and found a small place not far from the coffee shop, and he felt more relaxed there. He'd yet to return to Club Royal, though.

The idea of the club still held the usual joy in his heart, but his head had twisted it into something that made him cringe when he envisioned himself crossing the threshold. He'd spoken to his therapist several times over the past week because he wanted to visit the place that had become so important to him and his lifestyle.

He'd tried without it. Bella, one of his friends—after a drunk explanation from him—had offered to help him figure out if he had an issue with being sexually close to someone or if it was the BDSM aspect of it his mind was rebelling against. Bella was an angel, and although Eddie was gay and didn't think of women in that way, he'd wanted to try. His friend had donned a strap-on and fucked him with it with no problems from his side, but the moment she'd restrained him, he'd lost it.

That was five months ago, and they had worked on it through the following months. Now, his head had stopped complaining every time she tied him up. It was still anxiety-inducing, but it was better than before.

"Thank you."

Eddie blinked up at the man who'd spoken, knocked out of his thoughts at the deep voice. The man had shaggy brown hair and hazel eyes, but it was the pain behind them that held Eddie transfixed for a long second.

"You're welcome," he finally replied.

The corner of the man's mouth quirked up, and Eddie could see what he might've looked like had he been at ease. The man pivoted away, carrying his tray, and Eddie watched as he chose a table in a quiet corner. Shaking his head, he turned to the next receipt and set about making the drink.

"Did you know him?" Bella came over to his station, making a show of grabbing napkins, which he doubted she needed, to give her an excuse to talk to him.

"No. He seemed sad." Eddie glanced over to the corner of the shop the man had sat in. He had his elbow on the table, cup in his hand as he read the paperwork in front of him.

"Maybe you could offer to cheer him up?" Eddie rolled his eyes when Bella winked and nudged him before going back to her station.

The number of customers dwindled as the lunch rush ended, and he wiped the back of his hand over his forehead.

"Eddie."

He turned to Mel, the cashier, who waved a hand towards the man he'd been so struck by earlier.

"Hi, sorry. I just wanted to say thank you for the drink." The man seemed uncertain, not nervous but unsure. "I know it's just coffee to some people, but it was well made and tasted fantastic. So, thank you. It made my paperwork easier to finish." He gave a self-deprecating smile and turned as if to leave.

"You're welcome. I'm glad it helped." Eddie didn't know what else to say.

The man nodded once. "I'll be back again, I'm sure." He paused and held out his hand. "I'm Timothy."

Eddie lowered his head a little and shook his hand. "Eddie."

Eddie watched as he left the shop, trying not to pout when the man's suit jacket hid his ass. He had a studious, stern demeanour, which meant he was probably a teacher or something similar and taught at the college around the corner. Eddie's heart missed a beat when he realised he was hoping he'd see him again.

"I can't believe you got his name," Bella said.

He grinned at her, feeling a lightness he'd not felt in a while. He'd stunned his friend if her open-mouthed expression was anything to go by. He chuckled. "Are you coming over tonight? I thought we could have a movie night. I've already invited Terry."

Terry was his next-door neighbour. He was unapologetically, extravagantly gay and had a heart of gold. Unfortunately, he had the worst taste in men—almost as bad as Eddie—and had recently broken up with his latest in-the-closet boyfriend. Eddie wanted to cheer him up and had plans for a *Legally Blonde* marathon followed by *Clueless*.

"Yeah, I'll be there," Bella said.

"Count me in," Mel agreed.

The afternoon sped by, filled with laughter, pleasant conversation and the smell of coffee—a scent he loved. The only thing he didn't love about it was the side effects he got when he hadn't drunk enough of it. He also had a slight addiction to coffee-related slogans on T-shirts. He owned more than he needed, but it meant he had more than enough to cover all the different moods he could be feeling.

When the doors closed for the last time that day, he cleaned his station while Bella turned up the music. Mel went around wiping tables and putting the chairs upside down on the tables, ready for Bella to clean the floors in her wake.

"Let's go!" Bella said, linking her arm through Eddie's, and set off down the street towards Eddie's house.

"Eager much?"

"It's margarita time, baby!" she sang.

"I don't know if I have any tequila left after last time."

Bella smirked at him. "It's a good job I sent Terry a message earlier then. He's stocked up. We're all good."

Eddie plastered a smile on his face, knowing the headache he would have tomorrow would be better than arguing with her. She kept up the conversation as they wandered down the road. Upon entering Eddie's house, she pulled off her coat and drifted around the place as if she owned it. He didn't mind. He wouldn't be where he was today if it hadn't been for her these past few months. He wasn't in love with her, and nor she with him, but they were the best of friends.

"Do you think we could fit in *Practical Magic* as well?" Bella asked, plucking the glasses from the cupboard.

Eddie didn't have the proper margarita glasses, so they used basic tumblers, but the result was the same. Too much alcohol for the hours they had.

"I doubt it. We have four and a half hours of films, and that's without including time for snacks and drinks and god knows what else."

"It would round us out at around six hours, though." She batted her eyelids, and he sighed.

"We'll see. Unlike you, I have to get up early tomorrow."

"It's not my fault my classes don't start until eleven."

Eddie snorted. "I'm going for a shower."

He left her to it, grabbed a change of clothes from his bedroom, then locked the bathroom door behind him. He started the shower to let the water warm up while he undressed and groaned when the hot water hit his muscles. He moved his body back and forth in the water, the spray soothing and warming his skin. As he closed his eyes, hazel eyes came to mind, and he remembered the man from earlier that day. His body responded to the vision, but if he stroked himself to orgasm, he knew how empty it would feel. Ignoring the need, he washed and dried, slipping on the clothes he'd warmed on the radiator. After opening the window a small amount to counteract the steam, he met Bella and now Mel in his living room.

"Hey. I didn't hear you come in."

Mel grinned. "I'm a ninja," she said, holding her hands up in what he assumed was a fighting stance.

He raised his eyebrows. "Ok-ay."

"Are we staying in or going out?" Mel asked.

"In," he said.

Mel groaned and flopped onto the sofa with her leg hanging over the arm. "Can we not go out for a change? We haven't been anywhere for ages."

Eddie's shoulders dropped. She was right. If they ever gave him a choice, he stayed home, but he needed to go out again, just not tonight. He felt bad for them, though.

"Mel!" Bella chastised.

"No, she's right. I'm sorry. You can go out if you want. You don't have to wait for me to be ready."

Mel stood and enfolded him in her arms. "No, *I'm* sorry. I'm so restless at the moment, and I don't know why. We can movie it. I don't mind."

"Terry needs cheering up, anyway."

"Tell me he got rid of that asshole finally?" Mel asked, putting her hand together.

Eddie nodded. "He—"

"I did, darlings! I'm fabulously free and single again, and it's wonderful!"

Terry sashayed into the room, wearing tight purple jeans, a T-shirt saying "Spank Me!" and a feather boa.

"I see you dressed up," Mel said, rolling her eyes.

"We're celebrating being single, Mel. Of course, I dressed up." He stepped to Eddie, grasping his cheeks and pressing a kiss to each side of his face before dropping one on his lips. He repeated the process with Bella but ignored Mel. They all knew she wouldn't appreciate it.

When they all had margaritas in their hands, Eddie switched on the first film. As Elle Woods filled the screen, he wished he could be as confident as she was. He had joked with Bella about asking the guy out, but he didn't know if he could, especially because of his lifestyle choices. It was more difficult to induct someone into the lifestyle than it was to find someone already in it, but those already in it had differences of their own. He'd thought he'd found someone in Talon who worked well with him, but he was a fool. He was glad the man was behind bars now, but it wouldn't stop him from sending someone after Eddie to get revenge if he was inclined.

There was no way Eddie was going to find someone who could be everything he needed them to be when he sat at home every night. He had to find the courage to go back to Club Royal. It was his only choice. Although…he could go to another club, but he wouldn't know anyone there, and that seemed more dangerous than visiting the place where he'd originally been hurt.

He twisted his mouth, then firmed it. He'd go back to Club Royal the following night. He had nothing to lose, after all.

By midnight, everyone was dozing or yawning, so Eddie called it. "Right, that's it. We're done for tonight."

"But we didn't get to see *Practical Magic!*" Bella whined.

"You're *practically* asleep, so what's the point? Come on. We can watch it first another night."

Mel rose, stretching her arms to the ceiling and yawning. "I'm going. Thanks for the drinks." She pressed a kiss to his cheek, then waved a hand over her head as she strode for the door. She lived a couple of streets away, which used to worry him until he saw her take down someone who had grabbed her arm once. Since then, he was more worried about the state of anyone who tried to hurt her.

Eddie nudged Terry, who snuggled further into his blanket cocoon, and then pouted when Eddie kept it up.

"Time to go back to your place, sleeping beauty."

"If I must," he murmured.

"I'll see he gets there." Bella's eyebrows drew together. "Unless you need me?" she whispered.

Eddie smiled and shook his head. "I'm good, thank you. Get some rest. You have college tomorrow."

"I will. I'll be thinking of you when you have to get up in seven hours."

Eddie shoved her shoulder. "Yeah, thanks for the reminder."

He grabbed the glasses and carried them to the kitchen, repeating the action with the empty wrappers and rubbish they'd accumulated, then set the dishwashing going and headed to his bedroom. Without putting the light on, he drifted to his bedside table and switched on the lamp. It had a low-watt bulb in it, so it didn't flood the room and instead gave a yellow ambience to it. It helped him adjust to sleeping if there wasn't a bright light glaring at him.

He stripped down naked, washed up and slid between the cold sheets. Bringing the duvet to his ears, he snuggled under it, wishing he'd thought to warm the bed first. He rubbed his eyes and tried to relax as the sheets warmed to the temperature of his skin. His mind whirled with the decision he'd made earlier, and he found he couldn't sleep. Would people look at him strangely? Would anyone say anything to him? Did they all believe him? Did it matter if they didn't?

He rolled onto his back and exhaled. He needed something to relax him again. He considered calling Bella back because an orgasm usually helped, but it wasn't fair to use her all the time. He needed to figure out how to let go of the thoughts and whispers in his head.

He rolled to his side again, goosebumps pebbling his skin as he exposed it to the cold room, and opened his bedside table. The variety of sex toys in there could be overwhelming for a newbie, but there was something for every occasion as far as Eddie was concerned. He considered his choices, then reached for the one he thought would best serve him that night. The one he'd chosen he hadn't used for a while, so he tiptoed to the bathroom, not wanting his feet to touch the cold floor for longer than necessary, to rinse it before grabbing a towel and heading for the kitchen counter.

From experience, the side of one of the kitchen cupboards was the sturdiest place for him to attach the dildo to, and he could work without the light on because the glow from the oven clock was enough to see by. The suction attached to the melamine without issue, and Eddie laid down the towel. Although he didn't mind the rough floor on his knees—it was actually something he loved to feel—this floor had tiles, and where he needed to kneel was right on the grout between them, which was extremely uncomfortable and took him out of the scene, hence why he had the towel.

He grabbed the lube and dropped to his knees on the towel, his ass facing the dildo. Squirting some lube onto his fingers, he reached behind him and massaged his pucker, closing his eyes and enjoying the feel. He pressed harder and harder until the tip of his finger breached it, and he bit his lip, loving the small bite of burning. He pushed further in and out until it no longer burned, then he repeated the action with another finger. When he could take three fingers with minimal stinging, he slicked the dildo liberally, shoved some more in his ass, then faced forward.

He scooted back until he could feel the dildo press against his crack, and he wriggled to get it in the right place. When he had it at his hole, he pushed backwards, circling his hips over and over to encourage his plastic friend to enter him. As it slid through his ring, he gasped at the pressure and licked his dry lips. He worked it inside him, taking his time as it had been a while, then, when his ass touched the cold surface of the unit, he stopped, dropping to his forearms and resting his head on his hands.

There was nothing better than feeling full of cock, even if it was of the plastic variety. If he could've stayed plugged every hour of the day, he would. When it became too much for him to stay still, he pulled off a little, then pushed back again. The ribbed dildo tugged against his insides, and Eddie moaned. He increased his speed, envisioning a man behind him slamming into him. He needed more, though, and he knew what.

Opening his eyes, he saw the tea towel hanging on the drawer opposite him. He slid almost off the dildo and snatched it, then pushed back on the cock with a sigh. He wrapped the tea towel around his wrists, tight enough to feel it but not enough to stop the circulation. The moment the material cinched his wrists, his muscles relaxed. Using his forearms and legs, he began thrusting himself back onto the dildo with increasing speed.

Linking his fingers together, he clenched his fists and rose, bracing himself on them, which changed the angle of the dildo and finally reached where he needed it to. He saw stars with each push back. He refused to remove the restraint around his wrists to jerk off, instead, speeding up until he had no choice but to explode onto the towel beneath him.

His limbs trembled, and he slid off the dildo, moaning as it dragged against his sensitive channel, then collapsed to the floor, heaving breaths. He dropped his head to the floor and lay there for several long minutes. When the chill became too much, he unravelled the tea towel and climbed to his feet.

He folded the towel in half, then used it to wipe off the dildo before throwing it in the washing basket with the tea towel. He removed his plastic boyfriend, then trudged to the bathroom to clean it before wiping himself down and collapsing back on his bed.

He'd been right earlier. Even with the release, he felt empty. He rolled to his side, burrowed his head into the pillow and cried.

4

GEORGE

The club was busy as always. Douglas was working that night, and Freddie was wandering around with Damon somewhere. George had wanted to get away from his workload because he couldn't concentrate. Club Royal seemed as good a place as any to visit. He hadn't been able to find anyone he wanted to scene with, though.

"Master George."

George studied the submissive who stood to his side, head lowered, hands clasped in front of them. "How can I help you?"

"I wondered if you had time to do a bondage scene with me, sir."

"It just so happens I do. What is your name?" George faced the man, taking in his tall, defined body, covered only with a pair of tight, black shorts.

"Is everything all right, Eddie?"

George glanced at Douglas as he came up beside him, resting a hand on the submissive's shoulder. The sub—Eddie —peered up at Douglas and nodded.

"Yes, Master Douglas. I was asking Master George for a bondage scene."

Douglas exhaled and smiled. "I'm glad to see you back, Eddie. Master George will look after you."

"Thank you, sir."

Douglas leaned down and whispered in George's ear. "Eddie is the sub Talon abused. Eddie has only recently returned to the club after an absence."

George nodded and stared at Douglas, hoping he conveyed his promise through his gaze. He turned back to Eddie.

"I apologise for keeping you waiting. What bondage are you interested in?"

Eddie swallowed. "The suspension bar."

George narrowed his eyes. "Are you wanting people to watch?" Eddie shook his head. "Follow me, please."

He needed to get some more information from Eddie before they could start the scene, but he thought it would work better if he took it to a quieter room. He entered one of the private rooms, waving his hand for Eddie to enter, then closed the door.

"Please, take a seat. Would you like a drink?"

"Yes, please, sir."

George grabbed two bottles of water from the fridge and settled on the sofa beside Eddie, opening the lid for one and handing it to the sub. "I won't ignore what I know, Eddie, because it's important that we talk about it. Now, you had an awful experience here before, and I want to make sure you're ready for this step. Have you taken part in a scene since the incident?"

Eddie took a sip, eyes lowered. "I have done a couple of basic scenes with a friend. A chain around my wrists and a spreader bar. I was fine with them, and it gave me the confidence to come back here." He lifted his gaze, spearing George with his blue orbs. "I love it here, and I hate that he took that away. I want it back."

George slipped his arm around Eddie's shoulders. "We can get it back for you. Please understand, though, it might not happen today. We need to take things slowly."

Eddie relaxed back, fiddling with the label on the bottle. "I just want to get back to where I was before. I love bondage. I love being tied up. I enjoy the slight pain to ground me in the present, but not what he did." Eddie peered up at him, eyes wet but not overflowing. "I want someone to care for me."

George's heart broke. He knew what Eddie had been through from conversations with Freddie and Douglas, and he knew what it was like to want someone to love and be loved in return. He pressed his lips to Eddie's temple.

"I know, little one. I know." He inhaled. "Have you been seeing a therapist?"

Eddie nodded. "I have. Ever since it happened, and I'm still seeing her now."

"Does she know about this part of your life?"

"Yes. She's in the lifestyle herself. She's a friend of a friend."

"Good. Keep talking to her. It's an important part of this." He cleared his throat. "How about this? What if I were to help you get back to a new normal for *you*? You won't ever get back to the way you were before because our life experiences change us inside and out, but we can get you back to where you are comfortable in your skin and with your club life. How does that sound?"

Eddie's eyes widened. "You would help me?"

"Of course, I would. If you agree, and after we've spoken about boundaries and everything else, I can be your Dom at the club until you're steady on your feet again."

"That would be great. Are you sure? I don't want to put a crimp in your evenings here."

George chuckled. "You wouldn't, but I'm sure."

"Thank you, Master George. I appreciate it more than you know."

"Now that's decided, let's get a few details squared away. First, what's your safe word?"

Eddie's cheeks flushed a dark shade of pink, and he stared at his hands. "The traffic light system."

"Good. What are your hard limits?"

"Extreme pain. I only like a little. Spanking was always fine before...but I don't know about now." George tightened his arm. "Flogging and caning are too intense for me."

"Okay. What about the things you enjoy?"

"I like sensation play and all kinds of bondage. I enjoy being edged." His cheeks darkened again with those words.

"So, you like being restrained, giving control to someone else."

"Yes, sir."

"If you're happy to try this evening, I will ask you what your colours are more often than you're probably used to. I don't want you to *ever* feel like you can't say red. That is more important than anything else. If I don't believe you can stop me if it's too much, we can't do this."

Eddie inhaled and exhaled, a wealth of emotions passing over his face. "I can stop you, sir. I know I can."

"Good." He pressed another kiss to his temple. "What does your aftercare look like?"

"I tend to be emotional, like crying and such. I like to be

covered in a blanket and held. Running a hand through my hair helps me, too."

"All right. Would you like to try something easy tonight?"

Eddie smiled, though it was barely a twitching of the corners of his mouth. "I would."

"Well, as you're already deliciously dressed, how about we try the suspension bar but with your feet on the floor, to begin with? We can adapt as we go. There are no wrongs here."

George stood, but Eddie grabbed his hand before he moved away. "Thank you, Master George."

He cupped Eddie's jaw, smoothing his thumb along the soft skin. "You're welcome."

George stepped towards the wall and loosened the chain for the suspension bar that was pulled tightly to the ceiling when not in use. The clink of the chains was loud—and arousing—in the quiet room, and he glanced over at Eddie to see his cheeks flushed, but his eyes wary. Two emotions at war with each other. He'd have to be careful, but he would do anything to help Eddie become whole again. Or as whole as he could be.

Eddie was the same height as George, so when the bar was shoulder-height, he attached the chain to the wall again, holding the bar in place.

"Come here, Eddie," he murmured, not wanting to startle him.

Eddie turned wide eyes on George, then put his bottle down and rose from the sofa. With each step he took, his hands shook, and when he was within reach, George wrapped him in his arms, his front to Eddie's back.

"Touch the bar, Eddie," he said in his ear. "Feel how hard and cold the metal is. Listen to the clink of the chains as they move. Feel the softness of the leather cuffs. Remember a time when you were tied up to one and loved it. You can have that again."

Eddie reached forward, smoothing his hands over the bar, the chains and the cuffs as George had told him to.

"I love the sound of the chains. The only sound better is when someone is moaning in ecstasy from something I've done to them." Eddie's breath hitched, and his head dropped back on George's shoulder, eyes closed. "I bet someone has made you moan like that."

He hadn't been sure whether talking like this would help or hinder him with Eddie, but it seemed like words were a balm to the sub as well. He made a note of that.

"Shall we see what the cuffs feel like around your wrist?" Eddie nodded. "Words, Eddie. I need words."

"Yes, Sir."

"Open your eyes for me. I need to make sure you're with me."

He pulled away from Eddie and turned him to face him. Eddie opened his eyes, and George saw his pupils were already dilating. Reaching behind Eddie, George grabbed the first wrist cuff, bringing it forward. Eddie hissed when the bar touched his shoulder, and George paused.

"Colour?"

"Green, Sir. It was cold." Eddie chuckled.

George smiled. He held out the opened cuff. "Try it on."

Eddie slid his wrist into the cuff, and with slow motions, George secured the strap. Eddie's shoulders lowered, and he exhaled.

"Colour?"

"Green, Sir." Eddie's voice was breathy, his eyelids at half-mast.

If George wasn't mistaken, there was relief in Eddie's expression. "Other wrist." He repeated it on the other side.

Eddie stood facing George with his wrists secured at shoulder height and the bar behind his neck. His breathing had increased, but George could see no tension in his body.

He cupped Eddie's jaw, making the sub look at him. "I'm going to raise the bar. Tell me at any time if it's too much for you."

"Yes, Sir."

George stepped to the wall and unhooked the chain, pulling gently to raise the bar and Eddie's arms. He stopped when Eddie was just off his heels so he could feel the pull on his wrists and shoulders. George secured the chain again and stood in front of him. Eddie lifted his head, and the banked heat behind his eyes didn't surprise George at all. It was the calm ocean in those blue depths that shocked him. He knew Eddie had been worried about it, but George now knew the sub would find his way through. With every scene, from this point forward, Eddie would find another piece of himself and patch himself back together. George was glad to help.

"Colour?"

"Green, Sir."

No hesitation. Deciding not to push too hard, George tilted his head and stepped closer, using one finger from each hand to draw a soft path from Eddie's jaw, down his neck and over his chest and abs. Each circuit had Eddie's breath hitching, gasping inhales that jerked the bar above them, sending the chains rattling. Eddie's hands clenched on the grip, and he arched forward, seeking more as his head dropped back.

The reactions he was pulling from Eddie made George content. He never went into a scene thinking it would be sexual—the opposite, in fact. Unlike some members, BDSM for him didn't need to entail anything sexual happening at all. From his experience, it varied depending on what each person wanted from the scene. He chose not to have sexual relations with most of his partners in the club, not because he couldn't, but because he didn't need to. Occasionally, he did, but more often than not, he didn't.

He'd gone into this agreement with Eddie with no thought to his own gratification, but damn if the man's responses didn't light a fire inside George. With his hands still wandering over Eddie's body, he stepped behind him, blowing soft breaths across his skin, heightening the man's awareness. The strength in his body was undeniable. His muscles clenched and released with each pass of George's fingers.

If they were to continue after tonight, a contract would need to be arranged to cover them both. He would hate to think Eddie believed he had no choice when he held all the power.

George stepped around to the front again, seeing the prominent erection tenting Eddie's shorts.

"Colour?"

"Green, Sir," came the breathy reply.

Leaning closer, he whispered, "Shall I take you higher, Eddie?" His question took on two meanings.

"Please, Sir. Please." He swallowed, his Adam's apple bobbing hard.

George removed his hands with regret, and Eddie whimpered. Unhooking the chain once more, George pulled it until Eddie was on his tiptoes, then secured it once more.

The extra few inches elongated Eddie's body, putting every muscle, hill and valley in stark relief, and George had the overwhelming need to lick along every line. He frowned.

He returned his hands to the sweat-slicked skin, but this time, he curved his fingers, grazing his nails along the tensed body parts. He didn't go easy, although he checked for his colour every few minutes.

Eddie was panting erratically by the time George deemed them finished, and he brought the sub down by softening his touches once more. After a final rub of his hands, George released the bar a little, ensuring it kept some of Eddie's weight so the man didn't fall to the floor. George unfastened the wrist cuffs, wrapping his arm around Eddie's waist when he seemed to sag forward.

"Come on, Eddie. Let's get some snuggles in."

He took him over to the sofa and laid him down, covering him with a warm blanket while he went for water, orange juice and a straw. When he returned, he slid onto the sofa beside Eddie, repositioned the man over his chest and clasped him. He offered the orange juice with the straw in and held it steady when Eddie drank some. After resting the glass back on the floor beside them, he slid his arms around him again, kissing the top of his head while stroking his fingers through the blond strands.

The trembling started several minutes later, and soon, Eddie was crying as he had predicted before their scene. George was used to different types of sub-drop because no one was identical in the way they dealt with things, but the pain in Eddie's cries tore at George's heart, even though he knew they had nothing to do with what they'd just experienced. It didn't hurt any less.

George folded himself around Eddie as much as he could, hoping to tether him to the present. It was all he could do.

He lost track of how long they laid like that, but eventually, Eddie lifted his head, his eyes bright despite their redness. "Thank you, Master George. It was perfect."

George couldn't curb his impulse, and he dropped a kiss to Eddie's lips. "I'm glad." He pulled back, but Eddie reached up, cupping his jaw.

"Would I be out of order to request a kiss?"

Eddie spoke softly, but George heard every word. His eyes took in every part of Eddie's face, making sure he wanted a kiss instead of feeling he had to as "payment" for what they'd done, but he seemed sincere.

"Colour?"

Eddie smiled, sliding his hand to his neck. "Green, Sir."

George lowered his head, taking Eddie's lips. He sipped from his top lip, then his bottom lip, alternating several times before he felt Eddie's mouth open with a moan. Unable to stop himself and hoping Eddie would stop him if it was too much, he slid his tongue inside, exploring the warm cavern. Their tongues duelled, and Eddie's hand tightened on his neck. George could taste mint and something else he couldn't figure out, but the sounds from Eddie's throat rivalled the chains for the top spot on George's list.

He pulled back, pecking kisses along his mouth until Eddie settled against him again. There were no words spoken, but something had shifted within George. He couldn't figure out what.

Eddie dozed for around half an hour before George reluctantly woke him. The man peered up at him with a smile.

"Thank you."

George returned the smile. "You're welcome. I want you to think over what we spoke about earlier. You have no obligations to me at all. I need you to be sure this is what you want." Eddie opened his mouth, but George held up a hand.

"Please. Think it over. You need to do what's best for you. It would kill me if you felt pushed into something you're not sure you want."

"And if I decide I want to continue?" Eddie asked, tilting his head.

"Then let Clarice know, and we will meet to arrange a contract between us. It will keep us both safe and let us know exactly where we stand."

They moved to the door, but before Eddie opened it, he turned back to George. "I won't change my mind, but in case you do, can I have a goodbye kiss?"

George couldn't withhold his grin. "I can see I'm going to have to learn to become immune to your charms."

He stepped forward, crowding Eddie against the door, and cupped his jaw. Not wasting a moment, he fastened their lips together, stealing the air and giving his own in its place. Eddie's hands gripped at the back of George's leather shirt while George took what he offered and gave what he could. When air was imperative, he tore his mouth away and stared at the man, shaking his head.

"Hmm," he murmured, wishing he could figure out what his brain and body were trying to tell him. "Come on. I'll walk you out."

George rested his hand on Eddie's lower back and weaved through the crowd to the exit.

"George."

He turned to the voice, keeping his hand on Eddie. "Charles. What can I do for you?"

His cousin sneered at the hand on Eddie's back. Charles never hid his distaste for homosexuals despite it being a rule of the club that all people were allowed to attend. There had been a big blow out not long ago with Aunt

Charlotte and Charles leading the charge, and George's father had banned them from attending social events unless necessary. Unfortunately, he couldn't do the same at the club.

"I wanted to check in and make sure everyone was doing well so far."

Bullshit. George knew it was a load of crap, but he played along. "Yes, we're all doing well, thanks. How is Juliet and the kids?"

"They're good." Charles stared at George, not even disguising his contempt.

"Glad to hear it. I'm sorry, but I have to go. Give my regards to your family."

George smiled, then frowned when he'd given Charles his back. What had that been about? Charles was usually only there to rub salt into any wounds they may have, but there was nothing unusual happening. Had something happened he didn't know about?

George guided them into the less crowded "conversation area," as Douglas liked to call it, and through to the reception area, discarding Charles's strange visit for the time being. He stopped at the door to the changing rooms.

"Get some rest and think it over. I won't accept anything before three days, all right." He chuckled when Eddie pouted. "Three days."

"Yes, Sir."

George lifted Eddie's hand and kissed his knuckles. "See you soon."

Eddie's cheeks darkened as he disappeared into the changing rooms, and George swallowed hard. He turned, snorting when he caught Clarice jerking her head away from him.

"It's okay, Clarice. I was coming to tell you about it, anyway."

"Sorry, Prince George. I didn't mean to stare."

George rested against her desk and smirked. "There's too much happening in this place for you to worry about staring. You need to know everything that's happening, anyway; otherwise, how can you do your job?"

Clarice's back straightened. "How can I help?"

George sighed. "I've made a verbal agreement with Eddie that I will be his Dom inside these walls. Because of his circumstances, I want him to think things through first. I've told him no less than three days, then if he wants to continue, he's to contact you. If that happens, could you please arrange a time for him to come in to go through a contract?" He stared down at his hands. "I don't want him hurt again."

"You wouldn't hurt him, Prince George."

"Not intentionally." He gave a small smile. "Is that okay?"

"Of course. Are there any times you can't do?" Clarice clicked on her computer.

"I can't do next Thursday, but apart from that, I've no plans."

"I'll see to it."

George stood. "He might change his mind."

Clarice smiled. "No, he won't."

The changing room doors opened, and Eddie emerged dressed in trousers and a button-down shirt with a leather jacket over the top. George stared. He couldn't help it. Eddie looked as delicious in clothes as he did out of them.

The man in question cleared his throat and stepped to the desk, putting his thumb to the sensor to log him out of the building. "Goodnight, Clarice. Goodnight, Master George."

They stared at each other for several seconds, then Eddie dropped his head and strode to the lift. George didn't stop staring until the doors closed on Eddie's smiling face.

"Fuck if I know what's going on."

Clarice smiled at him. "I think these next three days are going to be a test of your patience, Prince George."

He narrowed his eyes on her and returned to the club, her laughter following him. She was correct. Despite not knowing why he was so drawn to Eddie, he couldn't deny it.

Three days.

Fuck.

He'd be lucky if he lasted three hours.

5

———

TIMOTHY

Timothy sat on the comfortable leather sofa, fiddling with his mug of tea, his eyes firmly fixed on the liquid inside and the gentle ripples his movements made. Some people would say he was procrastinating, but Derek's question was difficult for him to answer. Dr Derek Stamford was a therapist his previous therapist had recommended to him. Timothy hadn't been sure whether he was going to continue his sessions, but after speaking to Derek, he decided to stay on for at least the first few months of his stay in the new town. Timothy had wanted a fresh start, but he knew that big changes sometimes made it more difficult, and old wounds could easily reopen at such a large switch.

"If you have to think about it this hard, Timothy, then it's something we need to talk about." Derek crossed his legs, leaning his elbow on the arm of his chair and resting his hands in his lap.

Timothy narrowed his eyes at him and the corner of his mouth curled. He knew what Derek was doing, but damn if it didn't work.

"My answer is undetermined," Timothy said with a smile.

Derek's mouth curled. "You know from your training, and as most of the population can attest, taking your own advice is much more difficult than taking someone else's advice. If you take advice from someone else, you can blame them if it goes wrong. If you take your own advice, you only have yourself to blame."

Timothy glanced at his mug again. "That is true. It doesn't make it any easier to hear the advice from you when I've already told myself the same thing several hundred times."

"You need to forgive yourself, Timothy. Their deaths were not your fault." Derek cleared his throat. "Walk me through what happened that day."

Timothy inhaled and let the breath out slowly. The ripples in his tea increased, and he reached across to place the cup on the table. Resuming his position, this time threading his fingers, he tapped his thumbs together and hung his head. As fast as his heart was beating, he knew he needed to face this memory many times more before it would cause him less pain.

Timothy closed and locked the door behind him, setting his bag on the floor near the pile of shoes. Sliding off his damp coat, he hung it up to drip onto the tray he'd placed there for this reason. After kicking off his shoes, he headed towards the kitchen, trying to ignore the silence of the house that had once been full of noise and warmth whenever he entered. Memories of his life with Orlan tried to take his breath, but he refused to let it. Orlan had decided, and Timothy had to live with the consequences.

He grabbed a glass from the cupboard above the sink and ran the cold tap for several seconds before filling the glass to the top. As he drank, he stared out of the kitchen window into the pitch black of his back garden. The garden he had once hoped would be full of children. The garden Orlan had painstakingly landscaped to include a vegetable patch. Despite being unable to see it with his eyes, he could visualise the details he would prefer to hide from.

He drained the glass and rested his hands on the counter, head lowered.

"I didn't hear you come in."

Timothy jerked so hard he knocked the glass into the sink, where it smashed to pieces. He whirled around and watched Yanni step closer. His heart raced, knowing instinctively that his life was in danger. Yanni stood before him in jogging bottoms and a T-shirt with bare feet, his hands visible but relaxed.

Timothy licked his lips. "What are you doing here, Yanni?"

Yanni took another step forward, and Timothy pressed his lower back against the counter, resting his hands to the side. He kept his eyes on Yanni, watching for any movements that might telegraph his intent.

"I came to keep you company. I know you've been lonely since he left. I wanted you to know you're not alone anymore."

Timothy knew he needed to contact his colleague to explain the situation, but there was no way of doing that without Yanni knowing.

"Why don't you put the TV on and choose something to watch. I'll get us some drinks and snacks." He had no idea whether Yanni would listen, but he had to try.

Yanni's face lit up, and his smile stretched. "Can we have popcorn?"

"Yes, of course. We have some in the pantry. I'll bring it with the drinks." Timothy indicated the sink. "I just need to clean this, too."

"Okay. I will choose a film."

He watched as Yanni exited the kitchen and disappeared into the living room. Fumbling for his phone, Timothy dialled his colleague, but there was no answer. "Call me the minute you get this, please." He didn't know whether he would get the message in time, but he had no other choice.

He placed his phone to the side, then grabbed some kitchen roll and picked up the glass pieces from the sink. He picked up a small shard when a click sounded behind him, and something cold rested against the base of his skull. Timothy froze, lifting his gaze to the window and seeing the reflection of Yanni with a gun pressed to his head.

"What…What are you doing?"

Yanni pressed the gun harder against his head, and Timothy braced himself to stop his forward movement, forgetting about the glass in his hand until it sliced deep.

"I thought we could have a really pleasant evening, just the two of us, but you had to ruin it by making a phone call. We don't need anyone interfering in our relationship, Timothy. We just need each other."

"I won't call anyone else." Timothy tried to focus on Yanni, but his hand was burning and bleeding.

"Wrong. You will call Orlan and get him to come over."

Timothy's head pounded in time with his heartbeat, and he knew there was no way he could ask Orlan to face Yanni in this situation. Fortunately, they had a code for such a scenario. Orlan had insisted on it when their relationship had become more serious because he was concerned about Timothy's safety.

"Okay, I will call him."

He reached his uninjured hand out to grab his phone and dialled Orlan.

"It's late, Timothy. What is so important it couldn't wait until tomorrow?"

"I wondered if you could drop by tonight and bring some cheese and crackers with you. I have some wine we can share."

Orlan was quiet for a moment, then he agreed, saying he would be there in fifteen minutes. After ending the call, Timothy put the phone down.

"He'll be here in fifteen minutes, Yanni."

"Good. Let's go to the living room." The gun pulled back a little, but Timothy could still see Yanni pointing it at him in the reflection in the window.

Timothy, moving slowly, turned to the side and showed Yanni his hand. "Can I clean this up first, please?"

Yanni's expression softened, and he nodded. The man moved to his side, nearest his phone, and watched as Timothy pulled the shard from his hand with a wince. He washed the cut and probed the area to see if he could feel any other bits, but he couldn't. He took a step back and opened the second drawer, grabbing the box of plasters and covering his palm with one before wrapping some surgical tape around to keep it in place. It was in the worst position.

"We can watch the TV while we wait," Yanni said.

Timothy walked slightly in front of Yanni and entered the living room, sitting in the armchair Yanni pointed to, the gun still trained on him with a surprisingly steady hand. Even though he'd been seeing Yanni for several months, he hadn't believed him capable of doing this.

Yanni reached forward and set the TV running, the choice of film a little unnerving. As The Jacket *started playing, Timothy's brain tried to figure a way out of this mess. Orlan appeared to understand his coded message, and hopefully, the police would quietly approach the house. He didn't want anyone getting hurt because of this situation. Orlan knew better than to come to the house, but Timothy wouldn't put it past him to be outside waiting.*

He didn't know how long it had been when he heard the key in the door, and his heart lurched when Yanni jumped up from his seat and pointed his gun at the new arrival. Timothy shook his head at Orlan.

Orlan held out his hands to Yanni. "It's okay. No one needs to get hurt."

"You broke his heart," Yanni shouted at Orlan. "You hurt him, and you deserve nothing."

"Yanni…" Timothy said.

"No! He deserves nothing when he hurt you to the degree that he did. I can see the pain you're in, Timothy. He shouldn't get away with it."

"It was my fault, Yanni. I did this to us, not him."

The hand holding the gun trembled as Yanni waved it around, his empty hand resting against his head as if there was too much noise.

"No, no, no! You're perfect. It's him. He's the evil. It must be stopped. It must be stopped." Yanni lifted his head and stared at Orlan. "I must stop it."

"No!"

Timothy raised from his chair as the gun fired, and he watched Orlan fall backwards onto the hallway floor. Seconds later, another shot fired, and Yanni hit the floor. Timothy's gaze flicked between his ex and his patient, unable to understand how it had come to this.

The door flew open, suddenly, and the room filled with people, although he couldn't hear what they were saying. He could only stare at the devastation that lay before him.

"He wasn't supposed to be there. He was supposed to call the police and stay away. We had a plan," Timothy said, his throat sore.

Derek said nothing because what was there to say? Orlan's death was unnecessary, and Timothy could've prevented it by stopping Yanni from visiting, by telling someone else what was happening, by talking Yanni down. Anything but sit there and watch.

Timothy stood, drifting to the window, and watched the stop and start of the traffic. He slid his hands into his pocket and played with the ring that he always kept there as a reminder.

"You're an amazing therapist, Timothy, but some people need more help than we can give them. You know this," Derek said.

He knew that, but when it was close to home, the usual platitudes and knowledge didn't help. Emotion takes over. It was a strange sensation to be on the other side of the sofa, so to speak. The questions Derek threw at him were much harder to answer than he'd thought when Timothy had been the one asking them. Everything had seemed straightforward. Everything had seemed black and white. Now, there were so many shades of grey, he couldn't keep up. So many variations of emotions, emotions that drag other emotions along with it, emotions that start as one thing and become something different.

There was no clear path, just a landscape of twists and turns with his future hidden behind a mountain too tall to climb.

If he ever went back to being a therapist—which was highly unlikely—he could help the patients better because he knew the other side of it now. He knew what they often couldn't articulate themselves.

And it was painful.

As the gates closed behind his car, Timothy's shoulders dropped. Although the house was far too big for him alone, the ability to keep everyone else out was a bonus. He parked the car in the garage and let himself into the main house through a doorway to what he had started to call a mudroom. There was another doorway at the other end of the narrow room that led to the kitchen. He took off his shoes and coat but took his bag to the kitchen table. He skirted around the island and flicked the switch on the kettle, grabbing a mug from the lower cupboard and making himself a cup of tea. His therapy sessions always took a lot out of him, but he had never turned to alcohol to blunt the pain. He couldn't. It wasn't how he was wired.

He checked his watch and headed for the living room. He sat in the centre of the sofa, propping his laptop onto a couple of books, then opening it and waiting for it to load.

The moment his sisters and mother filled the screen, he found his smile. It might not have been as big and carefree as a few years ago, but it was there.

"You look like you could do with a dash of whiskey in that cup," Talia said.

"Who said I haven't?" Timothy grinned, taking a sip.

"How are you, sweetheart?" his mum said.

Timothy's smile dimmed, but he hid nothing from them. "It's been a rough day, but I'm working through it."

His mum gave him a small smile, strained as it was. "You'll get there. I know you will."

"Have you still not got rid of those boxes?" Briony said.

Timothy glanced over his shoulder to see the pile of boxes behind the sofa. "There's no rush, Bri. It'll get done."

"Have you unpacked anything yet?" Imogen said.

He knew his sisters meant well, but they were also nosy as hell.

"I've opened the things that I use most often. The rest can wait."

Bri sighed. "I suppose it would make things easier to decorate if we don't have to worry about moving so much stuff," she said

"Have you eaten yet?" his mum asked.

Timothy's mouth twitched. "Yes, Mum, I have."

"Fantastic! That means you're ready for movie night," Imogen said.

"No, he's not ready yet. He hasn't got any snacks," Talia said.

"I don't need any snacks. I'm not like you three." Timothy chuckled when they started arguing about who ate the most snacks during a movie. Timothy would have said Talia, but all three could easily eat a bag of popcorn, two bags of sweets and a tube of crisps without batting an eyelid. The idea of eating that much junk food made him feel sick. Now give him pizza. That was another matter.

As his sisters disappeared to grab their snacks of choice, his mother leaned closer to the camera.

"Are you sure you're okay?"

"I'm better than I was."

When they all settled down, and their movie was ready, they set the laptops so they could see each other and pressed play. It wasn't as good as if he had been with them physically, but it was enough to bring him some sense of normality to help him ground himself further. They did this after every therapy session he had, and he loved it.

The only downside he'd found was that their movie never played at the same time. So, one of them would be several seconds ahead of the other, but he could live with that. That he could *visit* with them was more than enough for him.

They laughed their way through *Shazam*, occasionally having to explain something to their mother, then paused it halfway through to replenish their drinks. It wasn't quite the same atmosphere as being at a cinema, but it was still good.

When the film ended, they said their goodbyes and Timothy gave them the date of his next session. As he went to close his laptop, his eyes caught on the folder named "Pictures," and he hesitated. He didn't look at them very often, and he wasn't sure if it was the best time to do it, feeling as raw as he was, but his fingers had other ideas. Before he'd realised it, a picture of him and Orlan on holiday in Spain filled his screen.

Orlan had been completely correct in ending their relationship because Timothy hadn't been able to give him what he needed. There was only so much of Timothy to go around, but it seemed like he kept most of it for his patients instead of his husband. Orlan deserved better than that, and he'd been on his way to getting it. Timothy had never met Orlan's new boyfriend, but he knew he'd been happy.

Timothy flicked through a few more pictures before that tear in his chest became too wide. He slammed the lid of the laptop and lay down on the sofa, hugging a cushion to his chest as tears leaked out. He'd allow himself another hour, and then he'd pick himself up, get some sleep and begin again tomorrow.

He had the future of psychology to teach the following day, and he wanted to make sure they understood both sides of the therapy process. Being in the position he was in gave him something some therapists didn't have—the experience of the very pain they were treating.

Though he didn't wish pain on anyone, maybe explaining his version would help them. He wouldn't flay himself alive, but he would call on his incident to help them understand what the textbooks couldn't.

6

EDDIE

Saturdays were the busiest day of Eddie's week. He worked a full shift from eight in the morning until five-thirty in the afternoon, with an hour for lunch in the middle. That day, though, felt like it dragged. He knew why. He was meeting with Master George tonight and excitement coursed through him every time he thought about it. He couldn't stop his silly grin from spreading across his face. He'd lost count of the times Bella and Mel had asked him what was wrong, but because of the NDA he'd signed when he'd first become a member of Club Royal, he couldn't tell them anything except that he'd met someone he thought would help him.

They both knew something else was going on, but Eddie couldn't tell them. What were the chances that he—a lowly barista, who lived month to month on his wages and had nothing to offer anyone—could catch and keep the eye of a prince? Little to none. He was going to allow Master George to help him, then say goodbye and thank you at the end.

He didn't expect Master George to treat him any differently to how he would treat other subs at the club, but if Eddie could show him with actions how appreciative he was, maybe Master George would help him find a Master who would treat him right. He didn't trust his judgement any longer.

"What are you humming?" Bella asked. "I recognise it but can't figure it out."

Eddie frowned, having no idea he had been. "I don't know. I wasn't paying attention." He glanced at the clock and groaned. "How is it only two o'clock? I swear time is going backwards instead of forwards today."

"Try not to think about tonight, and you might get through the shift without complaining," Mel said, hip-checking him.

Eddie bumped her back and chuckled. "Shut up. You'd be the same if you had a date."

"Ooh, it's a date, is it?" Bella jumped on that phrase quicker than Eddie could backtrack.

"No, it's not. It's just a..." He peered around and lowered his voice, "scene, not a date. I'm just glad I've found someone who might help and who I know won't give me any trouble."

"How do you know?" Bella asked.

Eddie lowered his head, focusing on the floor. "I just know. I can't explain why. Trust me. He's a good guy. One of the best."

"You've caught his eye. Maybe he'll make this a long-term thing," Mel said, smiling at the next customer. "How can I help you?"

Eddie turned to Bella. "It won't be long-term. I promise you that, but for the moment, I know I can trust him."

Bella seemed unsure, but she smiled and hugged him.

"Promise you'll keep in touch and let me know you're okay at the end of the night. I don't like the idea of something happening and me not knowing about it until the next day."

Eddie nodded. "I will text you before I leave for home. Promise."

Mel passed him a slip of paper, and he started on the next drink order, his thoughts moving back to that night. He had no idea what to expect, but he would take whatever Master George wanted to give him.

Three and a half hours later, Eddie shucked his apron, grabbed his bag and coat and ran for the door.

"Don't forget to open it before you careen through it!" Bella called with a laugh.

Eddie held his middle finger up in the air, pointed in her direction. "See you Monday."

"Wow, you're going to be gone that long? Whoever the guy is, I want him. Stamina much?" Mel snorted, and Bella laughed again.

Eddie ignored them, although he smiled at their teasing. He had the best friends in the world.

By the time he'd arrived home, the nerves were settling in. His previous visit had taken several hours of working himself up to it before he could walk through the doors. This time, he had next to no time to prepare.

He jumped in the shower, washed and dried, then threw on some clothes and stopped in front of his bed. A bag waited for him, open and ready to fill with whatever outfit he chose for the night. He'd get changed into it when he arrived as most of the club members did, but he wasn't sure which to choose. Master George hadn't seemed averse to the shorts he'd worn, but would he want Eddie to uncover himself more if they were going to be a regular thing?

Eddie went to his wardrobe and flicked through the hangers. He could pair his shorts with a mesh shirt. It wouldn't show as much skin but would still be enticing. He didn't want to let Master George down. He threw the shirt into the bag and chose a more modest black shirt as well. He could always get changed if Master George wasn't happy.

He paused, resting the clothes on the top of the bag and sat down on the bed. Staring at his hands, he watched them tremble and inhaled, trying to calm down and remind himself of something. Despite his title, Master George had no right to tell Eddie how to dress. What he wore was Eddie's choice and no other, except if he went into a relationship with someone, and even then, there should be compromise and discussions about it. Eddie liked how he dressed, but Talon hadn't. More than once, Talon had ripped items of clothing off Eddie's body because he wanted him naked whenever he was present.

Eddie fought the urge to throw up and gripped his fingers tightly. Inhaling again, he reminded himself that Talon was now in prison and would never hurt him again.

He firmed his jaw and stood, throwing the shirt back towards the wardrobe and leaving the mesh shirt in the bag. If Master George didn't like it, then he'd have to deal with it because Eddie wanted to wear it. He would take his life back if it was the last thing he did.

Zipping the bag, he hitched it on his shoulder and headed for the door. The club didn't need membership cards or anything like that. They used thumbprints, which made it easier to get in as far as Eddie was concerned. He didn't have to remember to bring a card with him. He only needed to remember to take himself. He chuckled as he wandered to his car. Talking to himself in his head was becoming a habit.

The drive didn't take as long as Eddie thought it would, and he parked in the underground car park. The lift took him to the reception area, and he smiled as he strode towards Clarice.

"Good evening, Clarice."

"Good evening, Mr Ward. How are you tonight?"

"Very well, thank you." He pressed his thumbprint to the reader and cleared his throat. "Is Master George around, please?"

Clarice did an admirable job of hiding her smile while she nodded. "He's already inside. He'll be pleased to know you're here."

Eddie's heart jumped. "Really?"

Clarice glanced behind her as if someone might be there, then leaned forward. "It's not my place to say, but he's been waiting for tonight."

Eddie's eyebrows rose, and he bit his lip. "Thank you," he whispered and headed for the changing rooms.

His thumbprint let him into the room, and he glanced towards the room the monitors used to change. They were given a separate room, he assumed, because of their status. As for Eddie, he found his locker, opened it with his thumb and started stripping. His hands trembled as he pulled his shorts up and his shirt on. He slid on his fabric shoes to protect him from anything that might have been dropped on the floors of the club. They were like swimming shoes but had a sturdier sole to them. He preferred to be barefoot, but he'd once stood on a piece of tile that had been sticking up and cut the sole of his foot. It hadn't been pleasant and took ages to heal. Talon hadn't been pleased with that.

He shook away thoughts of that man and concentrated on who might be waiting for him on the other side of the wall.

Eddie stared at his reflection, making sure he looked the part, then took a deep breath and exhaled. Thinking about the possible positive outcome made him smile, and he closed his locker, aiming for the door. Clarice gave him a nod as he passed, and he felt his cheeks heating.

The bar area wasn't busy, and Eddie headed over to grab a bottle of water before going to the main club area.

"Good evening, Eddie. How are things?" Oliver asked. The man had been the bartender at the club for the entire time Eddie had been coming, and his husband also attended, although he could often "roam" the club. They had a good relationship and boundaries they both adhered to, which gave Eddie something to aim for. He'd love nothing more than to have what they had.

"Good, thanks. I'm glad to be back."

Oliver raised his eyes when Eddie's hand trembled as he reached for the bottle. Eddie chuckled. "I *am* glad to be back, but it's a little stressful."

Oliver leaned on the bar towards him. "I can imagine. Just remember, that asshole is in jail. He can't hurt you anymore."

"No, but someone else could," he murmured.

Oliver conceded the point with a tilt of his head. "If you tarnish every other person with *his* failures, you won't be able to see those worthy, even if they're right before your eyes."

Eddie frowned. Had he been doing that? Probably. "You're right. It's easier said than done."

"Definitely, but worth it." Oliver winked and tapped the bar before leaving Eddie with his thoughts.

He cracked the lid on the bottle and took a small sip, trying to calm his nerves. They hadn't set a time to meet or anything like that, but Eddie didn't want to waste any time they might have. Inhaling through his nose, he capped his bottle and aimed for the double doors. He could hear the bass reverberating through the floor before he'd even opened the door. The music wasn't particularly loud; it was just deep and ran through his body like someone was playing *him.*

He glanced around the room, noting the different scenes happening on the stages. Someone was on the fuck bench, and Eddie jerked his head away. He couldn't watch that yet.

"Eddie!"

He searched the room for the voice but couldn't see anyone until Master George stepped through the parted crowd.

Eddie lowered his head. "Master George." Eddie's heart raced, and he couldn't contain his smile.

"Clarice didn't hear from you. Does that mean you've decided not to go ahead with what we talked about?"

Was he supposed to have called her? "Oh, um, I still want to go ahead with it. I forgot to call her and tell her. I was excited about coming tonight and didn't think about calling ahead."

"Shh. Eddie, breathe. It's fine." Master George slipped an arm around Eddie's shoulders. "I wanted to go through a contract with you, that's all. Can we do that now?"

Eddie didn't want to read a contract. He wanted Master George. "Can we do it later?" he asked, eyes still lowered.

Master George was quiet, then a finger curved under his chin, lifting his head. When he met the vibrant blue eyes, he relaxed.

"Better. Yes, we can do it later, but we *must* do it if you want to go ahead."

"I do, Sir. Definitely."

Master George smiled. "What would you like to do tonight?"

Eddie licked his lips. "I'm not really sure."

"Do you trust me?"

"Implicitly," Eddie said in a firm voice.

Master George nodded once. "Come on."

Eddie went with Master George to one of the private rooms but hesitated at the threshold, even though Master George still had his arm around him.

"What's wrong?" Master George stepped in front of him and cupped his jaw, bringing their gazes together. "Talk to me."

"This is the room…Master Douglas found me in." Eddie's heart pounded. He knew he'd have to face the room eventually because it was ridiculous to think a space could have this much of a hold over him.

"Let's try another room."

"No! Sir. No." He stared into Master George's eyes. "Will you help me?"

"With anything and everything I can. What do you need?"

"I want to do it here. I need something good to wash away the bad memories of this room."

"Are you sure, Eddie? There is no weakness in not being ready."

"I'm sure." He nodded to emphasise his answer.

Master George stared at him for a long minute, then nodded in return. He slid his hands into Eddie's and gripped them hard. "I'm here." He stepped backwards, tugging Eddie into the room with him.

Every step had Eddie's palms sweating and his heart jumping, but when they finally stopped in the centre of the room, Eddie sighed. He glanced around, never letting go of Master George's hands.

"Master Douglas helped me to the bed. He's a good man. Talon, not so much," he murmured, unsure if his words were supposed to be loud enough to be heard. Staring to his left, his gaze caught on the table where Talon had bent him over and paddled his ass until he bled. "The table has moved. It used to be in the centre of the room."

"Most things in the room move around as the occupants need them. If the table was in the centre, it was where they had left it before you entered the room."

"Can we use it?" Eddie trembled as he asked.

"I don't think it's a good idea at the moment, Eddie. The room has thrown you off. I don't want you to tip over the edge. Why not try something else first, then we can work towards the table." Master George's hand left his and slid against his jaw, turning his face towards him. "You can beat this, Eddie. One step at a time."

"Can I have a kiss, Sir?"

Master George smirked. "Charmer." He lowered his head and set a small, delicate kiss on Eddie's lips.

Eddie could've easily lost himself in the kiss, but Master George lifted his head too soon. "I think something a little less stressful. Please strip and lay on your back on the bed. I'm going to close the door."

Eddie hadn't realised the door was still open, but a sense of peace flowed through Eddie at the order, and he stepped towards the bed, already yanking the shirt over his head. He slipped off his shoes and placed them tidily to the side of the room, resting his shirt on top, then his shorts when he was ready. He climbed onto the bed and stared at the ceiling, listening to Master George's movements around the room.

Despite the location, he knew he was with Master George, not Talon.

His Master came into view. "I would like to tie your wrists and your ankles to the bed while you're on your stomach, then I will use a flogger over your skin as a tease, but no actual flogging. Does that sound okay?"

Eddie closed his eyes and smiled. He inhaled and opened his eyes again. "Yes, Sir."

"What are your safe words?"

"Red for stop, yellow for unsure and green for continue."

"Perfect. Onto your stomach, then."

Eddie scrambled to obey, wanting what Master George was willing to give him. He put his hands above his head and spread his legs. The ankle restraints settled around him, and he sighed as his muscles relaxed. There was something about not having to make decisions, about not having to think that made this perfect for him.

"I'm going to strap your wrists together. That way, you can open them yourself if you need to." He did just that.

The thoughtfulness brought tears to his eyes. Never had anyone ever taken so much care with him.

"Eddie, are you okay?"

He nodded as best he could with his head burrowed into the covers.

"No, Eddie. Look at me. You're crying, and I need to know you're okay; otherwise, I will remove the restraints."

"No, Sir!" Eddie lifted his head and inhaled. "I'm fine. It's just...you're so much. You care. It's...overwhelming."

Master George's jaw clenched, then he sighed. "There are many people who care, Eddie. Unfortunately, you got one of the bad ones. I promise most of us are not like that." He skimmed his hand through Eddie's hair, and Eddie's eyelids fluttered.

"Do you want to continue?"

"Yes, please, Sir."

"Colour?"

"Green."

Master George stood from where he'd been sitting by Eddie's head. "Just a gentle tease, Eddie."

Eddie lay waiting and waiting, getting tenser by the minute until he realised what Master George was waiting for. Eddie inhaled deeply and relaxed into the bed, pillowing his head on the cover. The moment he did, a tickle started from his calf and rose up his legs, ass, back and shoulders, then down the other side. Goosebumps followed the path, and Eddie shivered.

"Colour?"

"Green, Sir," he breathed, fighting not to squirm against the sensation. He tightened his grip on the chain attached to his wrist restraints.

After a few minutes, the sensitivity lessened, his body becoming accustomed to it. Master George flicked the leather straps against the skin of his legs.

"Colour?"

"Green, Sir."

His cock was squashed between his body and the covers, and the friction was nowhere near what he needed to come.

"Please, Sir."

The flogger hit him a little harder, the small bite of pain perfect for him. He thrust against the bed, needing more. His arms ached with how hard he was pulling against his restraints, but he couldn't help himself. All he could focus on was where the next sting would come from and how close to orgasm he was. He trembled with the force of holding back, needing the command from Master George before he would allow himself to fly.

"Oh, god, please, Sir!"

"Come for me, Eddie."

Eddie's entire body clenched as his climax barrelled through him. His muscles jerked and throbbed until he slumped into the bed, depleted of energy. His lungs heaved as he inhaled the air he so desperately needed. He stayed floating, enjoying the relaxation that coursed through him.

Something wet touched his stomach, and he jumped, having not expected it.

"Sorry. Clean up time."

Eddie opened his eyes several times before they would stay open. He hadn't realised Master George had unlocked his restraints or turned him onto his back. The moment Master George had finished cleaning him, he covered him in a blanket and his arms and brought a straw to his lips. Eddie drank the orange juice, sighing when he finished. He snuggled in closer.

"Thank you, Sir."

"You're welcome. Now, rest. I'll be here."

Safe in the warmth of Master George's arms, Eddie slipped into slumber.

7

GEORGE

$\mathcal{H}$olding Eddie in his arms gave George something he'd not felt for a while. A sense of comfort. A sense of being needed. He'd always thought he was submissive, even when he'd been "acting" dominant to appease his family because he'd never felt this before. He felt a sense of accomplishment for giving a submissive what they needed, but he'd never felt it about himself. This time was different. What did that make him? A switch, maybe?

Could he cull his need to submit and become what Eddie needed?

Despite his thoughts, he knew the answer before he'd even finished thinking the question. No, he couldn't. He wouldn't expect someone else to change who they were, so why would he allow himself to?

When Eddie stirred, George loosened his grip and threaded his fingers through Eddie's hair, helping him to wake without being startled. The man's blue eyes blinked up at him, and George's heart jumped. He looked so innocent, so sweet.

"Hey. How are you feeling?"

Eddie smiled and wriggled in place. "Wonderful, thank you."

"You're welcome. Let's get you back into your clothes, and we can grab a drink from the bar and go over the contract."

"Yes, Sir."

George helped Eddie stand and took over the dressing of him because he couldn't help himself. Eddie chuckled when George slipped his shoes on.

"Ticklish feet?" he asked.

"A little."

"Good to know." He winked, and Eddie flushed.

"Come on."

George threaded their fingers together, and they left the room, no more talk about the terrible memories from it. At least for the moment. They weaved through the crowds and exited into the quieter conversation area. He grabbed two bottles of water from Oliver, asking him to request Clarice send a contract through to them, then led Eddie to a sofa, tucking him close when they were there.

"Is this okay?"

"Yes, Sir."

They sat in silence, but it wasn't uncomfortable for George. He didn't feel like he had to keep a conversation going.

"Master George?"

He hadn't even seen the server arrive. "Yes, sorry."

"Here is the paperwork you requested from Clarice."

George thanked her and encouraged Eddie to sit up. "All right. We're going to spend some time going over the details in this contract, then we'll talk and add or remove what we need to. This will make sure you're safe and happy with what we do here."

"Thank you, Master George. I appreciate you taking the time for me."

George scooted closer. "This is as much a pleasure for me as it is for you, Eddie." He smiled at the man. "Let's decide how we want this to play out."

They spent over an hour going through the details, with George ordering some snacks in between. When they finally had something they were both happy with, they signed it, and George gave it to Clarice. In the changing rooms, George kissed Eddie on the cheek before he went to his room. Before they separated, Eddie caught hold of George's hand.

"Could we start now, Sir?"

Eddie's words were quiet, his head lowered.

"Start what?"

"The contract. The…" He waved his hand back and forth.

George thought he understood what Eddie was trying to say. "Would you like a kiss to end the night, Eddie?"

Eddie sighed. "Yes, please, Sir."

George cupped Eddie's jaw, lifting his head to look into his eyes. "All you ever have to do is ask." He dropped his mouth onto Eddie's, starting gently and sipping at his lips. He licked and nipped until Eddie opened, then dipped in for a taste. George tilted their heads to deepen the kiss, and Eddie's hands grasped George's arms. He wanted more, but he wouldn't push. Softening the kiss again, he pulled back, watching as Eddie's eyelids fluttered.

"Thank you, Sir."

George pressed his lips to Eddie's again, then smiled. "You're always welcome."

"Sweetheart, if you have work to finish, I don't mind going in your place. Our plans have changed this evening anyway because the prime minister has called your father away to a meeting."

George's mother draped herself over the comfortable armchair in his room, looking completely at ease but every inch the queen consort at the same time. Her porcelain skin tone gave her an ethereal appearance that never seemed to leave, along with a sense of calm complemented by her favourite honeysuckle scent. Whenever birthdays or Christmas arrived, George always bought her something with honeysuckle in it. It was a scent that would forever remind him of his mother.

"No, don't worry. I'll send a message to the client and let them know it will be a couple of days later than planned. It's my fault." George stepped away from his computer, moving towards his bedroom.

"George." He faced her. "I don't mind. I haven't been to an official opening for months. It would be a pleasure to do this one."

George scrunched his nose. "I feel bad when you hadn't planned for this."

Louisa waved her hand. "Pfft. Plans always go awry. You should know that by now." Her tinkling laughter filled the space, and George grinned.

"If you're sure, Mother. Thank you. It will give me time to finish the speech tonight."

Louisa rose and held her arms out to him. "I don't mind at all." She enclosed him in her arms, and warmth filled his chest when he inhaled a lungful of her scent before she pulled back. "Now, you, my dear, get to work." She pointed a finger at him.

"Yes, ma'am." She laughed again and headed to the door. "Have a good evening, Mother. Please send my apologies."

"I will, sweetheart. Love you to the moon and back."

"Love you to infinity and beyond."

Their ritual goodbye had him smiling as he settled back in his chair in front of his computer. Focusing on the screen, he scowled at the amendments the client had sent back to him. The idea of writing speeches for other people came about when his mother had mentioned struggling with how to word something several years ago. George had read through her scribbles and added his own, and once Louisa had read it, she had called Randall, his father's personal assistant, in for a meeting.

Before George had known what was happening, Randall had approved Louisa's idea and set George on an alternative career path. Due to his familial link, they had decided to keep his identity anonymous, and they did everything through Randall. Clients would contact Randall, and he would book them in on George's calendar. Sometimes, though, George wished he could contact the client directly because they were so...bloody annoying.

Most clients were happy with the product he sent back to them, but occasionally, one client wanted to tweak things in a bad way, and George had to figure out how to accommodate their requests while still making sure the speech had the overall feeling it needed to have to stop the speech holder from making waves that would drown them. If that happened, it would be on George's shoulders.

This client wanted to add in some personal, humorous anecdotes, which weren't a good idea for the audience they would be addressing. It would take him several hours to work them into the speech, and he contemplated declining the changes.

Irate, he stood and stretched, feeling and hearing his spine and neck click in response. He was only thirty-two, but his body sounded well over middle-aged. He wandered over to the coffee machine and filled a large mug with the bitter brew before adding in one sugar and a splash of milk to make it what he considered coffee-coloured.

While he sipped the brew, his mind went back to the evening he'd spent with Eddie. It was the reason his speech was late because he couldn't stay away from the man. Since they'd signed the contract, he'd met up with Eddie three times. Three times in five days. He needed to get a grip.

His phone chimed, and he pulled it from his pocket, smiling when he saw Jason's name.

JASON: What goes red, black, red, black, red, black? A penguin rolling down a hill. I won't see you at the event tonight after all. Father wants me to stay home for dinner with the family.

Unfortunately, his best friend's father was strict and demanding, and although Jason was in his thirties, he had to jump when his father told him to. George hated his friend's situation, but Jason knew he could come to George whenever he needed to.

GEORGE: That was a terrible joke. Try again. Although I'm not glad you have to be with your family, it's good that you're not going. I forgot to message you and tell you Mother is going in my stead. This client is a pain in the arse, and I still have work to do before tomorrow. Ring me later or tomorrow.

After he sent that, he messaged his other friend, Katrina. She was Douglas's best friend, but George knew her from the club he frequented in disguise. She knew him as Georgie Cliff, a submissive who rarely visited the club. When he did, he tried to find her because he knew he could trust her, even if she didn't know who he was.

GEORGE: Can you message Jason later, please. He's being kept at home tonight, and I'm worried about him. You have more sway with him sometimes than I do. Thanks, and I hope you're well. Georgie.

He didn't speak to her often, but he had her number because of Jason. Between the pair of them, they could ensure Jason's father wasn't too hard on him.

Settling in front of the computer once more, he turned on the music and dived into the speech. He loved the aspect of tweaking and refining, editing and moving, making it the best he could make it, even when clients had to interfere.

A knock sounded, and he squinted at the clock, raising his eyebrows when he saw it was six-thirty in the evening. He'd been working for three hours already.

"Come in," he called and shut off his music.

Frederick entered, and George smiled, standing to greet him, but paused when he saw Freddie's expression. The usually unflappable heir to the throne had tears threatening to overflow, and his hands trembled as he brushed down the front of his suit jacket.

"Freddie, what's wrong?"

"There…" His voice broke, and he inhaled and exhaled. "There's been…Someone…I can't…"

George glanced behind his brother, expecting someone else to be with him, but no one was there. His heart raced, and his breathing increased as wave after wave of foreboding threaded its way through him.

"You're scaring me," he whispered.

A tear ran down Freddie's cheek. "Mother's gone."

George frowned, not understanding. "Of course, she is. She went to the opening celebration. I was supposed to go, but she said I could finish my work instead. She should be there by now because it started at six."

Freddie swallowed hard. "She's…"

"She's what?"

"Gone. She's gone, George."

"I don't understand!" He threw his hands up. "Gone where?"

Freddie stepped closer, tracks visible down his cheeks. He grasped George's biceps. "She's dead, George. The car exploded. She's gone."

George shook his head, his eyes filling. His lungs couldn't get enough air, and his gaze darted around the room as the walls drew closer. "No. She's just gone out for the evening. She told me to finish my work." He pushed away from Freddie, his lower lip trembling while he paced to the window.

"There was nothing they could do." Freddie's voice sounded distant.

George tried to inhale, but his lungs didn't work. He held onto the windowsill, lowering his head between his arms. "No. They've got the wrong person. I was supposed to be in that car. It's the wrong car. It has to be the wrong car," he murmured.

"She's gone, George."

He gripped his hair. "STOP SAYING THAT! She's not! They've got it wrong! They've got it…"

His words stopped when a sob caught in his throat, and

his knees buckled, taking him to the floor. A loud keening cry filled the air, and George wished it would stop. He tightened his grip on his hair, resting his head on the floor, jerking when the sound intensified. He rolled to his side, closing his arms over his ears to block out the noise, but all it did was change the tone.

They were wrong.

Images of his mother floated through his mind, and he tried to grasp onto each one, but the noise distracted him. He tried to tell them to stop, and that was when he realised *he* was the one making the sound, and he couldn't stop.

Arms surrounded him, but he couldn't acknowledge them. His head spun and pounded in time with his heartbeat. All sense of time ceased while he tried to find something to grasp hold of. Some anchor who could tether him. A *new* anchor because his old one had been…

His mother.

Who would stop him from floating away now? Who would tell him whether he was making the right choices? Who would he ask for advice?

He couldn't do this without her.

He woke cocooned in warmth, and he snuggled into the pillow beneath his head. There was nothing better than a soft pillow and a warm cover, even in the heat of summer. A movement beside him had him freezing, his breath stalling in his chest. He didn't remember inviting anyone to stay over.

Moving carefully, he glanced over his shoulder and saw Freddie sitting against the headboard, wearing a shirt with the sleeves rolled to his elbows. He rested his arms on his bent knees and gazed straight ahead of him.

George rolled to his back, and Freddie glanced at him. The minute he saw the bloodshot eyes and tear-stained face, a memory hit him, and his eyes widened, tears instantly blurring his vision.

"No," he said, voice firm. "No." He stared at Freddie, who just stared back.

"George…"

George glanced over to the corner of the room where an armchair sat, seeing Douglas there in a similar condition to Freddie.

George rolled over again and pulled the cover over his head, the wetness from his cheeks soaking into the pillow.

She couldn't be gone. She was invincible. They had it wrong.

He scrambled from the bed and rushed to the living room. He grabbed the remote and switched the TV on, flicking until he found the news. Then he dropped to his knees when the explosion played in full colour. He couldn't tear his gaze away, watching the replay repeatedly.

"That would've been me. That *should've* been me! Why her? What did she ever do to the world except love them for who they were?"

"They don't know who set the bomb yet. No one has claimed it as theirs." Freddie's voice was devoid of emotion except for the catch now and then. "Father is dealing with it all, but I have to help. There are plans to start. Things that need to be done…" Freddie drifted over to the window, crossing his arms over his chest and falling silent.

George returned his focus to the TV, which was showing pictures of his mother. He'd never see her again. He closed his eyes and tried to recall the scent of her, the look in her eyes as she joked with him before she left for the opening.

"Why? I don't understand why?" George said, leaning forward and resting his hand on the TV screen.

No one could answer him because they didn't know any more than he did.

He didn't know how long he sat in front of the TV, but his ass complained, his head pounded, and his eyes ached. He couldn't remember if he'd eaten or drunk anything. He didn't care, in all honesty. Over the hours, he watched the country and the world mourn the loss of their queen while he mourned the loss of his mother.

The news anchors gave no more information than they had the previous hours of the reports, but George couldn't take his gaze off in case they did.

Someone had to find out what the reason was for this travesty.

Someone knew.

Someone did this.

And when George found out who…they had better hide.

8

TIMOTHY

Timothy glanced around the class from his seat at his desk. He'd dropped a surprise test on them to see if they'd remembered anything from the first part of the year and to give them something else to focus on apart from the sad news of the queen's death.

The test would tell him what he needed to focus on the rest of his curriculum. Every student was scribbling away, and no one seemed to be confused from the expressions he could see. That was a win in his book.

He opened his desk drawer and sneakily checked his phone, though he didn't know why because only his family ever messaged. He saw two missed calls from Portia, and his stomach churned as a tendril of worry went through him. Portia usually called him instead of messaging, but to have two calls in quick succession when she knew he was teaching was concerning, especially with what had happened the evening before.

"Ten minutes left."

There wasn't anything he could do until the class ended

in ten minutes, so he pushed the drawer shut and tried to focus on the paperwork in front of him. Visions of police and hospital visits flowed through his head, and he rubbed a hand over his face to wipe them away.

The bell made him jump, and he exhaled as the students rushed to pack their things away and hand in their test.

"Well done, everyone. I'll have these marked by next week at the latest. Have a good day," he said.

The moment the door closed behind the last student, he fished out his phone and dialled Portia.

"Thank god!" Portia's voice was thick with tears. "Timothy, I know you don't want to be a therapist anymore, but I don't know who else to ask. I need your help. *We* need your help."

We? "I'm not the right person to ask, Portia. I don't know if I could do any good—"

"Please, Timothy. Prince George has not left his rooms since they gave him the news. I know that doesn't seem like a long time, and I know he has to have time to grieve, but this is so unlike him. He's the one who keeps our spirits up. He needs to talk to someone. Please, Timothy. You don't have to see him more than once if you can't, but *please help him.*"

Portia's voice cracked on the last words, and Timothy exhaled, knowing his answer. It wouldn't be a good idea—for him—but he hated seeing someone in pain when he might be able to help.

"Don't you have royal therapists or something?"

"He won't see anyone. Not even his brothers."

Timothy's mind swirled. "What makes you think he'll see me?"

"I don't, but I have to try." She sniffed.

Timothy exhaled as his next class filtered in. "I'm going to have to go, but yes. I will come and see him, but I won't be able to get there until after my last class."

"That's fine. Thank you, Timothy."

"You're welcome. I'll call you when I'm on my way. I'll have to go home first as there are some things I might need." He ended the call. "I apologise for that, class. There was a personal issue I needed to deal with." He glanced around the room, seeing drawn and pinched faces. "Okay, who needs to vent?"

Several hands went up. Timothy's chest ached for the people who felt adrift now the queen consort was no longer here. The heart of the royal family had died, and it would be difficult to fill it. The royal family had a difficult time ahead of them, and if Timothy could help, he would. His own issues aside, he knew he could still do his job. He just hadn't wanted to. It felt fake to advise people when he needed that advice himself. He made a mental note to ring Derek on his way home. He had a feeling he was going to need extra support for this.

"Let's go one at a time. Take your time, say what you need to say, and when someone is talking, remember their feelings and thoughts are valid even if you don't agree."

"I know you can do this, Timothy. You might not have faith in yourself, but I do. Try not to second-guess yourself. Follow your instincts as you would normally," Derek said.

Timothy concentrated on the road and Derek's voice as he drove the five minutes home. Luckily, Derek had been between patients when he'd called and could spare the few minutes to reassure Timothy he was making the right choice.

"Thanks, Derek. I'll let you get back to your patients."

"You're my patient, too. You'll be fine. Trust yourself."

They hung up, and Timothy turned into his driveway, waiting while the gates opened automatically, then carried on to the house. He left the car in front and jogged inside. He grabbed a shower, changed his clothes and headed for his office to get his bag ready. He didn't know what to expect from the royal family, but he would do his best, regardless. There was no guarantee the prince would even see him.

When he was ready, he jumped back into his car and rang Portia.

"Hey, I'm leaving now. Where am I heading?"

"Windsor Castle. Prince George has holed up in his room here. I'll call the guards and let them know you're coming. Make sure you have your ID with you."

"I will. I'll be there soon."

His stomach fluttered and churned the closer he got to his destination. He'd been expecting to drive into London, even though he knew the king and queen preferred Windsor Castle. Losing the queen had barely sunk in for Timothy, so her closest family must be distraught. Like he had been when Orlan had died.

His breath caught, and he inhaled and exhaled a few times to clear his head. He couldn't bring his own grief into the room with the prince. That wouldn't help. Timothy frowned. Or would it? He wasn't sure. He'd leave his grief aside unless he needed to use it as a way to make the prince see he wasn't alone in whatever he was feeling.

At the gates, he showed his ID and was told where to

park his car. Portia met him as he climbed out. He wrapped his arms around her.

"I'm so sorry, Portia."

She tightened her grip, then pulled back. "Thanks." She inhaled. "The king's PA would like to speak with you first."

He grabbed his bag and locked his car. "Lead the way."

He tried to keep his awe inside as Portia led him through elegantly decorated hallways, stone-walled corridors and several enormous rooms with high ceilings, fabric tapestries with gilded frames on the walls, highly polished wooden panelling and thick carpets. When he'd first seen the tapestries, he'd thought they were paintings until he saw the fabric. They must've taken hours and hours to complete. Portia told him a few things about the castle as they wandered.

They stopped at a wooden door, and Portia knocked.

"Come in!"

She entered the room, holding the door for Timothy. This room, though no less expensively decorated, was smaller than those he'd been through. A desk sat in front of a large window overlooking The Quadrangle—the large outdoor courtyard used for ceremonial processions. He'd seen it on the TV before, and it was a little overwhelming to see it in person.

"Randall, this is Dr Timothy Dixon. Timothy, this is Randall, the king's personal assistant."

Timothy stepped forward, holding out his hand. "Nice to meet you, though I wish it were under better circumstances. I'm sorry for your loss."

Randall's mouth tightened, and he nodded. "Thank you." His voice was quiet but firm, and Timothy immediately knew the man could get things done, even without the backing of the king. "I wanted to touch base with you before you attempted to see Prince George." Randall sat in his chair and waved his hand for Timothy to follow suit. "Prince George is…our shining beacon. He's the person who always found the fun, the joy, the crazy side of things. It kept us all grounded, I think. The rest of the family have their moments, don't get me wrong, but Prince George had that extra something. Something Queen Louisa wanted to cultivate. Her death," Randall's voice caught on the words, "has upset the balance she wanted to keep. You might get nowhere with Prince George, but I'm glad you're willing to try. We all are."

Timothy could feel the pain in the man's words. The pain of a family, a country, a world. He was one person. How could he help a prince? Especially one who wasn't interested in being helped.

"I will do everything I can." It was all he could promise.

Randall picked up some papers from his desk. "I need you to sign this NDA before you continue. I know you're bound by your confidentiality clauses, but George might discuss things that need to be covered by this one."

Timothy raised his eyebrows and took the papers. He read through them quickly, then signed his name, handing them back to Randall.

"Thank you. Portia will show you the way to Prince George's room. If he accepts your help, Dr Dixon, you will be welcome here whenever you deem it necessary. As often as you think he needs."

"Thank you." Timothy stood and followed Portia back into the hallway. He blew out his cheeks. "No pressure," he murmured.

"I'm sorry. I know you didn't want this. I didn't know who else to ask." Portia crossed her arms over her waist, staring at the floor as they weaved their way through the castle.

"It's fine. I'll be fine." Maybe if he said it enough, it would be true.

They said nothing more until Portia stopped at a door. "This is his room. You'll be able to get into the main living area, but he has secluded himself inside his bedroom, which is on the far left corner of the living room."

"Are you not coming with me?" He didn't need his hand held, but he felt uneasy walking into a prince's private area without an escort.

Portia shook her head and tried for a smile. "He doesn't want to see me because I remind him too much of his mother."

Timothy squeezed her shoulder and pressed a kiss to her cheek. "Get some rest. I'll find someone to escort me to my car when I'm done."

Portia nodded and wandered off down the hallway, her shoes clicking against the tile flooring. When she disappeared around a corner, he faced the door. He didn't want to barge in, so he knocked and waited. No answer. He tried again, and when the same thing happened, he twisted the knob and opened the door a short distance, calling through the gap, "Prince George?"

Still no answer. He entered the room, surprised by the change of decoration. Although the rest of the castle appeared to be decorated extravagantly and in keeping with the history of the royal family, Prince George's room was more modern. There were still gilded accents to the frames and walls, but the furniture was modern with sleek lines and sharp edges instead of fancy embellishments. The only other aspect that gave a nod to the prince's heritage was the royal blue colour of the walls.

Timothy tried to stop his analytical brain from figuring out the meaning of the decorations instead of the prince himself.

"Prince George?" he called again.

No answer. He placed his bag on the floor next to the dark brown sofa and stepped closer to the bedroom Portia had told him was Prince George's.

He knocked. "Prince George?"

"I don't need anything, thank you."

The soft, pain-filled voice broke Timothy's heart. "I'm sorry to interrupt you, Your Highness. My name is Timothy Dixon. I'm a therapist and friends with Portia." He wasn't entirely sure that giving Prince George the information about his friendship with his late mother's assistant was the best way to gain his trust, but he had nothing to lose when the man didn't want to see him, anyway.

The prince said nothing for several long minutes, and Timothy was about to try another tact when the man spoke again.

"I don't need a therapist, Dr Dixon. I need to find the people who killed my mother."

Timothy's eyes fell shut, and he pursed his lips. It seemed Prince George was in the anger stage of the grieving process.

"I understand that, Your Highness. Maybe you could have a break and a cup of tea while we talk for a few minutes before you get back to your work?"

Silence greeted him, and Timothy backed away from the

door, not wanting to push too hard. He would sit and wait for a short time to see if the man would emerge from his cocoon. He refused to push so much that the prince felt cornered. He knew how that felt, but he hadn't tried all the tricks in his repertoire yet.

He pulled out a book from his bag and settled himself in the corner of the sofa, facing the prince's bedroom door, and flicked through the pages of the book, not taking in the words. His mind remembered his anger phase, where he broke several items as the burning rage swept through him. Wincing, he thought about the hateful words he spewed to his friends and family when they tried to help, and he steeled himself for a similar response if Prince George ever faced him. It was a standard reaction to grief, but it didn't stop the pain of loss from tearing them apart.

He jerked his head towards the bedroom door when it clicked open, and a ruffled-looking Prince George emerged, his clothes wrinkled, his hair unkempt, but his eyes burned behind the strained, tired features.

Prince George stared at him, saying nothing. Timothy moved slowly and rose, stepping towards the table where the cups were held. He boiled the kettle and brewed two cups of tea, his mouth curling at the sight of a bowl of love heart sweets. He didn't ignore the prince, but he gave him time to accept Timothy was in his space.

When he carried the two cups over to the sofa, Prince George had seated himself across from where Timothy had been. He handed the cup over to the man, who took it with steady hands, then Timothy sat and crossed his legs.

"Thank you," Prince George said.

"You're welcome, Your Highness."

"Please just call me George. I've always hated the titles and honorifics."

Timothy nodded. "Of course...George." It felt strange on his tongue, but he wanted the prince as relaxed as possible. "I won't ask how you are. You'll only give me the same platitudes you give everyone else. What I will ask...have you spoken or seen your brothers or father since the news came to you?"

He sipped his tea, keeping his gaze on George, who diverted his focus to the cup in his hand.

"They're busy with arrangements and meetings. There's a lot to be done when the country loses its queen."

The last three words were whispered as if saying them louder would cause another catastrophic event.

"Do you not want to help with the arrangements?"

George turned the cup in circles on the saucer. "Someone needs to look for her killer."

"Are the police investigating?"

"They are, but they're taking too long. They have a lot of red tape they have to go through before they can get answers."

Timothy read between the lines: George had excellent computer skills. "Are you having any luck?"

"I've found where the car was before they drove it here to pick...her up, but I can't understand why they would want to kill *me*." The prince shrugged, and a frown marred his face.

Timothy was sure his frown matched when the prince's words sank in. "Why would you think they wanted to kill you?"

George lifted his gaze, and Timothy would forever remember the look in his eyes.

"Because I was supposed to be in that car, not her."

Timothy leaned forward to place his cup on the coffee table, hiding his reaction. No wonder George felt such pain if he was blaming himself for his mother's death.

"What do you mean?"

George snorted. "There was an opening celebration that I should've been attending, but I had a job I needed to finish, and…Mother told me to finish it and that she would go in my place." He sighed. "If I'd known what the outcome would be, I would've gone."

"It's not your fault, George. The only person to blame here is the one who caused this. That's not you. That's the person who planted the bomb. If roles were reversed, and they killed you instead, would you expect the person who arranged for you to attend to blame themselves because they booked you in?"

"Of course not, but that doesn't change the fact that I was the target, not her."

"Okay, but that's still not your fault."

The corner of George's mouth quirked up. "We're going to have to agree to disagree there, Doc."

Timothy canted his head to accept the declaration. A phone rang, and George glanced towards his bedroom but made no move to answer it. "Have you eaten?"

George raised his eyebrows. "Sorry?"

He cleared his throat and felt his cheeks heat. "I meant, have you been eating and drinking enough? You need to keep up your energy levels if you're doing a lot of research."

George stared at him, and Timothy fought not to fidget under the scrutiny. The ocean blue eyes were deceiving. He was sure they could see more than other people could.

"I'll make sure I eat and drink," George mumbled.

The silence settled for a short time, and Timothy was at a

loss for how to proceed. For the first time in his therapist career, he didn't know what to say or ask to help the patient. He was unnerved.

"I'll leave you to your day, Your Highness." Timothy stood.

"You're not going to push?"

He turned to face the prince. "Do I need to?"

The crease between George's eyebrows increased. "No, I just…Everyone else does. They think I should be out of my room and 'keeping it together.'"

Timothy huffed a laugh. "Everyone deals with things differently. There is no right or wrong answer on how to get through the loss of someone close to you." Timothy swallowed hard. "You have to deal with it how you have to deal with it. Just don't let it define you. Don't let it change who you are deep inside. It's not what your mother would have wanted."

George closed his eyes, and his nostrils flared, but he said nothing.

"I would like to visit again if you'll permit it?"

George lifted his eyelids and speared him with a gaze so filled with pain, it was all Timothy could do to stay rooted to the spot and not enfold the man in his arms and hold him as tightly as he could to stop anything from hurting him again.

"You remind me of Jake Gyllenhaal when his hair was longer and shaggier."

Timothy blinked. "Sorry?"

George shook his head. "Never mind. Yes, you can visit."

Timothy inhaled. "Tomorrow? Same time?" George nodded. "Words, please, George. I need verbal communication here."

George lowered his head. "Tomorrow is fine…"

Timothy waited, thinking George had something else to say, but he didn't continue, just bit his bottom lip. "Okay, I'll see you tomorrow. Please eat."

He grabbed his bag and left the room, closing the door behind him before resting against the wall and rubbing a hand over his mouth. He'd made some progress at least, but what the hell was that at the end?

9

—

EDDIE

*E*ddie sat on his mother's sofa with his knees to his chest, a blanket around his shoulders and a hot cup of coffee in his hands. He stared at the steam rising from the cup, lost in his thoughts. Was George okay? He sighed. Of course, he wasn't. He'd lost his mother. He wished he'd asked for his phone number now because Eddie had no way of contacting him except through the club, but he didn't think Clarice would be happy to pass a message along for him, so he hadn't left one. Yet.

He didn't know what George was going through, but just the idea of him losing his mother was devastating, and he could imagine the heartbreak. He wished he could be with him, although he wouldn't be able to help much.

"How are you feeling, sweetie?"

The cushion beside him lowered, and he tilted towards his mother when she sat. Righting himself, he tried for a smile.

"I'm all right. I wish I could help."

He'd told his mother that he was friends with George, but

not what their relationship status was because he wasn't sure himself. They'd only been meeting for a week, but it felt like a lot longer. During scenes, they focused on the bondage and sensations that George evoked from him, and during aftercare, they chatted about their lives and what they wanted. Neither went further than what they wanted from the club scene, but Eddie, even after such a short time, wanted whatever George could give him.

He wasn't stupid. He knew George was a prince and had obligations, and Eddie didn't delude himself into thinking they were a forever couple, but he couldn't help wishing it were true.

"I know. Maybe you should contact him. He might need a friendly face." Rose swept the hair from his forehead and ran the back of her knuckles down the side of his face in a move he had always found comforting.

"Maybe."

"He might need a distraction. Losing someone so close to him in such a way..." She shook her head. "He'll need someone."

"He has his family."

"Who is also grieving. Yes, family is wonderful when such a loss is experienced, but sometimes, they can't help another family member from dropping into despair. They're so... clouded by their own grief, they don't always see the signs. Contact him. Even if he tells you he's fine, at least he knows you're there."

Tears sprung to his eyes, and he closed them to stop them from falling. He wanted to be there. He wanted to hold George as George had held him so many times. He wanted to help George with anything and everything he needed. He wanted to help George forget, even for a few seconds.

"I will."

Rose left him to his thoughts again. He sipped at his coffee, the liquid cooling faster than he wanted it to. He needed warmth.

When he finished his drink, he uncurled and placed the cup on the table before grabbing his phone. He stared at it, wishing he had George's number instead of going through the official channels. Inhaling, he dialled the club.

"Good afternoon. How can I help you?"

Eddie recognised Clarice's voice and cleared his throat. "Hi, Clarice. Um, I wondered if, um, you could give a message to Master George, please? It's okay if you can't, but I haven't swapped numbers with him yet, and I wanted…"

"Mr Ward?" He stopped talking. "Prince George gave me permission to give you his number should you ever ask for it. I'm certain he would appreciate the call."

Eddie pressed his fingers against his lips and lowered his head as his shoulders relaxed. "Thank you."

She recited the number, which he programmed into his phone. "It's not my place to say anything, Mr Ward, but he needs you from what I've heard."

Eddie's eyes flicked open, and he stared at the fireplace. "What else has happened?"

"Nothing, sorry. Nothing has happened, but I've heard rumours. He needs someone to hold on to, and I believe that should be you."

They ended the call, although Eddie couldn't have told anyone what they said. It seemed like George wasn't dealing well. He knew George was close to his mother, but he had the strength inside him to keep himself together. Or was the loss so devastating he'd lost his ability? If that was the case, then he needed someone to help him put the pieces back together. Eddie would gladly do it.

His finger hovered over the call button, still uncertain George would want to hear from him. He inhaled and exhaled, his stomach roiling, and pressed the button. He held his breath as the ringing began. It clicked over to voicemail, and Eddie sighed. George probably didn't want to speak to him. He hesitated about leaving a message, but the beep gave him no choice.

"Hi, um. It's Eddie. Ward. From the club. Clarice gave me your number. I hope that's okay. Of course, it is. You told her she could. Sorry. Um. I'm so sorry to hear what happened. I wish there was something I could do to help you get through this. If you need anything, please let me know. Um, bye."

Eddie blew out a breath. He hated leaving messages, and he sounded like an idiot. Pulling the blanket tighter around him, he settled down with his head on the arm of the sofa, clutching his phone. It was now up to George to contact him.

He thought about their last scene, where George had told him he could call him George instead of Master George all the time, but Eddie had tried to fight him on it. In the end, George had persuaded him, but it had still taken a couple of days for the title to stop coming up in his thoughts. He couldn't think of George as someone other than his Master because they didn't socialise outside of the club. The corners of his mouth curled as he remembered George pleading with him to try before Eddie had reluctantly agreed.

His phone pinged, and he scrambled to check the screen, feeling deflated when it was Bella.

BELLA: How are you doing? Is everything okay?

He hadn't told her about George—at least, who he was—so she didn't know why he'd requested the day off from work. How could he explain that he'd wanted to be free in case George had needed him? She wouldn't understand., which was saying something when he'd told her everything else about his life. Bella wouldn't want him to get involved in something so...big, and she would class the royal family as big in her book.

Before he could answer her, there was an incoming call, and his heart pounded as he answered.

"Hello?"

"Hey," George said.

They fell silent, Eddie listening to the sound of George's breathing.

"Thank you for the message. You don't know how much I needed that."

George's voice was softer than usual, without the tinge of humour it always held, and Eddie missed it.

"I'm glad I could help. I'm sorry about what happened. I know it's no consolation, but I am. Is there anything I can help with?"

He heard George sigh. "I'd love to see you, but I can't come to the club right now. I have a lot of things going on."

Eddie's eyes fluttered closed, and he pressed the phone harder to his ear. "Whatever you need. I'm here whenever."

"Would you...No, don't worry."

"Would I what?" He tried not to sound too eager to do whatever George wanted him to.

"Would you visit me? Here?"

Eddie frowned. "Where's here?"

"Windsor Castle."

His eyes widened, staring at the unlit fire. "I, um, yeah, okay. Um, are you sure?"

"It's less private than the club because several people will know you're here, but we will have privacy in my room. No one will disturb us. It's okay, though, if you don't want to."

"No! It's fine. I just don't want to cause any problems for you."

"You won't. Do you need me to send a car?"

"No, it's okay. I can drive. Will they let me in?"

George chuckled, and Eddie's heart soared at the sound. "I'll let them know, and I'll get Randall to meet you at the entrance."

"Who's Randall?"

"My father's personal assistant. He can keep a secret if he needs to."

Eddie exhaled slowly. "Are you sure? I don't want to—"

"Cause trouble. I know. It's fine. I promise." George went silent, and Eddie didn't rush to fill the gap. "I want to see you."

The whispered words sent a shiver through him. He doubted they would do anything there, but being with George was better than not knowing how he was. It would give Eddie the chance to make sure he was okay.

"I'll be there as soon as I can."

"Thank you, Eddie."

"You don't need to thank me." He would do this with no thanks. They ended the call with Bella's warnings echoing in his mind, *"Don't get too close. Don't fall for the first person who shows you kindness. Keep an emotional distance."* Had Eddie fallen for George already? No, he couldn't have. Yes, George was kind and careful and considerate, but Eddie knew better than to fall for that because Talon had been the same in the beginning. The moment the thought crossed his mind, he slapped it away. There was no way George was the same as Talon. That was doing George an injustice. Eddie needed that splash of cold water. He couldn't fall for a prince. He'd get his heart broken because there was no way Eddie could become part of that family. He had no connections or aspirations to become anything other than what he already was. He was content with his life.

Liar.

He ignored the voice in his head and rose from the sofa, folding the blanket over the back of the sofa where it lived, then went to find his mother. She was in the kitchen with the scent of meat wafting in the air.

"I'm going to head out, Mum. Thank you for having me."

Rose waved her hand. "Pfft. You don't need to thank me for letting you visit. You're always welcome."

"I know, but you raised me better than that." He smiled.

Rose shook her head, though her mouth curved. "Did you call him?"

Eddie nodded. "I'm going to see him." He wrung his hands together.

Rose's eyebrows raised. "Okay. Are you all right with that?"

Eddie blew out a breath and chuckled. "I have no idea, but I'm doing it, anyway."

"It'll be good for you."

"Mum, can you not…"

"I won't tell a soul. Except maybe your father. He'll need to know just in case." She smiled and patted his cheek. "Take care of him, sweetheart. I know you're worried about what you are to him, even if you haven't said anything about it, but if he's anything like the man I've seen on TV, you have nothing to worry about."

"Thanks."

He draped his arms around his mother and let her hold him tightly before he pulled back. He wasn't fit for company, royalty or not, so he drove home to change, then aimed the car towards the last place he ever expected to be invited to. Silence reigned in the car because anything else would've set his nerves alight, and when he finally pulled up to the gate, his hands trembled while he showed his driver's licence. The guard directed him, and he parked the car where he'd been told. Without getting out, he glanced around him at the extensive area of landscaped gardens. This was even more opulent than he'd seen from pictures and the TV.

A knock on his window had him jumping, and he stared at the tall, muscular man dressed in a suit standing by his door. When the man raised his eyebrows, Eddie jerked and scrambled for the door handle. He clambered out and slammed the door closed.

"Sorry."

The man smiled. "Don't worry. It can be overwhelming on your first visit. I'm Randall." He held out his hand, which Eddie shook. "Follow me."

Eddie did, his neck aching from the craning he did as he passed through the most expensively decorated hallways he'd ever seen. They stopped in front of a door.

"Prince George is waiting for you."

Eddie nodded, but he could see Randall wanted to say something else. "Is there anything I need to know?"

Randall pressed his lips together and stared at the floor. "It's not my place to say…"

"I've heard that a lot recently, but I've come to realise

those who shouldn't say something often have the most insight to offer." Eddie tilted his head.

Randall exhaled. "Except for a therapist, you're the first visitor he's had since..." He swallowed. "You do not need to say anything to anyone, but if there is anything you think he needs..."

Eddie smiled. "I'll let you know."

Randall relaxed. "Thank you."

The man turned, and Eddie watched as he disappeared through a doorway. He faced the heavy-looking, ornate, moulded door and knocked, not giving himself a chance to escape, although he would more than likely get lost in the maze trying to find his car.

Within seconds, the door opened, and there stood George. The deeply lined face, bloodshot eyes and dishevelled look showed, more than anything, how out of sorts the prince was. Uncaring about social expectations, Eddie stepped forward and threw his arms around George's neck. He heard the door close behind him, and then George's arms were around him. One held him above his hips, the other across his back to his shoulder, George's fingers gripping. George nestled his face between Eddie's neck and coat and sighed, the heat of it seeping through Eddie's jumper.

They stayed that way for several long minutes until George pulled back so that their foreheads were touching.

"I didn't realise how much I needed that," George said.

"You'll be running on empty. You need to rest, Master George."

"I'm not much of a master today, Eddie."

"You don't need to be. It's my turn to look after you." The idea of taking care of George appealed to him more and more. "How does it sound if we have a shower and snuggle in bed—no expectations—just holding each other?"

George's eyelids fluttered closed. "Amazing."

"Come on. Show me the way to the bathroom."

Eddie's expectations were high, and it didn't surprise him when he entered a large, tiled wet room with an open shower, enormous bathtub and two sinks. He ignored everything else and pulled George to a stop.

"Can I undress you, Sir?"

George nodded, lifting his hand to Eddie's cheek and skimming his fingers over his cheek to his lips. Eddie kissed the digits and reached for George's clothes. It was then he saw George was more casually dressed than he'd ever seen him before. The T-shirt, joggers and briefs were removed within minutes, and then he divested himself of his clothes. He placed the items on the side of the sink, then led the prince to the shower. George switched it on, and hot water sprayed over them.

They needed no words between them.

With each swipe of Eddie's hand over George's body, cleansing him from the physical toll of the day, George appeared to relax further. When Eddie shampooed George's hair, the man groaned, and Eddie massaged his scalp with firmer strokes until he washed the suds clear. He switched off the shower, having watched George earlier, then reached for the towel. Ignoring his nakedness, he dried George off, rubbing the towel over his hair at the end. He put the towel back over the heated towel rail and grabbed one for himself, quickly drying himself.

Before he could drag George to the bed, George opened the cupboard under the sink and held out a toothbrush for Eddie. He felt his cheeks heat but accepted the item without saying a word. Side by side, they brushed their teeth, then George threaded their fingers together and led the way to the bed.

"Do you want your underwear back on?" Eddie asked quietly.

"I'm okay if you are?"

Eddie lifted the covers and nudged George towards it, but the man pushed Eddie first. He rolled his eyes, but with a small smile, he slid between the covers and slid over to the other side, allowing George to climb in the same side. Rolling to his side to face George, he slid a hand under the pillow he rested his head on, getting comfortable, but George nudged him until he rolled to face the opposite direction. George rested an arm over his waist and pulled him until they lay as close as they could get, George's front to Eddie's back.

Eddie felt George's lips against his neck, and he held onto George's forearm as the man slackened into sleep. It was early, but he doubted George had been getting much sleep since the incident. If Eddie was good for nothing more than helping the man sleep, then he would take that as a win.

Eddie would watch over him as he slept. It was the least he could do after George had been so generous with him. Eddie would help George as much as he could, then he'd let him go. It would hurt, but it was the right thing to do. There was no future for them, but the present was all they needed to concentrate on at the moment.

As the shadows lengthened, he reminded himself of that several times, and when he could no longer distinguish the shapes of the furniture, he let the tears fall, his heart aching for the pain George was going through and the acceptance of their future.

10

GEORGE

George woke when someone beside him moved, and he found himself twined around a body that was trying to get free. He loosened his arms and opened his eyes.

"Sorry. I didn't mean to wake you. I need the bathroom."

George raised his eyebrows when Eddie spoke, surprised but happy he was there. He couldn't remember the last time he woke up next to someone. Had he invited him over? Eddie disappeared into the bathroom, and George frowned, trying to remember...a weight settled on his chest and his breath caught as memories swarmed. He inhaled through his nose and exhaled slowly, hoping to keep his tears at bay. Why did this happen every morning? Why couldn't he either stay lost in his dreams or remember while he slept, so there wasn't this stabbing pain and nausea every time he woke and remembered what he'd lost?

He turned his head into the pillow, letting those tears he couldn't restrain soak into the fabric. He clutched at the cover, holding it tight to his chest as pain wracked through him.

Arms came around him, and he tried to push them away, not wanting Eddie to see him like this, but he was insistent, wrapping him up, covers and all. In the safety of that cocoon, George stopped fighting, listening to the soft whispers that reached him until he was as exhausted as if he'd not slept at all.

When he finally peered up at Eddie, he saw a pained expression on Eddie's face, his chin trembling and tear tracks on his cheeks.

"Th—" He coughed when his voice didn't work. "Thank you."

Eddie nodded with a small smile.

George rolled onto his back and blew out a breath. "I need a shower." He turned his head to face Eddie. "Come with me?"

"Sure."

George fought himself free of the covers and climbed out of bed, Eddie meeting him on his side. He threaded their fingers together and tugged Eddie towards the bathroom. They needed no words, but George showed Eddie with his actions how grateful he was. He washed every inch of the man, then grabbed his wrists and pressed them above Eddie's head against the tiles. Eddie hissed and arched forwards when his back met the chilled surface.

Keeping them out of the spray, George stepped closer until his body was flush with Eddie's. He watched Eddie lick his lips, the need flaring between them.

George lowered his head, brushing his lips back and forth against Eddie's while Eddie's breaths changed to pants. He glanced to the side, spying a flannel. Grabbing it, he swathed it around Eddie's wrists.

"Grip the ends in your hands. You can let them go whenever you need to."

"Yes, Sir."

"Colour?"

"Green, Sir."

George lowered his mouth, taking Eddie in a soft kiss that grew in ferocity when Eddie opened his mouth for George's questing tongue. He speared inside, tasting mint and Eddie, wanting nothing more than to take everything the man could give him. Holding Eddie's jaw, George pressed harder into the kiss, needing to see and hear the effect he had on him. When Eddie whimpered, George pulled back, seeing the red, puffy lips and hooded eyes that Eddie wore. He could feel their cocks between them, hard and hot.

"Colour?"

"Green, Sir."

George tapped at the flannel on Eddie's wrists, and Eddie nodded. Then George tilted Eddie's head to the side and pressed a kiss to his jaw, following the path to his earlobe. When he reached the cord of muscles running down the column of Eddie's neck, he followed it with his teeth, gently scoring down to Eddie's collarbone. George sucked against the skin, leaving a red mark that would disappear in several minutes. He continued down Eddie's chest until he reached his nipples.

Flicking his tongue over the nub, he released Eddie's jaw and used his thumb to rub against the other nipple. Eddie's chest heaved with every touch, and George peered up at him, seeing the pink flush across his cheeks and his bottom lip stuck between his teeth. Eddie's body writhed, but George gave him no relief.

Not yet.

He swapped his mouth over to the other side, replacing his fingers with his mouth, then continued his ministrations until Eddie was thrusting his lower body into the air, undoubtedly seeking friction. George licked across his skin, noticing how visible his ribs were, and painted a stripe down his stomach, around his belly button, and lower. George dropped to his knees, although Eddie protested.

"Colour?"

"Green, Sir."

Having made sure Eddie was on board with what he was planning, George focused on the shaft straining for attention in front of his face. He licked his lips, his tongue catching the head, and encircled Eddie's cock at the base. He flicked his tongue out several times, teasing Eddie with what was to come. When Eddie was babbling above him, George slid the heavy weight into his mouth and along his tongue until it reached his throat. He pulled back again, sucking hard, then sliding down once more. This time, when the cock hit the back of his throat, George relaxed his muscles and took Eddie further.

He breathed through his nose, ignoring the need to expel what was not supposed to be there. He swallowed around the shaft. Eddie's words were unintelligible, but George understood their sound. He lifted off, breathing heavily to return oxygen to his lungs. He inhaled deeply and lowered his mouth, taking Eddie into his throat again. This time, he swallowed repeatedly and used his hand to hold his balls while his fingers on his other hand quested for his rosebud.

He could tell Eddie was close, so he pulled off, inhaled

and sank down, swallowing hard when his finger breached the pucker of Eddie's ass. Eddie cried out, his whole body tensing and shuddering as he released into George's throat.

Before Eddie was spent, George pulled off slightly, wanting the taste of him on his tongue. When Eddie slumped, George removed his finger and circled his hand around Eddie's cock while he cleaned him with his tongue. After he was done, he stood, the ache in his knees worth the look of bliss on Eddie's face.

George brushed his knuckles across Eddie's cheek, and Eddie's eyes fluttered open.

"Thank you, Sir."

"You're welcome. Let's rinse off, and we can go back to bed."

They snuggled into bed once they had dried off; Eddie's head pillowed on George's chest. George raked his fingers through Eddie's hair, helping him to calm. Just because they weren't at the club didn't mean George wouldn't take his role seriously. He had a small fridge in his room, which held several drinks and some fruit. Before they had settled, he had retrieved some drinks and fruit and placed them on the bedside table. He hand-fed Eddie the fruit, offering him sips of juice in between.

He hadn't brought Eddie here for sexual relief, and besides, George hadn't come. He gained as much pleasure from seeing his partner's release, and his own climax was secondary. Eddie must have been thinking along the same lines because, after several minutes, he fidgeted and said, "Do you not want me to reciprocate?"

The whispered words held a small amount of hurt. George curled his forefinger under Eddie's chin, lifting his head to ensure Eddie understood what he was about to say.

"I don't always need the release. I love seeing my partner fly apart because of something I gave them. Just because my dick is hard doesn't mean I need to do anything about it." Eddie seemed unsure, so George continued, "I promise you, Eddie. I don't need to orgasm to receive joy in a scene."

Eddie stared at him, and George could see his mind whirling behind those expressive eyes. He waited, sure Eddie would have something to say once George's words had settled.

"Okay. I trust you to tell me the truth."

George's phone vibrated on the bedside table, and he sighed. "Time to face the real world, I suppose." He reached for it and winced. He had several texts and voicemails. "Shit. I hadn't realised my phone was still on silent."

The messages were from his brothers and cousins. Nothing urgent, just a check-in. The voicemails were from them, too, although the final one was from Randall reminding him of his appointment with Dr Dixon that afternoon.

He replied to his brothers and cousins with generic answers, then confirmed the appointment with Randall. After replacing the phone on the side, he rolled towards Eddie.

"Can we hide under the covers for a few more hours?"

Eddie smiled. "As you wish, Sir."

They wrapped their arms around each other and left the world outside of the room while they talked about their lives and other mundane stuff. For the first time since the news had arrived, he felt relaxed and not whole but content. And it was to do with this man beside him. They didn't play around again, just changed positions occasionally to keep their bodies from becoming numb.

An hour before his therapist was due to arrive, George made moves to get ready.

"I have an appointment I have to keep, but you're welcome to stay."

George climbed out of bed and stepped towards his drawers. He pulled out some underwear and socks and headed across the room to the walk-in wardrobe on the opposite side. He pulled on his briefs while he stood in front of his clothing choices, having no idea what to wear. He felt Eddie's presence behind him. It wasn't until the man's arms slid around his waist that George released a breath he hadn't realised he'd been holding.

"I'd love to stay, but I don't have any more clothes to wear."

"You can wear mine."

Eddie chuckled. "Your clothes will bury me," he said. His eyes widened. "Sorry."

"Why are you apologising?" George said.

"I thought…My choice of word…"

Eddie pulled away, but George grabbed his arms and pulled him back. Despite a stab of pain arrowing through him, he smiled and cupped Eddie's jaw in both hands.

"I hadn't even realised until you said. There will be phrases and words that remind me of my mother and the situation, and I can't get away from them all."

"I'll try to talk normally. I make no promises, though."

"I can accept that." George smiled and lowered his mouth, giving Eddie a chaste kiss. "Now, help me decide what to wear." George turned back to his clothes and sighed.

"What events do you have?" Eddie asked.

"It's an appointment with my therapist, or rather, the person who seemed to have broken into my bubble." A thought came to George, and he turned to Eddie. "I'm so sorry for not messaging you before to tell you how I was. It's not that I didn't want you here. I was shutting everyone out. For some reason, this particular therapist managed to not only get me out of my bedroom but to talk to him, too. I swear he's a miracle worker."

"I'm glad you have him. I would hate for you to have to deal with all this by yourself. I'm no substitute for those who can help, but I'm a pleasant distraction if nothing else."

The tone he said those words did not sit well with George, but he couldn't figure out why. He pushed them aside to think about later and focused on his clothing dilemma.

"Jeans and a T-shirt, I think," George said. "Can't go wrong with that combo."

While George dressed, Eddie disappeared back into the bedroom. George exited the wardrobe, and Eddie was pulling on his jumper. He surrounded Eddie and dropped his head to Eddie's shoulder.

"Prince George?"

Despite having only met the man once the previous day, his voice was distinctive, and one George immediately recognised. He pulled back, pressing a kiss to Eddie's forehead.

"Will you come with me?"

Eddie searched his face for several seconds before nodding.

"Only for a few minutes, though. You need privacy for this."

George wasn't so sure, but he would take what he could get.

"Prince George? Are you here?"

George opened his bedroom door and entered the living

area, seeing Dr Dixon standing beside the table where the kettle was.

"Good afternoon, Prince George."

"Good afternoon, Doc."

He saw the man's eyes flick towards Eddie and back again. George cleared his throat.

"Dr Dixon, this is Eddie."

Eddie smiled. "Nice to meet you. I'm only here for a minute, then I'll leave you to your session."

Although breakfast and lunch had been served to them, George was hungry, and he bet Eddie was, too.

"I'm going to order some food. Would you like some, Doc?"

"I'm fine, thank you."

George released Eddie's hand and wandered over to the telephone they used to contact the kitchen. He ordered jacket potatoes for three people, ignoring the therapist's words. He strode to the table to make a cup of tea when he realised there was already a cup waiting for him. He glanced at Eddie, seeing a cup in his hands.

"Thank you, Doc," he said, taking a sip of the hot drink.

"I'm going to take this back into the bedroom," Eddie said.

"I'll bring the food to you when it arrives," George said.

"Thank you."

George pressed a kiss to Eddie's lips and watched as he retreated, closing the bedroom door behind him. He dragged his bottom lip through his teeth several times as he took a seat on the sofa opposite Dr Dixon.

"I didn't realise you had a boyfriend," the therapist said.

George glanced over his shoulder towards the bedroom door. "It's not as simple as that."

"You're welcome to talk about it if you need to."

"I appreciate the offer, Dr Dixon, but I think we're fine."

"Timothy."

George frowned. "Sorry?"

"You can call me Timothy instead of Dr Dixon."

George couldn't see any hint of…anything if he was honest. Timothy was good at hiding his reactions.

"I'll bear that in mind." George frowned. "Did you sign an NDA before you spoke to me?"

"Yes. Randall gave me one."

George relaxed. "Good." He wouldn't want to inadvertently say something, then realise he'd messed up.

"How are you feeling today?"

George peered down at his cup. "One of the worst things about all this is forgetting, then remembering." He lifted his gaze to Timothy, noticing the crease between his eyebrows deepened. He stared off to the side, not focusing on anything in particular. "I mean when you wake up. There is this brief moment when your brain lies to you and pretends everything is as it was. Then a flash of pain as the memories flood in." He refocused on Timothy, an expression flying across the man's face before George could figure out what it was.

Timothy sipped his tea. "Yes, that is not pleasant. That eases, but it will take time."

The words were softly spoken, and George wondered if he had experience with what he was saying or if he had a therapist spiel he told all clients. The thought that he was just giving a speech annoyed George.

"Have you still been researching?"

George froze, his mind throwing up visions of lying in bed with Eddie, of keeping the world out. His cup rattled and was removed from his hands. Warmth covered his nape as he dropped his head to his hands and panted. He hadn't once thought about the research he'd been doing into his mother's killer. He'd *forgotten*. Pushed it aside as if it didn't matter when it was one of the most important things he needed to do. How could he do that?

He speared his fingers through his hair and gripped. The bite of pain brought tears to his eyes. A hand brushed over his, encouraging him to let go, but he didn't want to. He didn't deserve to be free from pain when he'd forgotten his job. The hand was insistent, though, and George dropped his hands from his hair, a sob catching in his throat. He hated being weak in front of others except for his family.

He tried to stand, but hands pulled him closer to a body until his face was resting against a cool fabric, George's hands gripping at whatever he could. The hand on his nape left, then returned, slightly cooler, and George closed his eyes, moving closer.

He just needed to rest. Just for a minute.

11

TIMOTHY

He'd known the moment he'd clasped his arms around the prince that he'd made a huge mistake. Never, in all his past years as a therapist, had he held a patient as he now held Prince George. The man had lost his composure when Timothy had asked about his research. George had said no words, but Timothy had a feeling his boyfriend—or whatever he was—had distracted him enough to forget about his quest. Under normal circumstances, that wouldn't be a bad thing, but George would blame himself, which was not what Timothy wanted.

When Timothy had moved to sit next to George, resting his hand on his nape to help calm him, that was all he'd planned to do. But when the prince had gripped his hair so hard, Timothy had been concerned he would rip the strands out. His body had acted on instinct and curled George into his chest. He hadn't expected the man to climb into his lap and mould himself to Timothy's body, gripping his shirt as tightly as he'd held his hair.

Now, he was sitting with Prince George on his lap, Timo-

117

thy's arms around him and his cheek resting on his head. It was not the actions of a professional, but Timothy couldn't bring himself to care, especially when George's tears soaked through Timothy's shirt. He'd save his concerns about the ethics of the situation for when he was at home. Alone.

Timothy swallowed hard, trying to stop the tears he wanted to shed. He knew exactly what George was going through because he'd been through it himself, but it didn't make it any easier.

A knock sounded, but George didn't move.

Timothy lifted his head and cleared his throat. "One moment, please." He didn't think George would want whoever was on the other side of the door to see him like this.

"Prince George?" He tried to pull him away from him, but George burrowed closer if that was possible. "George? There's someone at the door." He ran his hands through George's hair, trying to bring him out from the self-recriminations he was undoubtedly thinking. "George?"

"It's okay. I'll answer it."

Timothy glanced over his shoulder to see Eddie striding for the door. "Don't let them in."

Eddie paused, glanced at him, then George, and nodded. Timothy watched the tall, slender man open the door and slip out. Heat invaded his cheeks when he thought about what they looked like. He hoped he could explain before Eddie got upset.

The man in question returned with a rolling cart, closing the door quickly behind him. He brought the cart over to the coffee table, then wrung his hands together.

Timothy opened his mouth, but Eddie said, "Is he okay?"

"He will be. I'm sorry if this appears to be something it's

not. I'm not trying to encroach on your relationship. He got upset. That's all."

Eddie waved him away. "It's fine. He's what's important, not me."

"You're important to him; otherwise, you wouldn't be here," Timothy said.

George moved then, startling Timothy. He held out his hand to Eddie, beckoning him with his fingers. Eddie stepped closer and grabbed George's hand. George pulled it closer to him, causing Eddie to fall forward, almost into Timothy's lap, too. Eddie caught himself on Timothy's shoulder, then lowered to sit beside them, their thighs pressed together. Timothy moved his hand that had been resting on George's nape, allowing Eddie to run his fingers through George's hair.

"Food's here, George. You said you were hungry."

George nuzzled his cheek against Timothy's shirt until his head rested on his shoulder instead. Timothy knew the moment George came back to them because he tensed.

"It's okay. There's nothing wrong. Take your time," Timothy said, trying to make him understand that there was nothing wrong with what had happened.

George stayed in the same position for a few seconds longer, then swung his legs off Timothy's lap, let go of Eddie's hand and scooted himself into the corner of the sofa. He hugged his arms around his legs and rested his forehead on his knees. Timothy brushed a hand over the front of his shirt, trying to regain some professional distance. He stood and rounded the coffee table to sit back on the opposite sofa.

"I think we should try again tomorrow," he said. "I'll leave you to your food." He gathered his things, but George's voice stopped him.

"Stay. I ordered you food." George's knees muffled the words, but they were still clear enough to understand.

"I think it's probably better—"

"Stay," Eddie said, staring at him with something in his eyes that Timothy didn't want to unravel.

He knew he should leave, but he couldn't bring himself to yet. He nodded and dropped his things back to the floor. Eddie rose and placed a tray of food in front of him, then gave George his, and finally, his own. The scent of baked potatoes, melted cheese, baked beans and salad made his mouth water. He watched Eddie sit on the floor and rest the tray on the coffee table. He glanced at George, watching him watch Eddie. When George glanced at him, Timothy stared back for a moment, then dropped his gaze to his tray and began eating.

His brain tried to figure out what the hell was happening, but he came up blank. No one said anything during the meal, and when Timothy finished, he cleared his throat.

"Thank you. It was delicious. I'm going to go. Tomorrow?"

George's jaw worked as he finished his mouthful. "Yes. Thank you, Doc."

Timothy nodded. "Goodbye, Eddie."

"Bye."

Timothy replaced the tray onto the cart, grabbed his belongings and slipped out of the door. He wandered through the corridors in the direction they'd come, recognising specific paintings or decorations he'd purposefully memorised to get himself back out of the place without an escort. He closed his car door and started the engine, berating himself for being unprofessional. Despite what George said about having an appointment tomorrow, Timothy expected a phone call to cancel before then.

He waved to the guard who allowed him to exit, then drove home. By the time he arrived, he'd called himself every name under the sun. His best option was to call Portia and tell her he couldn't do it anymore. She wouldn't be surprised, but he was reluctant to do so when he knew George needed help and had refused everyone else. Why George continued seeing Timothy was beyond him, and it was because of that he let it be.

He wasn't due to see Derek until two days later, but he considered whether he should talk it out with him before going back. He lifted his chin and climbed out of the car, slamming the door shut behind him. Throwing his keys on the small table near the front door, he dropped his bag at his feet, slipped off his shoes and jacket, and aimed for the kitchen. Beer called his name.

He opened the can, took a sip and stared into the back garden, resting his elbows on the counter. He was a bloody therapist, and he couldn't make heads nor tails of his thoughts and feelings at that moment. The only clear thought he could grab was that he wanted to see George again, and he worried it was for the wrong reasons. He shook his head, disabusing the notion because everything that had happened with Orlan still overwhelmed him.

He paused.

He'd not once thought about Orlan since he'd seen George the previous day, except when George's words had brought up the incident. What did that mean?

Timothy guzzled the beer in several swallows and grabbed three more before heading for his bedroom. He would watch

Supernatural in bed and drink his beers, hoping to drown out the inconsistencies in his brain.

Four beers before bed were more than he was used to, and he woke with a pounding head. Paracetamol and a hot shower helped, as did a fry-up, although cooking it took longer because he battled with keeping his stomach from revolting.

Despite the cool weather and intermittent drizzle, he sat on his back terrace and stared at the trees lining the property. His thoughts were still no clearer that morning, but he felt at peace. It gave him the idea of how to approach George that afternoon. From what Portia had told him, George had not left his rooms at all since his mother's death. That needed to change. He'd encourage George—and Eddie if he was there— to take a walk in the castle gardens and maybe a little further if he could.

Decision made, he returned inside and grabbed the homework his students had handed in at the end of the week. After making himself a hot chocolate to stave off the chill in the air, he sat at his desk and put the radio on. Page after page, he read about the students' thoughts on a real-life situation. He could tell which students had looked up the case because they had additional knowledge of certain aspects that had not been covered in their course yet. That was all well and good, but it didn't give Timothy the option to see what the student took from the case, only what their views were on the opinions of what they had read in the news. Timothy hadn't specifically said they couldn't look up the case, but maybe he would on the next one. With that in mind, he made a note of the students he believed had researched the case and would use it as a training exercise in their next class.

When the time came for him to get ready for his appointment with George, he had read through half his pile, two hot chocolates, three cups of tea and a quick lunch break.

He took a shower, changed his clothes and made sure he had everything he needed. He wouldn't take a bag with him this time because it had to be searched every time, and it was a ball ache.

Randall met him at the door when he arrived, and they wandered through the corridors.

"I was thinking of trying to get Prince George out of his room today. Can we go into the castle gardens? Does he need security?"

Randall cocked his head. "He doesn't have security unless he's going somewhere we think he would need it. The gardens are fine. You could even wander down The Long Walk if you wish. Don't go too far, though."

"Thanks."

"Let me give you a number to call if you run into any problems."

Timothy withdrew his phone and entered the number for the security team when they reached George's room.

"Thank you for doing this. We appreciate it," Randall said, his voice sad.

"You're welcome. He'll get through this."

Randall smiled and strode off. Timothy knocked on the door, expecting silence.

"Come in!"

He raised his eyebrows and opened the door. George sat on the sofa with a laptop resting on his legs, and Eddie sat on the opposite sofa with a book in his hand.

"Good afternoon," Timothy said, closing the door behind him.

"Afternoon, Doc." The corner of George's mouth quirked up. The darkness under his eyes had deepened since the previous day, but he appeared more alert.

"Hi," Eddie said, looking not as tired.

Timothy settled onto the sofa where Eddie sat and glanced at George. His focus was on the laptop, his fingers flying across the keys and mouse pad.

"It has engrossed him since he woke this morning," Eddie whispered. "He only stopped when I made him eat."

Timothy peered at Eddie. "Are you okay?"

Eddie smiled. "Yes, a little tired, but I'm fine."

Timothy refocused on George and raised his voice. "Prince George, we're going for a walk today."

George's hands froze, then resumed. "I have stuff to do, sorry."

As he expected. "You need to stop working while I'm here, Your Highness. It's only an hour, and you'll feel much better for it. You'll have more focus afterwards." *And more tiredness, hopefully.*

"Randall said we could go into the gardens. It's a little cold, so you might need a coat. The drizzle has been coming and going all day, so there's no guarantee we won't get wet."

George's fingers continued, but his jaw clenched. "I'm happy to stay here. You can go if you want."

"Prince George?" Timothy waited until the man peered at him. "We're going for a walk." He didn't look away, and he saw the moment George accepted it. "Please get ready."

George nodded once and closed his laptop, turning his back on them as he strode for his bedroom. When the door closed, Eddie turned towards Timothy and tucked his legs underneath him.

"He's been awake several times through the night. I didn't hear him have any nightmares, but that doesn't mean he didn't. I can sleep quite heavily." Eddie flushed and looked at his hands. "We're not in a relationship, in case you were wondering. He's been helping me—"

Timothy held up his hands. "You don't need to explain yourself, Eddie. Your relationship is only my concern if George brings it up."

"Oh. I thought...Never mind."

"You thought what?"

Eddie licked his lips and scrunched his face up. "I thought you needed to have as much information as you could so you can help him."

Timothy sighed and nodded. "Yes, sometimes, that is the case, but..." He winced. "I can't say much, but in his case, I need *him* to open up. I need to hear it from him because everyone feels things differently. No one can see inside his head, not even me. I need him to explain how he's feeling, so we can work on tweaking anything that's negatively affecting him."

Eddie nodded. "That makes sense."

George entered the room wearing jeans and a jumper. "Are you coming with us?" he asked Eddie.

"I can stay here. It's fine."

"You're welcome to join us if you'd like to and if George is okay with it."

George nodded. "Come with us?"

"Okay. I'll just..." He pointed to the bedroom and shuffled away.

George swallowed. "Eddie and I...We have a BDSM relationship. Most of the time." He shoved his hands in his pockets. "I was helping him after he'd been a victim of... something. It seems I've needed his help to the same extent he's needed mine."

"It's good to have people who can help you. It doesn't have to be on one person's shoulders. Everyone has unique abilities and ways to make you smile, remember, forget, whatever you need. Pushing people away won't help you or them."

George clenched his jaw and headed for the door. Timothy stood, putting his hands in his trouser pockets, and watched as George pulled on his coat, then took down another one. He brought it over to Timothy and held it out.

"I noticed you didn't bring a coat with you. It should fit."

Timothy's heart jumped. George wasn't as unaware as Timothy had thought he was. "Thank you." He slipped it on. It was snug around the shoulders, but it would be better than his suit jacket.

George returned to the coat hook and took another one down, draping it over his arm. They waited in silence until Eddie joined them, and George held out the coat for him, helping him slide it over his shoulders.

"Ready?" Timothy asked.

Eddie nodded, but George stared at the floor. Timothy approached him and placed a hand on his shoulder. "One step at a time. Outside these doors is nothing you don't know. You don't need to be worried."

George lifted his gaze to Timothy. "What if I'm afraid of the memories?"

Timothy's heart broke. "You have Eddie and me to help. If those memories get to be too much, tell us. We'll distract you or listen if you want to tell us about them. I'm sure your mother would love the idea of those memories being so readily available to help you heal."

Tears welled in his eyes, but he lifted his head to the ceiling and breathed deeply. When he dropped his head, the tears were gone, his jaw set. "Ready."

Timothy squeezed his shoulder. "Let's go. You'll have to lead us in the right direction, or we'll end up somewhere we're not supposed to be." Timothy chuckled.

He watched George take Eddie's hand and exit the room, focusing on the floor instead of their surroundings. He walked a step behind, watching the prince and Eddie, but also anyone they encountered. Several staff members bowed in George's direction with wide eyes. He saw George pull Eddie closer and Eddie wrap his free hand around George's biceps, whispering something in his ear.

George shook his head and stopped. Timothy stepped in front of him and rested his hand on George's nape as he had done the previous day. He lowered his head and his voice.

"Breathe for me, George. In…and out. In…and out. That's it. How close are we?"

"Left, then right." George panted.

"Okay. Breathe for me while we walk."

Keeping his hand where it was, he led them forward, hoping he was going in the right direction. They took the left, then drifted straight for a bit until George pulled to a stop.

"Right here. Through the doors."

Timothy could see the gardens but couldn't see how those doors would get them there, but he followed George's directions. After going through the doors, Timothy understood and headed for the outside door. Once they were all outside, Timothy closed the door again. They went down some steps but didn't move any further than the bottom step because George sat right there.

Timothy moved to give him some space, but George grabbed for him, tugging his hand to his neck. Ignoring the thump of his heart, he rested his hand on George's nape again, and George sighed.

"I'm sorry for saying this, Eddie, because I know it makes me seem weak, but I'm scared," George said.

Timothy knew the feeling.

EDDIE

*E*ddie felt like crying for him. "It doesn't make you weak, George. It makes you human. I was scared, too."

"But I'm supposed to be strong for you."

Eddie cupped George's jaw. "And you are when I need you to be, which is when we're doing a scene. If I didn't trust you, Master George, I wouldn't be here. *We* wouldn't be here."

"What are you scared of?" Timothy asked.

The man had surprised Eddie many times over in the last twenty-four hours. He wasn't like any therapist Eddie had ever seen, but he understood everyone did things differently. It had been a shock to see George curled up on his lap the previous day, especially with what he knew about George, but he could see how much George needed it. Maybe the therapist was who George needed instead of him. Timothy could get him through the pain of losing his mother, whereas Eddie was just in the way, unable to help with anything. If Timothy was the better choice for George, Eddie would step aside despite the fact that it would hurt. He was getting himself in too deep already, especially when they'd not agreed to anything except scenes at the club.

He would admit to being worried about leaving George on his own when he had to go home that night. He started back at work the following day and couldn't take any more time off. Timothy wouldn't be there all the time either, so George would be back to being alone. He needed to ask Timothy about it before he left.

"The same thing that happens when I wake up. Remembering her, then remembering she's gone," George said, his voice cracking.

Eddie rested his cheek against George's shoulder, his forehead brushing against Timothy's hand on George's neck. He wasn't sure what the significance of the gesture was, but he was happy Timothy didn't baulk at the idea of doing it, even if it wasn't within his job responsibilities.

Timothy exhaled audibly. "Yeah, that would be painful. But isn't that what happens whenever you think about her, anyway?"

George sniffed, blew out a breath and lifted his head, Eddie following suit. He took in the gravel pathways, conical-shaped bushes, grass sections and a circular fountain in the centre of it all. It looked bare because the flowers had yet to come into bloom, but he could see the magnificence of it. From what he gathered, the public could see the gardens when the castle was open for visitors, but he assumed it wasn't today because, otherwise, the three of them wouldn't be there.

"Shall we wander around a bit?" Timothy asked, standing and holding out his hand to them both.

Eddie slid his hand into Timothy's, the warmth spreading

across the tips of his chilled fingers. The man was warm despite the cold temperature outside. He stood, waiting for George to do the same, then slipped his hand into George's free one. It was only when George stepped closer that Eddie realised he still held Timothy's hand, and he let go, his cheeks heating as he lowered his gaze.

The stones crunched as they strolled through the gardens in silence. They veered to the right when they reached the fountain, and Eddie smiled as he stepped onto the stone edge and followed it around. Still, they didn't stop, climbing the steps on the opposite side of the garden to the house and down the other side. Eddie wasn't certain, but he thought this led to The Long Walk. He doubted they would attempt the entire distance because it was about two and a half miles. He didn't think George was up to that today, but he'd happily do whatever he wanted.

He followed along as George led the way, Timothy one step behind. When George led them off the path, Eddie frowned. He hoped he could find the way back afterwards. The muted sounds of traffic and the liveliness of nature settled Eddie in a way he'd never considered before. He needed to find a place like this to go to by himself sometimes.

"What's going through your head, George?" Timothy asked.

George pursed his lips like he did when he was thinking. "How much she's going to miss now that she's not here."

"Like what?"

"Douglas getting married—eventually. Frederick and me if we ever find someone. She'll miss Father..."

When George didn't continue, Eddie squeezed his hand.

"Have you been to see your father yet?" Timothy tilted his head to the side.

George lowered his head. "I don't know if I can. They were together more often than they were apart. They were so...perfect for each other. I don't know if I'd manage to keep my composure under the pain he'll surely have on his face."

"Do you need to keep your composure?"

"He's the king. I always need to be composed in front of him."

"But he's your father, first and foremost. I'm certain he would understand your pain."

George held Eddie's hand tighter. "I don't know."

"What about Prince Frederick and Prince Douglas? Have you seen them?"

George shook his head, a tear escaping and rolling down his cheek. Eddie wanted to hold him again and take away his hurt. They came out from the trees onto a path. Eddie expected George to turn around, but he continued.

"Don't you think they might need you as much as you need them?"

Eddie wanted to argue with Timothy about his words. How dare he tell George what he should be doing. George had a right to feel however he wanted to. Why was Timothy pushing him to see people that would make him hurt worse?

"I'm scared," George whispered before Eddie could say anything.

Eddie frowned and stared at George, not understanding what he feared concerning his brothers.

"Of what?" Timothy continued.

More tears flowed, and George let out little breaths as if trying to keep himself under control. "I'm scared they'll blame me."

"Like you blame yourself."

George stopped. "It was supposed to be me," he cried.

Eddie held onto George as tightly as he could when George bent over at the waist. "Shh, it's okay. You're okay." He didn't know what else to say, but he glared in Timothy's direction until he saw the discomfort in the man's eyes. It told Eddie that Timothy didn't like making George hurt. "Hold him," Eddie said, staring at Timothy.

Timothy shook his head once, then lowered his eyes and stepped closer. He pulled George—and Eddie—into his arms, wrapping one around Eddie's waist to hold them upright, and the other cupped the back of George's head. Eddie got a whiff of cologne that he knew wasn't George's. He savoured the scent. His eyes darted open when a hand brushed through his hair. He met Timothy's gaze, the man offering half a smile, then he went back to holding George.

Eddie had no idea how long they stayed that way, but eventually, George pulled away and wiped his face. He inhaled and blew it out in a rush, then began walking in the same direction they had been going in.

"Where is he going?" Eddie asked.

"Not sure," Timothy replied.

They reached a fork in the road, and George went left, then right onto another road until he stopped at some gates. He pressed the button to the side. The gates began opening, and George slipped through, stopping on the other side. Eddie and Timothy stopped beside him, Eddie's eyes widening at the sight of Prince Frederick's house. He doubted he should be here and kept back when Timothy stepped closer to George.

"Are you going to see him?" Timothy asked.

George continued to stare at the house, and Eddie saw

Prince Frederick step out into the driveway. He didn't move closer, just stood there with his hands in his pockets. George's tears overflowed again.

"I don't know what to say," George said, his voice scratchy.

"You don't need to say anything. Just be with them."

George reached for Timothy's hand, and Eddie saw him squeeze it. "Thank you."

Timothy let go of George's hand and rubbed his back. "I'll see Eddie back, and I'll return tomorrow evening."

George spun towards Eddie and threw his arms around him. "I'm sorry. I didn't mean to leave you alone."

Eddie hushed him. "I'm not alone. Go and see your brother. I'm at the other end of the phone if you need me."

George pulled back, cupping his face. "And I am for you, too."

Eddie smiled. "Thank you."

"Thank *you*." George dropped a kiss on his lips and let go.

Eddie immediately missed his warmth and crossed his arms over his chest to keep it with him. George stood before Timothy once more.

"Thank you."

The corners of Timothy's mouth curled. "I didn't do much. You found your way here by yourself."

George cleared his throat and shuffled, an unusual show of nervousness. "Would you..." He stopped. "Never mind."

George turned away, but Timothy stayed him with a hand on his forearm. "What were you going to say?"

The prince's cheeks pinked, and Eddie raised his eyebrows.

"Would you squeeze the back of my neck again?" he

murmured so softly Eddie could barely hear. "It helps. Somehow."

Timothy rested his hand on the back of George's neck, and some of the tension released. Eddie knew then that George needed whatever Timothy could give him. There was no doubt in his mind. Timothy leaned down and whispered something in George's ear. George nodded and stepped away, Timothy dropping his hand and sliding them into his pockets.

George sent a smile to Eddie, small as it was, then turned to where his brother was still waiting patiently. Eddie watched as George picked up speed the closer he got to Prince Frederick, then fell into his arms. Prince Frederick wrapped his arms around George and dropped his head to George's shoulder. Eddie cleared his throat and turned away, not wanting to intrude on such a moment. Timothy reached past him to press the button on the gates, which slowly opened.

Eddie sent one last look at George, then exited, walking next to Timothy. "I hope you can remember the way. I'm terrible with directions."

"I think I can get us there."

They walked in silence with about two feet between them. Eddie didn't know what to say to break the quiet, but he didn't find it uncomfortable.

"Are you okay with everything that's happening between you and George? He told me you were in a BDSM relationship."

Timothy's voice startled him, but he smiled. "Yeah. He's helping me through some issues I have. I just don't want to push more onto him now that this has happened. I'm going to let him get over this and step back a little, so he can heal without worrying about me."

"Do you think he's not going to worry about you if he doesn't see you?"

Eddie lowered his head. "Out of sight, out of mind?"

Timothy chuckled. "That phrase is extremely outdated. When you care about someone, that feeling doesn't go away when they're not there. I think you and Prince George are well suited. He takes care of you and you of him."

"I don't really, though. He's always doing stuff for me, and although I love taking care of people, I don't feel like I can with him. Our contract is just for the club. This," he waved his hand around their surroundings, "was unexpected. He needs someone to take care of him properly. I don't think that's me."

He glanced at Timothy from the corner of his eye and saw him frown. Eddie wasn't sure how to get his point across that Timothy would be good for George without making Timothy feel like he needed to step back. If he did that, Eddie would be mortified because Timothy was the only person George had spoken to besides Eddie. He didn't want to ruin that.

"I don't think you're right there, but you have to make your own decisions. Don't push him away. Take a step back if you need one, but don't disappear on him. He needs you more than you realise."

Eddie wasn't sure that was true because of what he witnessed at Prince Frederick's house, but he let it go. "Is he going to be okay alone now?"

Timothy tilted his head. "What do you mean?"

"Well, you know he wasn't seeing anyone before you came." He glanced at Timothy to see him nod. "I have to go home and back to work. Since I arrived yesterday, he's not been alone at all. I was worried he wouldn't manage it."

Timothy sighed and stared at the floor, kicking leaves as they moved onto the grassy area, which Eddie assumed was the shortcut George had taken them on earlier.

"Being alone is not a bad thing, but it could make him feel worse. Unfortunately, we won't know the result until he does it. I think he'll be fine, especially now that he's made strides to see his brother. He'll find his way back to them easy enough now."

Eddie fiddled with the strap on his coat. "Have you always been a therapist?" The words were out before he could stop them. "Sorry, that's none of my business."

Timothy chuckled. "I have until recently." His voice wavered, but when Eddie looked, he stared in front of them as strong as ever. "I'm a teacher at the college now. A friend asked me to speak with George, but I don't take patients on anymore."

There was a story there, but Eddie could tell it was off-limits. "What do you teach?"

"Psychology," they said together.

"Sorry, I answered my own question. It should've been obvious."

Timothy grinned. "Not always. A friend of mine went from being a therapist to teaching mathematics."

"Really?" Eddie stared at him, eyes wide. "How come?"

"He had a degree in it alongside psychology. He loved both." Timothy cleared his throat. "What do you do?"

"I'm a barista, which doesn't seem very interesting compared to what you do, but I like it."

"There's nothing wrong with that job. I love coffee—"

"You came into the cafe a couple of weeks ago!" Eddie's

cheeks flamed as he realised he'd interrupted. "I'm sorry. I didn't mean—"

Timothy stopped and raised his hands to Eddie's shoulders. "Eddie, stop. Breathe. It's fine. You're not my student, so I won't give you detention." He smiled. "What were you saying about a cafe?"

Eddie exhaled. "You came in and did some paperwork, then thanked me for the coffee afterwards. I haven't seen you there since."

"I remember." Timothy smiled. "I didn't realise it was you. It was amazing coffee."

Eddie pouted. "Not good enough to bring you back." He lowered his gaze when he realised he'd been flirting. He hadn't meant to. It had just come out.

"Look at me," Timothy said.

Eddie swallowed and raised his head. "I didn't mean it the way it sounded."

"I don't mind. If we weren't in the situation we are in..." He sighed. "From my perspective, it seems like you have a relationship with George, even if you say it's just a BDSM one. Until you know what's happening there, you shouldn't confuse matters."

Eddie's shoulders lowered. He felt ashamed.

"No, Eddie, no. It's not your fault. I'm a very cut and dry man. I won't cheat. Ever. Your relationship with George confuses me because I don't know where you both stand with it, and I don't think you do either. It's a conversation that needs to happen, Eddie. You can't be left hanging any more than George can." Hands cupped his cheeks. "Don't settle for less than what you want, Eddie. I have no doubt George could be that person for you, but you need to be sure."

Eddie stared up at Timothy, the hazel colour darker than it had seemed before. He dropped his gaze to his lips, then ducked his head. He had his hands on Timothy's chest and slowly pushed away, not realising how close they had become. He cleared his throat. "I think I need to get back."

Timothy nodded and pointed in the direction they needed to go. They exited the trees into the sunlight again, and Eddie recognised where they were.

"You have a good sense of direction."

Timothy smiled, more relaxed than before. It made his face light up, made him look younger. "I blame being a scout when I was a teenager."

Eddie chuckled. "I lasted about two visits before I realised it wasn't for me."

They climbed the steps and entered the gardens once more.

"I have no hope of finding my way through the castle, though," Timothy said. "It's much too big."

Eddie chuckled. "I don't think we need to worry." He pointed. "There's a staff member."

The woman came towards them, then enfolded Timothy in her arms.

"Randall asked me to find out where you all were."

Timothy grimaced. "Sorry, I thought it would be a good idea for Prince George to get some fresh air. I didn't think about telling anyone."

"Where is he?"

"At Prince Frederick's."

The woman closed her eyes and sighed. "Thank you," she said, her voice broken.

"There's no need for thanks, Portia." Timothy glanced at Eddie. "Portia, this is Eddie, one of George's friends."

Eddie was glad he hadn't introduced him as anything else. He held out his hand to shake the woman's. "Nice to meet you."

"I'm glad you're here for him. He's been very…isolated lately."

"He'll be fine, Portia. Give him time," Timothy said. "We need to get going. Could you show us the way back to Prince George's room so we can gather our belongings, please?"

"Of course."

Eddie followed them as they chatted their way through the corridors, then went into George's bedroom to gather his clothes. He quickly changed out of the ones George had let him borrow and shoved everything else into the small bag he'd originally brought with him. He wasn't sure when he'd see George again, but he would send him a message when he got home. He glanced around the room, feeling like this would be the last time he'd ever see it. Ignoring his sentimental feelings, he entered the living room. Timothy was waiting for him.

"I know the way from here. Can I walk you to your car?"

Eddie nodded. After another glance around, he headed for the door with Timothy's hand on his lower back. The further away from George he was, the worse he felt, but he knew it was the right thing to do. He had to work, after all.

When they got to their cars, which were parked next to each other handily, Eddie smiled. "Thank you for everything, Timothy."

"Take care of yourself, Eddie. I'll come into the cafe to see you soon."

Eddie smiled again but refused to hold his breath. He doubted he'd see either of them again after today, and his heart pounded painfully at the thought.

1 3

GEORGE

He wasn't sure how long he'd held onto Freddie, but his throat was sore by the end. Freddie had steered him into the house and closed them in the comfortable living room—because Freddie had a guest living room, too, and it was full of antique tables and uncomfortable furniture. He sat them on the sofa and continued holding George until George finally pulled back and wiped his face.

"Sorry."

"Don't be sorry. I'm glad you're here. I was getting worried about you."

George huffed a laugh. How could he explain that the thought of seeing the anger or hatred on his family's faces was more than he could bear? Even then, he hadn't looked Freddie in the eye. He didn't want to see it, but it didn't stop him from needing his brother.

"I've been—"

"I know. We're trying to find them, too. Everyone is."

"I'm sorry I haven't been helping with the arrangements."

Freddie rested his hand on George's shoulder. "It's fine, George. Enough people are scurrying around, getting things ready. Mother," He cleared his throat, "had things already in place. It was easy enough to set the plans in motion. We're not needed at the moment."

At that, George glanced up. Freddie appeared older. Lines that had been absent were now marking his brow and the corners of his eyes. He sounded pained by the thought of not being of use, which was a Freddie thing. His eyes, though, were full of pain, not anger, not hatred, not annoyance. Pain.

"It should've been me," he whispered.

"Stop!"

His father's voice rang out through the room, and George flinched, lowering his head. Andrew strode forward and cupped his chin, lifting it until George met his gaze.

"I have known your mother for forty years, and she would've thrown herself in front of *anything* to ensure her children were safe. *I* would throw myself in front of anything to ensure you're all safe." Andrew's nostrils flared, but George knew it was not in anger. "Louisa is up there, smiling down on you all because she stopped them from hurting you. Yes, okay, she didn't know it at the time, but I guarantee you, it does not upset her."

Tears leaked from the corners of George's eyes, dripping down. "I'm sorry, Father."

Andrew grabbed his arm and pulled him into a hug. "You have nothing to be sorry for." His voice caught.

George held onto his father and sobbed. His father's arm tightened, his head coming to rest against George's temple.

"My dear boy, I'm so glad it wasn't you."

The rest of his father's words disappeared into the sound of George crying and clinging to the man who had the weight of the country on his shoulders. Long minutes later, George sniffed and pulled back, grimacing at the state of his father's shirt. He grabbed a tissue from the table and wiped at the wet patch.

Andrew chuckled. "It's not the first time, and I doubt it will be the last." He patted George on the cheek. "I hear you've had a couple of visitors lately."

George's cheeks heated. "I'm sorry I've not been to see you—" He stopped when his father waved him away.

"It's fine. I was more worried that you'd cut yourself off from everybody. Now that I know you haven't completely, I feel better about not visiting you sooner."

"I didn't realise you were here," George said.

Andrew blew out a breath and sank into an armchair, rubbing a hand across his mouth. "It's my turn to say sorry. I should've been to see you all sooner. Today was the first day I've managed…" He watched his father's Adam's apple bob several times. "It was time I checked in on my children. I should've done it before now, so I'm sorry. I had planned to visit each of you today, but you arrived before I finished my visit with Frederick."

George's stomach dropped. "I can go?"

"Don't be silly. You're here now. In fact, Frederick, call Douglas. We may as well all meet here if that's all right with you?" Andrew glanced at Freddie.

"Fine by me." He pulled out his phone, pressed a few times on the screen and held it to his ear. "Doug, are you busy? Good. Come on over to my place, will you? No, nothing's wrong. Okay, bye." Freddie put the phone away. "He'll be here in a few minutes."

"You didn't tell him why." The corners of Andrew's mouth lifted.

Freddie gave a small smile. "It'll make him get here faster." He stood. "I'll speak with Adele and get some drinks for us." He left the room.

George stared at his hands, picking at the skin around his thumbnail.

"Have your friends helped you?"

The question made him jump, and he glanced at his father, nodding. "Eddie is a sub at the club."

His father narrowed his eyes. "Is that a good idea?"

"He's a good man, Father."

"I'm not worried about him, George. Is it a good idea to bring him into this if you're not serious about him?"

George pursed his lips. "I think I am, or at least, I could be. We met a couple of weeks ago and have spent several evenings together at the club. I think…no, I know he's becoming more to me, but he's a little skittish."

"I can imagine. With everything he went through, it must've been difficult for him to step back into the club."

It did not surprise George that his father knew who Eddie was. His father knew everything. "It was. He came to me to help him get through a scene, and we've grown close. I really like him."

Andrew rested his chin on his fist and stared at him. "All right. Please be careful. He's vulnerable because of what happened to him, and you're vulnerable because of what happened to us."

"I know."

"How is Dr Dixon?"

George dropped his gaze, though he didn't know why. "He's nice. He seems to know what he's talking about." George chuckled. "He got me here."

Andrew raised his eyebrows. "He did?"

George scrunched up his face. "Well, kind of. He got me out of my room and to the gardens. From there, I took the lead, and we ended up here."

Freddie entered the room with an older woman following behind. He dropped to the sofa while Adele placed the tray on the coffee table between them.

"Thank you, Adele."

"You're welcome, Your Highnesses," she said before leaving.

"How is Portia holding up?" Freddie asked their father.

Andrew exhaled. "She's finding it difficult, but she's the one who suggested Dr Dixon. They're friends."

George hadn't known that, but then, he knew little about Timothy, anyway. It reminded him that he'd left them to find their way back to the castle. For all he knew, they could be wandering around the trees still. He pulled out his phone and messaged Eddie.

GEORGE: Did you find your way back okay? Sorry, I never thought about that.

He put the phone on the table and picked up his drink, curling his legs underneath him. He savoured the heat seeping into his hands. The door opened, and George peered over to see Douglas come through.

"What's up?" He paused when he saw their father. "Is everything okay?"

Andrew stood. "Yes, everything's fine. I thought it high time I visit my children."

He stepped towards Douglas, enfolding him in a hug and whispering in his ear. Douglas tightened his hold, tucking his head into Andrew's neck, despite being several inches taller.

George's throat thickened, and he looked away, tears threatening to spill again. He should've done this before now, but at least he was here. He had to remember to thank Timothy when he next saw him.

His phone chimed, and he uncurled to reach it.

EDDIE: We did. Timothy has a good sense of direction, unlike me. If I'd been on my own, I'd still be there. I hope your visit is going well. I'll see you soon.

George frowned, not liking the tone of the last sentence. Eddie would see him soon because he was determined to help Eddie as he'd promised. He would have to brave a visit to the club again sooner rather than later. It wasn't fair for Eddie to keep coming here.

GEORGE: If you're free, meet me at the club on Tuesday.

EDDIE: I'm free. What time?

GEORGE: Eight.

Eddie replied with a smiling emoji, and George put his phone away, tuning into the conversation.

"—she wanted to be buried. They have arranged it for the 19th."

George swallowed hard. He'd never asked what was happening or where his mother was. "Is she...lying-in-state?"

Andrew nodded. "She's at Westminster Hall. She had always told me she would've preferred a quiet funeral, but she knew the public would need this, which was why she agreed to it."

"She was always thinking of others," Freddie said.

They spent several hours talking and eating, then their father left them alone after asking them to join him for lunch the following day.

"I didn't say a proper hello to you earlier," Douglas said, coming over to George and pulling him into his arms.

For once, George didn't feel like crying, and he was glad. He still gripped his brother.

"What are you going to do about Mav's birthday?" he asked when they sat again.

Douglas crossed his ankle over his opposite knee. "I don't know. He doesn't want to do anything, but I don't think that's the best thing to do."

"You know what Mother would've said," Freddie said, staring at Douglas.

"I know. I think Mav doesn't want to disrupt the grieving process the day after the funeral. It's not fair to him to not celebrate it, but if he'd feel uncomfortable doing it, I don't know what else to do."

George cocked his head. "What if we did something small instead of something bigger? I know he's a part of our family now; therefore, large events should happen, but we can do this quietly."

Douglas frowned. "I don't know."

"Ask him. If he says no, then fine. But it would be nice to have something to look forward to after the funeral, even if it's just us lot drinking our livers away," Freddie said.

George laughed. "He couldn't be against that!"

Douglas rolled his eyes. "Providing he doesn't have to do

any media damage control for—what do you call us now? The Naughty Nine?—he'll be fine, I'm sure."

"Good." He was quite proud of that name.

"So, how are things going with Eddie?" Douglas waggled his eyebrows, making him look ridiculous.

George rolled his eyes. "Good, thanks."

"That's all you're giving us?" Douglas pouted.

"Yes."

"How is that fair? We always spill our secrets to you!"

George chuckled. "Not because we want to know them."

Douglas gasped, mouth going wide. "How dare you?" He snorted. "Though it's probably true." Douglas sobered. "How are you really?"

George exhaled. "Better than I was this morning. I should have visited with you before now."

"You did it when you were ready," Freddie said. "It's fine."

"Is there anything that needs to be done?" he asked.

Freddie massaged the back of his neck. "Father is still in his eight days of mourning, so there'll be nothing that needs doing for now. We'll get information from Randall about the plans for the funeral, and then Father will stay within Windsor for the following thirty days. After that," He cleared his throat, "it will be back to normal."

George snorted. "Back to normal. As if that's possible."

"Okay, almost normal," Freddie amended.

"What's happening with finding who did this?" George asked.

Freddie sighed. "I haven't got much information, but Randall told me they have many people searching through the evidence and investigating what happened. From what he's told me so far, it doesn't seem to have been a terrorist threat."

George stared at Freddie. "Ask them to look at it as if *I* were the intended recipient."

Their gazes locked, and understanding flashed in Freddie's eyes. "They're looking in the wrong place," he murmured and reached for his phone. "Randall, do me a favour, please. Call your contact and tell them that the target was George, not Mother. Hardly anyone knew about the change of plans because it was a last-minute decision. See what they can find out if they take a different direction with it. Thank you." He put the phone down. "He'll get back to me."

"Who wants *you* dead, George?" Douglas asked. "Not that I wouldn't be thoroughly pissed if you had died, but what does it achieve? What do they get from targeting you?"

"I've no idea."

Throwing ideas back and forth didn't help, so George left them with a promise to visit them again tomorrow. Douglas offered to take him back, but George waved him off. Despite dusk having fallen, he looked forward to the silence of the evening as he walked. Glad for his coat and the packet of love heart sweets Freddie had given him, George shoved his hands deep in his pockets and aimed for home, crunching one of the hard sweets.

He wished he had Eddie to go home to, but he couldn't expect the man to be at his beck and call every second of the day. He had a job and a life that didn't include George. All they had was the club, although George was certain he would like something more. He'd always thought of himself as submissive, but Eddie called to a part of him that wanted to care for him, to protect him, to give him what he needed.

As for Timothy, George wasn't clueless. The man exuded dominance, and whenever his hand rested on George's nape, it felt like there was no other place he belonged. George wasn't averse to the idea of being a switch, but how could he choose which man? They both felt necessary to George, or maybe that was his grief talking. Maybe he needed to talk it through with Timothy before making plans. He wouldn't name names, although it would probably become obvious once he explained.

When he stepped out of the trees, he stopped and stared up at the sky. No stars were visible yet, but there was a stillness to the night that he loved. If only that stillness could help him clarify his thoughts.

He continued his journey, entering the gardens, then sat on the bottom step, facing the castle that was his home. He tugged his coat around him and popped another sweet into his mouth. He didn't want to face the silence in the house, but the quiet outside was comforting. He wished he'd ventured further than his room before now.

He closed his eyes and listened to the trickle of the water from the fountain, the brush of the leaves against each other in the wind and the occasional beep of cars in the distance. A plane sounded overhead, and he opened his eyes to watch the red lights flashing as it flew the distance to the airport. He'd never realised how peaceful it was to listen to the silence.

Inhaling the chilly air, he shivered and folded his arms around him. He was cold—in fact, his ass had gone numb—but he didn't want to move. Instead, he turned his thoughts to Eddie, the bright light in his darkened world. While they would probably frown upon it, he would go to the club and scene with Eddie. Having a small slice of normalcy would probably do him good, and he couldn't wait to see what Eddie looked like as he came apart beneath George's hands again. Eddie had mentioned the table in that room; it might be time to look at it and help the man get over one of the hurdles holding him back.

It could also help George understand whether being a Dominant was something he enjoyed or had been going through the motions of—which is what he'd thought before he'd met Eddie.

He had come out as submissive to his family when Henry had a few months ago but had been continuing his dominant facade because he hadn't wanted to change how things were for himself. He'd been considering coming out publicly— well, publicly as in at the club—over the past couple of weeks, but then he'd met Eddie and had become as confused as ever. Timothy was visiting him again tomorrow. He would speak to him about his dilemma and see what wise words the therapist might have for him.

He shivered again and stood, his legs wobbly, his ass smarting from the cold cement steps, then weaved his way through the bushes and statues. The chill was replaced with warmth as he wandered through the house and into his room.

With so many thoughts bombarding him, he didn't expect to sleep because, all in all, it had been an emotional day, but he couldn't have done it without Eddie and Timothy.

14

DOUGLAS

"If I find out Aunt Charlotte and Charles had something to do with this, no one will stop me from giving them what we all know they deserve."

Douglas stood, pacing from one side of the fireplace to the other, his hands clenching into fists repeatedly. It was bad enough that they had taken his mother, but for it to potentially be aimed at George was something he couldn't comprehend.

"Why would they target George?" he asked Freddie.

Freddie shrugged. "It could just be because he's bisexual. Although he fits all the other requirements Aunt Charlotte 'allows' in the family, that's one thing she wouldn't like."

"But enough to kill him?"

"They set fire to Robert's shop while he and Henry were inside. I think it's safe to say they would go to any lengths to get what they wanted."

Douglas stopped. "They're not going to stop, are they?"

Freddie rubbed his forehead with his finger and thumb. "I

highly doubt it. As far as I'm concerned, they're trying to overthrow the crown, but we have no proof."

Douglas linked his hands at the back of his neck. "This is fucking shit."

"I have some of my own people looking into this as well. Don't tell Father, although he probably knows."

"Have they found anything?"

Freddie shrugged. "Nothing."

Douglas strode over to the window and sighed. "Mother would've known what to do."

"Yes, she would," Freddie replied after a beat. "But that could also be a reason *she* was the target and not George."

The truth was just out of reach, and no matter how hard they tried, they couldn't get answers. Aunt Charlotte and Charles were too organised, too hidden. Too many people in the country were of a similar opinion to them, and Douglas knew they would back her should she ask them to. That she would be so public with her hatred was laughable because she would never do that in case it isolated her from the people. In public, she was the epitome of a do-gooder. It was in private that she could do with some training.

"Is there anything we can do?" Douglas asked, twisting to face Freddie.

"Not at the moment. We have to wait for the results of the investigations; otherwise, we'll show our hand, and they'll find another way to get out of it. Playing it close to our chest is the best option for now." Freddie rose and drifted to Douglas. "How are you holding up?"

Douglas snorted and averted his gaze. "I'm not."

Freddie rested a hand against his nape and their foreheads together. "She'll never be forgotten, that's for sure."

Douglas's nostrils flared as he inhaled and exhaled, trying

to keep hold of his emotions. "What are we going to do without her?" he whispered.

Freddie let go and hugged him tightly. Douglas nestled his face in Freddie's neck, tears soaking into the fabric beneath his cheek as Freddie said, "We live. For her. We find the bastards, and we survive. That's what we can do for her."

The break in Freddie's voice broke Douglas, and they both cried. After several minutes, they pulled back, eyes wet, and Freddie's were red-rimmed—he assumed his were the same.

"Go to Mav. Remember what you have. Mother wouldn't want us missing out on things because we're sad. You know that like I do. Persuade him to have a party. That's your sole goal today." Freddie smiled.

Douglas inhaled and blew out the breath in a rush. He sniffed and wiped his face. "Okay. I'll do what I can."

He left Freddie's house and climbed into his car. Mav waited for him at the apartment, so he headed straight there. Maybe he could persuade Mav that the party could be a celebration of Mother's life, alongside Mav's birthday. It would do them good to let off steam with those who knew what they were going through. Especially for George. He was glad his brother had finally escaped the confines of his room. Douglas had been worried about him.

Only time would tell if they could get through what was to come.

15

TIMOTHY

Timothy stood in front of his students while they found their seats, his hands clenched in his pockets. He hadn't been able to sleep after the conversation with Eddie the previous day because he was as confused as Eddie appeared. The pull towards Eddie at the cafe had been unexpected, but he hadn't realised he was the same person, even though he felt a pull towards him when they were with George, too. It was a similar pull he felt towards George, but he wondered if that was more because he wanted to "save" George from doing anything rash.

He glanced at his shoes, berating himself because he knew it was different. How could he find two people who gained his interest in the space of not even three weeks? Was he that desperate to not be alone?

The bell chimed for the start of the lesson, and Timothy shook the thoughts from his head. He'd have to deal with his personal life afterwards.

"Good morning, class." He smiled at them. "I have been through your tests from last week, and I have to say, I'm impressed. You have a sound knowledge of what you've already learned. There are a few areas that appear to be a sticky point for some of you, and I will go over those in class again over the next few weeks. I think it will help everyone. For this class, though, I have an experiment for you to do. First, I want Emily to put your hand up. Now, every other person, put your hand up." He chuckled when some of them got it wrong. "Okay, that looks right. You are all person A. Everyone with their hands down is person B. Person A swivel to your left to face person B, who will swivel to your right. Does anyone not have a partner?"

They all did. He had no idea if this was going to work but live and learn.

He handed a stack of paper to the nearest person and clapped his hands. "All right. Person A, you will need one of these sheets of paper and a pencil. While you're sorting that, I will explain what's going to happen. Person A is going to ask person B the questions on this sheet—they are yes and no answers—and when person B answers, person A needs to not only listen to the answer, they need to look at the person's body language. Make a note of anything you think might be a tell. Once you have done that, person A will need to evaluate those responses and comments and decide whether person B was telling the truth. Now person B, you need to tell both truths and lies for this, and please remember your answers."

The class laughed, and one student raised their hand.

"What if there is a question we don't want to answer?"

Timothy chuckled. "There shouldn't be questions that are personal enough that you wouldn't want to answer, but if there is, say you don't want to answer. It's a valid answer. The same as in everyday conversation. If someone asks a question, you have the right to say nothing." He waited to see if anyone else had a question. "Okay, you have ten minutes to ask your questions, five minutes to evaluate, then you'll swap."

While they were busy, he sat at his desk and set up the presentation he would show them before the end of the session. It had been one the previous teacher had provided, but Timothy had tweaked it a bit. Then he focused on his planning for the rest of the term, the end of which was only three weeks away. After that, he would have two weeks to ensure he was ready for the summer term.

He didn't know what he'd do in those two weeks. He could ask Bry, Talia or Imogen to visit for a few days. It would depend if they could get the time off work. Two weeks with nothing to do sounded appealing to some people, but Timothy hated not being busy. Would he still be visiting George by then? Or would he have stopped their visits because he felt better?

He hadn't heard from anyone to say he shouldn't visit again this evening; therefore, he intended to keep his appointment. He hoped George had found his visit with his brother helpful. If not, he was sure George would tell him. He didn't seem like the person to stand by and let others tell him what to do. At least in some situations.

Timothy's mind went to the gutter with that thought. He could see George on his knees in front of him, waiting for his command, and he rubbed at his eyes to wash away the image. It wasn't something he'd been interested in before, except for the "idea" of it, but since George had mentioned being into BDSM, the images had circled his mind. He knew it was pointless because George was a dominant, and Eddie was his submissive. He needed to remember that.

"Dr Dixon?"

Timothy jerked his head up. "Yes?"

"Ten minutes is up."

He glanced at his watch, seeing it was true. "Thank you, Emily. Okay, time to evaluate, then after five minutes, swap roles."

He refocused on his planning, trying to brush aside thoughts of a prince and a barista and ways around having them both, which was a crazy thought.

When the class ended, he packed up his bag, heading for his car. His phone rang.

"Hello?"

"Good afternoon, Dr Dixon. I believe we have a mutual acquaintance. I think it would be in your best interests to stay away from him. He doesn't need your…influence. The prince is quite content living his life as he is now. Don't push him to be something he doesn't need to be."

The line went dead before Timothy could reply, and he stared at the screen. They had withheld the number, so he had no idea who it was. Few people knew he was visiting George, though. He shrugged and made a note to mention it to George.

Timothy knocked on George's door and heard the shout for him to enter. When he did, George was sitting on the sofa with the laptop on his knees and his feet propped up on the coffee table.

"Isn't that an antique?" he said, nodding towards the table.

George's forehead furrowed until he followed Timothy's

gaze, then he jerked his feet off and to the floor. "I forget. Mother always scolds…scolded me for that."

He shed his coat and hung it up before settling into the chair opposite the prince, trying to ignore his stomach, which protested not having dinner before he came. "What are you working on?"

The chiselled cheekbones of the prince flushed an adorable shade of pink, and his lips pursed. "Um, I'm catching up on some work."

Timothy raised his eyebrows. "I thought you'd say something different. I never asked before, but do you have a specific job, or is this work for your family?"

George put the laptop on the table, closed the lid and threaded his fingers together, resting his elbows on his knees. "I do have a job. Two, actually. I've not been doing much with them, though."

"You have the right to take time off."

"I know. I find it easier to bury myself in something else sometimes."

Timothy nodded. "I know what you mean."

George cocked his head, studying him. "You do."

"Grief is not something where one size fits all. Everyone mourns differently. If throwing yourself into work is something that helps you cope, then it's fine, assuming you're not hiding from the truth of the matter."

"Which is?"

"Your mother is dead."

George's nostrils flared. Timothy watched his hands tighten, becoming white with the force he was using. He hated being so blunt, but he needed George to acknowledge it. George inhaled and blew out a breath.

"She is, yes. And I know she wouldn't want me to ruin or lose the jobs I have because of it."

"She was a remarkable woman who will be sorely missed by many people."

George smiled. "She loved it when the public came out to see her at events. Despite her security cursing continually at her, she always made time to talk to the crowds before or after finishing her royal duties."

Timothy crossed his legs. "I remember watching your father's coronation and seeing her spend time with the children along the route the car took. I think I was about eighteen at the time."

"Yeah, she didn't care that it was the procedure." George chuckled, though his eyes were wet. "I was ten, and it annoyed me because I wanted to walk with her, but the security guards wouldn't let me." He sniffed and sighed. "I sometimes forget that she wasn't just my mother; she was important to the country. To the people."

"She will always be your mother, regardless of what else she was." Embarrassingly, his stomach growled, and he pressed a hand to his abs. "God, I'm sorry."

"Have you had dinner?" George asked.

"I'm fine. You eat, though, if you haven't."

George narrowed his eyes. "That's not what I asked."

Timothy could understand why George was a dominant when he aimed that stare his way. Although it didn't make him want to bow down and do what George said, it had a way of making him want to let George take care of him, which was strange.

He rubbed his earlobe. "I haven't, no."

George stood. "Is there anything you're allergic to or you don't eat?"

Timothy held out his hand. "I'm fine. I can eat when I get home."

"Either answer the question, or you get whatever I order for you." George didn't look at him as he lifted the old-fashioned dial phone that had a cable connecting it to the wall. Timothy hadn't seen one of those in years.

He sighed. "No allergies, and I won't eat fish."

George spoke into the receiver and placed an order. "It should be about half an hour, give or take."

"Thank you, but you didn't need to."

"I can't have my therapist passing out on me when you're supposed to be talking to me, can I?" George's mouth quirked. "Would you like a drink?"

"Tea would be great, thanks."

George busied himself at the small table holding the kettle, and Timothy studied the man. What was it about him that called to Timothy? George could take care of himself. Why did Timothy feel a need to protect him from things that could harm him or soothe him when things got tough?

Visions of Orlan and Yanni whipped him from his thoughts, and he inhaled, trying to remind himself not to get too close to another patient. Last time ended badly, and although he was far away from his family, there were still people he cared about close by. He couldn't afford to let his guard down. He needed to stay on track with George and make sure he was dealing with his mother's death in the best way possible. After that, he would pass it on to someone else. Someone more equipped to deal with any other problems the prince might have.

"Are you okay?"

Timothy glanced up at George, who was standing closer

than he'd expected, holding out a cup. He took it and smiled. "Yes. I'm fine."

"You use that word a lot."

Timothy frowned. "What word?"

"Fine." George sat, curling his legs underneath him and resting the cup on his bended knee. He stared across the distance as if in a challenge.

Timothy nodded. "It's the easiest word to use. My problems are not your concern."

George flinched and set his jaw. "I want to ask you about a problem I have."

"Sure."

"This is all in confidence, isn't it?"

"Of course."

George stared at the mug in his hands. "I told you the other day that I was a dominant, but that's not strictly true. Well, it is, but it's not. God damn." He sighed. "I...Do you know about Club Royal?" Timothy shook his head. "Fantastic," he muttered, though Timothy could tell it wasn't. "Club Royal is a BDSM club owned and run by the royal family." Timothy raised his eyebrows. "It's not public knowledge. Everyone who knows about it must sign an NDA. No one has proven we own it yet."

"Is that where you go?"

George nodded. "It's not the only place, although that stays between you and me. Most of my family doesn't know about my visits to another club." He waved his hand. "Anyway, in my family, every member had to train and appear as a dominant. Old thoughts die hard that submissives were considered lower ranking than Dominants. Now, this idea has changed over recent years, but although people's opinions changed, the rules didn't. I am a dominant when it comes to the club, but I'm not in my heart. Or at least, I didn't think I was."

Timothy tried to follow George's thought processes, but it was difficult. "So, you're a submissive?"

"I thought so until I met Eddie."

Timothy's heart rate increased. "What has made you reconsider?"

"I want to look after him. I want him to be part of my life, but there's a part of me that feels empty—god, I hate saying this." George placed his cup on the table and rubbed his face.

"It's okay. Talk to me. We'll try to work through it." Timothy was confused, but talking it out always helped.

"I thought that when I met the person I wanted to spend my life with, I would be content, but something's missing." He stared at Timothy. "I still need that submissive side of me to be acknowledged, but it can't be Eddie because he's a sub, too. So where does that leave me?"

"Are you talking about being a switch? Is that what you call it?" Timothy asked.

"I don't know. Am I? Can I have one without the other?"

"You've already said that something was missing when you were with Eddie, so I don't know if you can. How do you feel about it? Think about spending your life with Eddie and having that space always missing. Can you live with it?"

"For Eddie, I can."

"What about for yourself?"

Timothy watched George's shoulders tense, then lower as he dropped his head into his hands as he understood his answer. Timothy, on the other hand, was sweating because he knew what he could suggest, but it was something someone would struggle with, even without being part of the royal family.

"Could you not have both?" he said in a low voice.

George's gaze met his, the furrow between his eyes prominent until it eased, and George's eyes widened when he realised what Timothy was saying. They both froze. Timothy had never considered having a BDSM relationship, but at that moment, he could see himself, George and Eddie and a future they could never have. No one would accept that in public, and which of them would have to hide if two of them went out as a couple?

Timothy snapped his gaze away when there was a knock at the door. George opened the door for the staff member, who wheeled in a trolley.

"Over by the window, please," George said.

The man set the small table with a tablecloth, cutlery, glasses and their covered plates of food, then pushed the trolley back out of the room with a bow in George's direction.

"Time to eat," George said, his voice strained.

They sat opposite each other, and Timothy's throat closed at the intimacy of it all. George reached forward to remove the dome covering Timothy's plate, and Timothy inhaled the scent of steak, potatoes and vegetables.

"Wow, this looks amazing."

"It'll taste it, too." George smiled and lowered his eyes to his plate.

They ate in silence. Timothy wished he could think of something to say to get back around to why he was there, but everything he thought of, he dismissed as being too nosey or too benign. The subject didn't seem like something that they could brush aside, but for once in his professional career, he wasn't sure which way to guide George.

The quiet continued until they had consumed the last morsel of food.

"Thank you. That was delicious," Timothy said. "I should probably leave you to your evening."

"No!" George grabbed his hand that had been resting on the table. "Please, stay. For a little while longer, at least."

Timothy stared at their hands, then turned his over and grasped George's, rubbing his thumb over his knuckles. "I'm not a dominant, George," he whispered.

George tilted his head back and forth. "Maybe. Maybe not. There's something about you that fills the emptiness."

"What about Eddie?" Timothy refused to take George away from Eddie.

"We can talk to him about it."

Yanni's face flew to the forefront of his mind. "I can't be what you need, George. I appreciate what you're saying, but my life is…" He threaded a hand through his hair. "I can't deal with any more media attention. I moved to get away from that."

George frowned and squeezed his hand. "What happened?"

"I dropped my guard. Thought I was invincible." He slid his hand from George's. "I can't be what you need," he repeated. "Talk to Eddie about your situation. Explain it to him. He'll understand." He stood, lifting his plate, then realising there was nowhere to put it, and replaced it again. "I need to go."

He whirled towards the door, ignoring George's protests. Sliding his coat on, he paused when arms came around his waist, and George rested his forehead on his shoulder.

"Please come back tomorrow," George said, his voice muffled by Timothy's coat.

Timothy dropped his head and covered George's hands. Then he squeezed and pulled them off him. "Talk to Eddie. I'll have someone arrange a new therapist for you. I'll find a good one. I promise."

He opened the door and heard, "But I want you," before he closed it behind him.

He hadn't realised how involved he'd become in George's world until the thought of not seeing him again carved a slice into his heart. The distance to his car felt like miles as he wandered further from George's room. He inhaled and exhaled slowly, trying to keep his emotions under wraps until he was safely in the confines of his home. He made it as far as through the gates before a tear slid down his cheek. Only one, though. George would not wilt because of him; he wouldn't allow it. George and Eddie needed to work it out together or needed someone who could give them both what they needed.

And it wasn't him, although it pained him to acknowlededge. He was cracked, though not broken; he had to heal himself first before he could heal someone else.

Or two someone else's.

16

EDDIE

"Do you have a break coming up?"

Eddie snapped his gaze to the side at the quiet words and stared into one set of eyes he'd been thinking about for the past two days. Timothy's expression gave nothing away, but Eddie could see something in his eyes. He glanced at the clock.

"I'm on break in twenty minutes, if that's okay?"

Timothy nodded and strode to the back of the line. Eddie's hands shook as he continued making drinks of all varieties. When Bella took over from him with a knowing grin, he rolled his eyes and removed his apron. He collected the drinks he'd made for them and wandered over to the table Timothy had chosen in the far back corner, away from anyone else.

"Hi. How are you?" Timothy asked when Eddie sat opposite him.

Eddie pushed a cup towards the man and tried for a smile. "I'm good. What about you? How's teaching?"

"Busy, but then I'm trying to find my feet, being new and all."

"I have faith in you." Eddie sipped his latte. "Is something wrong?"

"No! Nothing's wrong." Timothy frowned. "Well…I wanted to ask you to keep an eye on George."

It was Eddie's turn to frown. "Why? What's happened?"

Timothy rubbed his earlobe and stared at the table. "I'm looking for a new therapist for him, and I want to make sure it goes okay."

Eddie leaned back in his seat. "What! Why? You've been doing great with him. Even I can see that."

"Things are…complicated."

Eddie felt a simmer start in his stomach. "Life is complicated, Timothy. Why are you leaving him to face this?" *Alone.*

Timothy closed his eyes. "He will still have someone helping him, Eddie, and he has you. I'm interchangeable with the next therapist."

"Bollocks!" Eddie hissed. Timothy's gaze flew to his. "Other therapists tried, remember? He spoke to no one but you."

"That was then. He's more open-minded now."

"Open-minded because it's *you!*" Eddie leaned forward in his chair. "Don't leave him to drown, Timothy. Don't leave him to drown when you know you help him more than any other therapist would." There. He'd acknowledged what he'd seen without actually saying the words, although he would if he had to.

Timothy clenched his jaw. "Don't you see? That's why I need to step back. I've become too close to hi—the situation. I can't see clearly enough to help him."

"You're already helping him, Timothy."

"But am I?"

Timothy's gaze locked onto him, and Eddie could see what the man couldn't say. Strangely, Eddie didn't feel like he'd lost George to Timothy. He'd expected this to happen and had told himself he would step back if they found their way to each other, but it appeared as if they needed him to help bridge the gap until they each figured out their feelings. Having a purpose made Eddie feel better about the situation.

He leaned his elbows on the table, getting closer and lowering his voice. "For once in my life, I'm going to speak up, and you better listen. George needs *you*. You can settle him in ways I can't. You don't need to understand why or how. Just help him get through this and out the other side. See where you end up."

"And what about you?"

Eddie smiled. "I'll be there, too. For whatever reason, George has chosen us to help him through this. I, for one, am taking that as a compliment." He sipped his drink, checking his watch. "I only have a couple more minutes."

Gripping one hand in the other, Timothy pressed them to his mouth, closing his eyes. Eddie waited, leaving him to his thoughts. When his expression hardened, Eddie knew he would ignore his advice, so he gave it his last shot.

"Whatever you decide, see him one more time. Tomorrow evening. I'll be there as well if you want but talk to him. Don't ghost him. You know the same as I do that if you do that, he'll always wonder why."

Timothy sighed and stared at him for several long seconds before nodding once. "Tomorrow evening. Please be there."

"Of course."

Timothy smiled, and Eddie's heart missed a beat. "Thank you for the drink."

Eddie stood, placing the empty cups on the tray he'd brought them on. "You're welcome. Make sure you eat lunch. It'll help you get through the day."

Huffing a laugh, Timothy rose, buttoning his coat. "Yes, sir. Anything you say, sir."

Despite knowing he didn't mean it the way it sounded, Eddie bit his bottom lip and stared at the man. Timothy reached forward, pulling Eddie's lip from his teeth with his thumb.

"This gives away some of your thoughts, Eddie. Be careful," Timothy murmured.

Eddie's cheeks heated, and he lowered his head.

"I am so fucking confused," Timothy whispered.

The man pressed a kiss to Eddie's cheek and brushed past him, and Eddie let him go. If he moved at that moment, nothing would stop him from reaching for Timothy and saying so many things that needed to be kept inside. He swallowed hard and lifted the tray, taking it back to the kitchen for washing. He slid his apron back on and took over from Bella, who raised her eyebrows at him.

"Are you okay?"

Eddie inhaled. "No idea." He washed his hands and returned to his station.

Throughout the afternoon, he thought about George and Timothy, trying to figure out what was happening. He knew both men would be good together because even though Timothy didn't appear to be in the BDSM lifestyle, he was naturally a dominant person, which Eddie believed was what George responded to. He hadn't thought George was submissive but, looking back over their interactions, there were certain things Eddie had noticed that would put George in that description.

Eddie, despite being quiet and reserved most of the time, was willing to go outside his comfort zone a little to figure it out. He wasn't quite sure how yet, but he was meeting George at the club that night. He could think of something before then. And if he was…

That was the other image that kept returning to his mind all afternoon. The idea of several menage relationships he knew of. He wasn't stupid enough to think it was something the three of them could do, but the idea of it was enticing. Timothy would be the dominant of them both, although George would dominate Eddie sometimes, too. It would never happen, but it could fuel his fantasies.

Eddie took his time in the shower when he got home. He shaved and buffed and cleaned every inch of his body, then covered it in coconut body moisturiser. While he prepped, he put a plan together. It wasn't a solid plan, but it was something. When he was ready to leave, he threw his messenger bag over his shoulder and exited his house, locking the door behind him. He descended the steps to his driveway and threw his bag onto the passenger seat of the car. Terry called his name before he climbed in, and Eddie rested his arms on the roof of his car while the man jogged over to him.

"Off out?"

Eddie smiled. "Yeah. I'm meeting an old friend."

"Sounds good. Going anywhere nice?"

He couldn't tell Terry where he was going, but he could generalise. "Just a club, nothing fancy." Although it was. "What are your plans for the evening?"

Terry waved his hand. "Oh, you know. A movie and some ice cream. The usual."

"That's nice." Terry had a way of angling for an invitation to places, but this was one time Eddie would have to ignore the need to please everyone. "Have a good night, Terry. I'll sort out another movie marathon for us soon."

Terry wiggled his hips and threw his arms in the arms with a "Yay!" but Eddie could tell it was half-hearted. Unfortunately, Eddie had no choice in the matter.

"Take care of your *old friend*." Terry winked with enough suggestion to know what he was implying.

Eddie chuckled and climbed into the car. Terry stepped back towards his own house as Eddie started the engine. Terry didn't go inside. Instead, he watched while Eddie reversed into the road and drove off. It was something Terry had not done before, but Eddie brushed it off. He was lonely like Eddie had been.

By the time he reached the club, he was all kinds of nervous. First, he didn't know what to expect from the scene they would be doing, and second, he wasn't sure if his plan was going to make anything clearer. He'd have to wait and see.

He went through his routine, then entered the club, wearing his usual tight black shorts and not much else. There was already a crowd gathered, and Eddie wasn't sure where George wanted him to be. He grabbed a bottle of water from Oliver, then wandered around the floor, trying to find him.

When a hush descended over the crowd, he tried to see what had caused the reaction. Hushed words filtered through the members.

"I didn't expect to see them so soon."

"What are they doing here?"

"Nothing seems to keep them away."

"Aren't they still in the mourning period?"

With the last one, he knew who had arrived and weaved his way through the unmoving masses.

"Thank you all for your kind words regarding our mother. She will be sorely missed," Prince Frederick said, his voice strong but hoarse as if he hadn't used it for a while. "Whilst we are still in mourning, we wish to begin finding our way back to a new normal. That starts with the club. Please respect our wishes even if you don't agree with them. Enjoy the rest of your evening."

Reaching the front, he met George's gaze, then lowered his head.

"Eddie."

"Yes, Sir."

"Come with me."

Eddie followed George to the private rooms, hesitating for a split second when they entered the same room they had used the second time Eddie had requested George's help—the room Eddie had been abused in.

"Eddie?"

Eddie jumped. "Yes, Sir?"

George rested his hands on Eddie's shoulders, rubbing his thumbs back and forth against his collarbone. "Are you okay?"

"Yes, Sir."

George tilted his head and narrowed his eyes. "I'd like to try the table today," he said.

Eddie's gaze flicked to the hip-height wooden table, and he shivered. "Okay, Sir."

"I need to know you're with me, Eddie. Your colours are important. I don't want this to hurt you."

Eddie glanced at George and smiled. "I understand. I'm ready."

"First..." George's mouth quirked, and he fused his mouth to Eddie's. Being the same height meant they didn't need to stretch to reach each other. Although Eddie told his hands to stay at his sides, he found them gripping at the leather shirt George wore. George licked into Eddie's mouth, and Eddie sucked on his tongue. He tilted his head, wanting it deeper, harder. George slid his hand into Eddie's hair, tugging gently on the strands. A moan escaped, and Eddie held George tighter.

Even though he was running out of air, he pressed himself closer. George, though, pulled back, resting their foreheads together. Eddie kept his eyes closed, breathing unevenly into the space between them.

"Thank you, Sir."

George chuckled. "You're welcome." He pulled back, cupping Eddie's jaw. "Are you ready?"

"Yes, Sir."

George searched his face, then nodded. He turned to the table and moved it into the centre of the room. "I want you to lay your chest on the table and your arms down the sides."

Eddie inhaled and did as asked. The table, despite being wooden, was surprisingly comfortable when he wasn't being forced over it. It had curved edges to it, so they didn't bite into his skin and was smooth with no sharp bits on it. The chill made him gasp, but he continued until his torso met wood. He rested his cheek against the surface, staring at the opposite wall. He wasn't sure if he wanted to know what George had planned, but George started explaining.

"I'm going to strap your wrists and ankles to the legs of the table. Then, I'm going to take you to the edge as many times as I can before you fall."

Eddie's breath shuddered out of him at the idea.

"Colour?"

Eddie bit off a smile. George must've misinterpreted his body. "Green, Sir. I like the idea."

"Glad to hear it."

George strapped him down. When Eddie tested, there was no give in them at all. He couldn't lift his body from the table, only his head.

"Colour?"

"Green, Sir."

George smoothed his hands over Eddie's back several times, changing from the pads of his fingers to his nails with no rhyme or reason that Eddie could tell. Eddie's eyelids fell shut, and he blocked out everything except what George was doing.

George's hands moved further down his back, meeting the waistband of his shorts, and Eddie wished them gone. George's fingernails dug into his cheeks and continued down the back of his thighs, knees and calves. On the way back up, the touch was featherlight. Once the touch returned to his back, Eddie hummed at the feel of George's body against his. It felt like the early stages of a massage, bet Eddie wished for a different ending.

George's hands disappeared, and Eddie blew out a breath, trying to withhold his whimper of need. George's fingers slid between his waistband and his skin, gently working them down his legs to his ankles. This time, on his way up, George pressed kisses against his skin. Eddie released a groan when George ignored the area Eddie needed him most.

George disappeared, and Eddie knew this because cold air invaded where George had been. Eddie heard George fiddling with some items, then a careful hand rested against his lower back.

"This shouldn't be too cold," George said.

Eddie braced for the chill to touch his back, but instead, it touched his pucker. George spent ages stretching Eddie, and he wondered if George was going to fuck him. He wasn't opposed to the idea, but he'd leave the decision up to George.

"Get ready to bear down," George said.

Something cold but solid pressed against his hole, and he pushed down, allowing it entry. He breathed deeply, aware that he had only used his dildo about two weeks ago. His breathing increased, and his heart started a rapid beat.

"That's it," George said. "Just a little more."

Eddie wasn't sure he could take anymore with how full he already felt, but he trusted George.

"That's it. There we are. It's all the way in."

Eddie exhaled, trying to relax his muscles. He hadn't realised how tense he'd become. George's hands skimmed over his skin, setting all his nerve endings alight. Then George disappeared again. Within seconds, George was back, and something soft tickled his skin. Up and down, neck to ankle, from one wrist to the other, no skin left untouched, except for one. His cock was straining for attention, but he had nothing to rub against to find the sweet release that hovered on the horizon. He replaced the soft tickle with a rough texture, and Eddie tensed.

"Colour?" George asked.

Eddie checked in with himself, then answered, "Green, Sir."

The rough fabric followed the same path that the soft item had, and Eddie craved more. Once more, the item changed, and this time, it was hard and unyielding. Eddie's whole body locked into place, his breathing increasing more and more. He knew what it was.

"Colour?" George asked.

"Yellow, Sir," he panted.

The item disappeared, and Eddie felt George stand in front of him. George's hands took hold of his. He whispered something to him, but Eddie couldn't hear him over his breathing. He repeated the words until Eddie could make sense of them.

"Do you want me to untie you, or do you just need a breather?" George asked.

"Breathe," Eddie croaked.

George released one of his hands, running it up his arm and across his shoulder to the back of his neck.

"Can you open your eyes for me, sweetheart?" George said.

He tried, but it took several attempts before he could meet George's gaze.

"There you are." He smiled. "There is nothing wrong with acknowledging you are uncomfortable," George said. "Nobody has the right to make decisions for you. Would you like me to unstrap you?"

Eddie licked his lips and tried to shake his head but couldn't. "No," he said. "I want to keep going."

"Okay. Can you tell me what worried you?"

Eddie inhaled through his nose. "I knew it was a paddle. The moment I realised, I was thrown straight back there."

"Do you want to try again, or would you prefer a different item?" George asked.

Eddie was fed up with being held back, of being scared. "Try the paddle again, please, Sir."

"Are you sure?"

"Yes, Sir."

George brushed a kiss to Eddie's forehead, then rounded the table. Eddie tried to relax, but he knew he wouldn't be able to until the paddle had finished its path. At the first touch, Eddie jumped. After confirming he was okay, George moved to his back. The closer it came to his ass, the harder he clenched his fists. George requested his colour again.

"Green, Sir."

George dragged the hard wood over his cheeks and down the back of his legs. Eddie relaxed as it made its way back up again.

By the time George lifted the paddle from him, Eddie was back to feeling floaty and relaxed. He squirmed against the table, feeling the dildo moving inside him. George continued his ministrations, taking Eddie higher until he felt he couldn't take much more. George must have touched the dildo because it began vibrating, sending shock waves all over his body. He needed more friction on his cock to make him come, but it didn't seem like that would happen anytime soon.

17

GEORGE

George was so proud of Eddie. Not only because he had stopped him when it had become too much, but because he had succumbed to the sensations the paddle could give him. The paddle didn't always need to be a source of punishment or pain.

He watched Eddie squirm beneath the onslaught of the vibrations. He needed Eddie to fly. He wanted to remind him of all the good things that could happen within the club and banish all the terrible memories. Timothy's face swam before him, and George wished he could help ease those memories for him, too.

Refocusing on Eddie, he pushed against the base of the dildo, and Eddie's groans grew louder. A shiver went down George's spine, and his eyelids fluttered closed to savour everything.

He smoothed his hands up Eddie's back, then scraped his nails down again. Eddie hissed.

"Colour?"

Eddie exhaled. "Green…Sir," he breathed.

George leaned over Eddie's back, his groin pushing against Eddie's ass and eliciting more noises from the man. "Will you come for me, Eddie?"

"I want to. Please, I want to." Eddie pulled against the restraints.

George stood. He crouched behind Eddie. He gripped the base of the dildo and fucked Eddie with it while his other hand wrapped around Eddie's cock.

"Ah!" Eddie panted. "Oh, fuck!"

George squeezed his cock, using the precome to slick his way. He continued to withdraw and thrust the dildo but encircled the head of his cock, using his thumb to rub against the bundle of nerves underneath. Eddie gasped. George kept his movements steady and continuous. Eddie writhed, jerking against the fabric holding him down, his moans increasing.

George watched the sweat beading on Eddie's skin and wanted to taste it. He wanted to be the one thrusting into him and bringing him to orgasm, but it wasn't the right time. He didn't know why, but he knew it wasn't.

As his thumb continued its strumming, he slid his finger to the slit and rubbed it. Eddie's moans turned into whimpers. Pressing the button on the end of the dildo, George increased the vibrations, and Eddie became incoherent.

"Sir! Oh, *fuck*, please!"

George tilted the dildo, and Eddie shouted as he came. George continued until Eddie twitched and pulled away. He shut off the vibrations and pulled the dildo free, dropping it to the floor. His hand was covered with come, and George licked his lips. He stood, rounding to where Eddie's head rested against the table. Eddie's breathing was evening out, but his eyes were closed.

He knelt, running his clean hand over Eddie's head until the man's eyelids fluttered open. Those deep blue orbs settled on him, and Eddie smiled. George lifted his come-covered hand and, holding Eddie's gaze, licked it clean. Eddie's cheeks reddened, but his eyes never wavered.

Once his hand was clean, George unstrapped Eddie from the table and helped him to stand. He lifted him into his arms and strode to the bed, laying Eddie in the centre. Covering him with a blanket, George fetched some water, juice and some pineapple pieces from the fridge. He set them on the bedside table and lay beside Eddie, pulling him into his arms. He grabbed a carton of juice and held the straw to Eddie's lips. When it was all gone, he slid a piece of pineapple into his mouth, then stroked Eddie's hair.

"Thank you," Eddie whispered.

George pressed a kiss to his forehead and held him for a long time. He wasn't in a rush to go anywhere. No one thought he should be here, anyway, but he needed to be there for Eddie, to show him he wasn't just another man at the club. How to do that was something he'd have to figure out, especially after his conversation with Timothy.

"Timothy isn't coming back," he said, breaking the silence.

"He will," Eddie replied.

George glanced down at him. He had his eyes closed but a slight smile on his face. George wished he had as much faith as Eddie did.

"He didn't turn up today."

"He will tomorrow. I'm sure of it. He's a good man, George."

"He is, but I wish he'd see that." George kissed Eddie's

forehead again. "It shouldn't hurt so much." He wasn't sure if he was talking about Timothy or his mother.

"It's because he's more to you than a therapist."

Eddie's words made George flinch. He swallowed hard, needing to reassure Eddie. "He's…I'm focused on you, Eddie. You mean so much to me."

Eddie smiled and opened his eyes, cupping George's jaw. "As you do to me. That doesn't mean you don't also care for Timothy."

"I'd never cheat on you."

Eddie chuckled. "I know you wouldn't. You're too honourable for that." Eddie sighed and snuggled closer, closing his eyes again. "You don't need to decide. Timothy is perfect for you, and I will always be here."

It felt a lot like Eddie was passing the baton to Timothy, but George didn't want that, but he wasn't sure how to ask for what he wanted. Or even if he *should* ask for what he wanted. Silence descended again, leaving George to his confused thoughts.

After he'd tended to Eddie the previous evening, he'd made sure he was okay, then headed home himself. He hadn't felt like socialising. Now, though, he was back in Freddie's house, surrounded by his brothers and cousins—the Naughty Nine were in session.

George hadn't told them about his predicament, but he needed to. They were the only ones he trusted to tell him the truth and if he was being an idiot or not, but how did he start *that* conversation?

"Oh, gee, do you remember when I said I was a submissive? Well,

apparently, I was lying because I'm falling for a sub. On top of that, I'm also falling for my therapist. How's that for a funny story?"

It was only when the room went silent that he realised what he'd thought he'd been saying in his head, he'd said aloud.

He scrunched his eyes closed and dropped his head back against the sofa. "Why me?"

Robert cleared his throat. "You know, it's not unheard of to have more than two people in a relationship. I know of two relationships like that."

George groaned. "So do I, but do you honestly think our family will allow it?" Robert winced.

"Uncle Andrew has been good to us, George. I'm sure he won't mind," Henry said, resting his head on Robert's shoulder.

"I'm not worried about *Father*," George mumbled.

They sat in silence, their thoughts probably going to Aunt Charlotte just like George's had. He hadn't been concerned about figuring out the relationship with Eddie and Timothy as much as whether their lives would be in danger because of it. His eyes widened, and he sat upright.

"The car bomb...Aunt Charlotte?" He stared at Freddie, who slumped back in his seat, brushing shoulders with Damon.

"It would surprise me if it was. Only because of how visible the incident was. It brought a lot of media attention to it, and the public is gunning for the people responsible."

"She seems to have been behind most of the other things happening around here lately," Patrick said.

"Why would she be after you, though, George?" Mav asked.

"I came out as bisexual and submissive to several of the

family. I can almost guarantee that didn't stay within the four walls they were told in. Plus, I'm supporting you both." He indicated Douglas and Henry, who had recently found their other—male—partners. "You know she doesn't care for homosexuals. Could she be branching out to those who support them, too?"

George wouldn't put it past her at all. After the confrontation last month between his father and Aunt Charlotte, where her son, Albert, chose them over her, they hadn't heard from her, but that didn't mean she wasn't doing something behind the scenes.

"It is just as likely that it was a terrorist attack," Freddie said. "We are vulnerable to that as well."

"Is there no more news from anyone?" George asked.

Freddie shook his head. "They're still investigating. It won't be something that's figured out quickly, George. They need time."

George bit his lip to stop from saying something they already knew—that time was running out. The people would already be scattering, and leaving it longer made the trail harder to find. He stared at his lap, where his fingers were tapping out a rhythm on his leg.

"We have three days before the funeral. Let's concentrate on figuring out George's predicament before then," Douglas said, a smirk curving his lips.

George rolled his eyes and checked his phone, ignoring him. He had two hours until Eddie was coming over, and he was looking forward to spending more time with him. It was a shame he couldn't have Timothy there as well. They all needed to talk, but he was sure the therapist would run instead.

"So, George Henry Sutcliffe, what little mess have you got

yourself into now?" Douglas rested his chin on his fist and smiled.

"Shut up," George said without heat.

"Come on, George. We've had enough talk about us. Now, it's your turn." Henry pointed his finger and grinned.

His cousin had come out of his shell more since his relationship with Robert and since he'd announced it to the world. Maybe George should do that, then there wouldn't be any issues with secrets or not knowing.

He blew out a breath and leaned his forearms on his legs, spinning his phone between his thumb and forefinger. "I don't know what to tell you. I have no idea what's going on either."

"Start from the beginning," Damon said.

"A couple of weeks ago, Eddie approached me to help him work through the issues he had with…what had happened. I agreed. We did a few scenes over a few nights, then…" He inhaled, knowing he needed to say it but not wanting to. "Then Mother died. I had seen no one in that time, but Timothy arrived, and there was something about him I couldn't turn away. He appeared so sad, and I found myself talking. Eddie contacted me, and I invited him to visit. Not for any nefarious reason," he added when several eyebrows raised. "He comforted me," he whispered. "I wanted to be with him more, and I opened up to Timothy more. He understood how I felt without me having to explain it."

"And…" Henry asked when George stopped talking.

"He visited on Monday, and we had dinner because he'd forgotten to eat before coming. Afterwards, he said he would find me another therapist, but I don't want a new one. I want him. But I also want Eddie."

"So have them both." George blinked at Mav. "Yes, there

is the potential for danger, but isn't it better to have them in the fold of the family than out there with no protection at all?"

"But if I didn't start anything with them, they'd be safe."

Mav's mouth curled. "But haven't you already started something with them?"

George stared at him, then hung his head. "They're already in danger, aren't they?"

Freddie came to sit beside him, sliding his arm around his shoulders. "If this was to do with Aunt Charlotte, Eddie would most likely already be on her radar with how much time you've spent with him at the club. As for your therapist…he's probably not in any danger at the moment."

George dropped his hands into his head. "I shouldn't have started anything with anyone. I've no right to bring anyone into this mess when they don't know about it."

"You can't help who you fall for," Douglas said.

"I should've known better with everything we've been through. Everything you've been through." He waved his hand at Douglas and Mav and Henry and Robert.

"And I repeat, you can't help who you fall for."

George rose, Freddie's arm dropping from his shoulders. He paced across the room, raking his fingers through his hair.

"George, we're all here. We'll do everything we can to ensure they are safe. The same that we do for everyone."

"Mother was supposed to be safe!" he yelled, tears brimming. "She had protection. They took precautions, and still, they got her."

Douglas grabbed him in a hug, arms crushing him as his heart pounded painfully at the knowledge that there was little chance of keeping anyone completely safe if someone wanted them dead. George gripped his brother, tears soaking straight into Douglas's jumper. He wished he was as strong as his brothers were, standing strong despite the emotions that were no doubt battering at their insides because George's certainly were. He thought he'd got past the crying stage.

He pulled away from Douglas, wiping at his face. "Sorry." He cleared his throat. "I have to go. Eddie's going to be here soon." He headed for the door.

"Don't make any rash decisions, George," Christian said. It was one of the few sentences he'd said since he'd arrived, looking dishevelled and tired. "Happiness is what helps us get through this life. Don't sacrifice yours because of those who don't deserve it."

George glanced over his shoulder to look at him, something flashing behind the man's eyes. He wished Christian would open up to them, but it seemed George wasn't the only one who'd been keeping secrets lately. George nodded once and exited the room. The cool evening air helped him breathe for the first time in several minutes. He stood with his hands on his hips as he inhaled and exhaled. When he felt more composed, he aimed for home.

He had a lot to think about and only a short time to do it before Eddie was there. Could he knowingly allow Eddie to step into danger? He'd been through so much already with Talon. Then again, did he have any right to choose for him? George's head swam as he tried to figure out the best course of action.

Before he knew it, he was standing in his room, staring around him, no clearer about what he should do. He'd run out of time to decide.

A knock sounded, making him jump. His heart leapt,

emotions warring inside him. He inhaled and opened the door, eyes widening when he saw who was there.

"Can we come in?" Eddie asked.

George stepped back, coughing. "Of course, sorry." He closed the door. "I wasn't expecting to see you again."

Timothy shoved his hands into his pockets and glanced at Eddie. "I was persuaded not to leave things as they had been."

George peered at Eddie, who smiled at them both. "Really?"

"Look, I don't think it's a good idea for me to be your therapist. We've crossed lines that are there for a healthy professional relationship into something...I don't understand what. We need to stop."

"No, we don't."

George raised his eyebrows at Eddie's declaration. "We don't?"

Eddie raised his chin and pulled his coat sleeves over his hands. "There's something here. Between us all. We need to figure it out."

"I would never come between you," Timothy said, holding out his hands.

George continued to stare at Eddie. "That's not what he's saying," he murmured. "Keep going, Eddie." It appeared this amazing man would be brave enough to say what George couldn't or shouldn't.

"I met Timothy a few weeks ago in the cafe. There was a simmer of attraction from my side straight away." He smiled at Timothy, then at George. "I've always been in awe of your ability to make everyone at ease, especially in the club. That's why I asked you that first night. But that's who you are all the time. You genuinely care about people. It's easy to fall in love with someone like that." Eddie's cheeks darkened, and he crossed his arms over his stomach. "I can see something between you and Timothy. Something deep. Something raw. I came here tonight, ready to step aside, but I realised…we're pieces of a puzzle. We're all broken, but when we're together, we're complete."

George stared at the tears running down Eddie's face, and he took Eddie's hand, rubbing his knuckles with his thumb. He glanced at Timothy, seeing the indecision on his face. He had no idea which way Timothy would go.

"I don't know if I can," Timothy whispered. "I'm a long way from being fixed. I'm not a dominant. I have the media hounding me, even here. I'm not someone you want to rely on."

Eddie stepped forward, keeping hold of George's hand. "You don't need to be fixed. We'll heal each other. You don't need to be a dominant. You just need to care. There will be more media attention when our relationship goes public. You haven't let us down."

"There's no going public with this," Timothy said, waving his hand in a circle. "You'll be ruined." He stared at George. "One of us would have to hide each time, and it's not fair to you or us."

It was George's turn to move closer. "I want this. I don't care what the public would say, but I do have information I want to tell you before either of you decide."

George let go of Eddie's hand and invited them both to sit. He stayed standing, pacing the width of the room, unsure where to start. How could he explain years' worth of what could basically amount to treason?

"We have several members of the family who are homo-phobic. To an extreme level. They want to keep things as our ancestors made them. Douglas and Mav had problems when they announced their relationship, and so did Henry and Robert. Henry has been dealing with this for years. It's entirely possible…Mother was killed because they were trying to get to me. To clean up the 'gay' people." He tried to swallow down his tears. "If we do this, there is every chance they'll come after you, too."

1 8

───────

TIMOTHY

They were trying to get to me.

The words circled Timothy's mind, and he felt his stomach churn. He fisted his hands and clenched his jaw. How dare they? He lost some of what else George said and had to refocus on the conversation.

"I have no idea what we're doing here, but I want us to try. As Eddie said, there's something here, but I understand if the potential outcome is too much for either of you."

George sat opposite them, hands linked in his lap, head lowered. Timothy didn't like his expression, as if he was awaiting execution. Timothy imagined his life without being able to see either of them again, and he didn't like the idea of it. Understanding seeped into his body, and he covered his mouth with his hand. He was already in too deep. He wanted this, but as George had opened his life to them, it was time for Timothy to do the same.

"I have something I need to share before you make up your mind, too." Timothy swallowed hard and rubbed his earlobe.

"Let me get some drinks. I think we might need some for this entire conversation," Eddie said, wandering over to the drinks table.

While he did that, Timothy tried to figure out how to explain everything that had happened. The mistakes he'd made were glaringly obvious when he looked back, but it didn't change the outcome. Orlan was still dead, and it was Timothy's fault.

The cup of tea warmed his hands, but it didn't warm his insides. He placed it on the table, not wanting to drop it while he told his story. Timothy cleared his throat.

"Orlan and I were married for many years. He understood the long hours in the beginning because I had to make a name for myself while I was starting up. He stood by me for years, then it became too much when a patient found out where I lived. Yanni was a quiet patient, answered my questions when I asked, but was to the point and didn't give more detail than necessary. When he turned up at my house, I was surprised, but I stepped onto the steps and spoke to him for a while before he went home. This happened several times a week. Orlan was fed up with it. I couldn't see the harm in talking with Yanni. Not in the beginning anyway."

Timothy closed his eyes as images from that final night bombarded him. His chest hurt, but he breathed it away, leaning back in the sofa cushions.

"Orlan left me when I refused to push Yanni away. I couldn't understand why Orlan wouldn't support me. After that, I threw myself into my work, spending all hours of the day and night working. Yanni's visits continued until, one night, I came home and found Yanni *inside* my house. I could see the change in him and knew it wouldn't end well. I never realised how bad it would go, though."

The cushions depressed either side of him, and hands rested against his shoulders and legs. He opened his eyes, having not realised they were still closed. George and Eddie sat on either side of him, eyes showing concern. He stared at his hands.

"What happened?" George asked, his voice quiet.

"I got Yanni to think we would have a movie night, but he overheard me trying to call my colleague when I was in the kitchen. He pulled a gun." Timothy's breath caught. "He wanted me to call Orlan and get him to visit. I knew I couldn't, but luckily, we'd created a code for if this ever happened." Tears overflowed. "He was supposed to call the police and stay away. He wasn't supposed to come into the house as if nothing was wrong!"

George's arm slid around his shoulders, and Eddie rested his head on his shoulder, his arm across his stomach. Feeling surrounded made the last moments easier to talk about. He dropped his head onto the back of the sofa.

"Yanni shot Orlan. Then the police shot Yanni."

"Oh, god," Eddie whispered, tightening his hold.

George's thumbs swiped at Timothy's tears and pulled him until his head was on George's shoulder. "It wasn't your fault."

Timothy didn't answer, his throat too closed up to do anything but breathe. The heat from the two men surrounded him, making him feel tired.

"It wasn't your fault, Timothy. It wasn't."

Timothy cleared his throat again. "The media thought so. They hounded me, stating malpractice because I saw Yanni outside of my office. They spoke to so many people who knew me. Stalked my family and friends. I...I couldn't take anymore. That's why I moved here. Since I disappeared from

Bristol, the media has died down, but I'm already getting phone calls here. It's a matter of time until they come around."

"Some members of the media can be soulless demons. Mav helps with that for Douglas and occasionally with the rest of us if we need it. I bet he'd help you should anything happen," George said.

Timothy lifted his head and sniffed. "You have enough media attention because of your family. You don't want to add this into the mix."

"I'm willing to chance it." George smiled.

"Me, too," Eddie said.

"If it gets out that you were my patient..." Timothy raised his gaze to George.

"We'll deal with it." George's resolve was admirable, but Timothy wasn't so sure they could easily brush it under the carpet, despite how expensive said carpet was.

"I'm sorry you went through that," Eddie said, staring up at him.

Timothy realised he was running his hand up and down Eddie's arm, and George grasped his other, the back of his hand against George's palm. They surrounded him, and he loved it. He lifted the hand George had hold of and, not letting go, reached for Eddie's cheek, brushing their joined fingers across the soft skin. George moved closer, sliding his face closer to Timothy's and resting his chin on Timothy's shoulder.

Could this work? Could the three of them make something good from all the crap being thrown at them?

Eddie's eyes drifted closed, and Timothy felt an immense need to close the distance between them.

"He wants you to kiss him," George whispered in his ear, causing him to shiver.

"We haven't decided—"

"Haven't we?" George challenged.

They were all still there despite the problems they would likely encounter. Was that answer enough?

Timothy licked his lips and swallowed, using his and George's hands to lift Eddie's chin higher. His gaze roamed across the features of the man before lowering his head. The initial brush of lips resulted in a gasp from Eddie.

"Kiss him," George said. "He likes to feel it."

The idea that George knew that should've put him off, but instead, it sent goosebumps along his spine. He joined their mouths again, this time licking inside when Eddie opened for him. Timothy's eyes closed when a blast of warm air coated the side of his neck. He could feel Eddie in his arms and George surrounding him. It felt natural.

A whimper left Eddie's mouth when Timothy pulled back for air. George moved their joined hands to Timothy's cheek, turning Timothy's face towards him.

"My turn," George whispered.

George dropped his mouth to Timothy's, licking at his lips. Timothy opened, and their tongues slid alongside each other, harder than he had kissed Eddie, but just as tantalising. Timothy inhaled through his nose as George took from him and gave everything in return. Lightheaded, he pulled away with a gasp.

George quirked his mouth, then turned his attention to Eddie. Moving their hands again, George made them cup Eddie's neck and pull him forward. Eddie eagerly moved closer, and Timothy had a front seat view of them when their mouths joined. Their eyes closed, but Timothy fixed his gaze on the sight of their tongues sliding into each other's mouths. His cock tingled as blood began filling it.

Unable to resist, he leaned forward, slipping his tongue between both their mouths. Eddie whimpered again, and George gripped the back of Timothy's head, holding him close. It was a messy kiss, but it was everything Timothy had ever needed.

George released their hands, and Timothy slid it behind George's back, matching the one around Eddie. Eddie moved closer, straddling Timothy's leg. He widened them to make room for him, then moaned when Eddie's knee rested against his groin. George's mouth disappeared, and Timothy fused to Eddie, taking everything he could give him and, hopefully, giving everything back.

More pressure against his cock and balls, and Timothy ripped his mouth free from Eddie's. Eddie whined and writhed against his leg, but Timothy glanced at George, who had straddled Timothy's other leg. He had one man on each leg, and he didn't argue when George began unbuttoning his shirt. Timothy ran his thumb over Eddie's lips, pulling his bottom lip from between his teeth.

"What did I tell you about that, Eddie?" he murmured.

Eddie's eyes opened and closed several times before fixing on Timothy. He rested a hand on the back of the sofa and the other on Timothy's now bare chest, thrusting his hips against him. "I want it all," he said.

Timothy slid his hand around to Eddie's ass, encouraging his movements. George reached over and pulled Eddie's T-shirt over his head, throwing it behind them. Eddie lowered his upper body until his skin touched Timothy's. The shiver was instantaneous. Eddie rested his face in the crook of Timothy's neck, his warm pants pebbling Timothy's skin.

Glancing at George, he saw the prince smile before he yanked his T-shirt off. Eddie made soft whimpers of need while George unbuckled his own trousers. With no hint of embarrassment, George pulled his cock free, stroking the length a few times before leaning forward and kissing Timothy. The kiss was harder than before, and Timothy gripped the back of George's neck, keeping him in place.

Hands unfastened Timothy's trousers, and Timothy hissed into George's mouth when a hand surrounded his hard shaft. The friction continued amidst other fumbling. Timothy finally pulled back, dropping his head forward to watch. Eddie's hand encircled Timothy's cock, while George's hand wrapped around Eddie's dick. George's free hand joined Eddie's on Timothy's shaft, and he bit his lip. He reached between them to push George's hand from Eddie's cock. When he let go, Timothy slid his hands around their lower backs and urged them to rest against him.

"Ride my leg. Come over me." He didn't know where the need came from, but he wanted them to mark him.

Both men attached their mouths to his neck, and Timothy fought the urge to drop his head back. He didn't want to miss any part of this. They continued to stroke his cock as they thrust against him. Eddie's whimpers were music to his ears, and George panted against his skin.

Eddie's movements increased, and his hand faltered. Timothy felt the slight sting of teeth in his neck, then the warmth of fluid over his stomach as Eddie cried out. Timothy gripped his ass, encouraging him to ride it out. Timothy's spine tingled, and he knew he was close to coming. He wanted George to come first.

"Come for me, George. Take your pleasure from me."

George's hands tightened on his cock and neck, his

tongue painting patterns on Timothy's neck as he thrust. George dropped his forehead to Timothy's shoulder, then shuddered and growled, releasing over Timothy. George's hand let go of his cock, and Eddie leaned down, encasing it in wet heat. Timothy gasped and thrust his hips. Eddie's tongue fluttered against his nerve bundle, and Timothy was over the edge.

George pulled Eddie off, sending his come over Timothy's stomach to join theirs. When he lifted his head, George grinned and swiped a finger through their joint releases and licked his finger clean. Eddie followed suit, then George did it again, but this time, held it out for Timothy.

"You trust me without asking if I'm clean?"

George tilted his head. "You would've told us if you weren't."

It was a statement. Timothy opened his mouth, and George slid his finger inside. The burst of flavours was bitter on his tongue, but he swiped around George's finger until it was clean. George repeated the action, sharing the fluid between all three of them.

"Are you both okay?" he asked after swallowing, unable to curb his need to make sure they were good.

George quirked his mouth. "More than okay." He glanced at Eddie, who had curled himself against Timothy with his eyes closed.

Timothy dropped a kiss on his head. "Eddie?"

"Hmm?"

"Are you feeling okay?"

"Hmm."

George chuckled. "He loves to be held and petted afterwards."

Timothy expected jealousy to come rearing up because

George knew what Eddie liked when he didn't, but only softness and affection showed up.

George climbed off Timothy's lap, and a wave of cool air washed over him. He realised they still had their cocks hanging free from their clothes. Heat invaded Timothy's cheeks.

"This was not what I had planned for my visit today."

George snorted. "Let me guess, you were going to repeat the need to get me a new therapist?"

"Yes. I still think it's a good idea."

George shivered. "I don't need anything but you two."

Eddie snuggled closer, and Timothy slid his free arm around him, holding him close.

George smiled. "I knew we'd be good together." He grabbed his discarded T-shirt and wiped his front, tucking himself away afterwards. Stepping closer, he reached out and wiped at Timothy's stomach and cock before carefully putting him away.

"Thank you." Timothy reached out and grabbed the back of George's neck, pulling him near. George's eyes fluttered closed, and Timothy pressed a kiss to his forehead, his nose, then his mouth. He tugged George off balance until he knelt beside him, their foreheads resting together. "Thank you. There's no guarantee I won't second-guess myself after this, but I will never forget this."

George pointed a finger at his chest. "There is no leaving, Doc. You're ours."

"And we're yours," Eddie said with a yawn.

"Damn straight." George grinned and raked his fingers through Eddie's hair. "You up for a shower, sweetheart?"

"Hmm."

George laughed. "Come on, sleepyhead. I'll grab some

juice if Doc can get you into the bathroom." He kissed them both and stood.

Timothy dropped his head back against the sofa and sighed. This was probably a huge mistake, but if all the problems were in the light now, and they could only weather whatever was sent their way. He would still insist that they don't show up as a threesome because it was courting trouble. He'd happily stay in the background if it meant there would be fewer problems. He was over the media attention, anyway. He wanted solitude, which was a stupid thing to say when he wanted to be with the two people who were coming to mean so much to him.

Derek would have a field day with his thoughts. He had no idea how he was going to keep this from him, but it was imperative that he did. George seemed lighter now that they'd confirmed their relationship. Or at least, as confirmed as it could be after one conversation. He was sure there were many more conversations to have.

"Oh, I'd like you to meet my brothers and cousins at some point. Let me know when is best for you," George said as he disappeared into the bathroom with glasses.

Timothy's eyes widened, and his heart pounded. Eddie began giggling from his position.

"George! You should feel his heart rate! He's terrified!" Timothy snorted and grabbed at Eddie's sides, tickling him. "No! Stop!" Eddie's laughing increased, and he tried to squirm away, but instead, fell to the floor with Timothy on top of him, though he braced himself to stop his full weight from falling on the smaller man, especially as his cock was still out.

Eddie stared up at him, his laughter subsiding. He slid his hands up Timothy's still naked chest and cupped his face, running his fingers over his cheeks and mouth. "I'm glad you're still here."

Timothy kissed him, chasing his tongue when he opened his mouth. His taste differed from George's, who seemed to have a lingering sweetness. Eddie, on the other hand, tasted of coffee. He pulled back, but Eddie lifted his head to keep them locked. Timothy grabbed his wrists and pinned them to the floor, ripping his mouth away with a gasp.

Eddie undulated against him, and Timothy could feel the hardness springing back to life. He chuckled, then frowned. "How old are you?"

"Old enough," Eddie quipped with a wink.

"Sassy," Timothy said before raising his eyebrow and waiting.

Eddie sighed. "Twenty-seven."

Timothy hung his head. "Jesus. I'm a fucking cradle-robber."

"Hey, no, you're not. I'm old enough to know what I want. I'm old enough to be going to a BDSM club."

Timothy tilted his head. "True, but fuck. You're thirteen years younger than me."

"And?" George said.

Timothy glanced over to the bathroom, seeing George with his arms crossed as he leaned against the doorframe. He stared at him for a few seconds before returning to Eddie. He kissed him. "Never mind."

"Good. Come on, Doc. Time to get clean, then we can grab the Naughty Nine."

Timothy frowned. "The Naughty Nine?"

"My brothers, cousins and their partners." George stood upright. "Damn it!"

Timothy scrambled up, helping Eddie up. "What's wrong?"

"I'm going to have to find a new name again. Bloody hell."

"What?"

"When the new partners came into the group, I changed the name. We used to be the Scandalous Six."

"Why do you need another name?"

"Because of you two. We're now eleven people." George sighed. "Took me bloody ages to figure out the new name."

Eddie strode towards George. "We can always stay away."

George slid his arms around him. "No, that's not what I was saying. I think you're going to have to help me choose one. Something cheeky that rhymes with eleven."

"I'll think about it," Eddie said, sliding his arms around George's neck. He whispered something into George's ear, and a smile spread across his face as he glanced at Timothy.

Timothy had a sense of foreboding. "What?"

"Wouldn't you like to know?" George said, and they disappeared into the bathroom, leaving him with his hands on his hips and as confused as ever.

Despite knowing trouble would most likely follow them wherever they went, he didn't think he could walk away. Even though he thought it would be the best option, he realised he'd sealed his fate the moment he'd agreed to the appointment with Portia.

19

EDDIE

*E*ddie didn't know where his confidence came from. He felt strong whenever he was with the two men. He felt like he could take on the world and win. That was the only thing that could account for the words he whispered into George's ear.

I want to show him what we can do.

He wanted to show Timothy how they were when they were at the club. He wanted him to see the beauty they could see. At least, he *hoped* Timothy would see it.

"We can't do exactly what we could at the club because I don't have all the equipment," George said. "However, I have some leather restraints." He dropped a kiss to Eddie's neck as they wandered towards the shower. "Why don't you get in, and I'll grab them without him seeing?" He winked.

Eddie smiled and nodded. He turned towards the shower, switched it on and climbed under the spray. He dropped his head, letting the warm water pound onto his head and shoulders. He lost himself in the rhythm of the spray, enjoying the heat on his skin.

Hands slid around his waist, the hair of Timothy's goatee giving away who it was. Eddie smiled and dropped his head back to rest against the man whose exhale Eddie felt.

"What's wrong?" Eddie asked, pivoting to face him and slide his own arms around Timothy's neck.

"This seems so easy and so hard all at the same time. George is my patient. I shouldn't—"

"Is he, though? Does it state anywhere on paper that George is your patient?" Eddie stared at him. "If I know anything about this family, it's that they don't like to show weakness. I don't know if they'd consider therapy a weakness or not, but I would bet good money there is no record of your sessions, even if you got paid for it."

Timothy glanced to the side, his forehead creasing. "I have no idea."

"I don't think you have anything to worry about."

Eddie saw and felt George take his hand from around Timothy's neck and wrap a PVC cuff around his wrist. He slid his forearm down Timothy's arm, trying to keep the cuff out of sight, and reversed their positions so that Timothy was under the spray. George kept hold of the cuff and took Eddie's arm behind Eddie's back. Eddie, knowing what George wanted, released his other arm and put it behind him with the other one. George fastened the cuff around the other wrist, and Eddie relaxed his shoulders.

Timothy peered over Eddie's shoulder and raised his eyebrows, running his hands over them. "Are they tight?" Eddie nodded. "Too tight?" Eddie shook his head.

"Just right," he whispered. He tugged against them, the chains clinking above the sound of the water. He bit his lip when one of them grabbed the chain and held him still. His cock rose to the occasion once more, reaching for Timothy.

George closed in behind him, pressing his front to Eddie's back, trapping his hands between them. "Colour?"

"Green, Sir."

George stepped back again, and Eddie whimpered at the loss. A similar cuff went around his left ankle, then his right ankle, pushing his feet together.

"To your knees and spread them," George said.

Eddie knelt between the two men, spreading his knees as far as his cuffed ankles would let him. George fumbled with the chains and attached Eddie's wrists to the ankle chain, making it impossible for him to stand. He exhaled and relaxed. The position was not the most comfortable, but he enjoyed the freedom it represented.

"Colour?"

"Green, Sir."

"How do you feel, Eddie?" Timothy asked, curling a finger along his jaw.

Eddie felt a rush of energy and smiled. "Free."

There was silence, and Eddie glanced up at Timothy, noticing the crease between his eyes again.

"You don't understand?" Timothy shook his head, and Eddie licked his lips. "Despite the restraint making it so I cannot move freely, I can let go of everything I think I should do or second-guessing if I'm doing the right thing. Being restrained gives me the freedom to just be. To give my care over to George. To you. I know you'll give me what I need and want, and I don't have to think about it."

"You just have to follow orders," George added.

"Is it not uncomfortable?" Timothy asked.

"Sometimes, but it helps me focus on the here and now instead of the future."

Timothy caressed Eddie's face, and Eddie's eyelids fluttered.

"I think you need to thank Timothy for your release earlier," George whispered in Eddie's ear.

Eddie gasped and focused on Timothy's dick, long and dark red in appearance, spearing towards his face. He swallowed hard, remembering the taste of him from earlier. Could he make Timothy lose himself again?

Eddie used his knees to shuffle himself forward enough to reach the underside of his shaft. He licked the water droplets from it, his tongue curling around the girth. He couldn't lean forward easily, and he didn't have the use of his hands to pull the cock towards him, so he had to think creatively. He curled his tongue around the head again, firming it and trying to bring it closer. It slipped away several times, and Timothy's hand encircled the base, but George pulled his hand away.

"He can do it."

Eddie glanced up at Timothy, his eyes narrowed, his mouth tense. Refocusing, Eddie firmed his tongue again and slipped the head of Timothy's cock into his mouth. Along with the explosion of something that was uniquely Timothy, Eddie sighed at the butterfly feeling in his stomach from achieving what his Masters wanted him to.

He sucked at the head before taking him in further, the tip rubbing against the roof of his mouth to the back of his throat. Eddie savoured the experience. Timothy groaned, and a hand fisted his hair.

"Do you love it when he feeds you his cock, Eddie?"

Eddie moaned around the shaft, releasing part of it before taking it in once more. This time, when it reached the back of his throat, he swallowed, eliciting a groan from above him. He repeated the action several times before Timothy pulled away. Eddie chased after him, wanting more.

"I want this to last," Timothy said.

"You'll get more chances, don't you worry," George said, tilting Eddie's head back and hand-feeding Timothy's cock to him. "Let him swallow you."

Timothy and Eddie both groaned as his dick slid back into Eddie's mouth. George knelt behind him, encircling Eddie's cock with one hand and flicking against a nipple with the other. He rested his head on Eddie's shoulder, cheek to cheek, and Eddie wondered if George could feel the echo of the cock sliding deep. He wanted to see Timothy sliding into George's mouth. Eddie pulled back, whimpering at the image.

"What do you want, Eddie? Hmm? What dirty image went through your mind?"

Eddie couldn't speak, but Timothy slid his other hand into George's hair. "If it was anything like I was thinking of, it was the idea of you taking my cock alternately."

Timothy's voice was hoarse and barely audible above the shower.

George kissed Eddie's cheek, his hands never faltering from their seduction of Eddie's body, then opened his mouth, waiting, his eyes on Timothy. Eddie glanced up at Timothy, too, watching to see what he'd do. Timothy smirked and slid his cock deep into George's mouth.

As close as Eddie was, he could see the string of saliva that joined the two men when Timothy slid free. He aimed for Eddie's mouth, and he took him deep, swallowing around him before Timothy pulled away again and into George's mouth.

"Fucking hell," Timothy hissed between his clenched teeth.

Eddie's climax barrelled towards him, the sensation of Timothy's cock in his mouth, the visual of his cock in George's mouth, the feel of George's hand around his own shaft and George's dick thrusting against his lower back was more than he could take. He closed his eyes, breathing deeply when his mouth was free to do so, trying to withhold his release until he was told he could come. He winced with the effort.

"Timothy, he's nearly there," George said. "Fuck his mouth and take him over the edge. Eddie, don't come until Timothy does."

Eddie whimpered, not knowing if he could hold back much longer. Timothy thrust into his mouth, and Eddie swallowed, trying to get Timothy to come. He sucked and licked and focused on the nerve bundle while George stroked his cock, flicked his nipples, and sucked on his neck. A tingle began at the base of his spine, and he increased his movements on Timothy's shaft. He held the head of his cock in his mouth, flicking his tongue repeatedly over the nerves, knowing for some men, it would be sensitive enough for them to come. Not everyone, but some. Timothy was one of the former.

"Fuck!" Timothy thrust deeper, and Eddie sucked, tasting his release on his tongue, but his body burst into flames as he climaxed.

All he could focus on was the fireworks detonating in his body and how he wanted to get closer, yet further away from the sensations at the same time. His body jerked until the explosions subsided, and he relaxed, dropping his head back on George's shoulder, panting.

"Well done," George whispered in his ear, and Eddie realised George had orgasmed, too.

Eddie kept his eyes closed when he felt the restraints being released. They cleaned him with the soap he'd used when he'd showered here before, then George picked him up and carried him from the bathroom, still wet. He shivered when the cooler air of the bedroom met his skin, and he burrowed closer to George.

"Shh, sorry, you'll be warm again in a moment, sweetheart." George kissed his temple.

His back met some cool sheets, and George let him go but climbed in beside him. His own furnace. He snuggled close, then frowned, blinking his eyes open. He saw George staring at him with a half-smile, but where was Timothy. He saw him standing at the bottom of the bed with a towel around his waist.

"I'm going to head home," Timothy said.

Eddie simpered. "No, come here. I need you."

The crease returned to Timothy's forehead, and Eddie hated it. He vowed to remove that frown for all eternity.

"I don't think—"

"Don't think. Come." Eddie held out his hand, bending his fingers repeatedly in a "come here" movement and burrowed back under the covers with George. George nudged for him to drink his juice, but his eyes filled with tears, the usual comedown from a scene.

"Don't cry," Timothy said, sliding into bed behind him.

"It's his usual response. Don't panic, although he probably worried you wouldn't stay."

"I can't stay all night, but I can stay for a while."

Eddie snuggled between them, content in the warmth they exuded, both physically and emotionally.

"Would you like to check out our club?" George asked Timothy.

There was silence, and Eddie couldn't help but open his eyes and peer over his shoulder to see Timothy's expression. The frown was back again.

"I suppose it wouldn't hurt. I've never been to one or even been interested in BDSM before I met you both. I don't know if it's something I can do all the time."

"You don't have to do it all the time," George said. "And besides, it's not all whips and chains."

Eddie grinned and tucked himself against George again.

When he woke, it was dark apart from a lamp on the bedside table. Eddie lifted his head from where he was lying on his stomach and found George looking at him with a small smile on his face.

"You're so peaceful when you sleep," George whispered as if not wanting to talk too loud in the silence.

Eddie felt his cheeks heat. "Where's Timothy?"

"He had to leave. He had to prepare for his students tomorrow. Did you know he was a teacher? I didn't. I thought he was a full-time therapist."

"I did, yes. We spoke about it when we walked back from your brother's house." Eddie rolled onto his back and yawned. "What time is it?"

"A little after four in the morning." George scooted closer, wrapping his arms around Eddie, who pillowed his head on George's chest. "Timothy didn't seem like he was running, but I'm worried he'll change his mind after thinking on it alone."

"I don't think he will. It's the media that's worrying him the most, it seems. I hadn't realised they had harassed him. That's awful. The whole situation is."

"I'm going to speak to Mav about the media thing. He might have some advice on how to handle both Timothy's situation and our relationship. So far, the media have been incredibly supportive of Douglas's and Henry's relationships. I'm hoping that will continue when ours becomes public. Is that something you're ready for?"

Eddie thought about it. He had never, in his wildest dreams, expected to be in any kind of relationship with a prince, except for a BDSM kind that stays within the club. If anyone had asked him before he'd experienced anything with George, if he wanted to be in the spotlight, he would've adamantly declined. Now, though, it seemed such a small matter in the grand scheme of things.

"It comes with the territory, doesn't it?"

"That didn't answer my question."

Eddie kissed George's chest. "It will take some getting used to, but I'm not opposed to it. I will need to speak with my parents before we go public. There are a few things they'll need to get their heads around before being harassed by journalists."

"Do they know about your BDSM side?"

"Yes, although they don't know everything. I explained to them what it *was* rather than what they *thought* it was, and they were fine with it. I need to prepare them for what will undoubtedly get printed or thrown at them."

"I forget how different my life is to other people's. It's all I've known, and everything is second nature."

"That's not a bad thing, George. It's just different."

George nodded against Eddie's head. "It is." Silence fell for a few minutes, then he sighed. "Although it pains me that Timothy's been through everything he has, at least I know he told me the truth when we spoke about Mother."

"What do you mean?" Eddie glanced up.

George sighed. "Well, some people who go into the therapy profession don't know what they're talking about. It's all hypothetical from research and second-hand accounts. They're guessing how someone should behave or react. Don't get me wrong, they're awesome at it and have a lot of training, but they've never experienced it themselves. When Timothy arrived, I assumed he was the same and took some of what he said with a pinch of salt. I know now that he understood what he was talking about."

Eddie tightened his hold on George. "He definitely does. I, however, can't imagine what it must feel like to lose someone close to me, but the idea of losing you to these maniacs makes my heart freeze."

George kissed his head. "I'm not going anywhere. Except to make some coffee."

Eddie chuckled at the change of subject. "It's four in the morning. I don't think coffee is a good idea if you want to sleep."

"I won't be able to go back to sleep now. I'll get some work done while you rest. I know you have work tomorrow, too."

George rolled Eddie onto his back and kissed him, long and slow. When he pulled back, Eddie was lightheaded.

"That is not the way to help me fall asleep," Eddie said.

George snorted. "Sorry, couldn't resist." He kissed him once more, chastely, then climbed off the bed, tucking Eddie back under the covers. "Get some sleep. I'll wake you in a little while."

"Yes, Sir." Eddie smirked when George sucked in a breath.

"You're the one who wanted sleep, Mr Ward." George began crawling up Eddie's body, covering him with his own, separated only by the duvet. "If you're not careful, you'll be falling asleep at work," he growled, nipping at Eddie's lips.

"Sorry, Sir." Eddie gasped when George sucked at his neck, arching away but leaning forward for more.

George kissed him one more time, then climbed off again. "Sleep. That's an order." He punctuated the words with his finger.

Eddie smiled, snuggling under the soft, warm cover. He'd asked George to help him, knowing it would be a short-term agreement, never realising how much more it would become. He'd been content to see how things progressed and had thought George was everything he needed when they got more serious. Then Timothy had jumped into the mix, and now, Eddie couldn't imagine their relationship without him being part of it.

It was funny how life sometimes gave a person pain and suffering, then brought in someone—or two someone's—to help them weather it. After everything he'd been through with Talon, he'd never expected to find George, let alone Timothy, but Eddie knew, with every fibre of his being, that they were what each other needed to get them through the trials they'd already experienced.

Eddie was more than happy to forge a new future, even if it meant dealing with those who wished George harm. If Eddie had anything to do with it, no one would touch a hair on either of their heads. That was a promise.

20

GEORGE

An hour after Eddie had left, George tried to focus on the computer screen, reading through the manuscript they had sent him, but he couldn't focus. Instead, he closed his screen down and picked up his eReader. He had a narration to finish, and the deadline loomed. He wasn't sure if he could do it, but he had to try. He'd hate for the author to wait for the audio longer than George had said. Of course, he hadn't known something would happen to his mother, but he still felt bad.

He locked his door before entering his walk-in closet and unlocking the door of the furthest unit. Inside was a small table with audio equipment, a microphone and a comfortable chair. He had covered the walls with thick blankets to stop any echo from his voice. It wasn't a professional studio, by any means, but he was happy with it because it was within his room, and he could do it whenever he felt like it. His mother had told him to use one of the other rooms in Windsor, but he hadn't wanted people to know what he was doing. The fewer people who knew, the better.

He sat in the chair, opened the manuscript to the page he'd bookmarked and got everything ready to go. Although he'd read the book several times to get to know the characters, it had been a while, and he couldn't remember what the next section was about. After reading the first few lines, he froze. If he could get through this chapter, he'd be able to read anything.

Taking a fortifying breath, he began. It wasn't long before his voice closed up, and genuine emotion came out.

He crouched in front of her. "Lucy, as much as we don't want to do this, we need to say goodbye. You might be upset if you don't get the chance to do it. But if you don't want to see Dad, you can stay with Flynn, and I can tell Dad whatever you want me to."

Varying emotions flickered across her face too quickly for Mal to figure them all out, but she nodded and stood by his side when they entered the hospice center. Flynn took care of the details, thankfully. Mal tried to hold in his emotions, not wanting to cause Lucy to be any more upset. The problem was that by doing so, the only thing inside him was emptiness.

"Do you want to go in?" Mal asked Lucy.

She nodded. "To say goodbye, then I want to come back out again."

"That's fine, sweetheart."

Gripping her hand, they followed Gia to their dad's room, entering quietly. The only sounds in the room were the beeps of the machines.

Lucy's hands tightened on his, and he glanced at her. Her eyes were wide as she stared at their dad. Mal couldn't bring himself to look at the figure on the bed yet. "Do you want to move closer?" he whispered.

Lucy stepped closer until they were right next to the bed. She reached out with her free hand and touched their dad's hand. "Good-

night, Dad. Sleep well." She leaned down and kissed the back of his hand before running out of the room and into Flynn's arms.

George paused, inhaling through his nose. Tears had tracked their way down his cheeks, and he wiped them away. He knew it was just a story, but the emotion was there, in words and in George's mind and body. He sat back, staring at the equipment but not seeing anything. He remembered how his mother always greeted everyone with enthusiasm, even if they were horrible people. She never treated people differently in public. Behind the scenes, however, it was a different matter. She'd rant and rave about what they'd done and how it physically hurt her to be kind and magnanimous when all she wanted to do was throw up her middle finger and tell them where to go.

George chuckled. Feeling like she was there watching him do a job he loved, he inhaled through his nose again and exhaled it quickly. Refocusing on the words, he got through the chapter, then saved it to listen to another day. There would be a lot of editing and re-recording, but he'd got through the chapter. It was how he worked. He'd read the chapter, then listen to it to check for errors, noting where it was and what needed to be changed, and then re-record the amendments. Other narrators did things differently, but everyone had their intricacies.

Closing everything up, he emerged into his living area as his phone rang. He picked it up from the coffee table, where he'd left it, and answered with a smile. "Jason!"

"George! My man! How are you doing?"

"I'm doing all right. What are you up to?"

"Nothing much. Working as usual. I'm heading to The Den tonight. I wondered if you wanted to join in?"

George considered his options. There was no way they would clear Timothy for Club Royal in less than twelve hours, but The Den might be a suitable alternative. It would give him a chance to see things without the pressure of being watched by nosey members, especially if they all had masks on to hide their identities.

"I don't see why not. I need to double-check a couple of things, but it should be fine. What time?"

"Eight."

"All right. I hope to see you there."

"Before you go, how are you really?"

George snorted. "I've been better, but I've been much worse. I've had help to sort my brain out. I'm doing all right," he repeated.

"Well, you know where I am if you need me. Katrina, too."

"I know, thanks, man. How are things with your dad?"

Jason blew out a breath. "You know when you fry an egg, and you get to where it's nearly ready and bubbles and spits, but you're never too sure when it's going to happen and often get burnt? Yeah, that's my life."

"Shit, Jason. I'm sorry. Definitely tonight. We'll drown our sorrows."

"That's the plan."

They spoke for a few more minutes before ending the call, and George wished there was something he could do for his best friend. George felt bad for hardly speaking to him over the past week, but Jason wouldn't come to Windsor because the last time he had, his father went ballistic. Though why Jason wouldn't say.

He checked his watch and went to the kitchen for an early lunch. He'd call Eddie and Timothy when he had some food and see if they would join him that night. He expected a fight with Timothy, but hopefully, his charms would win out.

There was a slight kerfuffle when he entered the kitchen, as always, but the staff was happy to make him something to eat. He refused to use the dining room and instead found himself in a small library he often visited, even though he'd read most, if not all, of the books on the shelves. He dropped into a chair by the window that overlooked the vast gardens and smiled as he remembered the walk he'd taken with Eddie and Timothy. He couldn't remember how long ago that was now, but it seemed like a lifetime. The days merged into one when his mother died, but they were separating themselves now.

"I wondered if that was you."

George glanced over his shoulder at Henry and stood. "Hi. I wasn't expecting to see you." He embraced his cousin.

"I'm doing some research, and Freddie suggested this smaller library might hold some books to help."

"How is the research coming along? Wait, hold that thought. Have you had lunch?"

Henry spread his hands. "I was going to drop by the flower shop and surprise Robert, but if you have a better offer...?" Henry grinned.

"I wouldn't say I was the better option between Robert and me, but I have food. Or at least food I can order."

Henry chuckled. "Sure. I'll eat anything except—"

"Cheeseburgers. I know."

George placed an order with the kitchen staff and returned to his seat. "So, the research?"

Henry sighed. "Nothing specific is jumping out at me, but

there are rumours that there's an inner circle of royal family members that fight for justice. Whose justice, I don't know. I'm wondering whether the justice thing is a screen for what they're really doing."

"You mean like what happened with those men you saw when you were younger?"

Henry nodded. "I had always wondered how they had got away with it when there were so many people around. If they were couching it under justice being served, would anyone bat an eyelid?" Henry shrugged. "It's all circumstantial, though. I have no proof so far."

"Sounds about right, though. With everything we know about Aunt Charlotte, Uncle John, Aunt Miranda and Charles, I wouldn't put it past them. People would go along with it because they'd fear being on the receiving end."

"Exactly. This is why I don't have proof. It still scares people to talk about it, even as rumours."

"What are you hoping to find here?"

Henry studied their surroundings. "Any accounts of similar events. I found one that was buried in a story about a Christmas event. It was literally one sentence that said, 'after we dealt with the unrighteous, we celebrated.' I have nothing else to go on."

"When was this? It sounds ominous."

Henry nodded. "In 1953."

"Quite recent. I expected you to say the 1800s."

A knock sounded, and George called for them to enter. A household staff member entered with a tray of food for Henry, then disappeared again, closing the door behind them.

"Yes, I'm shocked. It could be nothing, but my instincts won't let me stop until I clarify."

George chuckled. "Those instincts..." He huffed. "I would've loved for mine to kick in last week."

Henry squeezed his shoulder. "I expect most of the family is saying a similar thing. How are you holding up?"

George swallowed his mouthful before answering. "Good minutes and bad minutes. Eddie and Timothy are helping."

Henry raised his eyebrows. "Have you sorted things out with them? Is it working?"

"We came to an arrangement yesterday, although I'm concerned once Timothy thinks too much about it, he'll change his mind. His relationship with the media is already an issue because of his past—which I can't tell you about without his permission—and I think he'd prefer to hide behind us instead of walk beside us." He rushed to continue when Henry frowned. "Not because he doesn't want to be with us, but because he'd suffered at the hands of the media and is jumpy about them."

"Understandable if he's had an unpleasant experience. If you go public, there will be a lot of scrutiny."

George nodded. "A lot." He sighed. "I'm going to The Den tonight. I need to persuade the two of them to join me."

Henry frowned again. "Make sure you take security and speak to Elton first."

"Elton already knows me." Henry gave George a pointed look. "Okay, he doesn't know I'm a bloody prince, but I've been there enough to be careful."

"Still, with everything that's happened, I don't want to take any chances."

George stared at his plate and swallowed hard. "I know."

"Maybe Kean would be interested in visiting."

"Kean? I didn't know it was his kind of thing. You never went to the club together, did you?"

Henry shook his head. "He was my best friend and had a membership, but he never went. I never asked why. Maybe it's time I did," Henry murmured.

They were lost in their thoughts for a few moments until George said, "I'm happy to meet him there if he wants to go, but he doesn't have to. I'll take some security, but I will ask them to meet us there. I don't want to walk into the place with several security members breathing down my neck. That's a loaded gun pointed at me straight away."

"Your lawyer friend, Mr Kiln, might be able to get in contact with the ones I had." Henry bit into his sandwich.

"Good idea."

They ate their lunch with gentle conversation and a promise from George to call Mr Kiln, then George exited the library, leaving Henry to his research. As he wandered down the corridors to his room, he dialled the lawyer.

"Mr Kiln, it's George Sutcliffe. Can you spare a minute of your time?"

By the time the call ended, he had the same two security members Henry had used meeting him at The Den for eight o'clock. They would wait inside at the bar, which George appreciated. He dialled again.

"Elton, it's Georgie Cliff."

"Well, I've not heard from you in a while. How are you?"

Keeping up the pretence of being someone else, he replied, "I'm doing good, thanks. I wanted to let you know that I'll be dropping by tonight with two of my friends. All three of us will wear our masks, but we won't cause any trouble."

Elton was quiet for a moment. "Will you be bringing any security staff, Mr Sutcliffe?"

George's eyes widened, and his mouth gaped. "I...Um, fuck. How the hell did you find out?"

Elton's laughter filled the line. "I have my ways, but I'm also very observant. I have no problem with it, Prince George, but I would prefer you to have security."

"I'll have the same two men that Henry had."

"Good man. I look forward to seeing you, in so many words."

"Thanks, Elton."

George chuckled as he entered his room. "How the hell did he figure that out?" He dropped a quick message to Henry, letting him know Elton knew who George was and was happy with the plan, then he messaged his men.

GEORGE: Hey, gorgeous. I hope you're having a good day. I have plans tonight and would like to invite you to join me at The Den for a night of anonymity and submission. If you choose to accept, I'll pick you up at seven-thirty. x

GEORGE: Hey, Doc. I hope you're not working too hard. Tonight, I would like to invite you to experience the BDSM lifestyle at a club I sometimes visit. We'll be wearing masks and will have security on the premises, plus I know the owner, and he's a tough guy. There won't be any trouble. If you like what you see, we could look into the membership at the other club. Don't think about this too hard because you'll hurt yourself and talk yourself out of it. I'll pick you up at seven-fifteen. x

He didn't want either of them to decline, but he wouldn't push if they didn't want to join him. Getting Timothy to experience a club would show him how it was on a deeper level, George hoped. Everyone was different, and they needed to figure out the logistics of their decision before any of them got into the relationship too far. He wouldn't want to hurt anyone on purpose. It scared him that the man could say no. Timothy had every right to, but George hoped he didn't.

As he had several hours before he needed to contemplate getting ready, he focused on the speech he had to write. He gave himself two hours before stopping for a break, then checked his phone.

EDDIE: I'll be ready. x

TIMOTHY: I don't know if this is the right time. We're so new and finding our feet. Plus, you've lost your mother. Is it a good idea? x

GEORGE: I think it's the perfect time because if it doesn't interest you, then we can regroup and figure it out. It doesn't matter if you don't like it, but at least we'll know, and we get to have some time together. And as for Mother, she wouldn't want us on hold. She'd be fighting for us to live our lives. x

Despite what he said to Timothy, George felt a little uneasy with the idea of celebrating their relationship when his mother had died a week ago, but what he'd said was true. Louisa wouldn't want anyone to wallow in grief for her passing, and it had taken Timothy, Eddie, Freddie and his father, plus others, telling him to understand that. To remember what she fought for. She wanted them to be as free as possible while remaining safe. She had always followed the rules for the royal family, but she had fought for her children to be given more freedom than others would have.

George could almost hear her telling him to stop being silly and have fun. A tear trickled down his cheek as he heard her say, "I'm so happy my death sent your loves to you. It was worth it. It was all worth it."

He knew it was in his head, but it felt so real, so freeing. He wished Eddie and Timothy could've met her. He knew his mother would've loved them.

TIMOTHY: Okay. I have nothing to wear, though. x

George chuckled, wiping his face. He closed his eyes and breathed deeply, bringing his mother's face to the forefront of his mind.

"Thank you, Mother."

GEORGE: Jeans and a T-shirt are fine. I'll see you at seven-fifteen. x

He switched on his music app on his phone and set it to shuffle through the god knows how many songs on there. When *You Will Be Found* by Sam Smith and Summer Walker started, he knew his mother was with him. A song about darkness and being found by someone. They had given him that. The darkness of his mother's death had lightened at his newfound relationship with Eddie and the appearance of the man made to complete them both.

He couldn't have asked for more.

TIMOTHY

Timothy was not sure about this at all.

He'd never been to a BDSM club; he only knew what he'd seen in the odd porn video he'd tried and from what he'd been told. He knew they all wore black; therefore, he opted for black jeans and a black T-shirt with a partially unbuttoned black shirt over the top. He tried to tame his shaggy hair, but it was a losing battle, as it had been since he was a young boy. His mother loved his hair, and his sisters teased him mercilessly about how his hair was a Venus flytrap for girls and boys.

Which reminded him. He took a mirror selfie and sent it to Bri, Talia and Imogen because they'd wanted to see what outfit he'd chosen. Bri had called him earlier that afternoon—luckily in his free period—and asked him what he was doing over the weekend.

He mentioned nothing about George, but he did mention Eddie. It seemed the safest option. Not that he didn't trust his siblings, but they often gossiped about things, and although they wouldn't if he said not to, he didn't want to take the chance that something might slip out. Timothy had told her he was going to a BDSM club to see what all the fuss was about, and she screamed down the phone at him. Literally screamed. For some unknown reason, she was excited about his adventure.

He missed being there with them, and before this had happened with Eddie and George, he might've considered returning home at the end of the school year. Now, though, that decision would happen once he knew where their relationship was heading.

BRI: Perfect! Gives you a menacing edge. x

Timothy snorted. There wasn't a menacing bone in his body, although he still felt the anger bubbling under his skin whenever he thought about the situation with George and those who might want him dead.

He brushed the thought away, not wanting it to sour his mood, and wandered into the kitchen for a drink. He'd barely drunk half of it when the buzzer for his gate sounded. Butterflies took flight in his stomach, and he inhaled and exhaled as he strode for the door.

On the video screen, he could see a black Audi, and he smiled when George's face came into view beneath a baseball cap.

"Come on in," Timothy said, pressing the button to open the gates. He checked his watch, seeing it was barely seven o'clock. So much for picking him up at seven-fifteen. Timothy chuckled.

He opened the front door and stood, leaning against the door frame with his arms crossed. George parked the car right in front of him and jumped out, eyes scanning him up and down. Timothy kept himself as still as possible.

"My god, you're gorgeous."

Timothy snorted and ducked his head. "Thanks." He looked at George's leather ensemble and wished there was another reason the man was there except to take him some-place other than there. "You look amazing."

George held his hands out to his sides and did a twirl, complete with his signature grin. "Thank you."

"You're early, Your Highness."

"I'm impatient, Doc."

George stepped closer and reached for him. Timothy grabbed his hands and pulled him inside the house before fusing their lips. He fumbled for the door and slammed it shut while pushing George against the wall. Moulding his body to George's, Timothy knocked the baseball cap off and slid his fingers through George's hair. The man tasted divine. Something sweet, almost sugary about it. He swept his tongue into George's mouth for more, and when George whimpered, Timothy backed off.

He rested their foreheads together and cupped George's face.

"Hello to you, too," George murmured.

Timothy chuckled and stepped back. "I just need to finish locking up, then I'll be ready."

"Don't I get a tour?"

"Well…" Timothy rubbed his earlobe.

"Come on, Doc. Out with it. What nefarious plans did you have for us?" George hugged his arms around Timothy's waist.

Timothy sighed and copied the action. "I was going to invite you both back here tonight."

"Ooh. I'd be happy to. Not sure about Eddie, though, because he has to work tomorrow."

"So do I." Timothy raised his eyebrows.

George stared up at him. "Good point." He stepped back and pushed his hands into his pockets, which Timothy was surprised he could do with how tight the trousers looked. "I'm not ignorant of other people's work, but I do sometimes forget not everyone is as lucky as me."

Timothy pulled him close again, cupping his face once more. "You're not ignorant. You remember more than you realise, and you take it into account when you talk to people. The occasional forgetfulness is not a problem, George."

"Sometimes, I wonder if people think I'm a stuck-up, spoilt, rich prince."

"They don't. They love you. No, they don't know every facet of your personality, but they don't need to. The face you show them is the compassionate, friendly one your mother and father brought you up to be." George tried to duck his head, but Timothy wouldn't let him. He kept their eyes locked. "You are that person, but you are also so much more."

Tears glistened in George's eyes, and Timothy kissed them away before kissing his lips gently. He pulled George close, the prince tucking his face into Timothy's neck and gripping the back of his shirt. They stayed that way for several moments before George pulled back with a tremulous smile.

"Shall we go fetch our other puzzle piece?"

Timothy laughed. "Yes. We wouldn't want to be late and worry him."

"We need to take a leaf out of Eddie's book. After what he

went through, he should run from a relationship like this. Instead, he's fighting for us," George said.

"He's stronger than he believes he is."

George bent down and picked up the baseball cap, and Timothy checked the back door was locked, then set the alarm system before climbing into George's car.

"Is this your car?"

George smirked. "One of them. This is the least flashy, which is why I chose it for tonight."

"I can't imagine what others you have."

"I'll show you one day."

They spoke about Timothy's classes while George navigated the streets of Windsor until he pulled up outside a two-storey house. There was a small, tidy, walled garden with a driveway to the right of it and steps leading up to a white door.

"Would you mind doing the honours?" George asked, pulling his cap further down.

"Of course."

He climbed out of the car and tugged the jacket tighter around him, the windchill having picked up since that afternoon. Timothy jogged up the steps and knocked on the door, glancing around him as he did. The neighbourhood seemed tidy and had nothing to make him think it was a dangerous area. The houses were well cared for, the gardens neat, and the cars were in good condition.

The door opened, and he spun around to glimpse Eddie peeking around the door.

"Come in."

Timothy held up a finger towards George's car, then stepped inside. "Everything okay?" he asked.

"Yes, I just need to grab my bag and didn't want you standing in the cold."

Eddie wore tight black leather pants, similar in style to what George wore, and a black shirt. Eddie cleared his throat, and Timothy's cheeks heated at being caught staring.

"You look fantastic."

"Thank you. It's not what I normally wear, but I've not been to this club before, and I wasn't comfortable wearing it."

"You definitely need to feel comfortable when you're going somewhere new."

Eddie rummaged through his bag, then closed it and slung it over his shoulder. "Let's go."

"George is excited to see you."

Eddie licked his lips and the corner of his mouth quirked up. "Just George?"

Timothy inhaled, leaning forward to press his lips to Eddie's. "No, not just George," he said when he pulled back.

"Good."

They descended the steps once Eddie had locked up his house, and Eddie climbed into the back seat. When Timothy slid into the seat, George and Eddie were lip-locked behind George's cap.

"Good evening, Eddie," George said when they pulled back.

Eddie smiled. "Good evening."

George set off through the streets once more, and they talked about their day apart. Or rather, Eddie and Timothy did. George was suspiciously quiet about his. Was George having second thoughts about the visit? Or about them?

"Are you okay?" he asked when they pulled into a car park. "We can go home again if you've changed your mind?"

George's eyes widened. "What? No! I want this."

"You've been quiet. Are you sure?"

George nodded. "Definitely."

Timothy narrowed his eyes at him. He'd get it out of George later.

George smiled and pulled a mask from his pocket. "I'm going incognito now. If you want to remain anonymous, there are masks for you in the glove compartment, but you don't have to. I do, for obvious reasons."

"Is it safe for us to be here?" Timothy asked, looking around the car park.

"I have two security guards inside, just in case. I'll grab the alarm from them before we head upstairs."

"Upstairs?" Eddie said.

George pulled on his mask, obscuring his face except for his eyes. "There are two floors to the club. The ground floor is the main area, where people dance, drink and enjoy the voyeuristic scenes, then the upstairs is for the more kink-orientated people."

"Have you been here before?" Timothy asked.

"Yes. Many times. Though few people know that. Henry and Robert do, and I think some of my other family suspects, but nothing has been confirmed. Yet."

Timothy's butterflies took flight again at the mention of his family. The day was coming when he would meet them, and he hoped they wouldn't look on him unfavourably for taking advantage of his therapist position. It would be understandable if they did. After all, he was breaking the law technically.

"Timothy?"

He blinked and glanced at George. "Yeah?"

"Ready?"

Timothy swallowed and nodded. He wasn't at all ready, but there was no going back now. George climbed out, and Eddie squeezed Timothy's shoulder.

"Just remember, George needs you. I need you. And you need us. Nothing else matters," Eddie said.

"Wise words," he murmured. His phone rang, and he checked the screen. Withheld number. He frowned. He'd forgotten to speak to George about the call he'd received the other day. He answered as Eddie exited the car.

"Hello?"

"Did you not heed our last call? Trust me when I say it would be in *your* and *their* best interests to stay away from him. I hope I don't need to contact you again."

The call ended as it had last time. He had no idea who it could be, but they didn't want him anywhere near George for some reason. Unfortunately, he didn't think that was possible. Not now. He'd mention it to George the next day because it might be relevant to the inquiry, and he didn't want to ruin the night they had planned.

He joined George and Eddie, and they strode for the entrance. The bouncer nodded and held the door open for them. The noise was instant, and Timothy flinched. It had been years since he'd last willingly entered a club, and his ears had got used to the quiet. The bass assaulted his eardrums, and he scrunched his face. George nudged him and indicated the bar. Timothy reached a hand backwards, and Eddie took hold.

George leaned over the bar, shouting to the bartender, then turned to the man beside him, leaning close to listen to what the man said. George nodded and pointed over his shoulder towards them. The man glanced at them and nodded once. He shook hands with George, then returned to his drink. Timothy assumed the man had propositioned George, who had turned the man down. The man didn't seem like he'd cause problems, despite his size and build.

George handed over some money, then grabbed the three bottles of water, met Timothy's gaze and tilted his head towards the back of the room. Timothy, pulling Eddie along with him, followed George to a set of stairs, which they ascended.

The music lessened as they rose, and soon, they entered another world—a quieter world. The bass was still audible, but it wasn't ear-splitting.

"Welcome to The Den," George said, and Timothy knew he was grinning.

Timothy studied the room. He knew some things he saw from his limited experience, but some he had no idea about. There were people dressed up in what he thought were animal outfits, some wearing little to nothing, and some wearing head-to-toe leather. Some submissives, he assumed, had leashes. Some knelt by their partners. Others were strapped to various equipment around the room. Groans, whimpers and exclamations seared the air where the music barely reached.

"What do you think?" George asked.

"It's a lot to take in," he said, and though it was the truth, he also felt a flutter of excitement when he watched those taking care of their partners.

"I like the look of that one," Eddie said from beside him, pointing to a swing.

Timothy couldn't understand how it worked, but George herded them towards it. The swing itself was made from a material that looked similar to what he knew hammocks were made from, but not exactly and a lot smaller. Four chains at each corner held it above floor level. A black voile curtain hung to the side, which George pulled around them, separating them from the rest of the room.

"How…?"

"We'll show you," Eddie breathed.

George held out his hand, and Eddie stepped forward. Timothy watched as Eddie climbed onto the swing with George holding it steady. Eddie slid around in the swing until the fabric was beneath his shoulders and back, and his legs, arms and head hung over the edge. It couldn't be comfortable for Eddie. Puzzling him even more, Eddie grabbed the chains by his head and lifted one of his legs. George grabbed Eddie's ankle and clasped a restraint Timothy hadn't noticed around it. He repeated the action with the other leg and both arms.

Timothy had one question. "Not that I'm expecting to have sex, but what is the point of this when he's dressed?"

George, despite wearing the mask, stared at him with a twinkle in his eye, then unfastened one side of Eddie's trousers, then the other. It soon became apparent to Timothy that the whole flap was separate, and George exposed Eddie's genitals to the room.

In an automatic move, Timothy stepped closer, shielding him from the room's occupants. "Okay, understood."

George and Eddie chuckled.

"I think you should stand by his head," George said. "I have work to do down here."

Timothy moved to the top, seeing the flush in Eddie's cheeks and the serenity in his eyes. "Are you okay like this?"

Eddie nodded and licked his lips. "I'm good, Sir."

"Eddie uses the traffic light system. If you ask him what his colour is, he'll tell you either green, which means he's fine; yellow, which means he needs you to stop so we can discuss it; or red, which means stop everything." George slid his hands down Eddie's thighs, resting on his hips. "He's very good at saying what he means."

Timothy had transferred his gaze to Eddie before George had said the last sentence, and he watched as pleasure suffused Eddie's face. A soft smile caressed his lips, and his eyelids fluttered closed. His head dropped back, exposing his long neck. Timothy couldn't help but draw a finger along the skin, sending Eddie arching upwards. He undid the buttons of Eddie's shirt, exposing his pale skin to them.

Everything else disappeared, and they were the only people he could see. From where he stood, he saw Eddie's body splayed out for them and George standing between his legs. He met George's gaze, and though his eyes were the only things he could see, he felt like he could see everything. He'd always thought the idea that the eyes were the windows to the soul was a euphemism, but it was true. He seemed to instinctively know what George wanted and undid his trousers, pulling his cock free.

Eddie pulled against his restraints, moving his head to reach him. The swing moved in his direction, and he glanced up at George, noticing him pushing it towards him. It meant Eddie could reach. At the first lick of Eddie's mouth, Timothy gripped hold of the chains. His arms extended when the swing moved away from him, and Eddie's mouth disappeared. Within seconds, Eddie was back, and he engulfed his cock in his mouth before he swung away again, and Timothy developed a newfound appreciation for the swing.

He stared at George as the prince manipulated the swing back and forth while he dropped to his knees between Eddie's legs and lowered his head. Eddie's muffled groan was the only other sign George was doing something to him.

Timothy watched George lick over Eddie's exposed pucker, and Eddie's mouth sucked harder.

He took over control of the swing, making it so Eddie kept the head of his dick in his mouth before being pulled back again so he could swallow him. Timothy alternated between watching Eddie's rapturous expression and the minute tells of his body and George's ministrations on Eddie's lower body. Eddie's toes curled, and his moan vibrated against Timothy's shaft when George pushed a finger inside of him.

Timothy wanted more.

"George, stand up. I want to see your cocks sliding against each other."

George did as he'd asked, unbuttoning his trousers to release his cock. He gave himself a few strokes, then slid closer to Eddie. Timothy watched as George's and Eddie's dicks slid together with every movement of the swing. George's cock slid up Eddie's as Eddie released Timothy from his mouth, then slid back down again when the wet warmth of Eddie's mouth encased Timothy's shaft in once more.

He couldn't escape the feeling this experience pulled from him. Here he was, with his dick hanging out, while two men were giving him attention. He'd never expected to have this. He couldn't believe he had two men who wanted to be with him despite everything he'd been through. He wanted to return the favour and give them everything he had.

Which he had to hope was enough.

22

EDDIE

Eddie was in heaven. The sensation of George's cock sliding alongside his own was indescribable. He wanted nothing more than to wrap his arms and legs around George to give him more friction because he was right on the edge. All he needed was a little more. He tugged against the restraints, excitement thrumming through him at the reminder that he remained bound and exposed. Although his neck was aching from its position, he had never felt more alive, more taken care of.

Timothy's dick slid between his lips and into Eddie's throat, making his eyes water, then withdrew. Eddie wanted to keep it in his mouth forever. Timothy growled, then pulled back.

"I'm going to come."

Instead of coming inside Eddie's mouth as Eddie wanted, Timothy stepped closer and glided his cock against Eddie's collarbone. George increased the pressure and speed of their movements, and Eddie whimpered when the heads of their cocks bumped against each other.

Timothy's hand cupped the back of Eddie's neck, giving him a reprieve from the ache. Their gazes caught and locked, and Eddie saw when Timothy lost control, the wash of warmth hitting his chest. Eddie's mouth opened on a gasp as his body seized, and Timothy's eyes were lost to the oblivion of his release. He was distantly aware of George climaxing and the flow of more heat across his stomach along with his own.

Eddie floated on the clouds of release. He fluttered his eyelids open when he felt someone unfasten the restraints but allowed them to close again. His hands and feet tingled with the change of position, but he revelled in the sensation. Timothy lifted him from the swing—he knew it was Timothy because he smelled different to George—and held him on his lap. Eddie snuggled close, jerking when a cloth wiped at his skin before they placed a blanket over him.

He sighed and enjoyed the warmth, even as tears streamed down his cheeks. He realised the tears were cathartic for him. A release of the tension, the stress, the memories, life itself. He'd have to remember to explain it to Timothy later because the man's muscles felt tight and tense as if he worried about Eddie.

"'m 'kay," he mumbled, trying to tell Timothy he was fine.

The arms tightened, and Eddie exhaled, brushing his cheek against Timothy's shirt.

"He's fine, Doc. Remember what I said about his tears. They're the usual reaction for him after a scene."

"I hate seeing him crying, no matter the reason." Timothy cleared his throat. "Can people see through those curtains?"

George chuckled. "Now, you ask? Yes, but not easily. They get the gist of what's happening but can't see details. It's like getting a teaser of a show, and those who like the idea of voyeurism or exhibitionism can get a taste of it before going full out." The sound of a kiss. "I'm going to get us some drinks and snacks. Back in a minute."

"Will they leave us alone?"

"I'll close the curtains behind me again, then they'll know not to bother you."

"Thanks."

"My pleasure."

Silence descended. Well, silence within their little bubble. As Eddie returned to the surface, the sounds surrounding them became louder and louder. The smacks of skin against skin or paddle against skin, the hum of conversation, the moans and groans of pleasure. It was the same as Club Royal but on a smaller scale. Eddie would love to visit again one day, but he knew it was risky for George to be here too often. Even with the two security guards downstairs, there was no telling what could happen before they got to them.

The idea of George being in danger brought Eddie into full awareness, and he craned his neck to see where George had gone.

"What's wrong?" Timothy asked, his hands gentling on him.

"Where's George? He shouldn't go too far away."

Timothy rubbed his hands over Eddie's back and arm. "He's just by the bar there. In fact, he's on his way back to us now."

George pushed through the curtain, eyes sparkling when he saw them. Eddie didn't think he could ever get over being looked at like that. Like they wanted him. Needed him. It had never been remotely like this with Talon. Eddie couldn't believe he hadn't seen how much of an asshole the man was. It pleased him that the shithead was in prison, although he wished it hadn't come at the cost of Kendal's physical abuse. No one deserved that kind of punishment.

"Hey, why the sad face?" George asked, crouching in front of them.

Eddie smiled and skimmed his fingers down the side of George's leather-covered face. "Just thinking about Kendal. Have you heard from him recently?"

George slid onto the sofa next to him and Timothy, resting the tray on his lap. "Not personally, but I know Father had been speaking with him before…" His voice caught. "Before Mother's death, and I know Douglas has been keeping an eye on him as well." George chuckled. "Kendal's probably fed up with us checking in with him."

The tension in Eddie released. "I'm glad. I've been worried about him, but I wasn't sure whether he'd want to talk to me or not with everything I represent."

"What do you represent?" Timothy asked.

Eddie glanced at him, then lowered his head, steeling himself to tell the story. "The man who abused Kendal did the same to me shortly before. Prince Douglas saved me from the possibility of worse, and he did the same for Kendal, but not as quickly. Kendal suffered badly."

"It's not your fault at all, Eddie," Timothy said. "The only person responsible for that act was the man himself. That *man*—and I use that word sparingly—is evil and shouldn't be around anyone." He glanced at George. "What happened to him?"

"He's in prison for the next seven years."

"Good." Timothy took the orange juice from the tray and held it up for Eddie. "Come on. Drink up."

"Yes, Sir." Eddie smiled and ducked his head, drinking slowly but steadily. He could easily fall asleep, but he wanted to savour every minute of their time here. He loved this, and it was even more special because Timothy was taking it all in his stride. He wasn't freaking out. Why wasn't he freaking out?

"You're frowning again," George said.

Eddie stared at him, wishing he could see George's face properly. He transferred his gaze to Timothy. "How do *you* feel about all this? You've not said anything about it. You've just gone ahead with it. Did you not want to do it?" The tension in his body was back at the idea they had forced Timothy into this situation.

Timothy smiled and ran a finger across Eddie's bottom lip. "Does it look like I didn't enjoy it?" Eddie wasn't sure. "I came, didn't I? And all across this exquisite body of yours. If that doesn't prove I was content with the situation, I don't know what will."

Eddie bit his lip. "Just because you came doesn't mean you were comfortable. Most men can climax with the right stimulation, even when they don't want to." Memories crowded into his head, and Eddie pushed them aside.

"Eddie, look at me." It took him several long seconds, but he lifted his gaze to Timothy's. "I loved every minute. The moment the curtains were closed around us, and I focused on you both, I forgot where we were. It didn't matter because I was here with you." He kissed Eddie's lips, then chuckled. "Don't get me wrong. I don't plan on standing in the middle of the city and doing this, but here, it's fine."

"Good. We're going to get you a membership to the club, so you can see the differences, and it's also more secure," George said.

"Are you in danger here?" Timothy asked.

George shook his head. "I'm fine because no one knows who I am."

"Well, that's not strictly true, is it?"

A voice from beside the curtain made Eddie jump. His heart raced as the implications of the man's words sank in. Eddie peered at George as horror wormed its way through him. They needed to get out of the place as soon as possible.

"Shut your pie-hole, Jason," George retorted, shaking his head.

"Hey! I've waited long enough for you lot to finish. The least you can do is be polite," Jason continued.

"And I bet you were so hard pushed to decline the offer of the quick fuck you had in the corner."

Jason laughed. "Touché."

"We'll be out in a few minutes. Go get a round of drinks. We'll meet you at the sofas soon."

"Yes, sir." The man wandered off.

Eddie's heart pounded, but George looked at ease. "Who was that?"

"One of my best friends, Jason. I told him we'd meet him here, but I got a bit…distracted."

Eddie ducked his head again, heat invading his cheeks.

Timothy's chuckle vibrated through his body into Eddie's. "Let's get cleaned up, then we can meet George's friend."

Eddie slid off Timothy's lap and stood on shaky legs with the blanket covering him. He allowed Timothy to wipe him over again, removing any dried-on come they'd missed prior, then he buttoned Eddie's shirt and trousers, setting him to rights. While Timothy tended to Eddie, George looked after Timothy, cleaning his flaccid cock and fastening his trousers. When Timothy had finished with Eddie, he turned to George and took care of him, too. It was pleasing to see Timothy taking on that role with George because Eddie had finally realised what had been bugging him about George's demeanour—George was a switch and needed Timothy as much as Eddie did. Had they already discussed that aspect during the therapy sessions? Was that how Timothy knew what George needed, or was it more instinctual? Did it matter?

Once they were decent, George used the spray specifically for cleaning the equipment and washed it all down. Then they left the area and followed George to the ring of sofas surrounding where the pets played. This type of play had always calmed Eddie, and he'd often watched the interactions at Club Royal whenever he wasn't in a scene himself. He didn't feel the rush to be one like he did being tied up, but they were all so adorable and playful, he could do nothing more than smile whenever he saw them.

George sat on a sofa, pulling Eddie to sit next to him, and wrapped his arm around him. Timothy hesitated before sitting beside George and sliding his arm around the prince's shoulders. Eddie couldn't have been happier with that result because George hadn't received the aftercare that Eddie had within their bubble, and he wanted George to have the same as what Eddie did. He wasn't sure why it was so important to him, but it was.

"Well, I would never have expected this, but I'm surprisingly unsurprised."

George's friend returned, carrying a tray full of drinks and wearing a grin. He placed the tray on the small table to the side of the sofa, then dropped into the chair sitting next to theirs.

"I bet you're less surprised than I was when I began figuring it out," George said.

"Probably, but then you had always known what you 'thought' your life should look like. It's nice to see you...complete."

Although Eddie couldn't see George's face, he guessed he'd be grinning.

"Jason, this is Timothy and Eddie," George said, pointing to each in turn. "Guys, this is my annoying best friend, Jason." George glanced around. "Is Katrina not here?"

Jason rolled his shoulders. "Not that I've seen. She messaged to say she would be here, but I've no idea."

George fidgeted and pulled out his phone. "Let me message her." Eddie watched as George one-handedly texted his friend, then rested the phone on his lap. "How have you been?"

Jason waved his hand, staring at the drink in his lap. "I'm good."

"Liar," George said. Eddie jumped at the venom in his tone and glanced at him. "Sorry, sweetheart. Jason's dad is... strict, to keep the word pleasant. Jason needs to move out, but he won't leave his sister and brother there alone."

"Would you?" Jason raised his eyebrows at George.

George sighed. "No. That doesn't mean I have to like the situation, though."

"You and me both."

"How old are your siblings?" Timothy asked.

"Fourteen and twelve." Jason chuckled. "Mum got busy with her new husband after the wedding."

"Are you worried about their situation?" Timothy said.

"No, not really. Stephen seems to be good towards them, at least for now. I don't know if that will change if I move out or when they get older. I don't want to take the chance."

"Could you find somewhere to live and take them with

you? It's not impossible if home life is not good for them," Timothy said.

"No one would ever find anything if they came to investigate. There's no evidence or anything untoward."

George sighed again. "I wish I could help."

Jason smiled. "I know you do, but I'm fine. I can take whatever he dishes out."

"You shouldn't have to," Eddie whispered, tears brimming.

George pulled him closer, tucking Eddie's head into his chest. The beat of his heart calmed Eddie. He hated the idea of anyone being in a similar situation to what he'd been in. Be it a romantic relationship or a familial one. No one should ever lay a hand on another person without their consent.

"Families should have contracts in addition to clubs," he murmured.

George chuckled. "Yes, they should." His phone vibrated, and George picked it up. "She's not coming. Something came up."

"Always the same. I've hardly seen her lately," Jason said.

Eddie assumed Katrina was another of George's friends.

"I'll have to ask if Douglas has heard from her." George held a kiss to Eddie's head. "Are you okay?" he whispered.

Eddie nodded his head. Now that he had relaxed, he felt tired.

"I think we should take this sleepy one home." Timothy smoothed his thumb over Eddie's cheek. "We both have work in the morning."

"It was nice to meet you, Jason," Eddie said.

"You, too. We'll meet again soon, I'm sure."

George passed Eddie to Timothy, who slid his arms around Eddie fully, holding him tightly while they watched

George hug Jason and whisper something in his ear. Jason bit his lip and met Eddie's gaze. Eddie recognised the pain inside of Jason and vowed to get help for him. Eddie firmed his jaw and nodded his head. Jason closed his eyes, then smiled brightly as George pulled back.

They bid goodbye, and Eddie held his tongue until George was driving them home. "He needs help, George."

George nodded his head, now free of the leather mask. "I know. I don't know what to do. Most of the people I've spoken to have said that because he's thirty, he should move out and distance himself from the situation. Jason won't do that."

"There has to be something we can do," Eddie said.

"Let me talk to a colleague and see what he says. No promises, but he might be able to help." Timothy reached back to hold his hand.

"Thank you."

They were silent for a short time until George said words that broke Eddie's heart, "It's Mother's funeral in two days." He swallowed hard. "I won't be able to see you for a few days, but please don't miss out on time with each other, okay?" He glanced at Timothy, then caught Eddie's gaze in the rearview mirror. "Spend some time together."

"We will. Don't worry about us. Just make sure you're okay. You know where we are if you need either of us," Timothy said.

George gave a half-smile. "I won't be attending the burial."

Eddie raised his eyebrows and tilted his head. "Why not?"

"I don't want that to be the last thing I remember about her—being lowered into the ground." He sniffed.

"Pull the car over, George," Timothy said. George did, and Timothy exited, rounding the car to the driver's side. "Climb over the middle. I'll drive."

Once George was in the passenger seat, Eddie reached an arm around to him. George rested his head on the back of the seat, looking at Eddie with tears in his eyes. "I don't want to see her that way. It's bad enough to have to watch her…coffin in the back of the hearse in the procession. I'm planning on watching the ground. I can't…" He broke off and gripped Eddie's hand.

Tears overflowed Eddie's eyes at the pain in George's voice and expression. "You do whatever you need to do to get through it, and we'll be waiting for you at the end."

"It still feels a little unreal. I still expect her to walk in the door any minute."

"That feeling will be there for a while, and it's not a bad thing. Keeping your mother at the front of your mind will help you keep her close when she can't do it physically," Timothy said, eyes focused on the road ahead. "You can weather this, George. No one can force you to visit the cemetery if you don't want to. You do what's best for you."

"Father will want me to go."

"Can you speak with Prince Frederick and Prince Douglas?" Eddie asked.

George chuckled, opening his wet eyes. "You can just call them Freddie and Douglas, you know."

Eddie's stomach churned. "I can't."

George snorted, then sobered. "I will talk to them tomorrow." He blew out a breath. "I hate it when it comes over me like this. One minute, I'll be enjoying myself, and the next, I'll be crying."

"It's natural when you're dealing with loss, George,"

Timothy said. "You'll find your feet, and things will become easier."

"Will I forget her?"

Eddie nearly burst into tears with those words.

Timothy glanced at George. "Never." He returned to the windscreen and inhaled. "You'll remember the good times, which will hurt as much as the bad times, but they will be just as bittersweet because they remind you of how human they were. Full of faults and imperfections along with humour and love. It hurts, George. I won't lie to you. It hurts for a long time, but each day, it becomes easier to live with that pain, that piece of your heart they took with them, even if they didn't mean to."

Eddie leaned forward and pressed a kiss to George's head. "We're here for whatever you need."

"I need you both. Nothing more, nothing less."

"You have us," Timothy said.

"You have us," Eddie agreed.

23

GEORGE

George hadn't slept well at all. After tossing and turning for over an hour, he'd got up, made himself a coffee and did some narrating. He didn't know whether he'd have to redo any of it, but it had kept him busy. When he'd finally given up, he'd sat on the chair by the window and watched the sunrise. Having no idea what time he'd sat there, he hadn't a clue how long he'd been there. It was only the protesting of his legs and back when he stood to answer the door that made him realise.

"Your Highness, I have some breakfast for you."

George noticed the household staff member didn't wish him a good morning, and he was glad of it. Yesterday, he'd spent his day with his father and brothers doing what needed to be done to prepare. Physically prepare, not mentally or emotionally. He wished Timothy and Eddie could be there with him, but he could imagine the uproar if they had been by his side. George didn't want that for them or his family.

When the staff member left, George stared at the cereal, toast and fruit but didn't move to eat it. He wasn't sure he could stomach anything, and the last thing he needed was to throw up while they were in the procession.

His stomach churned at the thought, and he breathed. He brought Timothy and Eddie to the forefront of his thoughts and concentrated on them. Though he hated to admit it, they had taken over his life for the past week or so. Even his brothers had mentioned not seeing him to the degree they had before. He felt guilty about that, but they were what he needed, and he wouldn't excuse that.

His phone beeped, and he strode over to the table where he'd left it, the sun having finally risen completely and bathing the phone in its light. At Eddie's name, he smiled.

EDDIE: As painful as this day will be, remember we are here for you. The second you need us to be there, let us know, and we will be. x

George sent back a kissing heart emoji, then placed the phone back on the table. Ignoring the breakfast, he wandered to the bathroom and spent a long time under the warm spray, then on autopilot, got dressed. He slid his phone into his pocket, ensuring it was on silent, and left the room, heading for Freddie's. George knew what to expect from the procession, but it didn't make it any easier to deal with, but at least his family would be with him. And the entire country, if not the world.

Freddie called for him to enter, and he closed the door behind him. His brother wore his black suit and white shirt with his medals pinned prominently on the jacket as their mother had requested in her funeral arrangements. Under other circumstances, Freddie and Douglas would've been wearing their military uniform, but their mother hadn't wanted that. George was the only brother to have not been in the military. He wondered whether that had gone into his mother's decision to make this stipulation, but he'd never know now.

"Morning," Freddie said, coming to stand in front of him. He rested a hand on George's shoulder. "You ready?"

"As I'll ever be."

Who could ever be ready to say goodbye to their mother?

"I said we'd knock for Douglas before we leave for Father's room."

Freddie picked up his phone and slipped it into his trouser pocket. They exited Freddie's room and wandered down the corridors in silence until they reached Douglas's. Freddie knocked and entered, George following. Douglas embraced Freddie, then George, and Mav did the same.

"Are you ready to go?" Douglas asked.

All three nodded. As they followed the twists and turns of the hallways, George's heart raced, and he inhaled and exhaled as Timothy had told him to do whenever he worried. It wasn't a panic attack, but he was extremely nervous. He lost track of how many times he checked his phone to ensure it was on silent.

George hesitated on the threshold of his parents' living room. It wasn't the first time he'd been there since his mother had died, but it didn't seem to get any easier. The scent of her permeated the room and made it seem like she'd just stepped out for a minute and would be back before they knew it. Obviously, that wasn't true, and it made it more difficult for George to remember she was no longer there.

"Morning, Father," Freddie said.

"Mornings, boys."

George glanced at his father, the man looking impeccable

in a black suit, white shirt and black tie. His skin appeared paler than usual, but apart from that, he was ever the king.

"Before we go, I want to say that I'm proud of you, and I know your mother would be, too. If she were here, she would want you to feel however you need to feel and show it however you need to. We're human. We're not robots. I don't care what the family has done before now. If you need to cry, you cry. I will not see you as weak, and those who do cannot understand how strong someone needs to be to walk behind a hearse with the world watching. I don't care what they say. We are who we are and nothing more."

By the time his father had finished talking, tears were already streaming down George's face. Andrew folded his arms around him and rubbed his back.

"Thank you, Father. That means a lot to us. I, for one, know I will be unlikely to stay stoic through this," Freddie said.

Although George thought Freddie was being kind towards him—he was, after all, known as being the most emotional of the three of them—he appreciated it all the same.

He wiped his eyes as he pulled back from his father. He sniffed and exhaled, clearing his throat. "I'm ready."

"I wish I was," Andrew said with a sad smile.

They got themselves ready and set out for the entrance, where many people were waiting. The plan would be for them to drive to the part of The Long Walk that the cortege would use for the last leg of the procession, then walk from there to St George's Chapel, where they were holding the ceremony. They had brought his mother to Windsor the previous evening, though George hadn't visited her. He didn't want to walk behind her—not because he thought she was unworthy, but because he wanted to grieve in private. Why did he need to show the public how upset he was? Why couldn't he shy away from the limelight as other mourners could?

When he climbed into the car, he let the scenery pass him by. His family left him alone, and he was grateful for it. He wanted nothing more than to call Timothy or Eddie so he could hear their voices to shore up his defences against the things to come, but he couldn't.

The journey was ten minutes, but it felt a lot quicker. He wished for time to stretch out to infinity so that he didn't have to go through with it. Timothy's voice sounded in his head.

"She wouldn't want you to be sad. She would want you to celebrate her life. Celebrate what she stood for."

He was right, but sadness was inevitable, and Timothy also knew that. Every aspect of life should be celebrated, but it was impossible to not let the sad times overrule the good on days like that.

"They will arrive in five minutes," the security guard in the front seat said.

"Thank you, Simon." His father adjusted his shirt sleeves, a move George knew belied his nerves.

George took a few deep breaths and nodded across at Douglas, who had raised his eyebrows at him.

The car stopped, and the four of them climbed out, moving to stand on the side of the road the coffin would turn onto. George went to stand beside Douglas, in age order, as was the usual stance at state funerals, but his father grabbed his shoulder and kept him beside him. George stood straight with his eyes fixed on a point in the distance straight ahead. He knew the public was lining the streets, but there was a hush over the entire area. Almost as if they didn't want to speak. To break the silence.

Time appeared to lengthen, but too soon, he got his first glimpse of the bed they had laid his mother to rest in. Though he couldn't see it, he knew the coffin was a beautiful mahogany colour because his father had told him so. They had draped the royal standard over, and a horse-drawn carriage carried it, surrounded by eight men from his parents' personal guards. Men who had been with them for many years.

George's throat closed up as he watched the carriage pass by, and he broke his gaze and inhaled, trying to keep his composure.

His father squeezed his shoulder, and George glanced at him. Andrew tilted his head, and they stepped behind, following the hearse in a slow-moving procession up The Long Walk. Members of the public lined the roads, and flowers decorated the ground as they wandered past.

George tried not to see the people because their grief was as palpable as his own. He turned his focus to his hands, trying to ignore everything, and thought about Timothy and Eddie instead. Were they watching this on TV? Were they together? He hoped they were, although Eddie was probably working. He closed his eyes and took himself back to when they'd first decided to give their relationship a try. He couldn't believe they had agreed to take a chance on him when he came with so much baggage. Lucky and honoured didn't even come close, but would the burden of royal life get to be too much for them one day?

He shook his head and refocused on his steps, watching the crowds from the corner of his eyes grow the closer they came to their destination. How many of them had suffered a similar loss? He hoped the number was less than he believed.

They continued until they reached the gates separating Windsor Castle from the public, and George breathed easier, knowing he was under less scrutiny now the public wasn't standing there. There were still journalists documenting the journey of the queen, but it wasn't as bad as it had been.

When they came to a stop outside St George's Chapel, George exhaled. His heart pounded, and his eyes burned. He wasn't ready. He didn't think he'd ever be ready.

"No one is ready to lose the people they love, but they'll always be a part of us."

George hadn't realised he'd spoken aloud, but Douglas had answered with the tone that had always reassured George as a child. He inhaled and lifted his head, coming to a stop beside his father and brothers. They waited in silence, hands linked in front of them, and George stared at the hearse.

When the pallbearers made their way to the coffin, George couldn't withhold it any longer. Tears ran down his face, and his breathing became erratic. The men lifted the coffin to their shoulders and began the procession into the chapel.

Freddie moved beside George and wrapped his arm around his shoulders, and Douglas rested his hand around his waist. George couldn't look at them. All he could do was stare at the red, blue, gold and white standard draped across the coffin as they carefully carried it up the multitude of steps as the bells rang.

Freddie and Douglas nudged George into motion, and they ascended the twenty steps—George counted them to distract himself, and hopefully, push back his emotions a bit.

As they proceeded into the chapel and down the aisle, the choir began singing a sombre song. His mother would've hated it. He could feel the attendees staring at him, but he gave them no attention. He couldn't.

The pressure on his chest increased as the procession stopped, and his mother's coffin was secured to a table in the centre of the chapel. Freddie and Douglas steered George over to the pews to the right, and he dropped into his seat, his eyes locked on his mother. It was stupid to think of the coffin as *being* his mother, but it was easier than remembering she was locked in a box.

Tears trickled down his cheeks in continuous rivers, but he ignored them. People spoke; they sang; they spoke some more, but George went through the motions without breaking his gaze.

Finally, the pallbearers returned, lifting the coffin to their shoulders, and headed down the aisle to the exit. George kept his gaze on her for as long as possible, then blinked rapidly when she disappeared to the sound of another sad song. He caught Aunt Charlotte's wet gaze. She stared at him, eyes narrowing. He felt a shiver go down his spine and averted his eyes, catching on Charles's bitter smile. George lowered his eyes. When the song finished, everyone descended into silence for one minute, and George fought to keep his balance as grief pulled down on him.

The silence ended when the bells rang loud and clear, and they exited the pews and made their way down the aisle to the hearse. Andrew, Freddie, Douglas and George stopped beside it, hands held in front of them as they rested her in the back of it.

"My condolences, brother."

George tensed at Aunt Charlotte's voice, but he remained staring forward.

"Thank you," Andrew said, his voice low and tight.

"Please let me know if there is anything I can do."

George saw his father nod from the corner of his eye, then Aunt Charlotte moved away. He didn't know why she needed to make a spectacle of it, but as usual, she made sure she was seen front and centre, even if it was only for a few seconds.

Within minutes, the horses pulled away from them, and a car stopped beside them. They climbed in, following the hearse on its journey to her final resting place at the Royal Mausoleum, close to Freddie's home. At the gates, George requested for the car to stop. His father's forehead creased, and George cleared his throat.

"I'm sorry, Father, but I cannot attend the burial. I don't —" He exhaled shakily. "I don't want to see her like that. I'm sorry, but I can't."

Andrew enveloped him in his arms and tightened his hold until George felt like he would break. "Never be sorry for doing what's right for you. You don't need to be there if you don't want to be."

George pulled back, wiping his face. "Thank you."

He gave a small smile at Freddie and Douglas, who both nodded in return, and exited the car. It was only a short walk to Freddie's house, a slightly longer one to his home, but George didn't mind. He shoved his hands deep into his pockets and headed away from his mother's last resting place. He would visit her, but not today, and maybe not tomorrow, but he would go when he was ready.

The crunch of the stones beneath his feet was loud in the almost silence of the deserted gardens. His mother would love the place. Although she had married into the family, she had made sure she knew her royal history and had visited the mausoleum several times with George to pay her respects to their ancestors. At the time, George had thought it was cool, although a little creepy, but when he thought back on those memories now, he felt a sense of peacefulness instead.

He stopped and closed his eyes, lifting his face to the sky and just listened and felt. The pain in his chest was still there, but it had eased some. His mother would get her revenge in the shape of her legacy. Something that would never be forgotten. They would eventually find those who were responsible for her death, but although they killed her body, they can never kill her light, her compassion, her love.

George smiled, inhaled deeply and let it go, then started walking again. He pulled his phone from his pocket and dialled.

"I want to see you." He didn't wait for them to answer.

"Do you want to come here to get away from the media?" Timothy asked.

"Yeah, I think I do. I'll be there as soon as I can."

"Whenever you get here, we'll be here."

"I—" He paused.

"Don't worry. Come to us."

George ended the call and picked up his pace. He'd borrow one of Freddie's cars. He wouldn't mind. One of Freddie's household staff helped him get the keys to one of the smaller cars, slightly less likely to be noticed as containing a royal family member, but just in case, George stripped his jacket and borrowed a jacket, too.

By the time he drove away from Freddie's house, he could breathe easier, knowing he would see the two men he was coming to love sooner rather than later.

24

HENRY

Henry couldn't be with his cousins during the funeral, though he wished he could. He sat on a pew with Robert beside him, their fingers entwined, and he stared at the coffin until it disappeared to the front of the church.

"Do you want to stay?" Robert asked.

Henry focused on him and frowned. "Sorry?"

"Do you want to stay, or shall we go?"

Henry swallowed hard and made the mistake of looking across to the other seats where his aunt sat. As if she had felt his stare, she turned and held his gaze. For a few seconds, she did nothing, then her mouth curled at the corners, and she lifted her head before turning away and following the rest of the congregation outside.

What had that been about? Had she been trying to be reassuring? Had she been happy at the turn of events? Had she been angry at him? He guessed it was one of the latter two, especially if she was the reason for it.

"Henry? Are you okay?"

Henry sighed. "I'll be fine." They stood and followed the guests to the exit. Henry inhaled and glanced at Robert. "Time to brave the photographers again."

"I'm getting used to it."

Henry lifted Robert's hand to his mouth and kissed the back of it. "I'm glad. I don't know what I'd do without you."

"You don't need to worry about that because I'm here."

The sunlight shone down on them on an unfairly bright day. Not that he wished for the rain, but it would better suit their mood. Losing one of their own, especially someone who was loved so much and by so many people, was unbearable. He'd hardly seen any of them since the incident, and he wanted nothing more than to go barging into their rooms or houses to see them, but he knew they needed time to themselves. Luckily, they were meeting up the following day to celebrate Mav's birthday. He'd received an invitation from Mav the previous day, which had been a shock because he hadn't thought they would do anything because of how close it was to the funeral.

By the time they made it down the steps, the hearse had already disappeared, as had Aunt Louisa's immediate family. He was at a loss where to go now, and he glanced around for his brother.

"Patrick, where are we going now? Or is this it?"

Patrick slid an arm around his shoulders. "This is it. We can hang around and meet some of the public if you want to, or you can go straight home."

Henry peered at Robert, seeing the strain on him. "Shall we go home?" he asked.

"I'll do whatever you want to do."

He turned back to Patrick. "What are you doing?"

"I'm going to stay for a few minutes. I can see some of

them have flowers. I'm going to rest them to the side of the gates for them."

"We can help," Robert said.

"Are you sure?"

Robert nodded. "It's a wonderful idea."

Henry nodded, and they wandered down the path to the main exit gate—Henry VIII Gate. The crowd waved the flags they held, amongst other things. They had blocked off part of the road to allow the hearse and cars to move freely, and the crowd was several people deep. They headed over to them, and Henry steeled himself.

"Thank you for coming," he said, shaking someone's hand. He repeated the action over and over. One woman held a bouquet. "Would you like me to put that down?"

Her eyes brimmed. "Would you mind?"

"Not at all."

He took the flowers and pivoted away from the people to set them on the grass verge to the left of the gate. He returned and continued his way down the row. Robert took the flowers from him as Henry received words of comfort and sorrow he would pass onto those who needed to hear it. The country would never forget the woman who had been a part of their lives for so long. Aunt Louisa may not have been queen the entire time, but she had been a princess for many years before that. A lot of the people there would have always known her as part of the royal family, even though she hadn't been when she was born.

By the time they called it quits, flowers of all colours and varieties covered the grass.

"There's almost as many there as there had been in your shop."

Robert snorted. "I think it's a lot more than what I had. She deserves every bit."

"That she does."

He waved to the crowd before heading to the car that would take them home.

"I don't want to go through that again anytime soon," he said, resting his head back.

"Fingers crossed."

25

TIMOTHY

Timothy's heart broke as he watched George walking behind the hearse. No one should ever have to do such a thing, but he wasn't naïve enough to know it didn't happen. The worst thing about the whole situation was that George had no closure. There was no one to rage against the injustice of it all because they hadn't found the people responsible yet. George hadn't spoken about it much, but Timothy assumed they were going all out on trying to find those people. He doubted the royal family would roll over and let them go when one of the nation's treasures had been taken from them.

Eddie sniffed, and Timothy tightened his hold. They cuddled on the sofa in his living room, watching the funeral on the TV. Eddie had taken the day off work to support George in the only way he could until George was able to come to them. Timothy didn't think it would be long after the funeral for him to call them, but he wasn't sure if he needed to complete other royal obligations before he could get away.

"He's crying! Oh, it's so unfair, Timothy. Why does he have to go through this?" Eddie rolled closer but kept his eyes on the screen.

"I know. It's not fair, but he's strong. He doesn't care who sees him grieve. He's being himself in public for one of the first times in his life, as far as I can tell." He pressed his lips to Eddie's forehead. "He'll be with us soon."

"I hope it doesn't take too long. He'll be a wreck by the end." Eddie wiped his nose with a tissue he held crumpled in his hand, then took another from the box on his lap. "Is this what we're going into? A life of media attention and scrutiny?"

Timothy swallowed hard and nodded. "This is just the tip of the iceberg, Eddie. I can't even explain how…intrusive it can be. Everything you've ever done will be thrown out for the entire population to dissect and discuss as they see fit. You'll have to justify things you never thought you would." He sighed. "I'll try to protect you from it if you want to go ahead with this relationship."

Eddie lifted his head. "Don't you?"

"Don't I, what?"

"Want to go ahead with the relationship?" Eddie pulled back, creating space between them. "If you want out, you need to let us know now because we're already deep in this, Timothy. For me, there's no option. I'm in. All in. I don't care what I have to go through. You and George are worth it as far as I'm concerned."

Timothy cupped his face. "I'm in, Eddie. As scared as I am about the future, I can't change how I feel about you both. I'd be a fool to let this slip through my fingers because of something I can't change. The media ripped my life apart when I was in Bristol. They can't do much worse here."

Eddie's hands covered his own. "I'm sorry you went through that, but you're here. You have us, and we will protect you like you'll protect us."

Timothy closed the distance between them, taking and giving what they both needed—reassurance. It was a chaste kiss, but Eddie had an enormous smile on his face when they separated.

"I can't wait until he gets here," Eddie said, settling back against Timothy.

"Hopefully, it won't be long."

"I'm glad the cameras aren't focusing on them in the chapel. That would be awful."

Timothy nodded. "It seems the media has certain limitations—or rules to follow, at least."

As the service continued, they made small talk until the minute silence. At that point, they held tight to each other, gazes locked onto the screen, although they couldn't see George. When the pallbearers continued, George appeared, looking tired and washed out. His brothers were the same. As for the king, well, he appeared poised and immaculate, but his eyes showed the turmoil he fought to keep hidden. The tension in his jaw and temple belied his feelings, and Timothy wished there was something he could do to help them all. Nothing but time would.

They watched the family climb into a car and follow the hearse through the streets until they reached the area where cameras weren't allowed. Now, it was a waiting game. The family had a private burial to attend, and then hopefully, they would be able to grieve in peace.

"Now, we wait," Eddie said. "Do you think he'll call?"

"I've no doubt. He might need some time alone first, though, but we'll see what he's like when he calls." Timothy rubbed his hand up and down Eddie's arm. "Do you want something to eat?"

Eddie flapped his hands. "I don't think I could stomach anything at the minute. It's churning for everything George is going through." He sighed. "I know losing parents is inevitable, but he's only thirty-two. It's so unfair." He picked at a thread on his trousers.

"It *is* unfair." Something must've shown in his voice because Eddie asked him what was wrong. "I lost my father when I was thirteen."

"Oh, god, Timothy. I didn't know!"

"It's okay. It was a long time ago now."

"What happened? If you want to talk about it, that is."

Timothy exhaled. "Dad had been at the supermarket picking up some things we'd forgotten for a birthday party. Some men came in with guns, taking everyone hostage until they had what they came for. Money. The victims thought they were getting out of there because the men began to leave, but the assistant stood too soon, and a gunman aimed at the man. Dad stood and pushed him aside, taking the bullet himself. He saved the life of the assistant at the cost of his own life." Timothy smiled. "It makes it easier, knowing he died saving someone else and knowing Dad would've been happy with that result."

"God, that's terrible. I'm so sorry."

"Thanks. I know what George is going through. As morbid as this sounds, I hope everyone dies before I do."

Eddie pulled back, eyebrows in his hairline. "Why?"

"Because then no one would feel the pain of loss except me. You'd all die happy and wouldn't have to deal with the grief. I would do anything to spare you the pain."

Eddie straddled his lap and rested his hands against the

sides of his neck. "You are an amazing man, Timothy Dixon. Don't let anyone tell you any different."

Timothy didn't think so, but he wouldn't dissuade Eddie from believing that. Maybe he could believe it enough for both of them. Eddie lowered his head and kissed Timothy. Timothy slid his hands around Eddie's back, one hand rising to the base of his neck and the other to his ass. He never wanted to lose them, and his heart raced at the implications of everything he'd exposed to Eddie. It was already too late for him.

He was in love with them.

How had that happened in such a short amount of time? They'd known each other just over a week, which seemed such a small timeframe to change your whole life for, but Timothy had no doubts. He'd walk through fire for them.

His phone rang, and they pulled apart. Timothy grabbed it from the side table. "It's George." He pressed to answer but didn't get any words out before George spoke.

"I want to see you."

Eddie smiled, and Timothy's heart rate increased. "Do you want to come here to get away from the media?" Timothy asked.

"Yeah, I think I do. I'll be there as soon as I can."

"Whenever you get here, we'll be here." He met Eddie's wet gaze.

"I—" George paused.

He wasn't sure what George wanted to say, but he could say it whenever he was ready. "Don't worry. Come to us."

The phone went dead, and Timothy placed the phone back on the table. "He's coming." He didn't know why he said it because Eddie heard what George had said.

"Shall we make some lunch in case he's hungry?"

"That sounds like a good idea. Something that can keep if he's not."

"Sandwiches?"

"Perfect."

They set about their task, and Timothy had an energy buzzing inside. The need to see George in person was overwhelming. When the gate bell went, Timothy jogged down the hallway to open it for George. Once he was clear, the gate closed behind him. Timothy would do whatever it took to ensure he had his privacy here. For the first time, he was glad for the house and land he'd bought. They'd keep the curtains and blinds closed to make sure, but they were as secure as they could be without being inside Windsor Castle.

When George pulled up in front of the house, Timothy opened the door, and Eddie ran past him and flung his arms around the prince. He couldn't hear what they were saying, but George had his eyes closed and a small smile on his face. Timothy stayed where he was, allowing them the time to reconnect after two days apart.

George encouraged Eddie to wrap his legs around his waist and carried him closer to the door. He tilted his head when he met Timothy's gaze. The pain was visible in his eyes, but so was a serenity that Timothy hadn't expected to see.

"Are you okay?"

"I am now."

George stepped inside, and Timothy closed the door behind them. George spun, making Eddie laugh, then moved closer to Timothy.

"Kiss me."

Timothy smiled and leaned forward, pressing his lips to George's. It felt like coming home. He was in no doubt he was irrevocably in love with these two men, and it didn't feel like the burden he'd expected. It felt freeing. Scary but freeing.

Eddie's lips joined theirs, and in a messy meeting, they became whole. At least, that was what it felt like to Timothy.

Reluctantly, he pulled back. "Are you hungry?"

"Only for you two."

Timothy shook his head with a smile and scratched at his goatee. "Shall we retire to the bedroom?"

"I thought you'd never ask."

Timothy chuckled and led the way, George never once relinquishing his hold of Eddie. Eddie rested his head on George's shoulder, and Timothy wrapped his arm around George's waist as they climbed the stairs. He aimed for his room and steered them into the bathroom.

"Let's wash away the stress for you first," he said, helping Eddie to the floor before they both bracketed George, front and back.

As they divested George of his clothes, one item at a time, with plenty of kisses on his exposed skin, Timothy kept up a quiet monologue, telling George how brave and strong he was. When he was naked, George turned his focus to Eddie, removing the man's clothes, and then they both turned to Timothy. Before they started on him, the three men attempted a three-way kiss again. This time they were more successful, but it was still a learning curve he knew they would be happy to take.

When they were free from clothes, they stepped under the large shower. It rivalled George's. Timothy and Eddie took turns soaping George, and Timothy washed his hair. He wanted nothing more than to take care of him, give him everything. He understood that George and Eddie would need time to get to the stage that Timothy had realised he'd already arrived at. He didn't mind. They were worth waiting for.

Once they were all clean, Timothy switched off the shower and held out towels for them. He didn't bother drying himself, just tucked the towel around his waist and focused on the other men. He led the way to his bedroom and turned to face them, a fluttering taking up residence in his stomach.

"What's wrong?" George asked.

"Nothing. I'm glad you're both here." He still had some reservations about how their relationship would play out, but in the here and now, he was glad.

George smiled and stepped closer, invading Timothy's personal space. "I'm glad we're all here." He held out his hand for Eddie. "If you both agree, I'd like us to celebrate instead of mourn."

"What do you have in mind?" Eddie asked.

"Being as close as we can get." George studied them in turn as if expecting them to decline. Timothy knew neither of them would. This was a natural next step for them, but it was the logistics that concerned him.

"Who...I mean, how..." He felt his cheeks heat even though he was as far from innocent as he could get.

"I think I should fuck Eddie, and you should fuck me."

Timothy tried to swallow the lump in his throat. He wanted that more than anything.

George faced Eddie and draped his arms around him, pulling his towel free and dropping it to the floor. He did the same with his own towel, then kissed Eddie. Timothy's gaze took in the display, every inch of him enjoying it. There were no feelings of jealousy, which he was glad about. It had been a worry of his, but so far, everyone seemed on board. He watched Eddie's hands slide and skim across George's back, the muscles bunching in reaction. His mouth watered, and he couldn't wait to have them both.

He moved in close, trapping Eddie's hands between his stomach and George's back. He lowered his head to George's shoulder, pressing kisses along it and up his neck to his ear. All the while, George kept kissing Eddie. One of his hands caressed George's side as his other hand reached for Eddie.

George released his mouth, and Timothy took advantage, fusing his own to Eddie's. After he had his fill, he pulled back and guided them over to the bed. When George carefully laid Eddie down, Timothy removed his towel and climbed on beside them. They looked beautiful together. Perfect. If he had thought it would benefit any of them, he would have backed off and let him be together, but he was selfish. He could no more deny his need for them as he could deny himself breath. He snorted at his poetic thoughts and smiled at his partners.

Once more, George pulled away, although Eddie grumbled. "Do you have supplies?" George asked.

Timothy smirked. He stood, reaching for the bedside table and removed some lube, two condoms and something he was glad he'd requested express delivery for. He dropped the two sets of leather wrist restraints onto the bed beside George and Eddie. Eddie's face flushed, and Timothy heard the hitch in his breath. George licked his lips, his gaze never wavering from the items.

"I want you both locked together." Timothy hadn't realised until he'd seen the restraints and then researched that this was something he could have and that maybe they wanted.

"Yes," breathed Eddie.

Timothy climbed back onto the bed, taking one set of restraints and lifting Eddie's arms above his head. He fastened the restraints around Eddie's wrists, the small chain between them preventing him from moving far.

"I want you to keep your hands above your head because I have nothing to tie you to. Yet." Timothy slid down the bed a little, locking gazes with George. "Do you want this?"

George cleared his throat. "Yes, Sir."

Timothy swallowed hard at the title. He'd had a feeling George needed this but hadn't wanted to push. It had seemed like the right time to ask.

"Slide your hands up to Eddie's."

George did as he'd asked. Timothy secured the first restraint around his wrist, and George gasped. Timothy repeated it on his other wrist, then clicked both chains together, attaching Eddie and George together. He watched as the two men threaded their fingers together, holding tight even as their hips began a gentle thrust.

"Colour?" he asked.

"Green," Eddie said.

"Green," George confirmed.

"As neither of you now have hands, I'll have to prepare you both."

The two men whimpered in unison, then George kissed Eddie. Timothy smiled as he squirted lube on his hands, moving lower on the bed until he rested by their asses. He pressed a finger against each of their puckers and massaged in a circle. Both rings of muscles clenched, then released before they leaned into him, and he pressed forward, sinking the tip of his finger into each man.

The men gasped and thrust their hips faster, and Timothy

smiled. He could get used to this, although he was a little worried about being able to keep up with them as he was much older. Shoving the thought aside, he slid his finger deeper, withdrawing and pressing forward until it was moving with no resistance. He removed his fingers and added a second to Eddie's hole, scissoring them to widen him for George's cock.

Instead of fingering George, he lowered his head, licking across the entrance. A long, drawn-out moan escaped from George, and Timothy smiled before continuing. Concentrating on both acts—his fingers opening Eddie and his tongue opening George—he lost himself to the feel of them both. Never had he imagined this. Being with two men at the same time.

That thought made him pause. Was that possible? Could he use a strap-on and fuck them both at the same time? He didn't know, but he knew what he'd be researching the minute he could. No point bringing it up if it wasn't physically possible.

Whimpers brought his attention back, and he pressed three fingers into Eddie, which was rewarded with his groan. He firmed his tongue and pushed into George, receiving a similar sound. Not wanting to hurt the man, he played with him for a few minutes, then returned his fingers to him instead, wanting him ready and eager.

"Please, Sir! I need him, you!" George said.

Timothy grabbed the condoms and opened one. "Lift your hips, George." When he did, he slid the condom onto George's dick and rolled it down, slicking it with the remains of the lube on his fingers. "There you go." He positioned George's cock at Eddie's entrance. "Hold still now. No entering yet."

He grabbed the second condom and rolled it on himself before slicking it, then rested against George's ass. "Are you ready? I want you to enter Eddie as I enter you. Let's see if we can do this in unison."

Eddie gasped. "Oh, god, yes!"

"Now!" Timothy said and pushed forward, sliding into George's warm, tight channel.

2 6

EDDIE

*E*ddie went cross-eyed when George's cock slid into him, and the pressure of Timothy on top of them made him go deep. Coupled with being locked to George, it was divine. Made more so because George couldn't keep the weight of his body off Eddie as his hands were above his head like Eddie's were. It meant his whole body was flush against him, and he loved it.

Eddie lay on his back with his knees near George's armpits, giving George access to him. Although, there wasn't much George could do except take whatever Timothy was giving them. After the first entry, Timothy had paused, waiting for them both to be ready after George had shouted, "God, damn!" The outburst had made Eddie laugh as joy suffused him. They were together. Timothy wasn't shying away from the BDSM aspect of their lives. Everything was great.

Now, Timothy took up a steady pace, rocking George into Eddie whenever he thrust forward. After the initial few movements, George pressed kisses to Eddie's face and whatever skin he could reach, and Eddie just lay there and experienced everything he could. Remembering it all in case it fell apart after this. He hoped it wouldn't.

"Jesus," George groaned. "I'm close already."

"That will be because you have your cock sunk into the tight heat of Eddie's ass and your own ass stuffed by mine. Bet you've never felt this full, have you?" Timothy growled, his voice hoarse.

"Never, Sir," George said.

"You want more?" Timothy asked.

George dropped his head to Eddie's forehead. "God, yes, please, Sir."

"Eddie?"

"Yes, please, Sir. I want it all." Eddie swallowed hard as he stared into George's eyes.

"Your wish is my command."

George and Eddie moaned in unison when Timothy increased the pace, slamming into them. "God, damn, you feel good. How are you going to make Eddie come, George?"

George hissed, his eyelids fluttering closed with every thrust. Eddie was watching George's face, so he saw when George inhaled and fixed his gaze on Eddie with a smirk gracing his lips. Moving their hands towards the ceiling, George could lower his head to Eddie's nipples, and once he teased and sucked one, Eddie flew. The tug on his wrists, the weight over him, the fullness in his ass, and the new suction on his nipple sent him over the edge.

"Ah!" A long, drawn-out moan left his mouth, and he arched his back as tiny explosions flowed all over his body.

"Fuck!" George shouted and went rigid above Eddie, tucking his face into Eddie's neck while his body trembled.

"Holy hell," Timothy groaned, increasing his speed until

he slammed into them both and held himself deep. He rested a hand over their bound ones, connecting the three of them outside and inside. Then he slumped, though he didn't put his weight on them. "Hold still."

Timothy withdrew with a wince, and George hissed again, undoubtedly sensitive after their activities. Eddie pressed kisses to George's face and hair while Timothy unfastened them. He disappeared when they were free, reappearing with a cloth. George had rested against Eddie and didn't seem able to move.

"Can you lift off so I can clean you?" Timothy asked.

George mumbled something, and Eddie chuckled. "I don't think he has the energy," Eddie said, running a hand through George's hair.

Timothy hummed, then Eddie felt a hand between his legs, and George's cock eased from his ass. He smiled at the ache in his ass. The cloth wiped his hole, and Eddie felt the condom being removed from George, then the cloth to clean him. He wasn't sure how Timothy planned on cleaning their stomachs because they were stuck together by this point. He should've known Timothy better, though, because he climbed onto the bed beside them and rolled George and Eddie towards him, so George was between them. It made a small gap, and Eddie grimaced at the cool air reaching the wet patches.

Timothy wiped George's stomach, then Eddie's stomach and cock before throwing the cloth over his shoulder. "We'll have a shower soon. I brought drinks."

Eddie hadn't even seen the items on the bedside table. He didn't know if they'd been there before they started. Timothy grabbed two cartons of orange juice and pulled the covers over them all. He opened both cartons, then slid an arm beneath George's and Eddie's necks, effectively holding them both. With his other hand, he held both cartons together but with the straws pointing in different directions—one towards George and one towards Eddie.

As usual, tears seeped from Eddie's eyes, but he was so happy. He hugged George, reaching for Timothy as well, and drank his juice, closing his eyes as warmth filled him from top to toe.

"Thank you," George said.

Eddie opened his eyes, blinking a few times to clear the tears, and met George's gaze. Tears filled the prince's eyes, and Eddie gave a small smile. "I'm glad we waited."

George nodded. "Me, too."

"Waited for what?" Timothy asked.

"For you," Eddie said.

Timothy frowned. "What do you mean?"

George cleared this throat. "We hadn't had intercourse with each other before today. We'd had each other's mouths or hands, but never our bodies. It seemed like we had been waiting for something, but I couldn't figure out what until I realised it was you."

Eddie nodded. "There was never any urgency to take things further with George. It wasn't because I didn't want him, because I did. I didn't realise George felt the same, but he's right. Something was missing, and I now know what it was."

George turned his head so he could see Timothy. "Without you, we're missing a piece of a puzzle. I, for one, would love to stay complete whilst we all want it." He glanced at Eddie. "It will be difficult. You might hate the attention, the threats, the royal life, but I'll protect you from it if I can. *If* you want to stay with me."

Eddie cupped George's cheeks. "For as long as you let me."

George kissed him, then peered over his shoulder at Timothy. "You don't have to. I know how difficult it has been for you."

Timothy rested his head on George's shoulder, bringing their faces closer. "It's not that I don't want to. I'm concerned about the backlash on you and your family. A… triad? Throuple? Menage?" He chuckled. "Whatever we call ourselves is something that isn't well recognised in the world. Not only will you have issues with your family, I'm sure, but you'll also have problems with the public. Are you ready for that?"

George lifted his arm around Timothy's head. "I am, if you're sure. I won't do this without all of us agreeing and understanding what could happen. I'm not at all concerned with my immediate family. They'll be happy, although Father might take a little time to come around to it. As far as the BDSM community, it won't phase them. The public and my extended family," he shrugged, "I don't know, but if you are both sure you want to do this, we'll weather it all."

"I'm sure," Eddie said.

"I'm sure," Timothy echoed.

"Then we'll figure it out along the way," George said with a smile. "First, I need a shower."

They cleaned up, despite wandering hands making the shower last longer than expected, and got dressed again, with Timothy lending George a T-shirt and jeans instead of his suit. They wandered to the living room, and Timothy left him and George there to choose a film while he grabbed some snacks and drinks.

George's phone rang, and he smiled and put it on speakerphone. "Freddie, you're on speaker. How are you doing?"

"They've found you," Freddie said.

George tensed. "What?"

"The media know where you are, George. Is it secure?"

"As secure as it can be, but I don't have security guards," Timothy answered as he entered the room, a frown on his face. "If they try hard enough, it won't be difficult to get onto the property."

"Okay, I'll send some security over to you. Don't go outside or even near the windows if you can help it," Freddie said.

"How did they find me?" George asked. His face pinched, and his cheeks flushed.

"We don't know exactly, but there's a picture of you in the car, then pulling up to Timothy's house," Douglas said. "It could be a drone or something similar because it seems to be from higher than a normal car could be."

"If it's a drone, it could easily get pictures we don't want it to," Eddie said, clenching his fingers together. "Do you think they…" He pointed up.

No one answered him, which wasn't a good omen.

"Eddie, can you help me close the curtains, please? I got distracted earlier when I was supposed to close them," Timothy said. "George, stay here for the moment."

Timothy and Eddie closed the curtains in the living room first, then went around the downstairs and upstairs, closing every curtain and blind they could find. The size of the place amazed Eddie. He couldn't even imagine living in a place like this. It was huge but beautiful.

"This house is amazing, Timothy."

Timothy smiled and ran a hand along Eddie's back. "Thank you, sweetheart. It was my mum's first choice. It has enough bedrooms so my family can visit and stay over if they want to."

"I'm sure they love that. Have they been yet?"

They wandered back towards the living room. "No, they're all working, but we're hoping sooner rather than later they can get here. I'd love for you both to meet them." He checked his watch. "In fact, they'll be calling tonight, so maybe I can introduce you unless you need to go home?"

"Not tonight, I don't. I'd love that."

Inside, Eddie preened at the idea of being able to meet his family. It meant he was taking this seriously. Not that Eddie didn't think he was in the first place, but sometimes, it was difficult to determine what the man thought about things because Eddie was an open book.

"—can't believe they're saying that! What the fuck does it matter?"

George's voice met them before they'd even reached the room, and they hurried inside, sinking onto the sofa beside him. Eddie slid his arm around his waist and laid his head on his shoulder.

"You know what they're like, George. They'll print anything they think will increase their reader numbers whether or not it's true."

George sighed and lowered his head.

"What's wrong?" Timothy asked.

George said nothing, but Douglas answered for him, "The media are up in arms because George didn't attend his mother's burial."

"They have no right to say anything about that," Timothy said.

"We know that. That doesn't mean it won't sell," Freddie said.

"Fuckers." George leaned back and rested his head against the sofa, dislodging Eddie's arm.

"Ignore what they're saying, George. You are entitled to do what is best for you," Timothy said.

"He's right, George," Freddie said. "Father also agrees, as you know from the car. We'll get through this. We'll fight it as we always do. We just need to collect ourselves and get the facts straight."

"What facts?" Timothy said.

Someone cleared their throat on the other line. "Hi, it's Mav. The first thing we need to do is decide how we're going to spin where you are, George. Do you want Timothy acknowledged as a friend, an acquaintance? You tell me."

"He's my boyfriend. As is Eddie." He met their gazes with raised eyebrows.

"Yes, boyfriend," Timothy agreed, though his expression appeared troubled.

Eddie nodded.

"You sly dog." Douglas chuckled. "Not content with one; you have two. Cheeky devil."

Eddie snorted and hid it behind his hand. George grinned and clasped hands with them both.

"They dug themselves into my heart, and I couldn't choose."

"You don't need to," Timothy said. "We're here."

"Is Eddie there, too?" Freddie asked.

Eddie coughed. "I'm here."

"Nice to meet you," Freddie said. "We're going to do this properly tomorrow."

"Tomorrow?" George frowned.

"Mav has agreed to let us visit him for his birthday. It's just going to be us."

A sigh sounded. "It's not without argument," Mav said.

"We're not letting this go without celebrating. You know Mother wouldn't want that," Douglas said.

"The Improper Eleven," George said with a grin.

"No!" various voices shouted.

"God, George. Stop with the names already," Douglas said.

Eddie chuckled, knowing George wouldn't. It wasn't a good name, though. Eddie would have to help him think of something.

"Well, you try for something that starts with E, then. It's next to impossible." George crossed his arms and pouted.

"Good. Leave it alone then," Douglas said.

"Timothy, the security guards should pull up at your gate in the next five minutes. One will get out and corral the photographers while the car gets inside, then he'll slip in and make sure no one else does. They'll stay outside, but there are four of them, so two will check the property and garden area to make sure no one has got in. They'll introduce themselves first, so you don't think they're the media," Freddie said.

"Thanks."

"You're welcome. You are family now, so we'll protect you as such."

Eddie sat back, his hands dropping to his lap. Family. "I need to call mine. Is that okay? Am I allowed to tell them about us?"

George leaned forward and kissed him. "Of course, you can. We don't keep secrets from family unless we can't trust them, and everyone gets a chance to prove they can be trusted."

Eddie smiled and checked with Timothy, who nodded. "I'll be telling mine tonight. No going back now." He winked.

Eddie's smile widened. "Okay, I'll go into the kitchen and call them."

"Do you know where it is?" Timothy asked.

"No, but I know it's in that direction. I'm sure I'll find it."

He wandered down the hallway, and as he'd thought, it was easy enough to find. He sat at the breakfast bar and stared at his phone. His parents wouldn't care about it, but he was still apprehensive about their reaction, especially to the news he was dating a prince. They probably wouldn't believe him.

He chuckled and dialled. "Hey, Mum."

"Eddie! Everything okay?"

"Yes, I just have some news to share with you. Is Dad there, too. Can you put me on speaker?"

"Okay. Are you sure everything's okay?"

Eddie smiled. "Yes, positive."

"Parker! Eddie's on the phone!"

Eddie held the phone away from his ear and laughed as his mother shouted.

"Okay, we're here. What's going on?"

"Well, you know last time I was there, I mentioned Prince George?" He didn't wait for their answer. "We're more than friends." He paused, hoping they figured out what he was trying to say.

"And?" his mother said.

Eddie blinked. "And what?"

"Oh, is that the news? I knew that already, sweetie. No

one is that worried about someone when they're just friends."

That threw him, but he still had more to tell them. "Okay, I'm glad you're all right with that, but, well, that's not all. I'm also seeing someone else. His name is Timothy."

"You're cheating on a prince with someone else?"

"No!" Eddie dropped his head into his hand. "I'm saying this wrong. We're all together. All three of us. Me, Prince George and Timothy." He waited.

"So, you're one of these new fandangled, three-way relationship things?" his dad said.

Eddie couldn't help it and burst out laughing. He could hear his parents talking in his ear, but he was laughing so much he couldn't hear what they were saying. An arm slid around him, startling him. He glanced up at Timothy, who had a bemused look on his face. Eddie wiped his face and inhaled.

"Mum, Dad. Yes, we're in one of those fandangled three-way relationships." He bit his lip when Timothy raised his eyebrows.

"How does that work, then?" Dad asked.

"Parker! You don't need to know the ins and outs of his relationship. So to speak, Eddie." Tears escaped his eyes. His parents were hilarious. "I'm glad you found someone. Or two someone's," Mum said.

"Thanks. What I need to ask is that you keep this to yourself for now. We already have the media following us, and a story won't be far behind, I don't think. Until then, we need to keep quiet until we know what's happening."

"Not a problem, sweetie. Just make sure those men treat you right. Not like that other one."

Memories of Talon tried to work their way into his head.

His parents didn't know everything about what happened, but there had been no hiding the evidence on his body, even two days after when he finally went home.

"We'll treat him like a prince. You have my word," Timothy said.

"Oh, I didn't realise we were on speaker," his mum said.

Eddie put the phone on speaker. "You weren't, but are now. He's standing next to me. Mum, Dad, this is Timothy."

"Nice to hear from you, Timothy. I hope we can meet you in person soon."

"I'd love that. Eddie speaks highly of you." Timothy kissed Eddie's head, and Eddie rested against Timothy's chest.

"I don't exactly know what's going on, but I can imagine this is going to be a tricky time for you all. If you need anything at all, let us know," Dad said.

"Thanks, Dad."

"We appreciate your offer. Once we have a plan of action, we'll let you know," Timothy said. "I'll leave you to your call, sweetheart. Just to let you know, the security team is here. I'll introduce you when you're finished." He kissed him, then smiled and wandered back towards the living room.

Eddie watched him until he disappeared, then focused back on his parents. "I never expected this to happen, but I like them."

"I can tell. Did I hear that you have security there?"

"Yes, they've just arrived as news has got out about George being here."

"Okay, stay safe. We'll let you get back to them, but remember, if you need anything…"

"I'll ask. Thank you. I love you both."

"Love you, too, sweetie."

"Love you, son. Make sure they take care of you," Dad said.

Eddie grinned. "They do."

He ended the call and sat staring at his phone. He needed to say something to Bella, Mel and Terry, but he couldn't until he knew what the plan was. It was going to be a learning curve for everyone involved, but especially his friends. He supposed he'd know eventually who would be on his side and who would sell him out to the media. He wasn't looking forward to finding out who was on which side.

27

GEORGE

George dropped his head into his hands. He wished he didn't have to put Timothy and Eddie through this, but the time had come for them to decide if they were all in or not.

"Stop worrying. We're right here with you," Timothy said while Eddie finished the call with his parents. Timothy had already met the security guards when they'd arrived, who were now waiting outside for anything that might happen.

"It's hard for me to believe you're willing to throw yourself to the lions for me."

Timothy crouched in front of him, resting his hands on George's knees. "There's nothing we wouldn't do for you."

George stared at him, reading the honesty in his expression, but he couldn't help the twinge of fear that they were only words that he could easily take back. "I'm going to Douglas's apartment tomorrow for Mav's birthday celebration. I'd love it if you and Eddie could be there."

"I'm happy to come, although please save me from your

family." Timothy smiled, but there was a hint of uneasiness behind his words.

"They'll love you."

"What about me?" Eddie said, entering the room.

"They already know you, but they'll love you, too," George said, opening his arms for the man. Eddie climbed next to him, snuggling close, and George kissed his head, staring over it at Timothy. "I'd love for you both to properly meet the people who mean so much to me."

"Then we'll be there," Timothy said.

Timothy sat beside George and surrounded them both. "The security guard said the media weren't trying to get onto the property at the moment, but that might change depending on whether they get anything exciting. If they're anything like they were in Bristol, they're tenacious and won't be happy if we're playing happy families inside where they can't see anything."

"They're probably worse here with us being royalty. I'm sorry. I didn't want this for you," George said.

"Stop apologising. You've done nothing wrong. We both agreed to the relationship. You didn't force us. We will get through this together." Timothy kissed George's cheek.

George sighed and nodded. "Okay."

"Did you ever decide on a film?" Timothy asked.

Eddie chuckled. "No, we didn't get the chance."

"What're you in the mood for?" Timothy reached for the remotes and settled back again, flicking the TV on.

"An action or comedy."

While Timothy searched for something, George closed his eyes, thinking about how quickly things had changed since that morning. He'd been in front of millions of viewers while he'd attended his mother's funeral, cemented his relationship with Timothy and Eddie and had the media chase him down. The only thing he wanted to do tonight was to relax with his men, watch a film and go to bed—to sleep. He was exhausted.

George woke to a phone ringing, and he fumbled for it before realising he was sandwiched between two people. He smiled, then sighed when the phone stopped. Sitting up, he rubbed his eyes, groaning when the phone started again. He reached for his phone on the bedside table and brought it to his ear with a yawned, "Hello?"

"Sorry to wake you so early, George, but I needed to let you know what's been happening overnight."

George concentrated hard enough to figure out it was Mav's voice. "Morning, Mav." George cleared his throat and rubbed at his face some more. "All right. Let me have it."

Mav sniffed. "You're not going to like it."

He opened his eyes and stared at the wall opposite, waiting for the axe to fall.

"What's happened?" Timothy asked, sitting up beside George.

"I'm putting you on speaker, Mav." George leaned over to Eddie, smoothing a hand over his back. "Sweetheart, you need to wake up." Eddie snuffled but opened his eyes.

"What?" The word was barely understandable, and George gave a small chuckle.

"Go ahead, Mav."

"I've been monitoring the news outlets and social media, seeing what the public's reaction was to yesterday. On the whole, it has been extremely positive. However," Mav paused, and George tensed, "there are several reports about you not attending the burial."

"How did they know?" Timothy asked when George said nothing.

"I'm assuming the timeframe. Photos show George leaving Windsor before the end of the ceremony. It wouldn't take a genius to figure out he didn't attend."

"What are they saying?" George asked.

"They're saying you and your mother were not on speaking terms when she died. They're making it all up, but you know what they're like. I can swing things and dampen them, but I need something to give them. What do you want me to say?"

George lowered his head. "Tell them the bloody truth. I didn't want to see my mother dropped into the ground. I didn't want that to be the last memory I had of her. I wanted to remember her as vibrant, as kind, as alive."

He threw the covers back and scrambled out of the bed, storming into the shower, not caring if anyone followed him. This was what the media did. This was what sold. It didn't mean he liked it. No one had the right to make him feel bad for his choices when they didn't hurt anyone.

Switching the shower on, he rigorously scrubbed at his skin, then dried off. He tucked the towel around his waist and strode into the bedroom to collect his clothes. At least, his borrowed clothes. He could hear Timothy and Mav talking, but he wasn't interested. He needed to do something to get his mind back on straight. Before he left the room, he called back, "Happy birthday, Mav," then continued on his path to the kitchen. Coffee was what he needed.

He wasn't sure how long it had been until Timothy and

Eddie joined him in the kitchen, but the moment Eddie's arms came around his neck, he relaxed.

"Sorry. I didn't mean to leave you to deal with that."

Timothy dropped into the seat beside him. "Don't be sorry. The whole lot of them are assholes."

Eddie climbed into George's lap. "Mav said they've been digging up on you and Timothy. They don't seem to know about me yet, probably because I was already here when you arrived yesterday."

George nodded. "Makes sense. Hopefully, no one got any photos after I first arrived yesterday."

Eddie flushed and ducked his head. George chuckled, tucking his finger under Eddie's chin to watch the colour bloom across his cheeks. "I forgot," George said. "Good morning." He pressed his lips to Eddie's in a slow exploration, then pulled back, leaning his head to the side. "Good morning," he said to Timothy and kissed him.

Having them here with him made things easier, but he knew they would get worse before they got better. The first thing they had to attempt was to get out of Timothy's house with no one seeing them. It was unlikely to happen, but they needed to do as much as possible, especially for Eddie's sake. If his identity hadn't been acknowledged yet, George wanted to keep it that way for a few more hours.

He rested his head on Timothy's shoulder. "I think we need to get some breakfast, then butt in on Douglas and Mav's morning. I'll speak with the security to see if they can figure out a way to get us out of here with limited followers."

"Are you sure? Would it not be better to stay here?" Eddie asked.

"Possibly, but we have things to discuss which are easier

done in person than over the phone or video call. Also, we can't hide here forever, despite the fact I'd love to."

Timothy smiled. "You'd be welcome to."

George kissed the underside of Timothy's jaw. "Thanks. Reality intrudes, though."

Eddie stood. "All right, then. You two, get yourselves ready to go. I'll make some breakfast, then when we're ready, we'll get out of here." His hands flew to his face. "Oh no! We've not got Mav a present!"

George chuckled. "Don't worry. I've already sorted that. Douglas should have it waiting for us when we get there."

"Phew. That's good. Right, off with you."

Eddie waved his hands and turned to the fridge. George and Timothy shared a smile and exited the kitchen. Timothy went to the bathroom while George went to the front door. He slid it open a small amount and gained the attention of the security guard. The man exited the car, which remained parked in front of the door.

The guard slipped into the house. "How can I help, Your Highness?"

"Sorry, what was your name again?"

"Isaac, sir."

"Isaac, we're going to Douglas's apartment. All three of us. The media doesn't seem to realise there are three of us here, so is there any way we could keep it that way?"

Isaac's brow furrowed. "We could potentially put one of you in the car as a security member. The windows aren't blacked out completely, so they will see into the vehicle, but if one of you wore clothing similar to ours, we might get away with it for the journey there."

"Sounds good. I'll see what I can do. We plan to leave after breakfast."

"Okay, sir. Let us know when you're ready. I'll get things organised now."

"Thank you, Isaac."

"You're welcome, sir."

Isaac slipped back out of the door, and George climbed the stairs to Timothy's bedroom. The man in question had his clothes on—unfortunately—and George explained the plan.

"I have a suit Eddie could wear, but it'll be too big for him. Not in height but the waist."

"We can make it work for now. Even if it doesn't throw them off, it'll help for a while."

George took off his clothes and replaced them with fresh clothes Timothy gave him. He had planned on wearing the suit from the previous day, but it wouldn't look any worse if he wore someone else's clothes than if he went out in the same clothes from the funeral. Everyone would know what they were.

"Breakfast!" Eddie called.

"I could get used to this," Timothy said with a smile, ducking into his wardrobe to bring out a black suit similar to the security guards and laying it on the bed.

They descended the stairs, hand in hand, and met Eddie in the kitchen doorway.

"I was about to shout for you again in case you didn't hear me," Eddie said.

"Thank you, Eddie," Timothy said, kissing his cheek.

George copied. "Thank you."

Eddie blushed and ducked his head. "It's nothing much, but you're welcome."

The scrambled eggs and toast tasted delicious, but too soon, they were ready to go. Eddie wore the black suit, and they had a change of clothes in a bag for him when they arrived at Douglas's apartment.

Isaac entered the house. "Are you ready?"

George nodded. "Okay, Mr Ward, I need you to walk with your head held high and as if you're scanning around you for danger. I'll walk beside him, and I'll need you and Dr Dixon to walk directly behind us. Once I open the back door, you get inside, then Mr Ward will climb in beside you. Mr Ward, I will need you to keep up appearances during the drive."

"Okay. I can do that."

Eddie didn't seem too sure. "You'll be perfect, Eddie. We'll be right beside you." George hugged him.

"Let's go. On the move," he said into his radio.

They exited the property into the bright morning sun and followed Isaac's directions without issues. George could hear the journalists shouting at them, but they were too far away to be distinguishable. Eddie climbed in beside them and shut the door, blocking out the noise.

"One step down," he murmured.

Timothy clasped hands with George, and he saw him slide his hand beneath Eddie's leg on the seat. He couldn't be seen holding his hand, but at least there was some connection between them. If any pictures came out, it would look like his hand was resting between them. George hoped so, anyway.

They didn't say much on the journey, and George was glad for the underground parking his brother had. The security guard pulled up directly outside the lift. George dialled his brother.

"We're here."

"Okay, I'm ready," Douglas said.

They climbed out of the car, and the moment they

reached the lift, the doors opened. All but Isaac stayed with the cars. George could see the tension in Eddie, and he wished he could take him in his arms, but he needed to wait a few minutes longer. When they arrived in Douglas's apartment, George grabbed hold of Eddie and held him, allowing the man to release the hold he'd had on himself.

"Oh my god! I was so scared I would do something wrong," Eddie said.

"Shh, you did great." Timothy stepped up behind Eddie, encasing him between them both.

George glanced at Isaac. "We either need a different plan for leaving here, or we're going to have to let the papers see what we are."

Isaac inclined his head. "I'll do some thinking. I'll be by the lift outside if you need anything."

"Thank you." George buried his head against Eddie's neck until the tremors subsided, then he pulled back. "Are you okay?"

Eddie nodded. "I am now."

"Ready to meet the family?" George winked.

"Oh, god!" Eddie covered his face with his hands.

George laughed and grabbed one of his hands and one of Timothy's. "No escaping now." He dragged them towards the living room area. Douglas and Mav were sitting on the sofa but stood when they entered.

"Hey." Douglas came over and yanked George into a hug. "I missed you yesterday."

"Sorry. I didn't think past wanting to see these guys. I should've come back to see Father." George stepped back.

Douglas waved his hand. "He's fine. He knew where you were. He said he might come over later for a few minutes, so be warned."

"Warned about what?"

"He wants to make sure you're doing okay."

George smiled and turned to Mav. "Happy birthday, Mav."

Mav sniffed. "Thanks. Sorry about the early wake-up call."

"It's fine." He glanced at Douglas and raised his eyebrows. "Did it arrive?"

Douglas grinned. "It did. Hold on." He disappeared down the hall.

"What's going on?" Mav asked.

George smiled. "Patience, dear brother-in-law. Patience."

Mav coughed. "I'm not your brother-in-law."

"Meh, give it time."

Douglas returned with an envelope and passed it to George, who gave it to Mav. "Happy birthday."

"God, you didn't have to get me anything." Mav was clearly happy, though, because his eyes lit up, and his hand smoothed across the embossed paper.

"Before you open it, let me introduce…" He went to stand beside his two men. "Timothy Dixon and Eddie Ward. This is Douglas and Mav."

Timothy stepped forward and held out his hand. "Nice to meet you, Your Highness."

"Just call me Douglas."

Mav snorted. "You've learnt your lesson, haven't you?"

George frowned. "What lesson?"

Douglas held up his hand. "Storytime can wait. Nice to meet you, too, Eddie."

"You, too, sir."

"Please, call me Douglas. Here, I'm not a prince. I'm not a Dom. I'm just Douglas."

"I'm glad to finally put faces to names," Mav said with a smile. "Come on in. Get comfortable. Grab seats while you can. When the rest of them descend, don't move because someone will steal your seat."

Eddie chuckled, and George silently thanked Mav for easing the atmosphere.

"Now, what lesson?" George asked. They had chosen a love seat opposite where Douglas and Mav were, and Eddie sat between their feet on the floor.

Mav grinned. "Well, when I introduced him to Zara—my best friend, who lives in Edinburgh—he said, '*Douglas is fine*,' as the response to her using his title. She replied with, '*I know he is*,' and since then, he's changed how he answers."

George chuckled. "I wouldn't have thought that would bother you, brother." He was glad to feel relaxed enough to tease, although he expected the tension to return when they addressed the subject of his relationship later on. "Come on, Mav, open it up."

Mav sighed but tore open the envelope. He read it and gasped. "No way."

George smiled. "I hope it's the right one."

"Oh, my god." Mav sat with his hand over his mouth, staring at the paper. "It's perfect."

"What is it?" Eddie whispered to George.

Mav answered, "It's a build your own custom guitar classes, but these are private lessons. This must've cost a fortune, George."

"If it's something you think you'd enjoy, price doesn't matter."

"It's going to be amazing. Thank you so much."

The smile on Mav's face was thanks enough.

"Who wants a drink?"

George grinned. "Well, as I'm not planning to move from this chair for the next," he checked his watch, "several hours,

I think alcohol is in order. A beer for me." He glanced at Timothy.

"Can I have coffee if it's not too much trouble?" he asked.

"Sure. Eddie?"

Eddie frowned, twisting his hands in his lap. "I don't know. Um…a beer, please."

Douglas nodded and disappeared into the kitchen. George leaned forward. "Are you okay?"

"Oh, yes. I'm a little out of my element here. I'm trying to find a happy medium between Timothy's house, where I was completely relaxed, and the club, where I'm usually submissive. It's strange." He chuckled.

"Just be you. Whatever that looks like. No one will mind," George said.

Douglas reappeared and threw something at George. He caught it on instinct and grinned. "Thanks." He unwrapped the packet of love heart sweets and offered one to Timothy and Eddie, neither of which took one. "Your loss." He popped two in his mouth and laid his head against the back of the seat.

Despite the upheavals in his emotions over the past two days, he felt more content than ever. He knew they had several bits of information to go over, which would put a slight dampener on the day, but it needed to be done. George hadn't checked in with anyone for the past few days about where the investigation was, but he assumed his brothers would've told him if anything important had risen.

"So, Timothy, what do you think of the media circus?" Mav asked, grabbing his tablet.

Timothy tensed beside him, and George leaned closer, resting his head on Timothy's shoulder. "You don't need to tell them anything you're uncomfortable telling them," he said.

Timothy cleared his throat. "If it's all the same to you, can we leave it that I know more about it than I want to? Then I'll explain it to everyone when they're here. I don't want to go through my experience more than necessary."

PATRICK

"I'm glad they persuaded Mav to celebrate. I think they all needed something bright to come from what they've been through," Robert said.

They were on their way to Douglas's apartment, and Patrick had been checking around them to see if they were being followed. The bomb had made him edgy and suspicious of everyone, but there was nothing he wouldn't do for his family. He glanced at the front of the car where his security guard, Kieren, sat. Their eyes met and locked in the rearview mirror. Patrick would never admit it, but he felt more secure when Kieren was with him, and when the man gave a small nod and returned his gaze to their surroundings, Patrick's tension eased.

"Patrick?"

He peered at Henry, who had raised eyebrows. "Sorry."

"It's okay. Are you all right?"

"Yes, just a lot of thoughts circling my head. What did you say?"

"I asked if you had remembered the present for Mav."

"I did." He grinned.

"Do you think it's wise to let him open it with so many other people there?" Henry's eyes twinkled, belying his words. He wanted to see Mav's face as much as Patrick did.

"No, I don't, but I'm going to make him do it, anyway." Patrick chuckled. "It's not like most of them don't know about the club and what goes on in there."

"Yeah, but there's knowing about it and *knowing* about it."

The emphasis on the word made Henry's point. "I'll think about it."

"Are you not going to tell me what you got?" Robert asked.

Patrick shook his head. "You're going to have to wait like the rest of them."

It wasn't as risqué as they thought it was. Patrick had thought about whether to get something that would enhance Mav's experience of the club, but at home, but when he found what he'd ultimately ended up with, that idea had been put to the side.

They pulled up next to the lift, and Patrick called Douglas. "We're here."

"All set. Go."

They exited the car and pressed the button for the lift. Usually, they would have to wait for Douglas to walk to the button in his apartment before they could gain entry, which would expose them for longer than was good, but by calling Douglas first, he was ready to open the lift immediately.

When they piled in, he found Kieren had come with them.

"I thought you were staying in the car?" he asked.

Kieren held his hands in front of him, staring at the walls

of the lift. "Prince Douglas asked for another guard in the hallway. I offered."

"Thanks."

Kieren nodded once but said nothing more.

The doors opened into the hallway leading to Douglas's apartment, and they strode down to the door. Henry knocked, and it opened straight away.

"Hey! More people!" Douglas sounded like he'd already been drinking—in a good way—and dragged them all inside. "Thank you, Kieren."

"You're welcome, Your Highness."

Patrick gave the guard one last glance before the door closed behind them. He followed the rest of them to the living room, where everyone else was. It looked like they were the last to arrive. As his gaze focused on each person in turn, he saw some who looked wrecked and others who appeared the same as usual. Mav was a bit of both, and when Patrick approached him, he took the man into his arms and whispered in his ear, "How are you holding up?"

"I'm fine."

"It might not have been your mother, but you spent time with her as much as some of the other people here. You have as much right to feel like crap."

They pulled back.

"I didn't really want this party, but I think *they* needed it," Mav said.

Patrick didn't need to ask who he referred to, and he agreed. "It will be good for them to let loose with those who won't judge them if they lose it. You did a good thing agreeing to this."

"Time will tell." Mav gave a small smile.

"Happy birthday." Patrick handed him the gift. "It's

completely up to you if you open it in full view of others, but be warned, you may not want them to see. That's why I want you to."

Mav's eyes widened, and he gripped the gift tighter to him. "What did you do?"

Patrick chuckled. "You'll thank me later." He winked and twisted around, heading for the kitchen. "What have we got to drink?"

"Pretty much anything you could want," Douglas said after hugging Patrick.

"Beer it is, then." They both grabbed a bottle and clinked it together, eyes locked. "For her."

Douglas's throat bobbed. "For her," he croaked.

29

TIMOTHY

The idea of everyone knowing about his past was not as scary as Timothy once thought. Maybe the old saying that a problem shared is a problem halved was true after all. He'd already told the story to George and Eddie, so maybe telling the rest would make it easier to live with.

He threaded his hands through his hair and inhaled when more of the family arrived. Although George had reassured him there would only be eleven of them, it was unnerving to see so many royal members in one place. Wouldn't it be a security nightmare? Wasn't it a bad idea after what happened to the queen? Surely, this type of meeting would be the best time for someone to kill them all.

"Timothy?"

He blinked and glanced at George. "Sorry, I was miles away." He smiled and stood when he saw some people in front of them.

"Timothy, this is Patrick, Henry and Robert."

Timothy shook hands with the three of them. "Nice to meet you."

"You, too. George has been quite tight-lipped about you," Patrick said with a grin in George's direction.

George backhanded his arm. "Hey! I had my reasons. Anyway, storytime will be here soon. There's plenty to discuss."

Timothy's phone rang, and he excused himself.

"What's going on, Moth? Your name is showing up in the news again, and you didn't call last night like you said you would," Bri said without a greeting.

"Good morning to you, too, Bri."

"Morning. Now, what's going on? Mum's worried."

Timothy sighed. "I've met someone."

"So I see. A prince, Moth. When were you going to tell us?"

He moved to the windows to look out over the town. "It's only just become a…thing, a relationship. I didn't tell you before because I wasn't sure if we were going anywhere."

"And now you do?"

"And now I do." He smiled, though his mind rebelled at the ethics of his situation. "I'm meeting his family now."

Bri squealed in his ear, and he winced. "Seriously? Let me change to video."

"No, Bri—" He sighed when the phone rang with a video call. Glancing over at George, he saw the man's gaze on him. He mouthed, "Sorry," then answered the call, holding the phone in front of his face but making sure the camera pointed to the view outside the window. "Bri…"

"You may as well get all the family meetings out of the way now, Moth."

"Moth?" George appeared beside him and rested his head on Timothy's shoulder.

Timothy sighed. "George, this is my sister, Briony. Moth is what my sisters call me."

George smiled. "Cute."

"Nice to meet you, Your Highness," Bri said, for once serious in her demeanour.

"Call me George."

"Is anyone else with you?" Timothy asked his sister.

Bri nodded. "I'll take the phone to them. Hold on."

"I'm sorry about this," Timothy said.

Eddie appeared. "Everything okay?"

"Yes, but my sister insisted on meeting you and you meeting my family," Timothy said, pulling Eddie in front of him and George so they could all get on screen. He lowered his voice so only George and Eddie could hear. "They don't know about you yet, Eddie, but watch their expressions. This will be hilarious."

"I can go…"

"No. You're part of me now. They can take it or leave it, but I know what their reaction will be. Just wait."

"Mum, Moth's on the phone, and he has news," Bri said.

Timothy watched as she rested the phone on something and his mother and sisters came into view.

"Hey, Mum."

"Sweetheart, are you okay? I've been hearing all sorts of strange things on the news." Her eyes moved, then her eyebrows rose. "I see some of it might be true."

Timothy smiled. "Mum, I'd like you to meet George and Eddie. My boyfriends."

As he'd expected, Bri, Talia and Imogen all screamed and

jumped around while a huge grin crept across his mother's face. George and Eddie laughed.

"Two! You're so selfish, keeping all the good ones to yourself," Talia said. "Can't you send any of them my way? The ones around here are not worth my time."

"I have plenty of family, Talia. I'm sure we can arrange a celebration so you can get to meet them," George said with a wink in Timothy's direction.

Talia screamed again, which Timothy took as acceptance.

"Hey, Moth. Where's the rest of the family?" Bri asked, a twinkle in her eye even through the screen.

Timothy sighed again and glanced at George. "Will they mind?" he asked, indicating the rest of the room.

George shook his head. "Hey, Naughty Nine, plus two—I really need to get a new name—put your pleasant faces on to meet Timothy's family." He grabbed the phone from Timothy and switched the camera, moving to his family to introduce them. Prince Frederick, Prince Christian and Damon had arrived while Timothy had been on the phone.

Timothy held onto Eddie, tucking his head into his neck and closing his eyes.

"Are you okay?" Eddie whispered.

Timothy nodded. "I knew they wouldn't care who I was with. It's just overwhelming, but as I teach everyone else, deep breaths, taking a few seconds to yourself and not letting it get to you is the best way to get through it." He chuckled. "I'm rubbish at taking my own advice."

Eddie turned in his arms and slid his hand around Timothy's neck. "Well, we're here to give you advice now, so you don't need to worry."

Timothy dropped his head, giving Eddie a small kiss.

Eddie wasn't content with that. He threaded his fingers through Timothy's hair and deepened the kiss, opening his mouth for Timothy's tongue. It was only when people whistled that he remembered where they were. Eddie gasped and hid his face in Timothy's neck, and Timothy laughed.

George stepped closer. "I think your mother saw more than she should have. Sorry."

Timothy took the phone from him. "Sorry, Mum. I got carried away."

"If you don't get carried away with those two now and then, you're not worthy of them," she said, punctuating the words with her finger. "You show them every day what they mean to you, especially on the tough days. *Your* tough days, I mean, not theirs. Although on theirs, too." She waved her hand. "What I mean is, life often gets in the way. To remember who you are, you need to remember what you have, and I don't mean physically. I mean love."

George embraced them both. "You're a very wise woman, Mrs Dixon. My mother would've loved to have met you."

"I would've loved to have met her, too. I'm so sorry for your loss. The pain of loss has a way of making everything clearer. The pain never goes away, but the clarity remains if you remember the people you have lost."

"Thank you," George said.

"Right, we're going to leave you to get to know everyone. Oh, while I remember, we're going to visit over Easter, if that's okay with you, Timothy?"

"Can't wait."

"Come on. Let me introduce you to everyone now that they're here. Your family got to meet some of these people before you did." George chuckled. "Okay, people. Let's do this quickly, then we can get down to business. I'm going to go around the room, even if you've already met them. Boys, this is Timothy and Eddie. Guys, this is Patrick, Henry, Robert, Douglas, Mav, Freddie, Damon and Christian."

"I'm sorry our family comes with a media circus," Freddie said, shaking Timothy's and Eddie's hands.

"It's fine. We'll get used to it," Timothy said.

"All right," George said when they sat. "First order of business is—"

"George, do you mind if I go first?" Timothy asked.

The man stared at him, forehead furrowed. "Are you sure?" Timothy nodded. "Okay, first order of business is over to Timothy."

"I have a past that some of you may be aware of if you've done your homework." He smiled when he saw several gazes drop. "I don't mind, but let me explain everything, then I can answer your questions."

He spent the next several minutes telling the story of Orlan and Yanni and why he moved. The funny thing was that while he spoke, he realised he didn't want to escape from the media this time. He wanted to face them. He wanted to shout to the world that George and Eddie were his, and he would do everything in his power to keep them safe, especially if someone was after George. He just hoped they could keep the therapist and client issue out of it.

When he finished answering their questions, George took over, "We can't hide from the media. That would show them we think we're doing something wrong, and we're not. I don't know where to go from here, Freddie. I'm worried about their safety."

Freddie's jaw clenched. "Well, first, we treat them as we

would any member of the family who has had a threat against them. They'll get security. Their families will get security if they need it. Hopefully, this will only be short-term until the 'newness' of the relationship dies down. It won't go away entirely, as you know, but the media will find something else to talk about."

"I'll work behind the scenes as well, trying to keep the media diverted with other royal events and appearances," Mav said, clicking away at his tablet.

"And Aunt Charlotte and Charles?" Henry asked.

Freddie exhaled, fingers tapping on his leg. "We know they're opposed to the LGBTQ+ community, so we need to expect a backlash from their part of the family. In what form that comes, I've no idea."

"They won't back down if they think they can get someone to turn on us," Patrick said, scooting forward on the chair.

Timothy frowned, remembering a voicemail that had been left for him that he'd not listened to yet. He'd pushed it to the back of his mind because it was from a withheld number again. Now, hearing Patrick's and Freddie's words, he wondered if this was someone they needed to trace.

"Hold on a second." He put the phone to his ear and played the voicemail.

"You should've let him go when I first told you to. Now, you're in deep, and there's nothing they won't do to destroy you all. Enjoy your quiet while you can."

A shiver ran down his spine.

"What's wrong?" George asked.

Timothy cleared his throat. "I've been getting phone calls for days now. I'd pushed them to the back of my mind because I thought someone was just being a pain, and then we had plans, and I forgot about them. After hearing you talk, I'm wondering if it's more."

"Who are they?" Freddie asked.

Timothy shrugged. "They've never given a name. They always withhold the number. I've had several missed calls from a withheld number before, but this is the first time they've left a message."

"Let's hear it," Christian said.

Timothy set it going and put it on speaker.

"That's Vincent's voice," Robert said when it finished, sharing a glance with Henry.

"Who's Vincent?" Timothy asked.

"A guy who gave me a bit of trouble not long ago. He wanted me to keep some packages at my shop—drugs undoubtedly. He didn't appreciate it when I said no." Robert grinned. "Until this lot stepped in."

Freddie asked, "How long have you been getting the calls? When did they start?"

Timothy scrolled through his phone log. "Monday was the first call. I've had withheld numbers before from doctors and hospitals and such, but not for a long time."

"Three days after you started visiting me," George said.

"What did he say before?" Christian asked.

"Telling me to stay away from George, basically." He frowned. "Although, there was something…" He tried to recall the last conversation. "He said something about it being in my and their best interest to stay away." His mind scrambled for why that didn't sound right. *Their* best interest. He glanced up. "He knows about Eddie, too. He said, '…my and *their* best interest.' Not *his* best interest. *Their*."

"Shit." Patrick squeezed his hands together, his thumbs duelling an agitated dance.

"Is that a bad thing?" Eddie asked, a tremor in his voice.

"No. It just means we don't have to hide." Timothy frowned and George continued, "Vincent was working with Charles, we believe, though we only have circumstantial evidence. It's a loose connection, but a connection, none-theless. Despite Charles and Aunt Charlotte not wanting gay people around, if they can get others to do their dirty work for them, they will," George said. "They'll probably leak it to the media, and the world will come at us because they will have provoked them."

"Would it be an idea to do what Henry did and pre-empt the release of the news?" Patrick asked, looking towards Freddie.

"I think we need to speak with Father," Freddie said.

They were silent for a moment before George asked, "Did you find anything more about the bomb?"

Freddie leaned his arms on his knees, and Damon rested his hand on Freddie's neck. Timothy noticed Freddie hadn't moved it away and wondered if something was going on between them because of how familiar they were with each other.

"We don't know who did it. No one has come forward saying it was them. No one has any proof of anything. No fingerprints on what was left. The only thing we know for certain is that the driver appears to have been in on it."

"How do you know that?" George asked.

"They found the control in what was left of the driver's footwell."

"Any connections to me?" Freddie shook his head. "Aunt Charlotte? Charles?"

"We've found nothing to link them to Mother's death."

George stood and stormed to the window. "This is bullshit." He whirled around, throwing his hands wide. "No one knew she was going to that event. We'd decided three hours before the car was due to leave. Not that many people would've known in such a short time. There must be something linking it back to me. It doesn't make sense."

Timothy clutched at him. "Shh, it's okay. We'll figure it out." George dropped his forehead to Timothy's shoulder, linking his fingers with Eddie when the man joined them.

"All right, enough," Robert said. "Time for more drinks and celebrations, not acts of treason." He stood. "Douglas, where are your drinks kept? I think we need something stronger to continue this party."

Douglas chuckled. "I'm all for it. Over there." He pointed to a large, ornate dresser, and when Robert opened the doors, he could see it was full of bottles and glasses.

"Perfect. I've never been a bartender, but I can try," Robert said.

Eddie stepped forward. "I'll do it. I was a bartender before I was a barista. I still remember how." His cheeks flushed, and Timothy couldn't help but kiss the rosiness.

Eddie and Robert worked together to get everyone a drink, then they sat silently around the living room as Douglas stood.

"There are two things I want to celebrate today. First is Mother. She was taken from us far too soon, but we all know what she would say. She would tell us to live our lives, to love, to hope, to dream. She would tell us to be happy, and I want to honour that by celebrating Mav's birthday. Although it seems the wrong time, it feels right. If we missed his birthday, she would probably haunt us." Chuckles rounded the room. "So, with that in mind, happy birthday, Mav."

They held up their drinks and repeated his words.

"Thank you," Mav said, sniffing.

"Music!" George shouted, dancing over to the TV.

"Do not let him be in charge of the music!" Freddie shouted.

Douglas grinned. "Don't worry. I have the remote." He pressed a few buttons, and some pop music came on over the speakers.

Timothy jumped when the music surrounded him. It wasn't particularly loud, but it was everywhere. He smiled at George's pout. He'd have to ask why George wasn't allowed to put music on. Leaning down, he pressed a kiss to Eddie's temple.

"How are you doing?"

Eddie dropped his head back on Timothy's knee. "I'm good. Don't let me drink too much, though. I have work tomorrow."

"I won't."

While Eddie moved to rest his cheek on Timothy's thigh, Timothy watched the interactions between the rest of the people in the room. Douglas and Mav were clearly in love, their actions very tactile, and were like an old married couple, even though they'd only been together for about a year from what George had told him. Henry and Robert were similar, although Henry deferred to Robert more, making Timothy think they were in a D/s relationship. Henry also played with Robert's bracelets if they were sitting together.

Patrick smiled and laughed a lot, but it wasn't visible in his eyes. He often watched his brother, but it didn't seem to be jealousy. It was almost as if he was checking he was okay. Protective.

Freddie and Damon were a conundrum. Earlier, he'd thought they might have been in a relationship, but it became apparent they weren't. Damon, however, wasn't hiding what he felt when Freddie wasn't looking at him. The man in question glanced at Timothy, and his eyes widened before dropping to his lap. Seconds later, Damon's gaze met his again, a request for silence in his eyes. Timothy nodded once, and Damon's shoulders relaxed.

Timothy moved his focus to Christian. He was a tough man to read. He sat right beside his cousins, but he appeared miles away. He drank almost mindlessly, without thought, but every time someone asked him a question, he answered without hesitation. It was as if he was caught between two worlds.

Arms came around his neck, and George startled him from his musings.

"Have you figured them all out yet?" George asked.

Timothy chuckled. "Almost," he joked.

"I'm sure they'd love that. Not."

"Psychoanalysis is never fun for those who aren't interested in it," Timothy said. "It always shows something they're not ready to face."

"True." George kissed his neck. "If you play with Eddie's hair much more, he'll be asleep."

"He needs his rest."

"Hmm."

Timothy smiled and turned his head to the side, meeting George's mouth in a soft kiss. "Are you having fun?"

"The best. I have my family and my...other family all together."

Family. Some parts of your family cannot be chosen, but other parts can. It was those that made it all worthwhile. Even when the king of Great Britain arrived.

"Where's my drink?" King Andrew said when he entered.

The men froze, then Freddie stepped forward. "What are you having?"

"Bourbon on the rocks, please."

Freddie moved to get it, but Eddie stood. "I'll do it."

At that moment, Timothy knew Eddie possessed more strength than Timothy could ever hope for.

30

EDDIE

Eddie trembled so hard, he wasn't sure he'd be able to make the drink, but he was determined. He felt the need to prove himself, especially because the king was his boyfriend's father. *Fuck.* His boyfriend's father was the king. Eddie swallowed hard and concentrated on making the drink. When it was ready, he pivoted to where the man sat and stepped forward.

"Your Majesty." Eddie couldn't help the honorific or the lowering of his head. Being a submissive was ingrained, and it felt almost necessary to act this way in front of this man.

"Thank you, Eddie. Please call me Andrew."

Eddie spluttered, eyes wide. "Okay," he squeaked.

George's arms encircled his waist, and he could breathe again. "Father, can I introduce my boyfriend, Eddie."

"I know you from the club, and I know you're a decent man, Eddie. I'm glad you are part of the family."

"Thank you, sir."

"Andrew."

Eddie swallowed again. "Andrew." At least that's what he tried to say.

"Father, this is Timothy."

Eddie watched Andrew's eyes narrow as he stood. "You and I need to have a few words, *Dr Dixon*."

Timothy inclined his head. "Now?"

"I think it would be better to clear the air, would it not?"

"As you wish." Timothy turned to Douglas. "Do you have somewhere I could speak with your father?"

"The study is through there," Douglas said, pointing.

"Thank you." Timothy turned back to the king. "If you would follow me."

"Father—" George started.

Andrew stared at him, and George nodded at him, then transferred his gaze to Timothy, who also nodded. They disappeared.

"What was that about?" Eddie asked.

George stared after them, his expression tense. "If I'd have to guess, it was because Father is worried Timothy used his position against me. It isn't allowed, after all."

"Will he be okay?" Eddie asked, his stomach churning with the need to go after them and stand beside Timothy.

"Father is strict, but he will always listen. If Timothy's words don't convince him, his actions eventually will." George tightened his hold on Eddie and dropped his shoulders, almost forcibly relaxing himself. "Come on. Let's dance."

"Dance?"

Eddie wasn't a big fan of dancing but surrounded by George as he was, he didn't care. They both kept an eye on where Timothy and Andrew would appear when they finished their discussion. Eddie had lost track of how many songs they had danced through when the two men finally appeared. Timothy looked pale, but Andrew had his arm resting on his shoulder, so Eddie took it as a good sign.

"Everything okay?" George asked, reaching for Timothy.

"Everything is fine, George. I wish you all well," Andrew said, pulling George into a hug. "Next time, though, tell me first, rather than letting me hear it from Randall just before the news broke. Randall and Portia had an earful when I found out they knew and hadn't told me."

Timothy winced. "Portia will give me a lashing when I see her next."

"We do have one issue, though. Club Royal won't accept Timothy at the moment because of the media issues he's had in the past. I can and will circumvent it, but it will take time. If you're going to The Den, *please*, be careful and take security." George made a sound beside him, and the king laughed. "Do you not know how many eyes and ears I have around the place?"

Eddie snorted. He couldn't help it. The king had just admitted his PA had kept a secret from him, so he obviously didn't have as much information as he thought. Not that Eddie would voice that opinion.

"We will be careful, but I think we're going to stick closer to home for the time being. The club is more secure for us, especially now."

"Good call." Andrew made Eddie jump when he hugged him, then he moved to George, then Timothy. "Welcome to the family."

After Andrew moved away from them, Eddie raised his eyebrows. "Did that just happen?"

George chuckled. "It did. Now, after we've partied for a little longer, we have a discussion to take part in."

When they arrived back at Timothy's house, the media were still hanging around, although in fewer numbers. They got inside with little trouble.

"George, why do you not talk about what you do during the day?" Eddie asked. It was something he'd noticed but had put it down to him being more interested in their lives than his own. Now, though, Eddie wanted to know as much about George as he could.

George sank onto the sofa. "I'm so used to not telling anyone; it's become second nature."

"Will you tell us?" Timothy asked, sitting beside him.

"I have two jobs. No one knows about either—well, I would've also said no one knew about me visiting The Den, but Father did, so he probably knows about this, too." He chuckled. "One of my jobs is a speechwriter. I started with Mother's speech one day, and she was impressed and coerced Randall to be the contact for more jobs. I've lost count of how many speeches I've written now. I've been doing it for about four years."

"Impressive. I bet it's difficult, too," Timothy said.

"It has its moments."

"What's the other job?" Eddie asked, throwing his legs over George's lap.

A flush tinted George's cheekbones. "I'm a narrator."

Eddie smiled. "Seriously? How awesome is that! What books?"

George fidgeted, which Eddie thought was cute. "Mainly gay romance."

"What made you want to do that?" Timothy asked.

George frowned. "I don't know. I was researching jobs

one day and came across a site where you could find audition pieces. I thought it would be fun to try. I did a few—I'm quite good at accents, I found out—but didn't think I'd hear from anyone. I did it for a bit of fun, that's all. Then an author contacted me, saying they wanted to use me for their book. From there, I got more." He shrugged. "It was something to pass the time."

"It sounds interesting. How long have you been doing that job?" Eddie asked.

"Close to ten years now."

"Ten years!" Eddie said. "That's amazing."

"Thanks. I enjoy it, although it can get tedious sometimes. I don't take on as many as I did in the beginning."

They were quiet for a few moments, and Eddie's thoughts turned to his friends. "I need to speak with my friends about what's happening. I don't want them to find out from the news."

George threaded their fingers together. "How do you think they're going to take it?"

Eddie rolled his lips inwards, trying to hide his smile. "They're going to know you're into BDSM."

George raised his eyebrows and glanced at Timothy before returning his focus to Eddie with a light smile on his face. "Have you been sharing your experiences, Eddie?"

Eddie stared at their joined hands. "A little. Nothing that will point towards Club Royal because they don't know I have a membership there. They just think it's for a general BDSM club. They don't know which one. Plus, after what happened, I needed to talk to someone. Bella helped me the best she could."

George's forehead creased. "I'm sorry you had to go

through that, but I'm glad your friends were there. Speak to them. If you need us to come with you, we will."

Eddie smiled. "I'll catch them tomorrow. If it's okay with you, I'll spend tomorrow evening with them."

Timothy reached across George and caressed his cheek. "You don't have to get permission from us, Eddie. As far as I'm concerned, if you're happy where you are and not held there without your consent, you can go wherever you want to."

"Thank you." Eddie basked in their presence. "I'm going to go home. I have work tomorrow."

"Okay. I'll speak with Isaac and make sure you leave with protection," George said, slipping out from beneath Eddie's legs.

"I'll be—"

"Non-negotiable. At least for now. Please." The expression on George's face showed how worried he was, and Eddie didn't have the heart to let him down, so he nodded. "Thank you." He leaned down and kissed him, then disappeared. Eddie rested his head against the back of the sofa and closed his eyes.

"He wants to keep you safe," Timothy said, moving closer.

"I know. I just feel like it's so much trouble."

"It's not. It will help us both to settle, knowing you're safe."

Eddie's mouth curved. "We've come such a long way in such a short time."

Timothy chuckled, and Eddie opened his eyes to catch the relaxed, open look on his face. Sometimes, he appeared like he held the world on his shoulders, and Eddie hated that, but then he would settle down, and the fun, domineering, caring guy would emerge.

"This is the beginning of our journey. We still have a long way to go before we come out the other side unscathed."

"I know, but we're stronger together than apart. I have to believe that." Eddie leaned his forehead against Timothy's shoulder.

"I believe it."

Eddie hadn't realised how much he needed the reassurance that he wasn't alone in his feelings. Although Timothy hadn't said the words, he could hear them in his voice. Eddie lifted his chin and puckered his lips, receiving a kiss from him.

"Thank you."

George returned. "Isaac said you can try the same routine as earlier. They could hide it as a shift change if you're happy to wait for the next shift to arrive in an hour?"

Eddie tapped his finger on his chin. "Hmm, go home now or wait here with two gorgeous men for another hour. Which should I choose?"

George tickled his sides, making Eddie screech. "No! Stop!" He laughed. "Stop!"

George did, and Eddie found himself lying beneath the man with his head on Timothy's lap. George braced himself over him, staring at him, and for once, Eddie didn't find it uncomfortable. He'd never felt more content than when George and Timothy surrounded him.

"Do you have any nicknames?" he asked, looking at George.

"No. George isn't easy to shorten or change, so no one ever did."

Eddie rolled his head to look at Timothy. "I know your sisters call you Moth, but what about you?"

Timothy stared back, and Eddie watched the pain flicker through his eyes. He didn't expect him to answer. "Orlan used to call me Tim, and my parents called me Timmy when I was a kid. When Dad died, I asked Mum to stop calling me that, and after Orlan…It's easier to keep it to Timothy now."

Eddie reached a hand up and touched his cheek. "Timothy is a good name."

He changed the subject, and they spent the next hour talking and kissing until it was time for him to leave. He didn't want to, but he knew he couldn't stay with them every minute of the day, even though he wished he could.

He spoke to them again before he went to bed, already tucked up but enjoying the sleepy sounds of the two men talking in his ear. He didn't remember saying good night, and he woke up with his phone in the bed with him, so he assumed he fell asleep while they were talking. He messaged George to ask before getting ready for work.

When he arrived, Bella and Mel were already there. Mel gave him the usual high-five greeting, but Bella barely cracked a smile.

"What's wrong?" he asked.

Bella shook her head. "I'm good. Did you have a good weekend?"

He couldn't answer it truthfully yet, but he could pretend with the best of them. "Yeah. I didn't do much. Went to see a friend. Stayed in. What about you?"

She shrugged. "I went to my parents to watch the funeral and help with the decorating. It was so sad." She stared at him.

Eddie's throat closed as he nodded. She didn't know the

half of it. "It was. Are you both free tonight? I thought we could have another marathon."

Mel agreed, and Bella stared at him again for a long moment before nodding. "I'll be there."

Eddie smiled and finished getting his station ready. He couldn't get the idea out of his head that Bella had something to say to him, but she kept quiet about it if there was. The day dragged, except for his lunch break because he could message George. Timothy only joined in when Eddie had to go back to work. The group chat had worked well, and they could each read all the messages the others had sent. It made his afternoon drag because he was eager to know what they were talking about. *If* they were talking once Timothy was back at work.

"Oh, thank god. I thought that day would never end," Mel said. "I'm ready for a nap. I don't know about anyone else." She chuckled.

"I know what you mean, but I'm sure we'll perk up when we get to mine. I think takeaway is in order tonight. What do you think?" Eddie grinned.

"You're on."

They finished cleaning up, then said goodbye to their boss before wandering down the street to Eddie's house. While Bella and Mel let themselves in, Eddie knocked on Terry's door. He felt a little bad for not being in touch with him for a while. Eddie had kind of got sucked into George and Timothy - he snorted at the word - and forgotten about everyone else.

"Hey! We're having a movie marathon again. Are you free?" He held his hands wide, palms up.

Terry grinned. "Always for you. I'll be over in ten minutes."

Eddie waved and entered his house.

"-barely said a word to him all day. What's your problem?" Mel said.

"I don't have a problem, but I think he's keeping secrets from us, and you know how that went last time. I'm worried, Mel."

Bella sounded sad and angry at the same time, and Eddie felt terrible.

"You're right," he said, stepping into the kitchen, making Bella whirl around with a hand to her chest. "I am keeping secrets, but I'm telling you all tonight. Let Terry get here, and I'll explain everything."

Bella nodded slowly, then disappeared into the living room.

"Do we need to worry?"

Eddie turned to Mel. "I don't think so, but you might have another opinion."

Mel sighed and collected some glasses. "Bring the vodka. I think we're going to need it."

By the time all four of them settled in the living room with drinks and *Miss Congeniality* playing in the background, Eddie's nerves were shot.

"Out with it; otherwise, we'll all be too drunk to think clearly," Terry said.

Bella exhaled. "Is it to do with Prince George?"

Eddie, Mel and Terry gasped in unison. How the heck did she know?

"How...?"

The corner of Bella's mouth curled. "I saw the photos of the car leaving that Timothy guy's place with him and Prince George in the back. I thought nothing of the guard climbing in the back with them until he sat next to them instead of opposite or to the side. One photo caught a side shot of him, and I thought I recognised him.”

Eddie dropped his head. “I have a lot to explain.”

“Was it you?” Bella asked.

He glanced at her and nodded.

“What?” Mel shouted. “You know the prince? A prince? One prince?”

“Most of them,” he said.

“You’ve met most of them?” she yelled again.

He nodded. “As I said, a lot to explain.” He inhaled and began at the beginning, trying to keep confidentiality where he could and not giving too much information that they could crucify them in the press. Although he loved and trusted his friends, it wasn’t just his life he held in his hands now.

“I’m in a relationship with George.” He waited until the excited shouts stopped, then added, “And Timothy.” Silence descended.

“Both of them?” Bella narrowed her eyes, her mouth firming. She stood and paced. “Tell me you’re joking, Eddie. Tell me they didn’t push you into this? Oh my god! What did I tell you? Don’t fall for the crap they spew!”

“Bella, calm down. They didn’t force me to do anything I didn’t want to do.”

“Jesus, Eddie. What the hell are you thinking?”

Eddie stood, putting his hands on his hips. “Don’t you dare!” He glared at her. “Don’t you dare talk to me like that! I appreciate everything you did and do for me, but don’t. You have no right. Yes, I made a mistake with Talon, but you messed up with Adam and Jack, oh and what about Marcus?” He pointed a finger at her. “Everyone makes mistakes.”

"He could've killed you!" She burst into tears and dropped to her knees, her hands covering her face.

Eddie held her, rocking back and forth. He shared looks with Mel and Terry, who appeared as shocked as he had been.

"I think I'll order takeaway," Mel said, slipping off the sofa and dragging Terry with her.

"I'm sorry, Eddie. I was so scared for you, and when I couldn't help, I thought I'd lose you." Bella sniffed.

"The only way you'll lose me is if you go to the media about this," Eddie joked.

"Never!"

"I know." He sighed. "I love them, Bella. I'm so glad I found them, and I know they won't hurt me. I can't explain how I know but comparing this to Talon...I can tell the difference."

She gazed at him with wet eyes. "You're in love with a prince."

"And a teacher."

They went silent, then burst out laughing.

31

GEORGE

"What?" George stared at his father.

Andrew nodded, a grim set to his mouth. "The driver and second guard. Both had high amounts of money transferred to their accounts the day of the bombing."

"Isn't that a little…convenient?" Freddie frowned.

Andrew sighed. "Yes. Although they received phone calls on several occasions from a blocked number in the weeks and days running up to it. Everything the police have found points to them."

"I don't know if I believe that," Douglas said.

George's mind worked overtime as he tried to grab an elusive thought. Why did the explanation not sit right?

"One of them had to set the bomb off. The police said the type of bomb used had to be set off in close proximity. Even if they refused initially, one of them—or both—caved. We'll never know who, but the finances make it look like they were both involved." Andrew wiped his mouth and set the napkin to the side of his plate.

"They must've known they were going to die?" Douglas

said. "If they knew it was a car bomb, they would know they wouldn't survive. Is there nothing to show they were preparing for it?"

Andrew sighed. "Not that the police have found. Life insurance amounts were unchanged, and nothing showed up when they interviewed the guard's partners and children." He stared at the table. "I can't hate them for what they did. If they used their family against them, I can understand why they would do it."

"That's no excuse for killing someone!" George said, throwing his napkin onto the table.

His father met his gaze. "Isn't it? If someone said I had to kill someone to stop them from killing one of you, I doubt I'd hesitate. Parents protect their kids, and if it's within their ability, they will do it without hesitation. More so when the children are younger. It's difficult to understand until you're a parent." Andrew gave a small smile.

George dropped his head into his hands.

"Is there no evidence of anyone else's involvement apart from those blocked calls?" Freddie asked.

"Nothing at all. No one's routines or behaviours changed. Nothing. We have investigated everyone," Andrew said.

George's mind went back to the funeral and the moment he locked gazes with Charles, who had been sitting on the opposite side of the chapel. The man looked smug, which wasn't any different from usual, but he also looked pained. It was a contradiction of expressions, which George had found confusing. He explained his thoughts to his family. "What if Charles was in on it, but he hadn't known about us swapping? Apart from the incident when you told Aunt Charlotte to stay away, Charles got on well with Mother, didn't he?"

Andrew nodded. "Yes. Even Charlotte did once they put aside their differences."

"Would that account for the pain in his expression, but also the smug look he sent in my direction? He was sad because Mother died, but he was happy because it hurt me."

"It's not impossible, but we have no proof," Freddie said, leaning back in his chair.

"We have no proof for a lot of things that appear to be their fault." Douglas tilted his head at Freddie.

"True."

"I have people watching them," Andrew said. "I have done ever since I found out what they'd been doing. There doesn't seem to be anything amiss, but that doesn't mean there isn't."

"What happens now?" George asked.

Andrew exhaled. "The police will close the case because, as far as they are concerned, they've found the people involved. The guards' families will return the money that had been 'paid' to them. The families themselves are being investigated, but I don't think they'll find anything. If they don't, they will leave the families alone. If they do, they'll arrest them."

"Are there any links from the families to us?" Freddie asked.

"No. None are members of the club. None have ties to the royal family, except through the guard. Nothing has been flagged."

"So, we have an answer that might not be the answer," George surmised. "Wonderful." He stood. "Please excuse me. I need to...go."

"George." His father's voice stopped him, but he didn't turn back. "I'm sorry I can't give you more."

George exhaled, then pivoted back and strode to his father. He leaned down and hugged him, his father's arms closing around him, too. "You don't need to be sorry, Father. I'm sorry about everything. I wish we could…"

"I know. I know."

George sniffed and pulled away. "Goodnight."

"Night, George," Douglas and Freddie said.

He strode from the dining room, not stopping until he reached his room. It was the second night he'd been without Eddie and the first without Timothy, and he wasn't sure he could handle it. People had surrounded him every day since the day after his mother's death, but he found himself alone and wasn't sure what to do about it.

He paced the living room, then pulled his phone free, dialling.

"Hey, how are you?" Timothy said, and George could hear the smile in his voice.

"I've been better."

"What's wrong?" His tone changed completely.

George sighed. "I can't remember how to be alone at night. I've had someone with me ever since you came that first afternoon, except for one night. Today is only the second time I've had no one with me."

Timothy was silent for a moment. "Do you need Dr Dixon, the therapist, or Timothy, the boyfriend right now?"

George chuckled. "I don't know the answer to that, but you made me smile, nonetheless."

"Grief is hard, George. There are no easy fixes. Having people around you, be it to chase away the quiet and loneliness or to help you remember or forget, is not a bad thing. You need to find a new normal. One just for you. When you have no one with you." He sighed. "What did you do before when no one was around?"

George thought back. "I'd work, or I'd visit the club or The Den."

"Well, visiting the club or The Den is not being alone." He chuckled. "Is there a reason you can't work now? I'm not saying you have to, but if that was what you did before, you could still do it."

"I'm not in the mood for it."

"What are you in the mood for?"

George laughed. "Something I can't have."

Timothy snorted. "Okay. Tell you what, I want you to have a shower and get into some comfortable clothes. Then you're going to ring the kitchen and get some snacks and drinks. While you're waiting for them, you put the TV on and choose three movies. When you have your snacks, sit and watch at least two of the films. Don't think, don't worry, do nothing except watch those films. After the second film, check in with yourself and see how you feel. If you still feel uneasy, call me. If not, watch the third film, then go to bed. Understood."

George exhaled, his shoulders lowering. "Yes, Sir," he whispered.

"Good. And George? Remember something for me."

"Yes?"

"I love you."

Tears filled his eyes, and he bit his lip to stop a sob from escaping. "I love you, too."

"Message me before you go to bed, okay?"

"Yes, Sir." George smiled.

He stared at the phone in his hand as the call ended. There was one thing he needed to do before he did what

Timothy had told him to.

GEORGE: Eddie, I love you. I will say it in person when I next see you, but I didn't want you not to know for a moment longer. x

He nodded once and set about following the instructions Timothy had laid out for him. It was nice to not have to think about anything except what he wanted to eat and drink. As he'd not long had his dinner, he had to think about what he might want in an hour or so because he was still full.

After he'd called the kitchen, his phone beeped.

EDDIE: Oh my god! I love you, too. And Timothy. Thank you for telling me. x

Heart full, he sat in front of the TV and chose *Call Me By Your Name*, *10 Things I Hate About You* and *The Shawshank Redemption*. After the household staff delivered his snacks and drinks, he got comfortable on the sofa and switched play on the first film. To begin with, his mind kept wandering to things, but by the end of the film, he had become invested in it and had forgotten about everything else. He immediately played the second film, working his way through the love heart sweets, popcorn and crisps.

He had a smile on his face when it ended. As Timothy had requested, he checked in and found himself calm and centred, which he hadn't expected. Flicking the blanket from the back of the sofa over his lower body, he fidgeted until he was comfortable again, then played the third film.

His ass was numb by the time the third had finished, but he was happy. Well, as happy as he could be without his men beside him. He climbed into bed when he was ready and checked the message thread for them.

TIMOTHY: Thank you, Eddie. I love you. x

EDDIE: I'm crying. Stop making me cry! I'm supposed to be watching a happy film with Mum, and you're making me cry.

TIMOTHY: Don't blame me. George started it. Tell your mum to switch to a sad film, then you have an excuse.

EDDIE: Ha ha. Too late. Now I have to explain how awesome you guys are.

EDDIE: She says you both have to visit soon. I tried to talk her out of it, but she won't listen. Can you?

TIMOTHY: I'm in. Whenever and wherever you need me to be.
   *EDDIE: Seriously, stop it. *blubbers**

George grinned at the exchange, then added his own.

GEORGE: You're allowed to cry whenever you want to. I've been told it's good for you. Eddie, I'm happy to meet your parents whenever you're ready. I'm going to bed. I love you both xx (one kiss for each of you)

He plugged in his phone and rolled over with a smile on his face.

"Have you had any luck with changing the decision on Timothy's membership?" George asked his father the following day.

"Almost. Give me a few more days."

"Why is it taking so long?"

Andrew sighed over the phone. "They're questioning my decisions because of how recently your mother died. They want to make sure I'm not being coerced into doing it. I can understand why. I have ultimate rule over the club, but I purposefully put this group in place to ensure I couldn't overrule these kinds of decisions without a good reason. I could overrule them, but then there wouldn't be any point of having them there in the first place." He chuckled. "Be patient, dear boy. It won't be long."

"Thank you, Father. Sorry. I am impatient because I want to show Timothy what you've created. The club is great, and I want to share that with him."

"I'm glad."

"How are you?" It was a question he'd only asked his father once since his mother's death, but he had vowed to ask it more often because it wasn't fair that his father shouldered so much when he was grieving himself.

"I'm getting there. Thank you for asking. Randall is fielding a lot of things that I don't need to do right now."

"If Randall needs me to do anything, tell him to find me. I'd be happy to do it."

"Thank you, George. Now, go and see your men."

George chuckled. "Yes, Father."

He climbed into his car and left Windsor Castle, knowing he had photographers following him but uncaring. He'd either lose them, or he wouldn't. Eddie and Timothy were meeting him at Eddie's parents' house for dinner. Although he was a little nervous, he was also excited because it had been four days since he'd seen his boyfriends in person. Eddie and Timothy had been working hard all week, and George had some royal duties he needed to attend to. Tonight, though, after dinner, they were going to Timothy's house to spend the weekend together. George couldn't wait.

He pulled up outside the house after trying to lose as many media followers as he could. Eddie opened the door the moment he stepped close, and George slipped inside before Eddie closed the photographers outside.

"Hi," Eddie said with a smile.

George grinned. "Hi." He leaned forward and kissed Eddie, raking his fingers through his hair as he deepened the kiss. When he pulled back, they were breathing hard. "I missed you."

"Missed you, too."

"Is Timothy already here?"

Eddie shook his head. "Not yet. He's probably got caught up at work."

George tilted his head and took in every inch of Eddie's face. "God, I love you," he said with a sigh.

Eddie beamed. "I love you." He kissed George. "Are you ready to meet Mum and Dad?"

"Let's do it."

Eddie threaded their fingers together and tugged George towards the kitchen. "Mum, Dad, this is George. George, this is Parker and Rose."

"Nice to meet you, Mr and Mrs Ward." George held his hand out to Parker first.

"The same to you, young man," Rose said. "Please don't bother with the formalities. Parker and Rose are fine with us."

"Thank you, and thank you for having me for dinner. I can't wait to get to know Eddie's parents."

"We have plenty of baby pictures to go through after dinner," Rose said.

Eddie clapped his hands to his face. "No! That's not happening, Mum."

Rose chuckled. "I love getting him worked up. The baby pictures are for the third visit, Eddie. You know that." She winked at George, and he laughed.

Eddie backhanded his shoulder. "You're supposed to be on my side."

George slid his arm around his waist. "I am, sweetheart. Always." He kissed his cheek.

"Is Timothy running late?" Parker asked, fetching glasses from the cupboard and placing them on the dining table.

Eddie frowned and pulled out his phone. "There's nothing on the chat. I'll message him and make sure he's not forgotten."

"He won't have forgotten, Eddie. This is important to him. As you said, he's probably caught up at work."

George's phone vibrated, and he checked it, but it was only Eddie's message in the group chat. He replaced it in his pocket. "Is there anything I can do to help?"

Rose waved her hand. "No, thank you. Have a seat and tell us about you."

Eddie pulled him to the table, never letting go of his hand. George thought Eddie was more nervous than he was, so George began telling his parents about him and what he did. They asked questions, and he answered them as best as he could.

"Has Timothy replied?" Rose asked.

Eddie frowned, checking his phone as he had been doing every few minutes. "No."

George pulled out his phone and dialled. Timothy's number went to voicemail. "He's not answering."

"Maybe he's driving or in the shower or something. We'll give him a little longer," Parker said with a reassuring smile.

George, however, wasn't reassured. This was unlike Timothy. Visions of car accidents filled his mind, and he breathed through his nose to slow his heart rate. Eddie squeezed his hand, and George tried to send him a smile. He lost track of the conversation and tried calling him again. Voicemail again.

"Excuse me a moment, please."

He left the table and ducked into the hallway, dialling. "Freddie, Timothy's not here. He should've been here over an hour ago. He's not answering his phone. Should I be concerned?"

"From what you've told me and what I've seen, that's unusual for him. What do you think might have happened?"

"I don't know. I keep envisioning a car accident, Freddie. No one would know to let us know about it. I don't know what to do."

"Where was he?"

"He's been working, so at the college."

"I'll send someone over there to check, and I'll send someone to his house. I'll call you back the instant we know."

George swallowed hard. "Okay, thanks."

He paced in the small space, dialling Timothy every few minutes.

"George?" Eddie appeared. "Is everything okay?"

"I don't know, sweetheart. Freddie's sending someone to

the college and his house to check if he's there. I'm probably overreacting. We don't need to worry, I'm sure."

He hadn't convinced Eddie any more than he'd convinced himself. He folded his arms around Eddie, holding him as close as he could. The phone ringing made him jump.

"Hello?"

"We've found him," Freddie said. "He's at the hospital."

"What! Why?" His heart pounded.

"He got attacked at the college."

"Who the hell…" He inhaled. "Okay, we'll be there in a few minutes." He hung up. "Eddie, apologise to your parents, but we have to go."

Eddie raced down the hallway, then returned with his parents in tow.

"Let me drive you. You're in no condition," Parker said, putting on his coat.

George opened his mouth to argue, but the sight of Eddie holding his arms across his stomach reminded him he had someone else to think about, not just himself. "Thank you." He grabbed Eddie's hands and squeezed. "He'll be fine."

And George would find whoever was responsible and return the favour if it was the last thing he did. No one hurt those around him. No one.

32

TIMOTHY

Timothy's head pounded more than when he'd experienced a hangover in the past, and the back of his head stung. Other than that and feeling a bit dazed, he felt fine. Even the bruises he undoubtedly had on his face didn't hurt, but that could be the pain relief the doctors had given him when he arrived at A&E.

The doctor had told him they had contacted his mother, who was on her way with his sisters. His mother was his next of kin, so that made sense, but he hated to worry her. He'd not heard from Eddie or George, but he knew they'd been calling him. They must have been out of their mind with worry.

There had been an impromptu staff meeting at work when his last class had finished, and he'd left the college over an hour later than planned. He scrambled to get to his car and throw all his bags in, ready for the weekend, when someone had grabbed him and spun him around, slamming him back against his car. The man—he assumed it was a man from his voice, but he wore a balaclava over his head, so he couldn't see his face—had got in his face and given him a message, then punched him. Timothy had hit his head on the open car door on the way down.

He must've lost consciousness because the next thing he knew, he had light shining into his eyes, making him feel sick. The paramedics had said he was lucky someone had been walking across the car park and had seen him on the ground.

"Oh my god."

A soft whisper had him blinking open his eyes, and the sight of Eddie and George in the doorway had the tension melting out of him. He held out his hand, shaky as it was, and they stepped closer, Eddie gripping his hand.

"How are you feeling?" George asked, resting a hand on his leg.

"Like I've drunk too many drinks." Timothy's eyes closed, and he smiled. "Glad you're here. Mum will be here soon." He frowned. "How did you find me?"

"Freddie found out what happened to you. We came immediately after he told us," George said.

Eddie's hand rested against his shoulder. "Sleep, sweetheart. We'll be here when you wake up."

Timothy tried to stay awake, but his eyelids were too heavy. He floated off with the feel of his boyfriends' hands on him.

Several hours later, the police had taken his statement, and the doctor had discharged him into his mother's care. He'd wanted to go with George and Eddie, but George had said they would be there, too; therefore, he didn't need to worry about the technicalities of his discharge paperwork.

He was ready to leave when a nurse came into the room.

"Um, I think it might be better if you left from a different exit," she said, wringing her hands together. "There are photographers out there."

George dropped his head back and exhaled to the ceiling. "Probably a good idea. Are you able to check which exit has the least number of photographers?"

The nurse nodded. "I'll contact the security staff." She hurried off, and George turned to him.

"I'm sorry. I forget about them. I'm usually surprised when there's not one tailing me."

"You have nothing to be sorry for," his mother said, squeezing George's arm. "My boy is happy. A few pictures don't matter."

His mother had bustled in with his sisters behind her, taking over the room. She hadn't batted an eyelid that George and Eddie were there. She just hugged them and set about making sure they had everything they needed. He was glad they'd had the chance to "meet" on the phone before this happened because it made things easier.

When the nurse came back, she told them which exit was the best to use, and they strode through the corridors with a couple of security guards that Freddie had sent. He'd played dumb when the police had asked what the attacker had said to him. He'd told them the guy had asked for money, but Timothy hadn't had his wallet on him, so he had nothing to give him. He'd caught George's eye when he'd fibbed, and George's eyes had hardened. Timothy knew he'd have to explain the truth when he got comfortable at home. He wasn't looking forward to it because he knew George would blame himself.

Eddie's dad, Parker, had offered to drive them to Timothy's house, and Freddie was arranging for Timothy's car to be brought to him. George and Timothy climbed into the back seat, and Eddie sat beside his father but twisted around to face them once he fastened his seatbelt. His mother and sisters would meet them at the house.

He rested his head against George's shoulder on the journey home, and the man gently woke him as they rolled up to the gates. Photographers swarmed across the front of his property. He had given the security guards in the car in front of them the code, and two of them climbed out before the gates opened. Timothy realised they were going to keep photographers from getting onto the property.

As the gates opened, the cars drove through, his mother's car pulling up behind them as they entered. Timothy yawned. Exhausted didn't come close to how he felt.

George helped him out of the car, into the house and onto the sofa after an argument about Timothy going to bed. Timothy needed to explain what had truly happened before he slept because he knew George would have to speak with Freddie and whoever needed to be involved.

"Would you like a drink or something to eat?" Eddie said.

Timothy shook his head and winced. "No. Come here." He spread his right arm, and Eddie sank into him, tears instantly soaking into Timothy's T-shirt as Eddie pressed his face into him. He opened his other arm, and George sat beside him, reaching across to cup Eddie's face.

"Sorry. I was so scared," Eddie said.

"I know, sweetheart, but I'm here. I'm fine." Timothy

pressed a kiss to his head, repeating the action on George's head.

"What really happened?" George asked.

"Yes, Timothy. Tell the truth," his mother said, eyes narrowing. "I know you weren't being completely honest with the police officers."

Timothy huffed. "One of the few people I can't fool with my body language." His smile dropped. "You're right, Mum. I wasn't completely honest because I wasn't sure if George needed to keep it quiet or not, and I hadn't had the opportunity to discuss it with him beforehand."

"Do you know who it was?" George looked up at him.

"Not exactly. Everything I told the police was true except for the man's words. He didn't want money. He said, '*Will it be as easy to get to the others as it was to you, I wonder?*' Then he hit me, and my head hit the open car door as I fell."

George had tensed at the words of his attacker. He pushed away and grabbed his phone. "I have to make a call." He strode from the room.

Timothy hoped the call would be to his brother instead of to who they believed was responsible for the trouble.

"Will he be okay?" Parker asked, staring after George.

"He will be." George would need Timothy's reassurance that he wasn't to blame. It would take a while before the words would sink in for the prince.

"We've made some sandwiches for now," Talia said, entering the room. "We've covered them over in the kitchen. You can help yourself when you're hungry."

"Thanks." He glanced at his mother. "I'm sorry. The rooms aren't quite ready for you. The covers and duvets still need to be taken out of the boxes."

His mother waved him away. "Don't worry about it. We'll

sort it between the four of us. You just take care of yourself and your two men. They need a reminder that you're alive." She winked.

Timothy groaned and tucked his head against Eddie's, who giggled against him.

"I could do with a nap, to be honest." Timothy's head was still pounding, which the doctor had assured him could continue for several days, including nausea and dizzy spells. He wouldn't be at work for a while, probably not until after Easter now, and couldn't drive until the symptoms stopped.

"Come on. I'll take you upstairs. You can shower the hospital from you and get some sleep." Eddie rose and crossed the room to his father. "Thank you, Dad. I appreciate it." He banded his arms around him.

"You're welcome. I'll head home because no doubt your mother is worried sick, even though I told her everything was fine. Make sure you call her later just so she can hear your voice."

"Okay."

Parker stepped towards Timothy. "I'm glad you're doing better. We'll rearrange dinner for when you're feeling up to it."

Timothy rose unsteadily, Parker helping him keep his balance. "Thank you, Parker. I appreciate you looking after them for me." He glanced at Eddie. "Eddie, can you find George so he can say goodbye? I know he'll want to."

"Sure." Eddie disappeared.

Timothy faced Parker again. "I love him." He locked gazes with the man. "I will do everything in my power to make sure he stays safe. You have my word."

Parker nodded once. "I'm sure he and George will do the

same for you." He turned to the door when Eddie returned with George in tow.

George held out his hand. "Thank you for helping. I can't thank you enough."

"You're welcome. I'm going to head home, but let me know if there's anything you need. Although I think you're sorted with these four fine women helping."

Timothy chuckled as he glanced at his mother, who preened under the words. "They will mother us like no tomorrow."

Parker laughed and left the room, George and Eddie following him. Timothy sighed and rubbed his head.

"Is this your life now?" Bri asked, sliding a hand around his waist.

He wouldn't tell her how much he needed the physical support at that moment. "Pretty much. Security, photographs, intrusive articles. Nothing I haven't been through before."

"But you moved away to stop it," Imogen said, coming into view.

Timothy nodded, unable to deny the words. "I love them. They're worth it."

"How is he holding up?" his mother asked quietly.

Timothy didn't have to guess who she was talking about. "He's good at hiding the pain from other people, but he lets it out when it's just the three of us, which is good. It'll take time. As you know." He gave a small smile.

His phone rang, and he winced when the sound pierced his head. He checked the screen and saw Derek's name. "Hey, Derek."

"Hi. I heard what happened. Are you okay?"

"How did you hear?" Timothy frowned.

Derek snorted. "It's all over the news already. *Prince George's new flame in hospital.* It all seems to be speculation at the moment, but I wanted to check on you."

"I have a concussion and a few bruises, but I'm good. If it's all right with you, can I call you tomorrow? I'm just about to have a nap. These old bones of mine aren't up to scratch nowadays." He chuckled.

A laugh came down the line. "You and me both. Sure. Leave a message if I don't answer, and I'll reply when I can."

"Thanks, Derek."

George and Eddie entered the room. "Everything okay?" George asked.

Timothy nodded. "Derek was checking that I was okay. I'm going to call him tomorrow."

"I sent Parker home with security. The media will undoubtedly follow him home and find out all they can about the occupants of the house. I want them protected." George shoved his hands in his pockets.

"Good idea." Timothy yawned. "Time for me to go to bed." He turned to his family, hugging each one in turn. "Night. Let me know if you need anything."

The three men climbed the stairs, one on either side of Timothy, which he was glad for because his steps were slow and heavy. They entered the bedroom, then the en-suite and closed the door. George and Eddie undressed him and themselves, and they climbed under the preheated spray. The warmth eased some of Timothy's aches and reduced his tension. He hadn't realised how tight he'd kept his body until the heat hit him.

Eddie and George cleaned him and washed his hair before stepping out and drying him with a soft towel. They didn't bother with clothes and slid between the cold covers, wrapping their limbs over, under, between and around each other.

"Who did you call earlier?" he murmured, sleep already invading.

George exhaled against Timothy's chest. "Freddie. He's going to speak to Father about it all and see if there's anything we can do about Charles and Aunt Charlotte. I believe they were behind the bomb, too. If we could only find some evidence, some proof that they were involved in bomb, we could do something about them, but they're too bloody good at hiding."

Timothy stroked against his hair. "From what you've told me about them, they've had many years of practice."

"Too many."

He tried to say something else, but his eyes were heavy.

"Shh, sleep."

When he woke, his mouth felt like a desert, his face hurt like he'd been fighting with the heavyweight champion, and his head had several chainsaws hacking away at his brain. He didn't want to move, but he groaned.

"Here, roll to your side and swallow this."

Timothy tried. He truly did, but every movement sent spikes of agony through his head. The bed dipped, and Eddie helped to move him. Timothy squeezed his eyes shut and breathed through his nose.

"The quicker you take these, the quicker the pain will ease. You can sleep again afterwards."

Timothy cracked one eyelid, wincing at the light, but tried for a smile when he saw Eddie's strained expression. "Bottom's up," he joked and threw the paracetamol into his mouth and swallowed some water. He stayed as still as he could for several minutes, not wanting to take the chance that the tablets would reappear if he moved too quickly.

"I would ask you how you are, but I can tell you feel like crap," Eddie whispered.

"I do, but I know it will pass. Are you okay?"

"I'm fine. Your mother made us breakfast, and George headed back to Windsor to speak with his father and brothers."

Timothy's mouth curled. "You still can't call him Andrew, can you?"

"Shut up." Eddie chuckled. "No, I can't. One day, maybe."

"How is he?"

Eddie didn't pretend to not know what Timothy was asking. "He's upset. He's pissed. He's sad."

All things Timothy had expected.

"Eddie! Come here! Quick!" Bri shouted.

Despite the fact it hurt, Timothy climbed out of bed and pulled on some joggers, following in Eddie's wake. When he made it downstairs, he found them in the living room, glued to the TV screen. Timothy sat beside Eddie.

"—is everything. Family is one of the most important things in our world. That family doesn't have to be blood, but whoever is in that family itself needs to have trust, loyalty and honesty. It also needs to be understanding and willing to learn. I stand before you as your king, as a father, as a widower, as a brother, as an uncle, as a servant of this country, and I ask you to be more understanding. Be more willing to learn new things. Be honest. Be loyal. Be trustworthy." Andrew inhaled and glanced at his sons, who stood strong behind him. "I shouldn't have to expose my family's choices to the world, but I am doing this with their permission, so we can start building a village, a town, a city, a country or even a world where differences are celebrated, not lamented."

Andrew stared out into the crowd that had gathered around an entrance to Windsor Castle. "One of my sons is heterosexual and single. One of my sons is gay and in a committed relationship. One of my sons is bisexual and in a relationship with two men." The crowd's murmurs rose. "I, myself, am bisexual." The noise rose, then fell when he continued talking. "Something my late wife knew and held dear to her. She once told me she couldn't believe I had chosen her over the entire eligible population. She didn't lament the differences that made us. She made us realise those differences make us unique. It is in her honour that I make it known that we are not weak because we are different. We are not weak because of who we love. We are not weak because we believe in something different than you. No one can ever be weak when they stand up for who they are. Anyone who wants to stand up, we stand here with you."

Andrew stepped back from the podium, and the crowd went wild. Timothy stared at the screen, mouth wide.

"Wow," Eddie said. "That certainly shows the world where they stand."

Timothy had never felt so free. The words the king had said had not been meant for him as such. He had undoubtedly meant them as a warning to those in the royal family who were against them, but to know they had the backing of the king in such a public way was undeniably uplifting. He couldn't wait to see George because he knew he had to be behind the speech writing, but the performance was solely the king.

"Those men are fucking amazing," Bri said.

Timothy couldn't disagree.

3 3

CHRISTIAN

Christian stared at the screen as his uncle told anyone who wanted to listen that his family would stand beside those who needed them to. He wished it were that simple for him. He couldn't stand up with them like he wanted to.

"Christian!"

He'd long ago learnt to hide his reactions. It was the only way to survive in this household. No matter what happened to him, he'd shown nothing because he knew his parents hated it. Hated that he could hide from them.

"Yes, Father?"

He strode to the doorway. John Sutcliffe stormed towards him, his face mottled and tense, and Christian braced himself. His father stopped millimetres from him, getting right in his face.

"Did you see what my stupid idiot of a brother has done? Visit with your cousins. Find out what caused this outrageous speech. I want to know everything."

"Yes, Father."

John narrowed his eyes at him. "And don't go disappearing again; otherwise, I'll contact your commanding officer and tell him exactly what kind of lowlife you truly are."

Christian stayed silent, focusing on a spot just below John's eyes. He refused to give the man the decency to look at him directly—another thing that annoyed his father. The seconds dragged out as John stared at him, but Christian didn't move a muscle. John exhaled and stepped back, pivoting and marching back the way he'd come.

"Twenty-four hours, Christian."

Christian didn't relax until he heard his father's office door slam shut, then he sighed. Another day in paradise. He snorted at his thought. He wasn't worried about his commanding officer. The man knew what Christian dealt with, which was why he had such a lenient working schedule, not that his father knew that.

He was grateful for the excuse to leave and did so quickly and quietly. He'd sleep at Windsor tonight to give him a breather from his family. Lottie wasn't too bad, but Arthur, Elizabeth and Diana followed too closely in their parents' footsteps. Christian pretended to do the same, but secretly, he didn't.

Whenever John—and he was John to him, not his father—wanted him to do something, Christian would twist the truth and make it seem like the "leading Sutcliffes," as John called them, were not as bright or careful as they actually were. It was the only way he could give his cousins the head start in what was fast becoming a war between siblings.

Since he found out his father had been involved with Aunt Charlotte's plans, everything had begun to make sense. He watched the interactions, listened at doorways and rifled through paperwork whenever he could get his hands on it. It wasn't enough. Aunt Louisa had lost her life, and Christian had found no evidence to point to anyone in the family.

His parents, Aunt Charlotte, Uncle Ernest and Uncle Arthur were working behind the scenes to rid the country of what they thought was a poisonous family, and Christian could do nothing to stop them.

Climbing into his car, he drove as fast as he dared to Windsor. He would help them in their fight to keep the crown. Even if it killed him.

John and Miranda, his mother, had no idea Christian was bisexual, and they wouldn't until Christian was ready for them to. He'd been very careful. He knew what would happen, and he needed to finish his job before that time came.

As he pulled up to Windsor, the guard waved him through, and he parked in his usual spot. Staring at the cloudy sky, he inhaled and exhaled, letting the tension seep out of his body. When he felt more human, he got out, grabbed his bag and strode for the doors. He wasn't sure who he should go to first. George would probably be with his new boyfriends and Douglas with Mav at his apartment. He'd try Freddie first.

Knocking on his cousin's door, he waited. It opened without warning, but Christian didn't flinch.

"Christian. Nice to see you. Come on in," Freddie said. As expected, Damon was perched on the sofa. "Everything okay?"

Christian nodded. "I saw your father's speech."

Freddie grinned. "I've never seen Father move so fast."

Christian dropped onto the opposite sofa from Damon. "What happened?"

"Timothy got attacked at the college when he was heading back to his car. They took him to hospital, and he's not long been home."

"Fuck. Is he okay?" Christian sat forward.

"Just concussion, but he blacked out."

"Is that why Uncle Andrew spoke out?"

Freddie nodded. "He was so angry. I've never seen him like that, not even when Mother died. He probably had been angry but hid it from us all. Behind closed doors and all that."

Christian knew what that was like. "I'm glad Timothy's doing better."

"Me, too. What brought you here, anyway?"

"I wanted to find out what I'd missed in my absence." Christian smiled.

"Well, I'm sure you'll see some fireworks if you look out of the window. George went to Timothy's to find out their reaction from the speech."

Christian raised his eyebrows. "He didn't tell them beforehand?"

Freddie exhaled. "He didn't have time."

"Uh oh."

They chuckled, and Christian wondered how understanding George's men would be.

34

EDDIE

When George had returned to Timothy's house, he had a sheepish smile on his face and an apology on his lips.

"I should've spoken to you first, but everything happened so fast. I've never seen Father so furious," he said.

Eddie curled himself into George's chest, hoping to convey a sense of relief for him. "It's fine by me. The public would've eventually found out who I was if they haven't already."

"And you know I'm fine with it." Timothy kissed George's temple.

"For the time being, Father has arranged for you both to have security whenever you're not at one of our houses. I need you to be safe." George tightened his grip.

"Is there one here now? I have to get to work soon," Eddie said.

George checked his watch. "Aren't you supposed to be there now?"

Eddie smiled. "Boss gave me the morning off when I

explained what had happened. I have to be there for twelve, which doesn't give us long. It'll give me the chance to speak with Bella and Mel, too."

"Oh, while I remember, invite your friends to a party next Saturday. We're arranging for all the friends of the group to attend a get-to-know-you party at Windsor. It'll be fun."

Eddie scrunched up his face. "If you're sure you want my brand of weirdos to join with yours, then by all means." He laughed when George narrowed his eyes at him.

George turned to Timothy. "How are you feeling this morning?"

Timothy nodded, then winced. "Assuming I don't move my head, I'm fine." He grinned. "I'm feeling better. It's just the occasional dizziness and nausea that's annoying. The headache I can deal with."

"Well, they said it should go soon. At least you have a few days to rest before you go back to work."

Timothy smiled. "I doubt I'll be back before the end of the term. I'm sure the students would be happy to be without me until the summer term. I actually make them work."

They laughed. Eddie left a little while later, along with a security guard called Sam. He went home first to shower and get changed, then headed for the cafe. He felt like he'd had more time off than he'd been there lately. Whistles and shouts greeted him when he entered, and he quickly got them up to speed on what had happened in between serving the customers.

"It's busy today," Bella said. "More so than usual on a Saturday."

"I wonder if it's because of the king's speech. Have they figured out about you?" Mel asked, studying Eddie.

Eddie surveyed the room, noticing a few people averting their gazes. His cheeks heated. "Possibly."

He checked Sam was still sitting at the small table nearby with a coffee and a tablet. As if sensing his perusal, Sam lifted his head and raised his eyebrows. Eddie gave a small smile and went back to his station.

The afternoon confirmed Mel's thought. It got busier and busier until people could hardly move, and there was a queue outside. Sam had called in reinforcements, and two men were working as bouncers at the entrance, letting in a certain number of customers at a time. Most of them asked Eddie to sign their cups, but after a glance at Sam, who shook his head, he didn't. He tried to be polite when answering their questions but ignored those that were too personal.

His boss had said he could leave if he wanted to, but Eddie had refused to stop doing something he enjoyed because other people were curious about him. It wouldn't change the outcome. If he went home now, they would come back another day, and the same thing would happen. If he stayed and stuck it out, soon he would become old news.

When they finally finished for the day, after having the bouncers stop people from entering, he dropped into the seat opposite Sam and groaned. "Is it always like this?"

Sam grinned. "In the beginning. You're new. You're like a shiny new toy for them to play with. Once they see you're just a regular guy, they'll back off."

"You sound so certain."

Sam shrugged. "That's been my experience, anyway."

"Oi, Eddie! Get back to work, slacker!" Mel shouted.

Eddie moaned and stood, his feet protesting as usual. They cleaned up the shop and stocked it for the next day. Before they left, Eddie told them about George's invitation.

"Hell, yes!" Mel said. "Tell me when and where, and I'll be there." She raised her hands above her head and swayed her hips as she sang the words to a beat only she could hear.

Bella snorted. "I'll be there."

"I'll let you know the details." Eddie nodded at Sam, and they left the building, heading straight for the car Sam used to drive them.

Eddie climbed into the passenger seat and sighed, leaning his head against the back of the seat. "That was crazy."

"Welcome to the world of the royals."

Eddie rolled his head to the side and glared at Sam, who chuckled and drove out of the car park into the traffic. It was nice to be able to relax after work and let someone else drive, but after a few minutes, he realised something was wrong.

"What's happening?"

Sam smiled across at him. "Nothing to worry about. I'm driving around a bit to hopefully lose some of the media following us. It won't get rid of them all, especially if they already have your address, but it will help a little. Don't worry. I won't let anything happen to you."

"I know. It's just weird."

Sam chuckled.

Eddie pulled out his phone and checked his messages. He'd called his mum before starting work and reassured her that Timothy was okay. She'd asked him to talk to George and Timothy and arrange for them all to go over for dinner. It seemed their social calendar was filling up.

EDDIE: Well, that was an interesting day. I've never had a request for my autograph before. I'm on my way xx

Within seconds, a reply came.

GEORGE: Are you okay? Nothing happened, did it?

EDDIE: I'm fine. Just tired. I'm safe. I'll explain my popularity when I get there xx

GEORGE: Good. See you soon xx

Eddie smiled and tucked his phone back in his pocket. They had decided to stay at Timothy's house until they could secure Eddie's house better. Naturally, Windsor would be the most secure, but it was also the busiest. Timothy's place was quieter and had good security, although even that was being increased now that the property held a prince occasionally.

Journalists were still sitting outside the gates, and they scrambled for their cameras when the car pulled up. Sam reached out of the window and pressed the button to call inside. They had agreed that they wouldn't use the code to get inside unless there was no one in the house, and once the code was used, they changed it. That way, if any of the photographers caught the code, they couldn't use it. The nitty-gritty details made Eddie's head swim, so he followed instructions without thinking too hard about the reasons for it. That way led to madness.

He climbed out of the car when Sam stopped and thanked the guard. Sam was his personal guard when he was at work, so it meant the man now had time off until Monday morning. He entered the property and was engulfed in arms the moment the door closed. Laughing, he held tightly and allowed himself to be manoeuvred into the living room.

"I'm happy to see you, too."

George took his mouth in a hard kiss, tasting of the sweets he loved. If George hadn't been meticulous about his dental care, Eddie would've been more worried about his sweets intake. After several long moments, George pulled back, and Timothy took over, but with a gentler claiming. He tasted of coffee. Eddie relaxed into them, allowing them to reaffirm he was there with them again.

This was what he'd always wanted. Someone to care for him as if he was precious, as if he was missed, loved. He'd walk through fire for these two men. A few pictures and questions didn't hurt anyone.

"He was about eight years old when he insisted he wanted to play the trumpet," his mother said, smiling. "He couldn't be dissuaded. So, we hired a trumpet and paid for lessons."

His father continued the story. "After four lessons, he told us he didn't want to do it anymore. We weren't surprised, but it was his reasoning that threw us."

Eddie covered his face. "I can't help it that I can't do the thing you need to with your mouth to be able to blow into the trumpet. It's impossible."

They all laughed, but Timothy came to his defence. "It's true. It's difficult. I gave up the trumpet to do piano lessons, but that didn't last long either."

"Did you play any instruments, George?" Eddie asked.

George spread his hands. "I don't have any musical ability, except that I'm not too bad at dancing. Not professionally or anything, but I can bust a move with the best of them." He chuckled. "No, Patrick got all the musical ability in the family. He can play a lot of instruments but keeps up with piano, flute, violin and clarinet."

"Wow, that's amazing," Eddie's mother said.

"It truly is, and he sounds great," George said.

"Does he do it professionally, like concerts and things?" Timothy asked.

"No, just for himself and family. It's a waste, I think, but he doesn't want to."

"Fair enough. I'd love to hear him one day. I love live music," Timothy said.

They continued talking music for a while, and Eddie listened as warmth flowed through him. He'd always hoped for this but had never believed he'd get it. Now, the only thing that would make this even better would be for Timothy to be accepted at the club. They refused to visit The Den while everything was still new, and although the response to Eddie's identity had subsided a little, there were still many people turning up to the cafe every day. In the four days since someone had leaked his information, he had become used to it, and he never thought that would happen. Was it because it seemed a little thing compared to what he had gained?

George's phone rang, and he excused himself to answer it. A shiver went down Eddie's spine, and he waited uneasily until George returned.

"Is everything okay?" he asked when George took his seat.

"That was Freddie. The police have finished their investigations into the bombing. Their official decision is that the two security guards were responsible, and they will announce it tomorrow."

"You don't think they did it?" Parker asked.

George shared a glance with Timothy and Eddie before sighing. "No, we don't believe it was them. We think they were set up to take the fall."

"For whom?" His father's forehead creased, and he rested his elbows on the table.

Eddie could see the indecision on George's face, and he didn't think he would answer.

"Some other members of the royal family."

Eddie's mother gasped. "What? Why would they do that?"

"To cut a very long-winded story short, there are several members of the family who do not appreciate the LGBTQ+ community and are fairly vocal about it. There have been incidents spanning many years that point towards them, but no proof has ever been found. We only have circumstantial evidence and several witnesses who could easily be... persuaded otherwise."

"My word! I can't believe it. Is that why you were so worried about being with Eddie?" Rose stared at George.

"Yes. I'm sorry for bringing your son into this."

"Don't be sorry," Eddie said, reaching across to squeeze his hand. "I don't regret a minute."

"Thank you. I don't know where my head would be at if it weren't for you both. I know it would've taken me a lot longer to drag myself from out of the hole I'd dug after Mother's death." George threaded his hands with Eddie's and Timothy's.

"I'm glad we could help." Timothy lifted George's hand and kissed the back of it. "You're worth it."

"What about Timothy's attacker?" Parker asked.

George clenched his fists. "No one has been found. The CCTV didn't catch his face or where he went after Timothy was knocked out. It's a dead end."

"But you know who was responsible." It wasn't a question.

"Yes. Not the person who actually did it, but the person behind it is my cousin, Charles. He's always been a thorn in our sides, even as kids, and he never grew out of it. He's always been vocal about his opinions."

"But you can't prove it."

"No. We only have a voicemail message and the information Timothy provided. It's not enough to do anything except piss Charles off, which we could do without." George sighed, then smiled. "Anyway, let's talk about something happier. We need your help."

Rose tilted her head. "What with?"

"Finding a new name for our little group."

Timothy and Eddie groaned and received a shoulder shove from George. "Hey! You've not been helpful with this. It can't be that hard to find a name that can go with the word 'eleven.'"

"It's not as easy as you seem to think it is," Eddie said. It was true. He'd been thinking about it for days and couldn't find anything suitable.

"Okay, so what are we looking for?" Parker asked.

"Well, when it was just me, my brothers and my cousins, I called us the 'Scandalous Six,' then when some partners joined us, I changed us to 'The Naughty Nine.' Now, though, we're at eleven, and I'm struggling to find something that goes with it."

"Hmm. Extreme. Edgy. Excessive. Exhilarating. Electrifying. Outrageous." His dad was a puzzle whizz and loved all kinds of word riddles.

George almost jumped out of his seat. "Outrageous! Although it's not an alliteration, it still works. The Outrageous Eleven. That does it."

"Or you could just call yourselves the Scandalous Six plus," his mother joked.

They laughed.

"Who would like dessert? It's apple pie and custard."

"Yes, please," he and George said in unison. They glanced at Timothy, who appeared divided.

"Oh, go on, then. You twisted my arm. I'd love some, thank you."

Overall, they spent about four hours with Eddie's parents, and it was fantastic. He still couldn't believe he had this, but he would hold on to it for as long as possible.

Their security guards were there when they exited the house and drove them back to Timothy's house. Eddie had hardly been back to his own home, but Terry had been keeping an eye on it for him. They were dividing their time between Timothy's house and George's…castle. Eddie chuckled, drawing the attention of his two men.

"What are you laughing at?" George asked.

Eddie grinned. "Just thinking about how you have a castle whereas we have houses."

George rolled his eyes. "I think of it as home rather than a castle."

"But it *is* a castle. It's in the name, after all. Mr Sutcliffe, where do you live? Oh, I live in Windsor Castle."

George tickled Eddie's side, which he took advantage of every time Eddie was a bit of a brat. When Eddie could get his breath, he soaked in the atmosphere of being happy. After everything that had happened with Talon, he hadn't believed he could find this. Talon had been clever enough to lower Eddie's expectations of a relationship and change what he believed he was worth. George and Timothy had helped build him back up again, as had his friends. He was one of the luckiest men on the planet.

"Is everything ready for the party?" Eddie asked, curling into George's body and threading his fingers into Timothy's.

"Yes, except for the music. I was going to ask Patrick if he wanted to serenade us for a bit but then thought it wouldn't be fair for him to 'work' when the rest of us were mingling. So, I need to decide what we're having."

"Maybe Patrick and Mav would do a few bits, then we could get a playlist together for the rest of the evening. A party isn't the same without dancing. We need dance music."

Timothy groaned. "Dance music? I'm hoping you mean something we can dance to and not the mind-numbing bass noise that most clubs have."

Eddie and George glanced at each other and burst out laughing. Timothy rolled his eyes and stared out of the window, but Eddie saw a slight curve to his lips. He couldn't resist and brought Timothy's face to his, kissing him until they were both panting. Then he did the same for George until a voice broke into the bubble.

"Sorry, sirs, but we're about to turn onto the road. I thought I should warn you."

They chuckled. "Thank you, Isaac," George said. "Paused until we're behind closed doors."

"Probably for the best, sir."

Eddie rested his head on George's shoulder and closed his eyes, soaking in the bliss as they laid in bed later that evening. If this was what his life would be like, he could be happy. In fact, he could be more than happy.

35

GEORGE

George stared at his father, a grin spreading across his face. "He's in?"

Andrew smiled. "Yes, Timothy can now visit Club Royal. You'll need to do the usual forms and NDA, but they won't decline him."

He threw his arms around his father. "Thank you!"

"You're welcome. Now, go. Have fun." Andrew turned him around and pushed him towards the door.

"Are you trying to get rid of me?" George pouted.

"Yes."

George gasped. "And I thought you were my father. I'm going off to cry now." He sniffed in jest, then grinned. "Have a good evening, Father."

"You, too. Tell the boys I said to behave."

"Which boys?"

Andrew sighed. "All of them."

George laughed as he exited his father's room and jogged down the corridors towards his own. He couldn't wait to tell Eddie and Timothy. Hopefully, neither of them had anything planned for that night because he didn't want to waste any more time. He wanted to show Timothy what the club offered. He rounded a corner and bumped into Douglas.

"Where's the fire?" he asked, steadying George with his hands on his shoulders.

"Father got Timothy accepted at the club. I need to tell them." He rushed past his brother and continued on his way.

"Let us know when you're going, and we'll be there!" Douglas called after him.

"Will do!"

When he was behind closed doors, he pulled out his phone and opened the chat.

GEORGE: Are you busy tonight? Timothy, they have accepted you at the club. I thought we could check it out if neither of you has plans xx

He knew neither of them would be able to answer straight away because, after checking the time, neither would be on a break. He paced around the room, tapping his phone against his other hand. He hadn't seen them for two days, and impatient as he knew he was, he needed to get some work done to distract himself; therefore, he strode to his desk and fired up his laptop. He had two speeches that needed finishing, though one had plenty of time before the deadline. Opening the first, he reminded himself of the details, then started working.

The distraction worked because his phone made him jump when it beeped with a notification. He saved the work, then picked up his phone.

EDDIE: I'm in. I have no plans but plenty of ideas

GEORGE: Hopefully, Doc will have time

EDDIE: This is going to be great

GEORGE: The rest of them want to come with us, too. I said I'd tell them when we were going. Moral support and all

EDDIE: Good idea. It can be unnerving the first time you set foot in there

George hoped Timothy wouldn't be too overwhelmed because he wanted their first visit to be perfect. He had a good idea of how to ease him into knowing what each of them could take, especially with everything that had happened to Eddie. As they all knew, Eddie needed to stay safe and content, and he wanted to make sure he wouldn't feel obliged to do anything he didn't want to.

TIMOTHY: I'm free. Is there a dress code?

GEORGE: No. All the club asks is that you don't wear club gear outside of the club itself. They insist you get changed at the club. Fewer people are likely to find out

EDDIE: Plus, it gets you into the right frame of mind

TIMOTHY: Well, I don't have any club gear, so will black jeans and a black shirt work?

GEORGE: Perfect

EDDIE: You'll look edible

GEORGE: *He always does*

EDDIE: *All right. More edible*

TIMOTHY: *Stop it, you're making me blush*

GEORGE: *You're not texting during class, are you?*

TIMOTHY: *No*

TIMOTHY: *Maybe*

TIMOTHY: *Yes, but don't tell anyone*

GEORGE: *You rule breaker!*

EDDIE: *Dr Dixon, what kind of example do you set?*

TIMOTHY: *Shut up. What time do you want me to be wherever it is you want me to be?*

GEORGE: *Eddie, I'll pick you up, then we'll pick you up, Doc. Around eight o'clock? Is that enough time for you both after work?*

EDDIE: *I'll be ready xx*

TIMOTHY: *Perfect for me xx*

GEORGE: *It's a date xx*

George's cheeks hurt from smiling so much, and he put his phone aside. He had several hours before he had to even consider getting ready, so he refocused on his speeches after he'd set his alarm. He also messaged his brothers and cousins to let them know they were going to the club that night. If everyone could make it, it would be fantastic.

By the time he'd picked up Eddie, George was vibrating with excitement. Club Royal had a few issues when it came to some members he wished weren't members, but the actual club itself was a dream. He couldn't wait to share it with Timothy.

The entire Outrageous Eleven would be in attendance, which was great news because they had hardly seen Christian lately. With the man's Army position and his father's requests, Christian hadn't been able to visit like he used to. It would be good to see him again.

They pulled up outside the gates of Timothy's house, several photographers still present, but not as many as before. He hoped they wouldn't follow the car when they left. George knew the driver would go the long way before heading to the club. It wouldn't be ideal to lead them straight there.

Once they'd parked outside the front door, Timothy exited and locked up before climbing into the back seat with them. He kissed them both chastely. Although George wanted more, he decided to be patient until they got to the club, but then all bets were off.

"Anything I need to know before we get there?" Timothy asked.

"I think I've told you everything. When we get there,

you'll have to sign an NDA and set up your fingerprints for the system, then we'll be ready to explore." George said.

Timothy nodded. "I'm going to be shocked, aren't I?"

Eddie chuckled. "I suppose it depends on how much BDSM you've seen in porn."

George snorted, putting his hand over Eddie's mouth. Timothy shook his head, a small smile gracing his lips. George loved it when he teased the man. As he stared at them, he couldn't believe how lucky he'd been when they'd come into his life.

When they entered the club, Clarice greeted them and handed the NDA to Timothy. While he read, Eddie and George whispered between themselves.

"I was thinking we could use the spanking bench," Eddie said.

George frowned. "Are you sure? We've not tried that yet."

"What better time to try and for you to teach Timothy what I can and can't take?"

It was a good idea. Timothy needed to know the difference between the two of them and how much each of them could take. George didn't mind a lick of pain, but Eddie didn't like a lot. It would give Timothy the confidence to try other things as well, he hoped.

"Okay. We'll take it into one of the private rooms, though. I don't think any of us are ready for the entire club to watch us."

Eddie shivered. "Not yet."

George rubbed his arm. "Don't worry. We'll never do what you don't want to do. You know that. We all need to be ready for something before we try it."

"I know." Eddie smiled. "It's sometimes difficult to separate the past from the present, but only when you don't have hold of me." He smiled. "The way you hold me is completely different. I can feel the difference between you."

George pecked Eddie's temple. "That's because we care. We love you," he whispered in his ear, making him shiver again, but he knew this was a good shiver.

"I think we're done, Your Highness," Clarice said.

George glanced at the receptionist with a smile. "Thank you, Clarice. Have you added them both to my locker?"

"Yes, sir. I've given them full access."

"Thank you. Have a good evening."

"You, too, Your Highnesses."

George didn't bother to correct her and turned Eddie towards the doors of the changing rooms when he saw his mouth open, undoubtedly to tell her they weren't royalty. Soon, they would realise that Clarice could see a lot deeper than most people could. She knew how he felt and gave them the respect she—and he—thought they deserved.

He led the way to the Monitors' changing room, explaining that this was where the royal family changed to reduce the risk of protection problems. Someone could gain entry to this room, but it was less likely when it was heavily monitored by cameras.

George and Eddie changed into their clubwear, but Timothy stayed the same, although he removed his jacket. He watched Timothy's eyes widen when Eddie stripped everything off and slid on his leather shorts. It was as good a time as any to give Eddie the gift they'd purchased for him. He caught Timothy's eye and nodded, receiving one in return.

"Eddie, we have something for you."

Eddie glanced up from where he was putting his soft shoes on, raising his eyebrows. "What?"

"Come here." George sat on the bench in the middle of

the room, Timothy sitting behind him but from the other side. He patted the bench in front of him, and Eddie sat, a crease in between his eyes.

"We wanted to get you something to show how much we care about you. To show you belong to us, but only if you want to," Timothy said, reaching to hold one of Eddie's hands.

Eddie's eyes were already filling with tears when George brought the box from behind his back. The black velvet box was about the size of a side plate and held something so precious—not in monetary value, but emotional value.

"We love you, Eddie."

George opened the lid, and Eddie gasped. They hadn't wanted something overtly BDSM related because they wanted Eddie to wear it day and night if he wanted to, so they had gone with a slim circle of metal, and instead of having a circle at the front, three letters were hanging from it —E, G and T—entwined together. It wasn't big and flashy, but they hoped it would make Eddie feel more secure and loved even when they weren't together.

Eddie reached out and skimmed his hand over the collar, tears tracking down his cheeks. "It's gorgeous."

George explained their reasoning behind its designs. "But if you want something more visible for the club, we can get you another one as well."

"No! I want this one. Always. I'm never taking it off."

George grinned. "Let's get it on then."

George and Timothy stood, and they fastened it around his neck, both pressing a kiss to Eddie's shoulder when it was secured. Eddie stood and faced the mirror, his fingers caressing the collar with a smile on his face.

"Thank you." Eddie spun around, throwing his arms

around them both. When he pulled back. "What about you?" he asked George.

George frowned. "What about me?"

"Don't you want a collar like me?" Eddie bit his lip.

George's heart pounded. He'd always loved the idea of having a collar around his neck, but he hadn't considered he'd ever have one. "I'm all right."

Timothy cleared his throat. "Well, actually…" He reached into the bag he'd brought with him, pulling out another velvet box but slightly smaller. "I wasn't sure if you wanted one, but I had one made, anyway. Don't feel pressured to wear it if you don't want to. I won't be offended. I just didn't want you to feel left out if you truly wanted one."

George stared at Timothy, flicking his gaze to Eddie to see if he was in on it, but Eddie had tears in his eyes again and a hand over his mouth, making it unlikely he knew about it. He refocused on Timothy. "Really?"

Timothy smiled, though it wasn't as sure as it normally was. "Yeah. If you don't like it, we can change it."

George took the box and opened it with shaky hands. Nestled inside was a chain with two hoops at the bottom, and hanging from it were their initials, just like on Eddie's. A lump sat in George's throat, and he couldn't say anything in response.

"Do you like it?" Timothy whispered. George nodded, unable to reply otherwise. "Do you want me to put it on?" He nodded again.

Timothy took the box and removed the chain, undoing one circle at the base and draping it around George's neck before refastening it. The letters settled beneath his neck, just above his sternum and perfectly placed for his leather waistcoat.

"I didn't want it too visible for you in case you needed to hide it for royal events. This way, you can put a shirt over it, and you can barely see it."

George gripped hold of the base and stared at the floor. "Thank you." His voice was hoarse. "Thank you for seeing me. For knowing me. For taking me as I am."

Timothy stepped closer and stole his arms around him. "We see you as you are. As you should be. We love you."

Tears ran down his face, and he burrowed his face into Timothy's neck, reaching his hand for Eddie's, who squeezed his when they threaded together. He sniffed and pulled back. "Wow. This has been way more emotional than I expected." He smiled. "Thank you."

"You're welcome. Always."

"Shall we find the others?" George asked.

"But what about Timothy?" Eddie said.

George tilted his head. "What do you mean?"

"Timothy gets nothing. He's given us both something but hasn't got anything for himself."

"But Dominants rarely wear anything," George said.

"I know, but it feels wrong to not have something for him."

"I have something," Timothy said, reaching up to unbutton his shirt.

As more skin showed, George swallowed. Timothy pulled his shirt to one side, revealing his left side. Over his heart were the same initials as on Eddie's and George's collars but tattooed on Timothy's skin.

"Oh my god," Eddie said, more tears escaping. George knew how he felt.

"When did you get that done?"

"Two days ago, just after I left you. Portia knows someone, and he was able to fit me in. I wanted it to be a surprise the next time we were together."

"It truly is a surprise, but I love it," Eddie said.

"I do, too."

The idea had sunk in, and he knew he would get the same tattoo as soon as possible. He met Eddie's gaze, his mouth curling, and he knew he had the same idea. Portia's friend would have two more customers once they could arrange it.

"Does it hurt?" Eddie asked.

"No. I should be able to take the cover off tomorrow."

George rubbed a hand over his face. "Right, let's get going. We have a lot to fill the guys in on."

They entered the main club and over to the bar, ordering drinks from Oliver. The rest of the group were settled on the numerous chairs and shouted greetings when they saw them. After settling into a loveseat with Eddie sitting on Timothy's lap with his legs over George's, he stared at Freddie, who winked at him. He couldn't explain how content he felt. It was something he'd never experienced even before his mother died. There had always been something missing. Now, he understood what it had been. Timothy and Eddie.

"Are we ready to induct the newbie?" Douglas said, his eyebrows waggling.

Everyone laughed.

"Might as well get it over with," Timothy said.

They rose and ambled towards the doors.

"Welcome to Club Royal," Freddie said, opening both doors with a flourish.

George watched Timothy's expression as they entered. His eyebrows rose, and his mouth curved. George took everything in and tried to see it through fresh eyes and ears. The sounds of meeting flesh, moans and screams of ecstasy met him, and his gaze took in the visuals of sex, discipline and pleasure. For someone who hadn't experienced it before, it could be overwhelming, but for him, it was a part of him. He was proud of what the club had accomplished.

He leaned closer to Timothy. "Let's do a quick tour, and then we can visit our room for the evening."

Timothy nodded, and George led the way through the people, him and Eddie pointing out different aspects of the club. As they went, they lost more and more of their group until the last people, Henry and Robert, disappeared into the pet play area. Once they'd looked their fill, George led them over to the private rooms on the opposite side of the club, then unlocked the door and held it for them to enter.

"Welcome to our home for the night." He grinned.

He'd purposefully asked Clarice for a room that wasn't the one Eddie had been in when he'd been abused. He hadn't wanted that hanging over them. Each room had the same equipment, anyway, so he wasn't worried they would miss out on something. The spanking bench was to the side, and he asked Timothy to help him slide it into the middle of the room, giving them enough space to move around it.

"Eddie." George crooked a finger at him, and he stepped forward, his cheeks colouring the closer he came. He held Eddie's chin and kissed him. "What are your safe words?"

"Red for stop, yellow for pause and green for keep going."

George nodded. "Shorts off, over the bench."

"Yes, Sir."

He glanced at Timothy as Eddie disrobed and leaned his stomach on the bench, gasping when his skin met the probably cool leather.

"Help me tie him," George said.

Timothy met his gaze and nodded. They worked together

to fasten the straps around Eddie's wrists and ankles. When they finished, Eddie had almost melted into the leather, his eyes closed, a peaceful expression on his face.

George smiled and stepped behind him. "Now, Eddie doesn't like extreme pain, but he likes a little bite of it. I thought I would show you what he liked, and then you could take over? What do you think?"

Timothy nodded. "Good idea. I don't want to hurt him. Either of you."

3 6

TIMOTHY

Never had truer words been spoken. Timothy didn't want to hurt anyone.

"Everyone has different levels they could withstand. I can take more than he can, but that's why we have safe words. If you're ever unsure if he can take it or not, ask him for his colour. Eddie, colour?" George said.

Eddie sighed. "Green, Sir."

George chuckled. "No falling asleep on us." He rested his hands on Eddie's lower back and massaged the area. "I'm getting him accustomed to my touch." He rubbed lower until he was caressing the globes of his ass. "I'm warming his skin a little, getting the circulation going."

Timothy moved so he could see Eddie's face and what George was doing. Eddie's eyes were closed, his mouth ajar, and his body relaxed. He glanced at George, who nodded and smacked his hand down on Eddie's skin. The slap was loud in the quiet room but not as loud as Eddie's moan. Eddie jerked, and a crease formed between his eyebrows. He focused on George again, whose hand met Eddie's skin once more, then rubbed over it.

"Timothy, come here," George said. Swallowing the lump in his throat, he stepped beside him. "You won't hurt him."

Timothy positioned himself as George had been while George moved to the other side. He skimmed his hands over the reddening cheeks, and Eddie squirmed. Bringing his hand back, he snapped it forward, connecting with Eddie's ass. His hand smarted, so he knew Eddie's backside would, too. He caressed the globes, and Eddie groaned and writhed, though he couldn't go anywhere.

"Colour?"

"Green, Sir," Eddie sighed.

He spanked Eddie over and over, asking his colour after every couple of smacks.

"Yellow, Sir," Eddie said.

Timothy stopped, racing to where Eddie's head rested. "Are you okay? Did I hurt you?" He shook his head at his words. "Of course, I hurt you, but you know what I mean."

"You didn't hurt me, Sir. I've just reached my threshold." Eddie fluttered open his eyes and smiled at him. "It's perfect."

"Let's unfasten him and cuddle up on the bed. After, you can try it on me," George said with a wink.

They worked together to get Eddie free, and Timothy carried Eddie over to the bed, noticing his straining cock, and laid him face down, settling beside him. George joined them with cream and some drinks and fruit.

"Aftercare is very important. As I've mentioned before, Eddie can be emotional, but don't let that worry you. It's just how his body reacts to the endorphins flowing around him. He needs hydrating with a sweet drink, given food if he wants it, and when he's been spanked, he needs some cream applied to the area," George explained.

Timothy took the cream, applying it to Eddie's ass as directed by George while George held the straw to Eddie's mouth and played with his hair. It truly felt like they were a team and all involved in the care of each other. He probably stroked Eddie's ass for longer than he needed to because Eddie began thrusting against the covers. He hadn't come after all, but an idea was taking root in Timothy's head.

"Keep still, Eddie. I have plans for that cock of yours." He met George's eyes and grinned. "When you're ready, it's George's turn."

Eddie perked up at that, and after inhaling several pieces of fruit and draining his drink, he rolled to his side, exposing his flushed shaft. "I'm ready."

Timothy chuckled and studied the room. "I think we should try something different this time. George, do you have an ankle spreader bar?"

George's eyes widened, then he nodded and headed over to the cupboard in the corner of the room. He brought out a bar around two feet in length with restraints at each end. Timothy nodded and checked out the restraints on the bed. He might need George's help to figure it out, but he would try to do it himself first, so it could be a bit of a surprise for the prince.

"Come here." George complied. "Eddie, help George strip."

George's throat bobbed, and he rested the spreader bar on the bed, his hands going to the buttons on his waist-coat, and Eddie joined him, focusing on his trousers. George's gaze never left Timothy's, and he saw when George's pupils dilated. He rested his hip against the bed, crossing his arms and enjoyed the sight of his two men undressing.

When George was naked, Timothy pushed off from his perch and crooked a finger at him. George stepped closer until they were chest to chest, their breaths mingling.

"Take off my shirt."

With excruciating slowness, George unbuttoned his shirt and threw it aside, being careful of his healing tattoo. Timothy dropped a kiss on his lips once he was done, then spun so that George had his back to the bed. Holding George's hips, he turned him to face the bed.

"Pass me the spreader bar," Timothy whispered in his ear, causing George to shiver. "Eddie, sit on the bed facing George and kiss him."

The bar was cool to the touch, and he kissed a path down George's back until he was on his knees. He placed the bar between George's feet, nudging them further apart, then strapped and secured the restraints around his ankles. Skimming his hands up George's legs when he'd finished, Timothy reached his hips and tightened his hold.

"Colour?"

"Green, Sir." George exhaled.

"To your knees." George dropped. "Rest your upper body on the bed, hands near your hips." The thrill that went through him at the sight of George doing exactly what he'd asked was something he hadn't expected, and his cock hardened. "I'm going to strap your wrists to the bed."

"Yes, Sir."

"Eddie, relax him with your hands while I work."

"Yes, Sir."

Timothy reached for the first chain and cuff, sliding it around George's wrist and securing it. He repeated the action on the other side, then took a moment to look at his men, both naked and waiting for him. Eddie's hand speared through George's hair while his other hand rubbed at his shoulders.

"George, colour?"

"Green, Sir." He had his eyes closed, his head resting on the bed. The rest of his body was splayed out for Timothy.

Timothy leaned forward, cupping Eddie's face and taking his mouth as his body pressed against George's ass and back. He then lowered his head to George's, taking what they both wanted. When he pulled away, he dragged his fingertips down George's back, remembering what he said about getting him used to being touched. He knelt behind George, kneading his ass cheeks and pressing kisses to his spine. Moving to the side, he got ready to deal the first smack.

"Colour?"

"Oh, god. Green, Sir." George sounded like he was already enjoying what was happening.

Timothy smiled and tapped at each of George's cheeks, warming the skin. George squirmed beneath him, and Timothy brought his hand down slightly harder several times in succession. After, he soothed the skin with his hand.

"Colour?"

"Green, Sir." George cleared his throat. "You can go harder with me, remember, Sir."

Timothy grazed his bottom lip, then pushed aside his worries, trusting that George would tell him if it was too much. He pulled his hand back and increased the force of his smacks, checking in several times. When George's ass was like a red beacon, and Timothy's hand tingled, he stopped.

"Eddie, we need lube and condoms, please."

Eddie scrambled to get the items, and Timothy pressed

his groin against George's sensitive ass, receiving a moan in return. He rained kisses down George's spine, then smiled at Eddie when he returned with the supplies.

"Sit back where you were. I have something for you in a minute." He kissed him, and Eddie melted into him.

He wasn't sure if Eddie would enjoy it, but he trusted them both to tell him if it was too much. Refocusing on George, he squirted some lube onto his fingers and massaged George's pucker. After the initial gasp—probably from the coolness of the gel and Timothy not having told him to expect it—George began pressing backwards for more. Timothy pressed past the muscles with one finger, spearing inside and stretching him. He leaned to the side to see George's face, pleased when a blissful expression met him. He used two, then three fingers to stretch him.

"Please, Sir! Oh, god, please!" The chain connected to George's wrists rattled.

Timothy twisted and curled his fingers, finding the spot he'd aimed for if George's reaction was anything to go by. He stimulated George's prostate for a few seconds before pulling out. Unfastening his trousers, Timothy hissed when his cock sprang free. He made quick work of rolling on a condom and slicking it with lube, then rested against George's hole.

Everything seemed to freeze. Breathing, heartbeat, blinking. Everything. Then George breathed, "Please," and Timothy pressed forward with a steady thrust until he sank balls deep. He gripped George's hips and closed his eyes, revelling in the feel of the warm, tight glove around his cock. He didn't move other than to breathe and, licking his lips, fixed his gaze on Eddie.

"Put your legs on either side of George's head and line up

your cock with his mouth. I want George to make you come with us."

Eddie swallowed hard but followed Timothy's instructions. He knew the moment George sucked at Eddie because George's body clenched along with Eddie's moan. Timothy withdrew slowly, then pushed in at the same slow rate. He couldn't see exactly what was happening, but he could imagine. He picked up speed, slamming into George, and heard him gag on Eddie's cock.

"Sorry!"

"George, colour?"

George pulled off Eddie. "Green, Sir!" He slid the cock back into his mouth.

"He's fine, Eddie. Keep going." Timothy set a punishing pace. "Hold his head, Eddie. Move him where and how you want him. Make yourself feel good."

George groaned and bucked against Timothy, and he smacked his ass in response.

"Fuck! Sir, I'm so close," Eddie gasped.

"Grip his head, Eddie. Fuck his mouth. He wants it. Give it to him." Timothy could barely get the words out with how close he was himself. He reached beneath George, encasing his cock and finding it dripping. He circled the head and rotated his wrist to rub against the nerves beneath his cock. George groaned and writhed. "That's it. Give to us, George. Come for us, Eddie. Now!"

Eddie dropped his head back and groaned to the ceiling, his fingers gripped in George's hair as he bucked forward, causing George to gag again. George didn't seem to care because he came all over Timothy's hand, his ass clenching around Timothy's cock, sending him right over the edge with them. The sounds of the three of them coming was music to

Timothy's ears and something he hoped they could repeatedly do.

George kept sucking Eddie, and Timothy kept stroking and fucking George until they were all too sensitive. Timothy let go of George and dropped his forehead to his back, sweat mingling. Eddie's hand came to rest on Timothy's head, and he lifted a hand to cover it, their fingers linking.

George groaned beneath them, and Timothy lifted off. "Colour?" he whispered.

"Luminescent green, Sir." He sighed. "Fuck, that was amazing."

Timothy smiled and withdrew with a wince. "Eddie, can you unfasten his wrists? I'll do his ankles."

They worked to get him free, then Timothy lifted George to his feet, catching him when his knees wouldn't lock, then swung him into his arms and deposited him on the bed next to Eddie.

"Snuggle up, you two. I'll grab the stuff we need."

He took off his trousers, got a warm, wet cloth and the same aftercare essentials George had fetched earlier, and knelt on the bed beside them. They looked so content with their arms clasped around each other and legs entwined. George's ass was as red as a traffic light, and Timothy grabbed the cloth first.

"Let's clean you up, then I can put cream on."

He suited actions to words and cleaned them both before rubbing cream into George's ass. Then he washed his hands and tucked himself behind George. He held two cartons of orange juice, which he held in one hand as he had done the other week. The straws pointed in opposite directions so Eddie and George could each reach one. They gulped it, and

Timothy put them aside, wrapping his arms around them as best he could.

"Thank you," George said, turning his head to see Timothy.

"For what?"

"Seeing what I need when I rarely see it myself."

Timothy tightened his hold and kissed George's cheek. "You're welcome."

They stayed tangled up for a long time, knowing no one would disturb them. When they finally roused, they dressed and set the room to rights, then exited into the club. The music was the first thing Timothy noticed. It wasn't the usual bass-thumping noise he usually linked to clubs. It still had bass to it, but it was softer, more musical than noise.

"Do you want to have another look around or meet up with the others?" George asked.

"Unless you want to go around again, I'm happy to sit with everyone and relax," Timothy said. "It's not like we can't come back another day."

George grinned. "True. I have to work tomorrow night as well."

George had explained to him what his job was at the club while they'd been resting in the room earlier. Initially, it had seemed harsh that George had to be something he wasn't—at least before he realised he was vers—but it was what it was, and things were changing for the better.

They met Douglas, Mav, Patrick, Robert, Damon and Christian in the conversation area, and George fetched them some drinks.

"What do you think of the club?" Douglas asked, his arm resting around Mav's shoulders. Mav had his eyes closed and a slight smile on his face.

"It's interesting. Has lots of nice gadgets to use."

Douglas smirked. "There's a lot more where that came from, I'm sure."

Timothy chuckled. "I'm happy to start slow." He tugged Eddie closer to him, kissing his temple. "Are you okay?" he whispered.

"Never better." Eddie sank into Timothy's arms.

Timothy felt the tension rise even before any words were spoken.

"Well, you don't seem to be the grieving types, do you?"

Timothy glanced over his shoulder and stared at Charles. He knew who it was because he'd seen a photo of him at the funeral. Even if Timothy wasn't an expert at body language, the hatred radiating off the man would be enough to know he wasn't a pleasant person.

"Mother would not want us unhappy, and you know it, Charles," Freddie stated, standing.

"Hmm." His gaze swept the group. "I see something is catching. Maybe I should warn people from getting too close." His mouth pursed.

"Maybe you should take your own advice," Timothy said, tightening his grip on Eddie when he felt the man trembling.

"No need. I know what I am."

"So do we, Charles. Have a good evening." Freddie crossed his arms over his chest, pointedly waiting for the hateful man to leave.

Charles's cheeks reddened, and his eyes narrowed. "Careful."

Damon and Douglas stood, and Charles took a step back before pivoting and entering the club. The group gave a collective sigh, and the three standing men settled in again.

"Are you enjoying teaching, Timothy?" Robert asked,

playing with his necklace. Despite his partner not being with him, he looked completely relaxed, though that telltale fiddling gave away his uneasiness at the previous conversation.

"I am. The students are doing well, and they seem to want to be there, which is half the battle when teaching." George returned with the drinks and settled beside him.

"I can imagine. I remember the struggle for some of the teachers I had when they couldn't control the classes, but that was in secondary school when the kids had no choice to be there or not. It was much different in college," Damon said.

Timothy nodded. "Definitely. Some of the immaturity is gone, too, which is good."

"Really?" Damon raised his eyebrows. "I'd expect them to be as immature as ever at that age."

"Well, the boys need a little reminder, but the girls are good."

"Usually the case." Damon grinned. "Girls are more mature than boys."

"I don't know what you mean," Douglas said, crossing his ankle over his knee. "There's nothing immature about us."

"Says the man who thought it would be funny to glue Freddie's phone to the table last month," Damon said.

Everyone laughed.

"What? It was hilarious. Don't knock it." Douglas chuckled. "It was the first time in a long time I'd seen Freddie as pissed off as he was. Although Damon's trick the other week might come close to the top."

Patrick snorted. "Yes, he blew a gasket after your stunt, but maybe it had been simmering for a while, and that just made it worse. It seems to have settled him again, though, so I wouldn't worry."

"Oh, I'm not worried. I have the next prank ready and waiting for the perfect moment."

Mav groaned. "You said you would stop."

"And I will. Eventually." Douglas smiled at his boyfriend and dropped a kiss to his nose.

"You should have seen some of the things he did as a child. He could never get away with it because Mother always knew it was him," George said.

Douglas sat forward. "That's not true. They weren't always me. Alice was just as bad, if not worse."

"Do you remember when Alice glued William's chair?" Patrick covered his mouth when he laughed. "They didn't realise that the glue would seep through his trousers and stick to his skin as well." Patrick winced. "That wasn't a pleasant experience, but it was still hilarious."

"My friend, Mel, once emptied my other friend's shampoo and replaced it with hair dye. Bella ended up with purple hair for weeks," Eddie said. "She was not amused but ended up liking it and redoing it when it got too light. She had purple hair for months."

"Do you have any tales, Doc?" George asked.

"Oh, I have plenty. Having three sisters gave me lots of time to perfect my stunts."

George gaped. "You? I thought it would be your sisters doing it to you."

Timothy shrugged. "I was a holy terror as a pre-teen. Even Bri, who's older than me, ended up on the wrong end of one of my tricks."

"You have to tell us now," Douglas said.

"Nah, I'll save it for the next get-together."

Everyone booed him, and he chuckled. The entire atmosphere reminded him of his family. They would love the whole royal tribe when they eventually met them. He slipped his arm around George's shoulders and pulled him close. Surrounded by everyone, he had a sense of contentment he hadn't felt for a long time. As the conversation continued around him, he thought back on Orlan and Yanni, and for the first time, it did not leave him with soul-destroying despair. Instead, he just felt sad about losing lives that could've been saved. For the first time, he realised he couldn't have saved them. For the first time, he understood what everyone had been telling him. It wasn't his fault.

3 7

FREDERICK

Frederick stood on the raised steps to the back of the room and skirted his gaze around the occupants. He spent several long seconds checking the stage areas to ensure everything was okay, and no one appeared to need help, then he returned to looking around. He winced as he twisted to the side. He wasn't sure if he'd trapped a nerve or was just really tense, but his back ached like he'd been hit by a wooden beam. He checked his watch. He had half an hour, and then Alice was taking over from him. He might say a quick hello to his family, but a shower would be better for him.

The pain grew with each minute, even though he changed positions and tried to ease it. By the time Alice arrived, he was gritting his teeth. They saw something was wrong, and they quickly went through the handover before Freddie climbed down and hissed his way through the crowd as they bumped and jostled him.

He sighed when he opened the doors to the conversation area. He'd grab a drink and head for the changing rooms.

"Freddie!"

He smiled at Douglas. "I'm going to grab a drink and a shower. I'll be back after."

He winced again as he turned for the bar, thanking Oliver for the water he'd passed to him. He gingerly headed for the door, but before it closed behind him, another person exited.

"What's wrong?" Damon asked.

"Nothing. Just aching in places. Go back. I'll be there in a few minutes."

"Freddie."

Freddie stared at him and sighed, inhaling deeply when the pain jerked his back. "I think I might have a trapped nerve or something. My back's killing me."

"Let's get you into the changing rooms, and I'll see if anything is visible."

Damon led the way, opening the doors for him, which Freddie was grateful for, even if he didn't say so. He didn't want to let on exactly how much it hurt.

"Take your shirt off."

Freddie grimaced. "You might have to help me," he said.

Damon narrowed his eyes. "On a scale of one to ten, how much does it hurt?"

Freddie tried for a smile and gave up all pretence. "Twenty?"

"Fuck, Freddie. How long has it been like this?" Damon stepped closer, undoing the straps and buckles of Freddie's leather top.

"A couple of days, although it got worse tonight as I was monitoring."

"A couple of days, he says." Damon huffed a breath.

Once Freddie was free of his shirt, Damon disappeared into the bathroom area and returned with two towels. One he laid on the wooden bench, the other he left folded. "Rest your head on the folded one and lie on your stomach. I'm going to work out the knots in your back and see if it helps."

"Sir, yes, sir," Freddie joked.

He straddled the bench, then braced his hands on it, lowering himself carefully and exhaling with every spike of pain until he was horizontal.

"I'm going to press over your whole back. Tell me the areas that hurt."

Damon's hands were warm as they softly pressed against him. Freddie closed his eyes, concentrating on the pain. He mentioned every bruise-like spot, then wished he hadn't because Damon would rub and press against it until the pain somehow disappeared. He hadn't realised Damon had been using some sort of cream until a scent he didn't recognise filled the air.

"What's that?"

"It's supposed to be a honey scent, but it doesn't smell like it to me."

Damon kept massaging his back until Freddie felt no pain at all, but he didn't want him to stop. Maybe he could hire Damon to be his masseuse every day.

Damon snorted. "You're delirious. I'm going to straddle the bench by your head and work down your spine for the last time. After that, you should be good to go."

Freddie felt the change in position but groaned in pleasure as Damon's hands worked magic on his spine. Damon dragged his hands slowly up his back, then lifted them off.

"All done." Damon cleared his throat.

Freddie lifted his head and came face to face with Damon's groin. He swallowed when he saw Damon was hard, but Damon moved away quickly, disappearing into the bathroom area. Freddie frowned, then shook his head. He carefully rose from his position and found his back didn't hurt as much as before. It still twinged in places, but he'd get it checked out by the doctor the following day.

What he was trying to get his head around was that he hadn't wanted Damon to stop.

Pushing the thought aside, he showered and dressed in a fresh shirt while Damon waited for him.

"All good?" he asked.

"Yep. Let's go."

They joined the rest of the group and passed the evening with plenty of conversation and laughter. Eventually, though, it was time to leave because Freddie had appointments the following day.

"I'll give you a lift home, Damon," Freddie said.

"Why do you say that every time?" George asked. "You always give him a lift."

Freddie smiled at George's question. "Habit."

They said goodbye and walked to the lift after signing out of the club.

"He's right, you know. You always give me a lift, so why do you say it?"

"As I said, habit." They reached his car, and Freddie scratched his jaw. "There's no me without you. We've been together too long to be separated now." He grinned and climbed into the car. His heart raced. Why had he said that? He blew out a breath and started the car, choosing to ignore whatever it was his brain was trying to tell him.

Damon was his best friend. That was all.

He needed to remain focused on what was happening around them. It wouldn't pay to be caught unawares now.

38

EDDIE

 *E*ddie was both excited and nervous to be around so many people, especially royals, but as they'd proven time and again, they were just people. It didn't stop him from wondering if he fit in with them. Luckily, he had two men who helped him remember his worth.

He glanced around the ballroom, searching out George amongst the guests. There were over fifty people who'd come to visit, including Bella, Mel and Terry. George had introduced him to all the new faces, but he could guarantee he wouldn't remember their names.

When he caught George's gaze, he weaved his way through the people, excusing himself with a smile, then slid his arm around George's waist.

"Hey, sweetheart. Everything okay?" George kissed his head, squeezing him.

"Mmhm." He closed his eyes and rested his cheek against George's shoulder.

George chuckled. "You can't be tired already."

"No, I'm not. I'm just…"

He couldn't explain the need to be close to them, but he preferred to be with one or both of them instead of alone. He wasn't dependent on them, but he felt happier when they were together. It made no sense when he tried to explain it to the others; he'd tried with Bella, and she thought he was being manipulated until she saw them together. It wasn't about not being *able* to be without them; it was about not *wanting* to be without them.

"I know." And George did. They had sat down and had a conversation about what they all wanted from their relationship and lives and were on the same page.

"Right, I'm stealing him," Robert announced, grabbing Eddie's hand and pulling him away.

"What! Why?" Eddie said, sharing a confused look with George as Robert dragged him to the other side of the room.

"We need to have a conversation."

With that sentence clearing nothing up, Eddie allowed himself to be deposited on a chair beside Mav while Damon sat Timothy beside him. Robert and Damon settled in.

"What's this about?" Timothy asked.

"Well, we're the partners of the future royal generation," Robert said. "There are certain things we need that only the people sitting around this table can give us." Robert stared around the table. "Solidarity. It's going to be overwhelming. Hell, I'm already in over my head, but I wouldn't change it for the world. Sometimes, though, I need someone who knows how I feel."

"Why is Damon here, though? He grew up with them and isn't in a relationship. No offence." Timothy winced, holding his hand palm forwards.

Damon gave a small smile, but it didn't reach his eyes. "None taken. I'm your spy if you like. I'm the bridge between the two areas: royals and non-royals because I'm part of both."

"The way I see it, there are things we might come across that we don't want to discuss with our partners. Damon is that for us." Robert drank from his glass.

"What about Mav? He's similar," Eddie said.

Robert nodded back and forth. "Yes, but he's only really seen the social side of things before becoming part of the family."

"Okay, so what do we need to know?" Timothy asked.

"You tell us. That's what this is for. If you're unsure about anything and don't feel you can ask your partners, or if they're not there, call me. If I don't know the answer, I probably know someone who does." Damon spread his hands.

"So, we're creating our own group, opposite to the Scandalous Six?" Eddie asked with a grin.

They all laughed.

"Yes, I suppose we are." Robert grinned.

"We'll need a name," Eddie said. "George won't take us seriously if we don't have a name."

Mav rolled his eyes. "We don't need a name."

Eddie tapped his chin. "Hmm, I'll have to think about it."

"George has created a monster," Damon said. "Does anyone have any questions?"

They all stayed quiet.

"What's all this?" Douglas asked, resting his hands on Mav's shoulders and leaning down to kiss his hair.

"We're starting a band," Damon said, standing when Freddie approached.

Freddie raised his eyebrows. "You're in a band? What are you going to play?"

Damon grinned. "Wouldn't you like to know?"

Eddie narrowed his eyes at them. He was never a good judge of things, but there was something about those two.

"Can anyone join, or is it just you five?" Christian asked. "Patrick plays a mean piano."

"Nah, I'm good, thanks." Patrick chuckled.

An arm came around Eddie's neck, and he glanced to the side, seeing George between him and Timothy.

"Miss me?"

Eddie kissed his cheek. "Always."

"Ladies and gentlemen, the fireworks are about to start," Andrew announced.

George grabbed Eddie's hand and tugged him towards the balcony. Despite the day being warm, the night had turned colder, but someone had thought ahead and, dotted around the open space, were piles of warm blankets. Timothy picked up a bundle and strode for a loveseat. He unfolded the enormous blanket and tucked it around his back before opening his arms for George and Eddie. Both dived for him with a laugh, and he pulled the edges around them. To make it easier, George and Eddie held onto each corner, tucking it closed. As Freddie passed, he threw another blanket over the front of them, covering their legs and the gap.

"Thank you," Timothy said.

"Enjoy."

Freddie continued towards where Damon stood in the far corner and draped another blanket around the man's shoulders before sliding it around his own. He knew Freddie was straight, but they would have made a good couple because they were so tuned to each other.

Eddie shifted his focus off them and to the man standing a few feet away. Christian stood tall, hands in his pockets, no blanket in sight, face lifted to the night sky. He had a feeling the man's eyes were closed, but he couldn't see from where he sat. His demeanour screamed to leave him alone, which was probably why there was no one with him.

As his gaze slid over the occupants of the balcony, he saw several groups, some bigger than others, and some people alone. It was none of his business, but he made a note of those singles, wondering if there was anything he could do to help them. He was only a barista, but sometimes, all someone needed was an ear to listen to them. He doubted he could be that for the king, but for Christian or Patrick or Henry's friend, Kean, he might. He could offer, even if they never took him up on it.

"Are you okay?" George asked, caressing his cheek with his thumb. "You look sad."

Eddie smiled. "Not at all. I was wishing everyone could be as happy as I am."

George studied the area, probably seeing exactly what Eddie had, and gave a half-smile. "Hopefully, everyone will be eventually."

"Which reminds me, George. I've spoken to a friend of mine about Jason. She's going to check into the situation discreetly and report back, then we can look at the options. We might be able to get Jason into the position of guardian for his siblings, but it depends on her findings," Timothy said.

Eddie watched George kiss Timothy like there was no tomorrow. "Thank you."

"You don't need to thank me. We'll help him. One way or another."

The telltale whistle of a firework shooting into the sky sounded, and Eddie transferred his gaze to the starlit sky. As it exploded into shimmering purple drops, he thought the journey of a firework was like that of joining the royal family. A gentle ripple in the air that is almost indistinguishable until the media realises who they are, then it explodes into a frenzy of camera flashes and attention before gently fading away as if they'd always been part of the family.

He smiled to himself, pleased with the analogy. Then he let all thought disappear and watched the colours shoot across the sky. Although the blankets helped keep the cold out, he was frozen by the time the display ended, and conversation resumed. It had been a wonderful finish to an amazing evening.

"We're going to head home," Mel said, her arm around Terry's shoulders. "Someone drank a little too much tequila." She rolled her eyes at Bella.

"It wasn't my fault," Bella said.

Eddie extricated himself from the blankets and hissed when the cold air hit him. He threw his arms around them. "Thank you for coming. I hope you had a good time."

"What are you talking about! It was fantastic. You royals sure know how to party," Mel said, steering Terry inside after giving Eddie a wave.

Eddie grinned. "How about you?"

Bella smiled, though it was weak. "I had fun. Thank you."

Eddie pulled her in for another hug. "Are you sure you're okay, Bella? You've not been your usual chatty self."

Bella stared at the ground, fiddling with the buttons on her coat. "I'm okay. I have things I need to work through, but I'm doing okay."

"You know you can talk to me if you need to, don't you?" Eddie said, ducking his head to see her eyes. "Just because I'm with George and Timothy now doesn't mean it's the end of our friendship."

She nodded. "I know." She kissed his cheek, smiled and disappeared after Mel and Terry. Eddie watched her go.

"Is she okay, sweetie?" his mother asked.

Eddie turned to her and smiled. "Yeah. It's a big change to wrap her head around, I guess."

"For everyone." Rose patted his cheek. "Your father and I are going to go home. It is way past our bedtime now."

"Okay. Thank you for coming. I'm glad you got to meet everyone."

Rose and Parker hugged the three men, then Eddie was pulled in yet another direction. "Oh, my god! I didn't see you arrive." He hugged Quinn and Kendal, holding tightly to the latter. "How long have you been here?"

"We arrived as the fireworks started. Later than planned. Sorry," Quinn said.

"It's okay. I'm so glad you came. Can I introduce you to my partners?"

Quinn glanced at Kendal, who nodded. "Of course."

"You know George, but this is Timothy. Guys, this is Quinn and Kendal."

Timothy stayed sitting but held out his hand. "Nice to meet you both."

"Nice to see you again," George said.

"Kendal?" Eddie glanced over his shoulder to see Andrew stalking towards them. "Is everything okay?"

Kendal dropped their gaze to the ground and nodded. "Yes, sir...Your Majesty."

The king rested a hand on Kendal's shoulder, a move that would've usually made the man flinch. "I've told you before that you can call me Andrew."

"Thank you, but it's difficult."

"I know what you mean," Eddie said. "He's said that to

me several times, too, but I still fumble before the name comes out." He winked at Kendal, trying to cut the tension. Kendal smiled, their cheeks pinking. "Do you have time for a drink with us?"

Again, Quinn deferred to Kendal, and Eddie assumed it was to ensure they were comfortable in the situation. Kendal nodded, and the king pulled several seats closer to where Timothy and George sat. Eddie joined his boyfriends on the loveseat, but this time, to one side. As some guests had bid goodbye, only a handful of people remained—the usual group of eleven, plus the king, Quinn, Kendal and Kean. Eddie was unsure about the king being there, only because he was older and all the other parents had left, but he said nothing.

"I won't disturb you for long," Andrew said as if hearing Eddie's unvoiced thoughts. He leaned back in his chair and sipped his drink. "It's rare I get the chance to see you all at once. I know this should be a celebration, but are there any issues we need to discuss?"

"Well, actually, Father, I'd like to ask about the police investigation," Freddie said, leaning forward. "I know what the police have announced, but are we leaving it at that, or are more investigations being carried out?"

Andrew sighed and stared at the glass in his hand, swirling it around and around. "You heard the Commissioner the same as me, Frederick. They have nothing to point towards any other outcome other than what conclusion they've come to. Vincent has been arrested for stalking Timothy, but I doubt he'll be kept in for too long. He either didn't have any or was unwilling to give us information about why he chose Timothy. But…the Commissioner is working on it and a new piece of evidence—potential evidence."

"Evidence?" George sat forward.

Andrew clenched his jaw. "The ignition key they found might not be the one that set off the bomb."

"What!" came from several people.

Andrew waved his hand. "The Commissioner is aware of the problems we have with certain members of the family, but unless we have proof, our hands are tied. All I can hope is that the true antagonists begin to feel safe and make a mistake in the future."

"We know who it was, Father," Douglas said, his expression hard.

Andrew nodded slowly. "More than likely. I promise you, their whereabouts and visitors are being monitored at all times. You have my word." He lifted his gaze and swept it around the room. "I'm so glad you're finding love, and those who haven't will soon enough. Having said that, I need you to be careful. By banishing Charlotte, I've done two things: increased her anger and taken her out of my immediate sight. No longer can I predict what she will do, and that scares me."

Eddie exhaled, his eyes widening. The king admitted to being scared, and that terrified Eddie. Timothy's arm tightened around him, and Eddie dropped his head onto his shoulder.

"We all have targets on our backs, and there is no way of knowing who she will go after next. She's clever. She hides well. You need to take precautions at all times, even with your friends. I'm sorry, but we can't let her win."

"She won't," Freddie said in a hard voice. "We won't let her."

Eddie studied the expressions of the remaining people and saw the agreement on their faces. No way would they let anyone get hurt if they had anything to do about it. Eddie would speak to his friends and make sure they knew the issues without saying too much. He knew they needed secrecy.

"Anyway, don't let this ruin your evening." Andrew stood, placing his glass on the table. "I'll let you enjoy the rest of the night." He turned to Quinn, who rose. "Thank you for coming." He touched a finger to his cheek, then focused on Kendal. "I'm glad you made it." He cupped Kendal's chin, and they stared at each other for a split second before he leaned forward and whispered something into Kendal's ear. Kendal nodded, and the king smiled at everyone before disappearing inside.

"Spin the bottle, anyone?" George said, munching on love heart sweets. Everyone chuckled, breaking the tension. "Well, I was serious until you laughed." George pouted.

"No, you weren't," Eddie said, threading his fingers through George's.

He sighed, listening to the hum of conversation rising. Despite the heaviness of the king's warning, Eddie felt a lightness inside. His instincts told him tsunamis were heading their way, but he believed they could get through them together.

Andrew had been right. Douglas, Henry and now George had found the people they wanted to spend their lives with, but Freddie, Damon, Christian, Patrick, Kean and Kendal were still waiting on their happily ever after. Eddie had to believe they would find it, even if that meant they were alone but happy. It was the contentment with their life that gave them their happy ending, not necessarily a relationship. Although, Eddie wished the happiness he had on everyone else because he had never been more ecstatic than he was now.

"Let's go to bed," Timothy whispered, his hot breath sending shivers down Eddie's spine.

Eddie smiled and nodded, not caring about the knowing glances and words that were sent their way.

"First band meeting is next week!" Damon called.

Eddie chuckled and waved back.

As they wandered through the corridors to George's room, Eddie's thoughts went to Queen Louisa. It pained him to think that by giving her life, she brought Timothy to them because he doubted they would've met if she hadn't died. Maybe George and Eddie would've had a relationship, but would it have lasted if they hadn't had Timothy to tie them together?

"Deep thoughts, Eddie?" Timothy asked.

Eddie stared at him. "Just what-ifs. I'm good."

Timothy slid his arm around his waist and pulled him closer. "What ifs are fine on the condition that you don't dwell on them."

"I won't."

Timothy kissed his temple.

"What are you two whispering about?" George said as they reached his door.

"Timothy was reminding me not to dwell on things." He smiled. "I enjoyed tonight. It was nice having everyone together."

"It was. Our group has expanded a lot since the relationships started," George said.

"It will continue to grow, too. Who do you think will be next?" Eddie asked, pulling off his clothes as he walked backwards into the bedroom.

Timothy and George stared at him. "I don't care," they said in unison, and Eddie laughed, twisting and racing into the room. He got tackled before he even made it to the bathroom.

"Give me that mouth," George said, lowering his head.

As soon as their lips touched, Eddie flew, and when Timothy's arms came around them, he felt like a shot of espresso had been injected straight into his veins. A feeling he would never deny. Lust, heat, adoration, contentment and, most of all, love.

He lived for moments like these. Moments with the men he loved. Moments where he felt the love the men had for him.

Love. The most addictive feeling in the world.

39

GEORGE

Six months later

George entered the bookshop and wandered around, trying to find something he thought Christian might like. He knew the man was an avid reader, but other than he liked science-fiction and crime genres, George had no idea what to choose as a birthday present.

The more he explored, the more he loved the place. It was a mix of a bookshop, cafe and library because customers could choose a selection of books to read while they had a drink, and they could buy the books, too. He'd never been in a shop like it before, and he was enamoured.

His security guard pointed to an aisle of crime books, and George thanked him. They had taken Isaac on as his permanent security, which George was pleased about because they got on well. Eddie and Timothy didn't have any guards, except for when they were going to places they hadn't been before or to royal events.

Their relationship had gone from strength to strength. They spent most of their time at Timothy's house with some additional protection added in around the place. Timothy hadn't minded, and although they hadn't discussed it, they were pretty much living together. George grinned at the thought. He'd never thought he'd leave home, but he loved Timothy's place as much as his own. He planned to ask them about the logistics of their living arrangements soon because he wanted them permanently together, but it was probably too soon. His family were never ones to go slowly, though.

He sighed when no books jumped out at him as something Christian might like, but then he caught sight of a figure he recognised. There went his surprise.

"Hey, I didn't expect to see you today." George sat across from Christian, who had been buried in a book in an armchair in the corner of the bookshop.

Christian didn't flinch, but George knew he'd not noticed him. "Morning. What brought you out today?" he asked, closing his book and resting it on his lap.

"I'm not answering that for secrecy reasons." George smiled. "I thought you were at work this weekend?"

Christian gave a half shrug. "They swapped my rota. I thought I'd get in some reading while I could." He shifted. "Do you want a drink?"

George waved him away. "No, I won't disturb you any more than I have done. I'll let you get back to your book." He stood, then paused beside his cousin. "Remember, I'm here if you need anything."

"I know, and thank you. I appreciate it."

George left the shop, walking aimlessly with Isaac beside

him. There had been a lot of changes in Christian's life over the past few months, but he still needed the alone time he'd always needed. That much hadn't changed. He hoped Christian could let go of the things that troubled him, but with no one to focus his anger on, Christian was stuck.

"Where to, Your Highness?" Isaac said, snapping him out of his melancholy.

"Hmm. Timothy's, I think. I'm going to have to find something else for the man who is impossible to buy for."

Isaac chuckled. "Good luck with that."

"I should make you find something, then you wouldn't be so gleeful." George pouted, then snorted. "Maybe Freddie has some ideas."

They made the journey home in near silence, and when George emerged from the car, Eddie jumped into his arms, barely giving George enough time to brace himself. Eddie's legs went around George's waist, and George buried his face in Eddie's neck.

"What are you doing home so early?"

"My boss gave me the afternoon off." Eddie pulled back and stood on his own two feet before cupping George's face. "I thought we could visit your mother."

George smiled. "That would be nice. Is Doc still at work?"

"Yes. He gave them a surprise quiz and now has to face the aftereffects of marking them."

"Ooh. More fool him." George chuckled. "Let me get a drink, and we'll go. Isaac..."

"We'll be ready," Isaac said with a nod.

George and Eddie entered the house and headed straight for the kitchen. "I saw Christian while I was out."

"Was he at the bookshop again?" Eddie asked.

George stared at him. "How did you know?"

"Where else would he be?"

George frowned and grabbed a bottle of apple juice from the fridge and offered Eddie one. Cracking the lid, he asked, "Have you had lunch?"

"Yes, I ate when I got home. Have you?"

George shook his head. "I'm not that hungry, though, so I'll get something when we get back."

He drained the bottle and threw it in the recycling. He wrapped his arms around Eddie's waist and rested his chin on his shoulder while Eddie finished his drink. Everything about their lives revolved around each other, and George loved it. They'd cook meals together on the weekends, and George often cooked for them during the week—after several lessons with Windsor Castle's chefs—so they didn't live on takeaways. After they'd eat, they'd curl up on the sofa together and watch a film while chatting and catching up on the hours they'd been apart. George still did his jobs, but apart from the narrating, which he continued to do in his room at Windsor, everything else was portable.

Eddie's hand slid against his cheek. "Are you okay?"

"Perfect. Ready?"

"Let's do it."

Isaac drove them towards the royal mausoleum, and they climbed out into the brisk October air. Autumn had truly set in, and a blanket of multi-coloured leaves carpeted the ground. The walk from the car to the mausoleum was beautiful. The trees swaying in the breeze, the water reflecting the sunlight, and a magnificent bridge across that water leading to the cream-coloured Romanesque-style building.

They drifted across the stone bridge, and George was once again awed by the attention to detail on the exterior of the building. They climbed the steps, passed between two angel statues and under the arches. The large doors opened at a push of his hand, and immediately the atmosphere changed. The temperature dropped, but the interior design was incredible.

"I remember the first time I ever came here," he said, moving further into the building. "Mother and Father took us for a walk when I was around eight, I think, and pointed out the different parts of the land." He chuckled. "It fascinated me why they called it Frogmore, and Mother told me the story about the frogs visiting day and night and disturbing the peace. I went searching for frogs for months afterwards, but I forgot about them the moment I saw this place that day."

"I bet it seemed gigantic for an eight-year-old."

"It did. I remember thinking there weren't many places to hide." He snorted.

He wandered around the area, taking in the pictures, the stained-glass windows, the marble details as if it was the first time he'd ever seen them. Even all these years later, it still fascinated him how someone had made something so beautiful.

He came to a stop next to the sarcophagus where his mother rested. Six months had dulled the loss to a bearable level, but his breath still caught when he remembered that fateful day. In an instant, he was back there, experiencing the same excruciating grief. He dropped to his knees beside her and bowed his head, tears streaming down his face. This time, though, they were not tears of pain; they were tears of what could've been, of what *she* had missed in the time she'd been gone.

He knew no one could live forever, and there would

always be something someone missed when they died, but she had so many years ahead of her. All he could hope was that she could look down on them all and see what they had achieved.

Inhaling, he lifted his head and twisted around to sit at the base of her resting place. Eddie joined him, and as always, George regaled him with stories of his childhood and the mischief they got up to. It was only when his ass went numb that he stood and helped Eddie up. He rested a hand on the cool granite.

"I love you, Mother. Rest in peace. Father has it covered." He smiled, knowing his mother would've laughed at that last sentence.

They exited the mausoleum, zipping their coats when the air proved chillier than when they'd entered.

"Thank you for encouraging me to visit. I still can't believe it took me two months before I could face it." George lowered his head.

"Everyone is ready at different times. It wouldn't have mattered if you were never ready. At least, you can say you've seen her. I'm positive she hears every word and is probably cursing up a storm when you tell some of your stories."

"Undoubtedly. I may embellish a few things, but purely for entertainment reasons." George chuckled.

He slid his arm around Eddie's shoulders and pulled him close, kissing his temple as they wandered back to the car. They had been lucky with the journalists. Their story, however unusual, was old news as quickly as any other, except for one photographer, who had followed Eddie around until Randall and Mav got involved. Mav threatened to expose all his secrets, and Randall did something no one was privy to, and the guy eventually backed off. He hadn't been stalking him or anything, but he was always hanging around at the cafe. Now, though, it seemed he'd got the picture and buggered off.

On the other hand, they had pestered Timothy for a while, having his ordeal in Bristol dragged back up but into the national newspapers this time, not just the local ones. It had weighed heavily on him, and he'd increased his visits to Derek for a while, but then, he'd come out the other side stronger and happier. In his own words, he'd "become accustomed to the media, and it no longer hurts like a strike with a vicious sword."

When they were encased in the warmth of the car, they cuddled close.

"As glad as I am that you're here with me, there always seems to be a piece missing whenever one of us isn't here," Eddie said.

"Definitely." George sat upright and fumbled to get his phone from his pocket.

GEORGE: If you get your ass home quick enough, we might be able to have dessert before dinner xx

Eddie chuckled when he saw what he'd written. It was mid-afternoon, but Timothy should've finished his last class and been working through his marking if George had timed it right.

"Do you think he'll take the bait?" Eddie asked.

"We'll soon see."

After bidding goodnight to Isaac, they shrugged out of their coats and kicked off their boots before heading for the kitchen.

"I'll make spaghetti carbonara for dinner. It doesn't take

long, especially if we prep it now." George winked at Eddie, and they rushed to get it ready.

George had just finished grating the cheese when the front door opened and closed. He grinned at Eddie. "Seems like our wish came true."

Timothy filled the doorway, his tie haphazardly dangling from his neck and his hands unbuttoning his shirt. "Why are you still dressed?"

George sat on the wide window seat in the back living room, the one they rarely used. It faced the back garden, and George found himself mesmerised and calmed by the sway of the trees. It had become his sanctuary. The place he went when his brain was too full of thoughts and images, and he needed to decompress. He wore Timothy's hoodie over his pyjama trousers and had bare feet, which he had regretted since he'd sat down in the cold room.

Promising to replace the hoodie, he'd pulled it over his bent knees and tucked his feet inside, too, knowing it would get pulled out of shape, but being surrounded by their scents comforted him as not much else could. He rested his forehead against the windowpane, the ice-cold a shock for a second before his skin adapted to the change in temperature. They had security lights in the garden that only came on when something moved, and in between those moments, it was dark, but George didn't mind.

He's woken from a dream two hours ago and hadn't been able to get back to sleep, so instead of tossing and turning and potentially waking Timothy and Eddie, he'd left the bed and settled at his window. He couldn't remember what the dream had been about, but it had left him with a sense of uneasiness and the vision of his mother wearing white. She'd worn white several times over the years, but he couldn't figure out if it was a memory or not. The rest of it had faded away the instant he'd opened his eyes.

George was not one for listening to omens in dreams, but something was niggling at him, and he tried to work out what it was. His phone beeped, and he frowned. He had no idea who would message him at three o'clock in the morning.

FREDDIE: Are you awake?

GEORGE: Yes. Why are you awake?

FREDDIE: No idea. I had a weird dream and can't get back to sleep.

GEORGE: Me too. I feel like we've missed something, Freddie. Something that's right in front of us.

FREDDIE: Like what?

GEORGE: No idea. I just have that feeling. It's not over, is it?

FREDDIE: Aunt Charlotte and Charles won't give up that easily. They want the crown, but they'll never get it while we're alive.

GEORGE: Are they going to kill us?

FREDDIE: They can try. I won't stop until they're in prison. I have people working on it. Hopefully, soon, they will have something we can use against them.

GEORGE: Who's next? They tried to drag Douglas through the mud. They scared the life out of Henry. They tried to kill me and succeeded with Mother. Who's next?

FREDDIE: I believe they were also responsible for the helicopter crash two years ago.

GEORGE: What! So, they started with you?

FREDDIE: Looks like it. We have to be careful, George. Eight people are standing between Aunt Charlotte and the crown, and four of us have had attempts to remove us from the line. I doubt she'll stop.

GEORGE: There has got to be evidence somewhere. Have you spoken to Albert?

FREDDIE: Yes. From what I can tell, they kept him in the dark about most things, except for their hatred of us. I just wish I knew why.

GEORGE: I don't know if I want to know why.

FREDDIE: What do you mean?

GEORGE: If I found out it was something trivial and meaningless, then Mother's death was pointless.

Freddie didn't reply for several minutes, and George wiped away the tears on his cheeks.

FREDDIE: Try to sleep. Come over for breakfast tomorrow.

GEORGE: I'll be there.

FREDDIE: CU

Most people would see Freddie's last message as a "see you," but it meant chin up. George returned the gesture and put his phone back beside him. He hugged his arms around his legs and rested his cheek on his knees, staring into the black night. Freddie's words swirled around his head.

"Hey," whispered Timothy. "Are you okay?"

George smiled. "I'm fine. Couldn't sleep."

"You should have woken me."

George opened his arms, but Timothy lifted him and sat on the window seat before settling George on his lap and enfolding him in his arms. George snuggled close.

"Want to talk?" Timothy asked.

"Maybe tomorrow. Tonight is for calm and quiet."

"Understood."

They were still for several minutes before soft padding sounded, and Eddie climbed onto the window seat with them.

"I wondered where you two had gone."

Timothy pulled Eddie onto his lap as well, but in the opposite direction, and they held tightly to each other. George closed his eyes and breathed in the scent of coffee and mint, the two smells he associated with his men. He sighed, and Timothy tightened his grip. No matter what came, no matter *who* came, they would stop them. Family or not, they would be stopped.

In the meantime, he had the love of these two men, and he would never take that for granted.

"Forever," he whispered.

Did you enjoy this book? Order Disowned Royal to see what happens to Christian when his family turns their back on him. Who has *his* back now?

Sign up to my newsletter to get a free prequel from Club Royal called Royal Firsts.

ABOUT ELOUISE EAST

I am Elouise East but feel free to call me Elli. I write sweet and steamy connections in gay romance. I also touch on taboo stories under the name Elouise R East.

Books that tell the stories where friendship and family are the focal point - be it blood family or chosen - is very important to me. That's why I include a variety of personalities, talents, ages, situations and abilities as I believe a story or a character needs. I want my characters to be real, to be relatable, to be free to have whatever views they tell me they have. And trust me, most of the time, I do not have *any* say in the matter!

My characters come to life on the page for me as well as my readers. Their stories unfold in front of me, and I have very little input into how they want to be shown. Just like real life, the lives of my characters change with every choice, every interaction and every conversation. And I wouldn't have it any other way.

I write books that are emotionally realistic, even if liberties are taken with other aspects of my stories. I don't know any other way to write. It comes from deep inside.

Who am I? A single parent to two children who make life worth living. An avid reader who still devours every book she can get her hands on. A student of learning about any subject that takes her fancy. An author of books she would read herself. And a romantic at heart who loves anything cheesy.

Who's in?

<u>Stalk me here... ;-)</u>
Website
https://elouiseeast.com/

Newsletter
https://elouiseeast.com/newsletter

All links
https://linktr.ee/elouiseeastauthor

BOOKS BY ELOUISE EAST

<u>CLUB ROYAL</u>

Rogue Royal

Secretive Royal

Grieving Royal

Disowned Royal

<u>LOVE IN FLAMES</u>

Out of the Frying Pan

Smokescreen

Breathing Fire

<u>CRUSH</u>

Love Conquers

First Kiss

Instant Desire

Primary Seduction

Deep Down

A Crush for Christmas

Life Support

Covert Strength

Love Scene

Lawful Attraction

Crush Box Set 1: Books 1-3